NORTHERN
GIRLS ♥ GRAVY

KAREN WOODS

EMPIRE
PUBLICATIONS

First published in 2011

EMPIRE PUBLICATIONS
1 Newton Street, Manchester M1 1HW
© Karen Woods 2011

ISBN 1 901 746 79 8 - 9781901746792

Printed in Great Britain.

Acknowledgments

WRITING THIS BOOK has left a smile all over my face. Since writing Broken Youth and Black Tears the public have shown they love my work. I write from my heart and always with a sense of humour. I would like to thank all my friends on face book friends and all my friends on Twitter.

I would also want to thank all my family and friends for their support especially my children Ashley, Blake, Declan and Darcy. I have now three grandchildren, Dolton, Cruz and Marci, and they have been patient with me while I have been writing. My husband James also needs a mention because without his support none of these books would have been written, so big kisses to him.

A big thanks to my mother Margaret and father Alan who have supported me all the way. Thanks to Ashley Shaw and John Ireland from Empire Publications for believing in me from the start. Also thanks to Judith Broadbent, a true Yorkshire lass – she will always be a friend. I would also like to thank Debbie Manley for all her help and encouragement and Rowetta Idah – a star in her own right and an inspirational lady.

Broken Youth, my first novel, is now being turned into a TV Drama and I would like to thank Glen Mortimer TV director for reading my book and believing in the story line. We both wrote the screen play for the TV drama and we laughed along the way. Every day I'm learning a new skill and hope to go the full circle with my dreams.

My fourth novel "Bag Heads" is nearly half way done

and I know people will love the raw, real edge of it. I've dedicated it to my brother Darren and when he reads it I know he will laugh and cry.

Dreams are there to be followed and I urge everyone to follow theirs. My finally words are to my son Dale in heaven. I know I never held you in my arms, but I will always hold your memory in my heart. Thanks everyone for your support I will be forever grateful.

Thanks

Karen x

1

VICTORIA GREYBANK HAD everything a woman could ever dream of but, as she stood tall in the full length mirror, she pulled at her expensive clothes and hated her life. To the outside world it seemed she was fulfilled in every way. She ran a successful business with her husband Oscar and they wanted for nothing.

Victoria was thirty-five but her life hadn't always been easy and she'd struggled for many years before she met Oscar. Her father Dennis was a Jack The Lad who'd begged, borrowed and stolen to get the family where they were today.

Standing in the mirror she clipped her raven black hair up from her face. Her eyes always looked filled with sadness. As she applied her green eye shadow, she tried to hide the emptiness she felt inside.

Victoria's figure was perfect and many women would have killed for it. Her appetite had always been small and she never ate a full meal.

Children had always been a dream for her in her early years of marriage but somehow it never happened. The couple thought about seeking medical help to try to conceive but both Victoria and Oscar never found the time in their busy lives.

The jewellery business they owned had been running for more than fifteen years. It had always kept them busy. Victoria was the dynamo of it, she covered the financial side of the business and always made sure the books were in order and up to date. Many a night she'd still be at the shop until the late hours. It really got her down sometimes.

The business had been Victoria's idea. When she first married Oscar he'd given her the money to set up the shop. All Victoria's family were proud of her and her dad loved that she married into money. He was always telling her "don't fuck it up."

Diamonds were Victoria's life and she could tell a fake at a glance thanks to the help from her dad. She loved dealing with customers who came into the shop. If they needed help to pick out a ring or a necklace for that special someone in their lives, she was quickly by their side. She always guided them within their budget and always tried on the jewellery for the customer. Most of her customers were men. Some of the stories they told her regarding their purchases really shocked her. The men quite often bought two rings at the same time – one for the wife and the other for their bit on the side.

Victoria never understood them. She couldn't understand why they would buy gifts for the other women in their lives. After all, weren't they just there for sex and weren't supposed to mean anything?

Victoria lived in a large four bed roomed house in Prestwich, an affluent suburb of Manchester. Her life before had been on a council estate in Miles Platting and completely different from the life she now led. Her circle of friends included some very rich people. She always thought they were up their own arses and only socialised with them to keep Oscar happy. Victoria felt false among them and always out of place.

Money had never been a problem for her since she married Oscar and she could just jet off to any destination at the drop of a hat. Many of her holidays were with her friends. Oscar never seemed to care if he went on holiday with her or not and she liked it that way.

Oscar was a lot shorter than Victoria. He hated her wearing high-heels when they were together as it made him look like a dwarf. His hair was dark brown. He always complained that he was going to go bald, and the egg in the nest at the top of his head suggested he was right. His build was strange. His head was quite large but his frame was quite small compared to it. Sometimes Victoria had seriously wondered if he was abnormal in some kind of way.

They had met when Victoria was just eighteen. From the moment he cast eyes on her he knew she was everything his heart desired. Victoria wasn't keen on him at first but as soon as she knew he had cash she had seen him as her ticket to a better life.

Oscar's parents were wealthy. He was an only child and had never worked for anything in his life. Victoria sometimes hated him for this and told him straight he was "a lucky fucker." Her life had been spent on the breadline and she knew what it meant to struggle for money. Oscar's parents had looked down on her when they first met and she knew they didn't think she was good enough for their only son. Victoria's father had a lot to do with her marrying Oscar because once he knew he had cash, he made sure his daughter did everything she could to keep him interested.

Oscar loved that they could go their separate ways without either of them batting an eyelid. He often went on golfing holidays with his friends and spent many a weekend away at business meetings. The situation had always been fine between them and neither of them bothered if they didn't see each other from one week to the next.

Victoria had everything in her life that money could

buy but her heart was empty. Love was a vague, distant memory. Her first love was always on her mind when she felt low. She hated herself for marrying for money and not for love.

Sex had been boring with Oscar. He was a complete let down in the bedroom. She wanted so much more from sex but always felt she had to be prim and proper with him because of his background. In the years that passed, she'd been denied the loving that her body craved. Sex with him made her cringe and some of his sexual habits made her think he was perverted.

Victoria often fantasised about having sex with other men. The thought of putting her plan into action made her tremble inside and she always had to remember he was her meal ticket and she couldn't chance losing him.

One of Victoria's friends had previously confided in her. She'd told her of an escort agency that was very discreet. Her face dropped with shock when she told her details about the men she'd met.

Fantasy was Victoria's only escape and for now that was all she needed. The thought of a hunky man tearing her knickers off and chewing on her vagina always kept her on her toes and she lived in hope that one day her dream would come true.

Victoria's life looked perfect to the outside world until the day she found a condom in her husband's pocket. At first, she just studied it. Her face screwed up as she tried to think how it had landed in his possession. She sat motionless on the bed as she pulled at it with a distraught look on her face. Never in a million years did she think the bastard was playing around.

The condom wasn't smooth, it had little thin lines on it. It looked ribbed. As she read the packet, she saw it was mint flavoured. Curiosity eventually got a grip of her and she slowly started to open it. Her hands were shaky and she had to use her teeth to open it. As she pulled the condom out of the golden wrapper, she was apprehensive as she felt the lubrication around it. Victoria hurried downstairs to lock the front door. As she ran back upstairs she struggled for breath.

Heading back to the bedroom she examined it further. She'd never felt a condom before and was amazed that it felt so nice. Quickly closing her bedroom door, she positioned herself on the bed. The thought of anyone catching her with a condom in her hands terrified her. She felt naughty.

Her bedroom was spotless. The gold silk curtains hung from the bay window giving it an elegant feel. The dark mahogany wooden frame bed stood in the middle of the room. It looked like a centrepiece in an art exhibition.

Victoria sat on the bed and kicked off her shoes as she made herself comfortable. The condom was now unfolded to its full length as she placed it on the bed. She sighed at the size of it slowly licking her lips.

Oscar only had a very small manhood and the thought of someone filling the condom in front of her made her smile. Sometimes she'd call him pickle dick under her breath, because that is what it reminded her of on some cold mornings when he got out of bed. Victoria had only ever had one sexual partner before him and she knew Oscar was small compared to what she'd had in the past. Victoria knew by some films she'd seen on TV that there were men out there with much bigger willies and she always felt cheated.

Staring in deep thought, she looked hypnotised, worried. Her fingers were tapping on the bed. Could he be having an affair? Her voice became higher now as she spoke aloud to herself. "I bet he's having an affair. Why else would he have a condom in his fucking pocket?"

The black pants where she found the condom stared back at her, almost as if they were laughing. He'd worn them several nights before, she remembered.

"He was supposed to have been at some business meeting. I remember, he didn't come home until late." She sighed to the cream wall in front of her, tried to get a grip of her thoughts, and pulled at the condom with anger written all over her face.

Within seconds, her face changed. Looking at the photo of Oscar by her bedside, she knew he wasn't the sort who played about. The sound of relief filled the room and the worried look on her face soon disappeared.

She sniggered to herself and thought that her husband would have had to put an elastic band round the condom to keep it on his small member.

She held the condom like a dead mouse as she raised it up to her nose. The long transparent plastic smelt of mints. Feeling more curious, she stuck her tongue out and softly licked the side of it. Her lips started to tingle. Touching her lips, she blew on them feeling the menthol reaction.

Victoria looked aroused. She tickled her tongue up and down the condom in a slow, sexual manner. Her cheeks looked slightly red and her body looked hot.

She caught her reflection on the wardrobe mirror. She felt extremely horny as she watched herself. The taste of the condom was now all over her mouth and she licked her lips as the mint flavour filled it. Victoria collapsed on the bed. She lifted her head and made sure she could see herself still in the mirror. As she unbuttoned her white cotton shirt, she pulled her nipples from her bra. Her vagina was now beating with excitement and she could hear her breath quickening.

Caressing her nipples, she hitched her skirt up and parted her legs. She was like a caged animal and she knew she had to pleasure herself there and then to release the frustration she felt. Her fingers slowly sneaked into the top of her knickers. She fondled her lady garden like she was stroking a cat. The condom was now hanging from her mouth and she licked at it with a frenzied look on her face. Victoria's fingers now took control and there wasn't a thing she could do to stop herself finding heaven. She groaned with pleasure as they sunk in and out of her and within minutes, she was reaching orgasm.

Once Victoria had answered her body's call for pleasure, she lay on the bed caressing her nipples feeling slightly embarrassed. Looking at herself in the mirror, she thought how sexy she looked as she held her nipples still in her fingers. Speaking to the mirror, she asked it if it thought she was sexy.

Sex with Oscar was like her periods, once a month. Even when they had sex, he just seemed to rush it and couldn't wait until it was over. Victoria had been quite shy in the bedroom. She'd never experimented with different positions or any love tools.

Oscar seem to have been brought up with the notion that sex was only for making babies. He didn't know all the kinky gadgets you could get to use in the bedroom. She'd often wondered if she was some kind of pervert because the things she wanted to do was something you would only see in porn movies.

Victoria had never told anyone about her fantasies, she felt too ashamed and was scared what people might have thought of her. After straightening her clothes, she stood up from the bed. She looked at the condom one last time and decided to throw it away without any more thought. Her husband loved her dearly and would never stray to another woman because he had everything he'd wanted from her, she told herself. She made her way to the bathroom and dropped the evil thing inside the silver pedal bin next to the sink.

★

For the next few weeks Victoria's head was in bits. The condom she'd found made her look at her husband more closely. He never came home until the late hours and he never asked her for sex anymore, not even the regular once a month.

Victoria had asked him if everything was all right between them and he assured her nothing had changed in their relationship. He just told her that he'd been wrapped up in some big business deals lately and was worried that he'd made a mistake investing in it.

Things went on in much the same vein between them and Victoria tried to put her unease to the back of her mind until she found something in his briefcase. Victoria had been searching for some paperwork one afternoon at work, and the last place she thought it could possibly be was in her husband's briefcase. She opened the black leather case. As she searched through all the letters, she noticed a black small box in the corner. At first, she didn't think anything and opened it slowly. Once the leather box opened, her eyes lit up with excitement. The large diamond shone like a thousand stars at her and she couldn't wait to place it on her finger. Victoria held her hand up in front of her and admired it. She knew the ring was expensive just by looking at it and took it off to examine it further.

The words engraved inside the ring were hard to make out at first and she had to get an eyepiece from a nearby drawer to look at it closer. Holding the ring in her fingers, she focused on the writing inside. Her heart leapt as she read the words engraved on it, 'Love you always sweetheart'.

The noise of someone outside the room made her jump. She closed the briefcase as quickly as she could. Victoria held her arms round her body and hated herself for even thinking her husband could be unfaithful. How could she have been so stupid, she thought and quickly placed the ring back into the box before anyone saw her.

The shop assistant was a lovely woman who had been with the company for the last three years. Katie was twenty-eight years of age and had a long, slender figure. She had a gift of chatting to the customers and she had always made a sale once she worked her magic. When they'd first employed Katie, Victoria hadn't been keen on her. She thought she was too flirty with her husband for her own good but as time went on she started to like her and eventually she trusted her with her life.

That night when Victoria returned home, she made her husband a special tea and waited patiently for him to arrive home. She'd told him to be back for no later than seven o'clock and he'd agreed. Everything was set and Victoria thought of the diamond ring. She wondered if tonight was the night he would place it on her finger and tell her that she still rocked his world.

Victoria had prepared Oscar's favourite meal. Chicken in white wine sauce with sauté potatoes. His mother had shown her how to make it several months before. If it was left to Victoria, beans and toast would have been her speciality most nights. The table was set for the two of them. Two large scented candles burned in the middle of the pine table. The lighting was soft and everything was ready for when her husband walked in through the doors.

She wore her sexy black dress and had clipped her hair back from her face just the way he liked it. The noise of Oscar coming in the house made her jump.

"Hi love, come and sit down" she said in a high-pitched voice as he trudged into the room. "I've made you your favourite tea. I'm going to spoil you tonight my little chucky egg, because I love you so much." Victoria could always turn on the charm when she knew a present awaited for her. Oscar took off his coat and threw it on the side cabinet that was next to the dining table.

Oscar took a curious look round the room and asked why they had candles on the table instead of the large chandelier lights switched on. Victoria smiled and told him she thought they would have a romantic night together and the candles would help set the mood. Oscar plodded to the table with a grumpy look on his face. You could tell he really couldn't be arsed with all the fuss and he was just doing it to please his wife.

The meal went well and Victoria had tried feeding her husband some of his food. When she placed a piece of chicken on her folk and slowly placed it into his mouth, he looked at her as if she had gone mad.

"Bloody hell. What's up with you tonight? What have I done to deserve all this treatment?" Victoria laughed and carried on feeding him his food, trying to make it as sexy as possible.

"Oscar, I think we should spend more nights like this. We need to find time for each other don't you think?" You could tell by his face that he couldn't have given a flying fuck and he just nodded to keep her happy. Still, Victoria waited for her surprise but it never came. She'd even tried hinting to him that she would like a new ring for her index finger but he didn't twig.

Pudding was next on the menu and Oscar rubbed his belly once the last spoonful of his chocolate cake and custard hit his lips. He had already made it quite clear that he was tired and the chance of any loving that night was definitely off the agenda.

Later, Victoria lay in bed tossing and turning as her husband slept at the side of her. She couldn't stop thinking about the whereabouts of the ring as she stoked her bare finger. Slowly she rolled out of bed and headed downstairs in search of his briefcase.

Her eyes scanned the area and she finally located it on the floor near the dining table. She slowly seated herself at the table before she opened it. Her ear turned to the door and she made sure there was no sign of Oscar as she listened. Her face showed signs of strain as her fingers struggled to open the first two locks. After a few attempts, a clicking noise brought a smile to her face.

She searched from top to bottom but couldn't find it. She became like a wild woman, throwing the contents across the table. Moments passed and she concluded the ring wasn't there. Sinking her head into her hands, she tried to think; where else would he have put it? Her eyes scanned the room and she noticed his jacket swinging from the chair. As if she'd shit her knickers she jumped up to search it.

Victoria searched every pocket in the coat and still there was no sign. His wallet was there but nothing else only a few old toffee wrappers. She slowly paced the front room and tried to gather her thoughts, but no matter how much she tried, the same scenario came into her head.

"The bastard's got another woman, I know he has," she

mumbled under her breath. "Oh let me find out and I'll make him pay through his teeth."

Her temper was flowing and she poured herself a glass of Vodka from the drinks cabinet to calm her nerves. She needed a plan to catch him and she racked her brains trying to find a solution.

The next morning Victoria wasn't in work and she'd planned to meet her friend Tina for lunch. Tina was a wise head who had been through a terrible time with her partner in the past. Her husband had previously cheated on her and she was now trying to rebuild her life without him.

Victoria met Tina in Manchester city centre. They sat in their favourite coffee shop waiting to get served. Tina knew almost instantly that something was wrong with Victoria by her body language. She waited until their coffee had arrived before she spoke. The waiter eventually placed the two coffees on the table. They both reached over and sipped at them before the conversation began.

It was Tina who spoke first and she commented on the weather to break the ice.

"Oh it's so cold today. I'm so sick of this English weather I need sunshine in my life." Victoria smiled but she could tell something was lying heavy on her mind.

"So love what's been happening in your life? You look like you have the worries of the world on your shoulders."

Victoria felt uneasy and she didn't really like discussing her private life with anyone but her worries were driving her mad and she needed to get them off her chest.

Victoria reached for her coffee and prepared herself to tell Tina exactly what was on her mind. The café was unusually quiet. The weather might have had a lot to do with it as it was pissing down outside and it may have caused shoppers to stay indoors.

Costa was a popular place in Manchester to go and meet up with friends. The leather sofas scattered around the shop made the customers feel at home. The deep red walls made the place feel warm and friendly. Tina watched Victoria eagerly, prompting her to reveal what was on her mind.

"Are you going to tell me what's the matter with you or not? Because a problem shared is a problem halved." Victoria pulled at her coat and fidgeted. She took a deep breath as her head turned from looking out of the window.

"It's Oscar, I think the bastard is having an affair." The silence filtered through Costa's walls and it seemed forever before any of them spoke.

"Don't be silly, Oscar loves you to death. He would never jeopardize what he has with you for some silly little slut." Victoria moved closer to Tina and kept her voice low as she continued.

"Don't be so sure love. I have a gut feeling and I know I'm right. How could I ever prove it?" Tina looked at her and remembered the way she'd felt when her husband was found out. Her heart went out to her.

"If he's got another woman, take the no good twat for every penny he's got," Tina ranted in an angry voice. "That's where I made my mistake. I missed out on a lot of money, you know? You need evidence love, and lots of it, because once you go to court, you need it to prove he was being unfaithful. He wouldn't have a leg to stand on if you've got evidence. You can take the cunt for every penny he's got." Tina's face looked angry as she chewed on her finger nails.

Victoria listened and by the end of their meeting, they had decided to get a private detective to find the required evidence. The more Tina heard about Oscar's behaviour the more she decided that Victoria was right. As the pair parted, Victoria felt happier that she'd shared her problems. The thought of Oscar cheating on her with another woman sent hate through her and as soon as she got home, she decided she would make plans to catch him in the act.

Victoria drove home with haste. Her heart raced at the thought of her husband seeing another woman. She listened to the radio and listened to some old song they were playing, she would have usually sung along with the tune but not today. Arriving home, she looked at the driveway and knew she was returning to an empty house once again. Victoria had taken a couple of days off work and planned to spend them relaxing but in her state of mind she was far from relaxed.

Searching for the phone directory, she sat on the chair in the front room looking at a list of Private Detectives. The names stood out from the page and she realised how serious the whole matter really was. They were listed all over the page and she didn't have a clue where to start. She finally came across an advert that seemed exactly what she was looking for. She read the words over and over again before she picked up the phone and dialled the number.

Once someone had picked up the phone she could barely bring herself to speak and it took a few moments before she answered.

"Hello Bernadette speaking, how can I help you?"

Victoria cleared her throat and after taking several deep breaths she replied.

"Hello, my name is Victoria Greybank, and I was wondering if you could help me." The woman's voice was very pleasant and she urged her to continue.

"What is it you require my love? We do lots of different kinds of work." Victoria poured her heart out to the voice at the end of the phone and sobbed as she told her she thought her husband was having an affair.

Bernadette was sympathetic and she told her that they would have to meet up to start the ball rolling. She also told her that many other women had gone through the same scenario and she wasn't alone in doubting her husband's infidelity.

The meeting was set for the next morning and Victoria decided she would meet her at a discreet place on the outskirts of the city centre. The phone call ended and Victoria fell back into the chair exhausted.

Looking round the front room, she stared at every piece of furniture and remembered how they had shopped together for most of the items. Victoria played with her white gold wedding ring and slowly twisted it round her finger. Anger seeped through her and the thought of her husband being unfaithful made her die deep inside.

Victoria put the phone directory back in its place and she decided to go and see Oscar in the shop. She knew it was her day off but she just felt like she needed to see her husband for some strange reason.

She'd already run over the idea of him having an affair in her mind and the outcome was more or less the same. She would make him pay big time she thought and as the days passed his penance would get bigger every day. She planned to ruin him and the slut he was shagging too.

Victoria walked into the shop. Katie looked shocked to see her and tried to make quick conversation.

"Hello love, thought you were having a few days off?" Victoria made her way round the counter past her and started to look at the new rings in the display cabinet.

"You know me Katie; I can't keep away from the place. Where's my devoted husband? In the back?" Katie smiled and told her Oscar was doing some paperwork in the office. As she came to join her to look at some more rings, she noticed Katie was acting strange.

"There are some really nice rings aren't there?" Victoria opened the glass cabinet and looked at a ring in more detail. Katie stood by her side and pointed to a ring she had liked. As she pointed to the ring, Victoria caught a glimpse of a sparkling diamond on her finger.

At first she remained silent but as she looked at it closely she realised it was the ring she'd seen in her husband's briefcase days before. Victoria's heart pumped with anger and she had wanted to rag Katie about the shop there and then but she gathered her thoughts and quickly brought the ring into the conversation.

"That's an amazing ring; let me have a closer look." Victoria grabbed her hand and helped slide it from her finger.

Katie couldn't hide her embarrassment and passed it to Victoria. The silence was deadly as Victoria focused on the engraved words in the ring. Now she knew what she felt in her heart was true and the truth was staring her right in the face. Her husband was having an affair.

Half of Victoria wanted to shout out that she knew their seedy secret and the other half wanted to remain calm. She remembered what Tina had told her and knew that without evidence, she wouldn't have a leg to stand on in court.

"Oh, it's lovely Katie. It must have cost your boyfriend quite a lot of money." Katie's head couldn't keep still and she looked everywhere in the shop except into Victoria's face.

They both chatted for a short while and Victoria knew one hundred percent her husband was shagging Katie's brains out. She now looked at Katie and weighed up what she had that she didn't.

Katie tried to make out she was busy and pulled a tray of rings out from the counter pretending to clean them. Victoria watched her every move and desperately tried not to let her know that she knew of her guilt.

"Dirty little trollop" she mumbled under her breath. At one stage, she nearly lost her cool and went to punch the slapper in the face but she managed to master her emotions.

"Better go and see my devoted husband then hadn't I?" Katie didn't answer and Victoria made her way to the small back office ready to face Oscar.

The corridor was narrow and poorly lit as she walked down it. Holding her back against the wall, she tried to remain calm.

"Dirty fucking bastard! Dirty bald bastard!" she mumbled under her breath. She now pulled at her hair in the hallway. "How dare he shag another woman, when I'm here for him? I've been starved of sex and the dirty twat has been going elsewhere." Victoria opened the door slowly. She crept inside. Oscar didn't notice her.

She looked at his cocky face as he sat with his legs up on the wooden desk. He was laughing loudly as he spoke on the phone. How could he be so happy, she thought, when her world was crumbling down around her?

The office was only small and the red carpet looked like it hadn't seen a Hoover in months. The bin was overflowing with paper and several cups were still on the table from days before.

Victoria remained in the same position and tapped her finger on her tooth as she watched him. Everything seemed so obvious now, how could she have been so foolish and not seen what was in front of her very own eyes? No wonder he was always working late and going on weekends away.

Revenge filtered through her and she left the office without speaking to him. On her way out, she smiled at Katie and let her know in a roundabout way she was on to her little secret.

Victoria shouted goodbye as she left the shop and headed towards her car. Once there she sobbed her heart out. As she headed home the tears fell onto her cheek. The journey seemed to take forever and she felt like she was in a daze. Once she pulled up on her driveway she looked at her eyes in the mirror and tried to wipe away the mascara that had spread all over them.

The home she loved so much seemed nothing more than a possession now. She wanted to burn it down there and then. Grabbing her handbag from the passenger side she walked up to the front door like it was some kind of trial. As she entered, she collapsed onto the carpet and screamed at the top of her voice.

"Fucking dirty, dirty bald fucker! I've given you the best years of my life and this is how you treat me." Victoria hit the carpet with her clenched fist and kicked her legs liked a spoilt child. She knew she would never be the same again and the man she'd once loved was about to find out exactly just what his wife was capable of.

★

Oscar came home from work that night and Victoria tried to remain as calm as ever. As she sat facing him on the chair, she watched his every movement. Every line in his face now seemed obvious. As she watched him eat, her heart sank. Oscar was oblivious to his wife as he sat watching some documentary on the television.Victoria now thought she'd start a conversation with him and watched his face as he tried to hide his guilt.

"I called in the shop today but you were busy so I left you to it. I was talking to Katie for a while and she showed me her new ring. It's amazing isn't it? Someone must really think the world of her to give her something like that." Oscar fidgeted around trying to find the remote control for the television and she could tell he wasn't going to answer her so she continued probing him.

"I've never heard Katie talk about any boyfriends have you? In fact, I've never known her to have a boyfriend. She's such an attractive woman. She could have the pick of the men out there, what do you think?" Oscar knew he couldn't ignore her again and mumbled under his breath.

"Never really took much interest of her love. I only have eyes for you my sweetheart."Victoria wanted to run at him and plunge a fist into his face as he continued. "There are always men phoning the shop for her, so I don't think she's going short. She's not my type anyway. She's too up her own arse for my liking. Katie's always in the mirror every time you look at her."Victoria couldn't believe her ears and the sooner she had the evidence to shove in the bastard's face the better.

They both went to bed at the same time that night, and as they got under the covers, he cuddled into the small of her back. His arms reached round her body and he dragged her closer to him. She could feel his manhood sticking into her back and she wondered if he wanted sex.

Oscar now began to kiss her neck and once she turned

to face him he said goodnight and turned the other way. Victoria felt like she wanted to turn him round and tell him to fuck her brains out, but her words were glued to her lips. She wondered now if he was capable of shagging someone else and hoped when she met the detective tomorrow they wouldn't find a thing on her husband and she could love him again like she always had.

Sleep didn't come easily for Victoria that night and she lay restless all night long. Morning came and Oscar left the house as usual at around eight thirty. Victoria had made him his usual piece of toast and he asked her what she had planned for her last day off work.

"I'm going into town to get a few bits, and then I might meet up with Tina for lunch. What do you fancy for tea, because I can pick something up for us in town?" Oscar quickly looked for his coat and told her that he had a business meeting that night and wouldn't be home until late. Oscar had always worked late and she had never been bothered by it until now. He could tell by her face she was a bit upset and came to where she was stood.

"It's an important meeting love, otherwise you know I would be at home with you don't you?" Victoria nodded but she had to turn her head from view, as her eyes were ready to burst. Oscar quickly kissed her and said goodbye. Victoria sat at the kitchen table and her heart jumped about in her chest. She checked her watch and knew she would have to get a move on to go and meet Bernadette.

Looking through her wardrobe, she searched for something to wear. Her black pants looked at her and gave her the signal that they were the right thing to wear. She also grabbed a red top that showed off her terrific breasts. Victoria hurried and quickly ran the brush through her hair and tied it back with a black and gold bobble. Once she'd put her black boots on she was ready to go and meet the woman who could end the torment she'd had been feeling for the last few weeks.

Victoria planned her speech in her mind as she drove to where they had planned to meet. She decided she was going to be as blunt as possible and tell her exactly what she wanted from her. As she pulled up in the car park, she checked herself one last time in the mirror and set off on the short walk to the café.

Bernadette sat waiting as Victoria approached the café. At first, Victoria hadn't been sure she was the person she had arranged to meet. Bernadette was quite young and had shoulder length hair. Her hair was a soft brown colour and she was dressed casually in a pair of jeans and a pale blue jumper. As Victoria neared the café, Bernadette stood and walked towards her.

"Hi I'm Bernadette are you Victoria?" Victoria smiled softly and nodded her head. She was quite surprised that Bernadette had known she was the one she was meeting and asked her how she knew.

"How did you know it was me you were meeting, am I that obvious?" Bernadette smiled and started to walk inside the café before she spoke.

"Listen honey, I've been doing this job quite a long time and I can always tell a woman who's got problems at a glance." Victoria smiled as they sat and ordered them both a cup of coffee. As they waited for their drinks Victoria looked around the café and checked there was no one inside she knew. The place was deserted at this time and the employees were busy cleaning and getting everything ready for the afternoon rush.

Once their drinks arrived, Victoria could feel Bernadette's eyes on her and she took a deep breath before she started the conversation.

"I don't know where to start with this, so I'm just going to say it how it is. I think my husband is having an affair and I want to know for sure so I can make the bastard pay. I need evidence though, photographs or something like that so he can't deny it."

Bernadette now took a small note pad from her black leather bag and started to ask her some questions. She wrote a full description of her husband and asked her a lot about his everyday habits including where he would eat lunch. She also asked her if she had any suspicions about who he was seeing and asked how long she had suspected her husband was having an affair.

Bernadette had dealt with so many cases where the husband had been unfaithful but she still knew the results would be heartbreaking. The women she'd previously worked with all had been quite well off and once she had handed them the information that their husbands had been cheating she had seen them fall to the ground and sob like their lives were over.

She now explained to Victoria about the service she offered and told her about the fee. Victoria would have given everything she owned to find out the truth and told Bernadette the money wasn't a problem.

Once they had chatted for a while, Victoria told her that her husband had told her he was at a business meeting that same night. Bernadette's eyes lit up and she knew she could start her investigations straight away.

The two women spoke for about an hour and agreed that that night her surveillance of Oscar would begin. They both left at the same time and parted company as if they were old friends. As Victoria walked to the car, her mind was working overtime as she imagined her husband with another woman. Her body felt weak as she entered the car and she knew that one way or another her torment would soon be over.

Victoria called into the shop on her way home. As she looked at Katie and Oscar it was quite obvious they were close. Victoria could have kicked herself now and slowly made her way to the both of them as they stood chatting at the counter.

"You two look lost in each other's eyes," she said pointedly.

Oscar immediately lifted his head and stared right at her. "Hello sweetheart, I didn't see you there." Oscar continued talking to Katie as Victoria came to join them. Victoria's eyes focused on Katie as she spoke and watched her expression as she tried to make her move on Oscar. Victoria's hands slid round his neck and she ruffled his thin hair as she spoke.

"I've been missing you my darling husband, and couldn't keep away so I thought I would come and take you out for lunch." Oscar wriggled his body to remove her hands and you could see he felt uncomfortable.

"I've got no time love, I'm so busy today. I've got shit loads of paperwork to get through, perhaps some other time." Victoria cringed and his words felt like a knife was being plunged deep into her heart. Her face showed how disappointed she was as she tried again to win some affection.

"Well what about if we go out tonight? We can go to that little restaurant in town that you like." Oscar turned his back on her and searched a drawer looking for some paperwork before he spoke.

Katie stood looking like she wanted the ground to swallow her up. She dipped her head and continued to read a letter in front of her. Oscar could feel his wife's eyes burning into his back and slowly turned to finish the conversation.

"Victoria you already know I've got a business meeting tonight, so how can we possibly go out? Tell you what; we can go out on Friday night instead." He felt both the women's eyes on him and Katie looked like she was going to burst. Victoria loved the way they were both feeling and wanted to take it a step further just to watch Katie's face drop.

"Oh alright love. You know Katie I love him so much, he does anything to make me happy. Don't you love?" Oscar's face was red with embarrassment and he couldn't look at Katie whilst Victoria was still in the room. Victoria told them both she was leaving and kissed her husband before she left. Katie had already left the room and it was obvious she couldn't stand his wife getting more attention than she did.

As night fell, Bernadette phoned Victoria to tell her they were going to follow Oscar. On hearing the news she quickly phoned her friend Tina and told her to come over as soon as possible as she didn't want to be alone. Tina arrived sometime later with a large bottle of wine under her arm. Victoria couldn't wait until she sat down.

"Tina, what if they find him with someone, what will I do? I'm so scared of being by myself and I don't know if I could ever cope without him. What am I going to do?"

Tina looked at her and told her to get a couple of glasses. Once she'd filled them, Tina started talking and made no secret of the way she felt.

"If he's fucking around love, there is only one option.

Take the bastard for every penny he's got. You are always saying you would like a holiday home, so now would be the time to get one. You have to learn that most men are dirty conniving bastards and they don't give a fuck about you once they have got a bit of attention from some little slut."Victoria took a large drink of her wine and listened as Tina bad mouthed her ex-husband once again.

"Look at that bastard of a husband I had. I gave him the best years of my life and he's walking round as if I never existed. Twats the lot of them Victoria and the sooner you realise that the better."Victoria just gazed at her and didn't want to put her husband in the same circle of men Tina was talking about and tried her best to defend him.

"Oscar hasn't been found guilty yet Tina. I'm just suspicious that's all and need to put my mind at rest one way or the other."Tina laughed and lit a cigarette.

"My dear you're so fucking vulnerable. I've told you before, get yourself a toy boy and have some fun yourself." Tina laughed and started to tell her about the times she'd spent with her own toy boy, "I've never had it so good Victoria. Sex is great, and these young ones can go all night, not like that husband of mine. I've started to get kinky as well. Anything I ask for he's only too willing to please me. These men will do anything for money love, and I love the way they make me feel, you should try one."

At the moment Victoria couldn't think of anything else and she watched the clock like a dog waiting for its owner to come home, as Tina continued to talk about her ex.

★

Bernadette watched Oscar leave the jewellery shop and she kept a low profile as she watched him get into his car to leave. She'd done this so many times in the past; she knew exactly how to catch a cheating spouse.

Peter sat next to her; he was her wingman as he watched Oscar's every move in the car. Oscar drove for about fifteen minutes and finally pulled into a car park that belonged to a hotel. Bernadette didn't pull in straight behind him; she waited a few minutes to see where he was going and parked opposite him in the car park. Oscar rummaged round in his car for a few moments and he looked like he was speaking to someone on the phone. Bernadette and Peter locked their car up and headed into the hotel as Oscar chatted on his phone.

When they got inside, the hotel looked quite busy and a few people were stood chatting at the reception. The hotel was immaculate and the marble floors looked like an ice rink. Bernadette and Peter headed to the bar to get a good vantage point from there they could see all the goings on.

As they sat down they scanned the bar area. They noticed quite a few women sat on their own and one stood out like a sore thumb. As they looked closer at her, she was checking her watch and watching the door as if her life depended on it.

She was dressed in a long black coat. It buttoned up to the top of her neck and they could see she felt uncomfortable in it. Her black lace tights were visible at the hem of her coat. The black patent shoes had heels that made her look a lot taller than she actually was. As they sipped at their drinks, the door opened and they watched the woman's face light up with excitement.

To Bernadette and Peter this was great news, because sometimes in their line of work they would have to wait weeks before they uncovered anything, but tonight they had struck gold first time. As they watched Oscar came over and was all over her like a rash.

"Well, looks like this will be a short case Bernie. All we need now is some evidence and our job will be done. Fucking hell you wouldn't think a girl like her would be interested in a man like him would you?" Bernie agreed and carried on watching them as she spoke.

"See the thing with men is, all the blood rushes from their brain to their dicks and they can't think straight. As for her, she's probably being well rewarded for whatever she's doing for him. It's such a shame because his wife is lovely." Peter smiled and watched the two of them as they made their way to a small corner of the room. As they sat down they could see Oscar stroking her legs and it was obvious she aroused him.

The other people in the bar were oblivious to the couple and carried on enjoying their night. The bar was getting livelier now and music playing. The bar had a country theme to it and the walls were covered in rich red wallpaper. The open fire was so relaxing to watch and several of the customers sat near it to feel the warmth. The furniture was made of oak and the tops of the chairs had a dark red cushion on them. Bernadette looked at the couple and she knew it wouldn't be long before they left. She nudged Peter in his side as she saw them stand to leave. They knew the next part of their job was about to begin.

As they watched them depart, Peter followed behind while Bernadette nipped to the toilets. Oscar strolled into reception and picked up a key. As Peter stood near the entrance pretending to read something, he could hear the receptionist saying 'Room 112'. The receptionist was no stranger to Oscar and told him to have a good night. He winked at her as he walked off holding Katie's hand.

Peter headed back to the bar and greeted Bernadette

as she came out of the toilets. "Room 112. Ground floor I think. We need to see where it is so I can see if I can get anything from outside."

Bernadette quickly went to the receptionist and tried to keep her busy while Peter sneaked into the main hall and tried to locate the room where Oscar and Katie were staying. The corridors were very narrow and the pale blue carpet complimented the gold wallpaper. On each side of the corridor were several doors with brass numbers on them. Peter listened carefully as he headed round the corner. He could hear giggling not far in front of him. His body froze. Slowly he peeped round the corner.

As he looked he could see Katie and Oscar fooling around outside their room. He saw Oscar lift up her long black coat and slide his hands onto her thighs. Peter nearly exploded with excitement as he watched and he could feel his own manhood swelling in his trousers. Katie was wearing nothing but a black Basque under her coat. Her suspenders had little red ribbons on them – she looked like sex on legs.

"Lucky, lucky bastard," he whispered to himself before he made his way back. When he arrived at reception Bernadette was still talking to the receptionist. He sneaked at the back of her and squeezed her bum cheeks. "Come on gas bags. We've got work to do."

Peter walked round the building and told Bernadette to get the camera from the car. He counted the room numbers under his breath as he walked around the perimeter of the hotel, and finally stopped when he found the room he required. Bernadette crept behind him and passed him the camera. They both tried to conceal themselves in nearby bushes. When they were ready, Peter stood up to try to get a glimpse through the window. He crouched and moved towards it. As he stood on his tiptoes he could just about see through the small gap in the curtains. The light in the room was poor and he had to get up closer to see what was going on.

Looking through the small gap he nearly fell to the ground with shock. Oscar was on all fours on the bed wearing what looked like a black silken thong and a dog collar round his neck. He nearly pissed himself laughing and urged Bernadette to come and have a look.

"Get your arse up here Bernie. He's a proper kinky fucker is our Oscar." As she joined him, she got the shock of her life.

Katie stood with one leg on the bed and Oscar was licking her black lacy tights. She looked amazing and her confidence showed in the bedroom. She now kicked at Oscar's body softly and he looked like he knew what the kick meant.

Oscar leant towards her and pulled down the top of her Basque revealing two erect nipples. Katie grabbed his collar and threw him back onto the bed and it was obvious she was cross with him. They could see her now straddling over him, as he lay defenceless on the bed. As they watched her grab, his face she spoke with an angry expression. Oscar could be seen removing his thong.

Bernadette and Peter nearly pissed themselves laughing but had to stop themselves. They had witnessed many sex scenes before in their line of work but nothing as kinky as this.

"Get the snaps quick Peter, before they get on to us."

Peter placed the camera between the small gaps in the curtains as Bernadette checked the area to make sure they hadn't been spotted. As Peter's camera started to take the pictures all Bernadette could hear was a clicking noise.

The photos were taken and they both made a quick exit towards the car. As they were seated in the car Peter shook his head and burst into laughter as he scanned through the thumbnails on the display.

"That's what I call fucking saucy! Who would have thought Oscar was a kinky fucker?" Bernadette smiled. She loved his way with words and he had her doubled over with laughter within minutes.

"We should have knocked on the window and he would have died a thousand deaths. Imagine his face. How could he ever explain why he was wearing a kinky thong and a dog collar? There must be something wrong with him in the head. Whatever happened to a good old knee trembler?" Bernadette nudged him in the side as he started to drive from the car park. He would have secretly stayed and watched more of the action if he had been alone, but he knew Bernadette would have gone mad if he had started getting aroused while he was working.

Bernadette had worked with Peter for a few years now and they got on really well. She'd met him first as a client when he needed help to find out whether his wife was having an affair. Once she had given him the damning evidence he needed, he'd got rid of his wife as quickly as possible and never looked back.

Things had always been good with Peter and they had a brief fling together after his divorce, but they realised immediately they were wrong for each other and remained friends. Instead they became business partners.

It was getting late and the pair couldn't wait to get back to the office to look at the pictures close up on the laptop. Once they had uploaded them they could see the hard evidence clearly. Once they saw it with their own eyes, the reality of what they had really witnessed hit home.

"Fucking hell Bernie, I feel sorry for his wife when she sees these shots. They're really sick photos. You would only see something like this in a porno movie or something like that." Bernadette nodded and when they printed out a large close up of the picture to show Victoria, she knew he was right. The photo showed Katie dressed in her black Basque and fishnet stockings. At the bottom of the snap, it revealed Oscar looking a prize prick wearing only his black thong and dog collar.

"I will phone his wife tomorrow and arrange to meet her. I don't think anything will prepare her for what I have to show her. I just hope she gets rid of the twat and makes him pay big time." Peter shook his head.

"I bet he gets out of it and blames it all on his wife. That's what usually happens. The wife always starts to find excuses for their partners and blames themselves for their infidelity."

"Well I don't think Victoria will be that kind. I think she's going to destroy the bastard once she finds out for sure. She's a stunner you know. It makes you wonder why he was cheating on her when he has a gorgeous wife at home. They say the grass is always greener but if men just mowed their own lawns a bit more, they would realise exactly what they had."

Peter agreed with her for a change and once they'd printed all the pictures out they went their separate ways for some well deserved rest.

The sound of Oscar getting into bed in the early hours of the morning disturbed Victoria. As she inhaled, she could smell perfume all over him as he lay beside her. She wanted to hit him there and then, but something inside her told her to wait until she had all the evidence she needed to convict him. Within minutes he was snoring and the sound of him next to her made her feel physically sick.

Sleep was a million miles away as Victoria stared around the bedroom thinking how different things would be without him in her life. She had already started planning what she was going to do with his money and the first thing on the agenda was a holiday home. All her friends had villas abroad and she couldn't see why she should be any different. The weather in England was shite and perhaps she needed some sunshine in her life

The following morning Victoria sat in the kitchen listening to the kettle boil. She could hear Oscar get out of bed and prepared herself. As he walked into the kitchen, he yawned and asked her for a coffee. Victoria didn't speak a word and placed another cup on the side. Oscar reached for the morning paper and started to read it as Victoria finished making the brews for them both.

"What time did you get in last night, because I was dead to the world and didn't hear a thing." Oscar carried on reading the paper and mumbled under his breath.

"Oh I don't know, it wasn't that late, but you know what these meetings are like they go on all night."

Victoria cringed and clenched her fist tightly. She wanted to punch right through the paper but until she knew for sure what the dirty bastard was up to, she had to bite her lip.

Oscar left the house at the normal time and Victoria couldn't wait to see the back of him so she could get to work herself.

She now rushed about the house and started to get ready. As she went into the bathroom, she looked into the mirror, her fingers pulled at her eyes and she moved her face closer to the mirror.

Victoria now started to talk to herself as she washed her face. "You've let yourself go girl, you need to start looking after yourself again. No wonder your husband doesn't come home at nights. You need to get your arse in gear."

The sound of her phone ringing stopped Victoria in her tracks and she rushed to her handbag to answer it.

"Hello, Victoria Greybank speaking." The voice she heard made her concentrate and she sat on the bed wearing only a towel. Bernadette told her they needed a meeting. Her heart pounded in her chest. She asked her why but the private detective kept her cards close to her chest and just said there had been a few developments in her husband's case.

Victoria told her she could meet her in the next hour and told her they could meet at the same café as before. Bernadette agreed and the phone call ended. Victoria felt like a nervous wreck and remained on the bed for a few moments to regain her thoughts.

She now phoned Oscar and told him she would be a little late as she had to nip into town to put her dress in the dry-cleaners. He never questioned her and told her not to rush into work, as it wasn't that busy.

Victoria hurried to get ready. Half of her wanted to stay at home and never know the truth but the other half of her was like a woman possessed and wanted to know the truth as soon as possible. Everything she did now seemed to go in slow motion and it seemed forever before she located her car keys from her bag. She checked herself one last time in the mirror and her grey suit and white shirt looked fine. She picked up her handbag and headed for the car as if her life depended on it.

The traffic was quiet that morning and the rush hour seemed to have passed. Victoria was driving quite quickly and she had to calm herself before she caused an accident. It was cold and the winter months were now kicking in. As she waited at the traffic lights, she watched people snuggling up in their winter coats, rubbing their cold bodies as they waited at the bus stop.

The lights finally changed and Victoria was the first away. Every scenario was now going through her mind. She even considered phoning her friend Tina, but the thought of her down her ear telling her she told her so made her think again.

As she made her way to the café, she could see Bernadette waiting for her with a large brown envelope in her hand. At first, she didn't think anything of it, and then it clicked in her mind. Victoria wanted to turn and run. She wanted to run far, far away where no one could ever find her. She felt sadness and her face was grief stricken.

"Hello Victoria," Bernadette said in a soft voice, "do you want a coffee or something?" Victoria told Bernadette to take a seat and she went to order them. She tried to make out what was happening by Bernadette's face but as she looked over to her, she was looking in her handbag for something. Victoria carried the drinks back to the table and tried desperately to stop her hands shaking.

"Oh it's bloody cold out there today I can't seem to get warm." Bernadette agreed and sipped at her drink before she began. She had thought over and over in her mind how to tell Victoria but finally just passed her the envelope and waited for her reaction.

Victoria looked at the envelope and slowly touched it with her fingers as she stared at Bernadette. Her heart pounded inside her chest and she pulled at her blouse trying to feel the cold air on her body.

"What is it?" she asked in a trembling voice.

"I don't know how to tell you this love, but you were right about your husband and he has been cheating." Victoria now ripped open the envelope and pulled the glossy photos out on the table. Bernadette watched her every movement and braced herself for the moment she saw her husband with the other woman.

Victoria studied the first picture for what seemed a lifetime time and shook her head with disgust as she moved to the next one. You could tell by her face she was distraught and Bernadette felt every bit of her pain alongside her.

"The dirty, perverted cunt. I can't believe this is my husband all dressed up in fucking sexy shit." Bernadette looked round the café and she felt embarrassed as Victoria's voice got louder. "Fucking business meeting. How could I have not known? And look who he's with. Fucking Katie!" Victoria held her head back, scratching at her scalp. You could tell she was already planning revenge and her face was white as she continued.

"The pair of dirty, no-good fuckers. I've given him the best years of my life and he does something like this. He doesn't even like sex, so I can't understand it all."

Bernadette came closer to her side, and cradled her in her arms as she could see her heart was breaking into a million pieces right in front of her. She tried to console her as she passed her a tissue from her bag. Victoria dried her eyes and sniffled as she spoke.

"Well, I knew deep down inside he was playing around but I never thought he would be into kinky sex. You think you know someone don't you? They just prove you so wrong at the drop of a hat. He has never done anything remotely sexy with me in all the years we've been married, so why is he doing it now?" Bernadette had been asked these questions so many times before and each time her answer had been the same.

"Men are funny creatures love and nobody understands why they go elsewhere when they have everything at home. I think when men reach a certain age they panic and think they need some kind of adventure and excitement in their life but they don't think of the consequences do they? Usually when they're found out they can't apologise enough for their actions"

Victoria sat up straight and placed the photos back in the envelope. She quickly settled the bill with Bernadette and wrote her a cheque. Once she'd finished writing she reached her hand to Bernadette and shook it firmly. She thanked her for her help and stood up from the chair. Just before she left she looked at Bernadette and smiled.

Somehow, Bernadette knew she was a survivor and knew her husband would get his payback some way or another. Her phone now started to ring and as she reached for it, she waved to Victoria one last time before she disappeared.

Victoria sat in her car for a few minutes before she started the engine. She knew her life with Oscar was definitely over and she planned her next move as she drove to the shop.

Once parked outside it she stared at the shop doors as she checked her face once last time in the mirror. The walk to the doors seemed to take forever and her legs shook as she pulled open the shop door. Katie greeted Victoria with her usual sweet smile and carried on with her work without a care in the world as Victoria slowly walked by her. Victoria clenched her fist and found it hard not to rip her hair out there and then but she held herself well and walked through to the back office.

Shouting Oscar's name she waited for him to reply, but there was none. She looked in every room then decided to go and ask Katie. Her husband's concubine told her he'd just nipped out and he shouldn't be long and told her of the parcel he had to get posted. Victoria remained as quiet as a mouse. Her mind was made up and she planned her next move. She got the shop keys off the side and slowly walked to the front door and locked it.

Katie lifted her head as she heard the noise of the front door being locked and looked at Victoria with concerned eyes.

Victoria stood in front of her and reached into her handbag to pull out the envelope that contained the photos. She placed the envelope on the side and now walked round the counter to face Katie.

"What's the matter Victoria, you look like you've seen a ghost?" said Katie now confronted by her boss.

"Good question Katie. What could be possibly wrong with me?" she stared at Katie and moved closer to her face. "Should I tell you what's wrong with me love or do you already know?" Katie never thought for one minute that her secret had been uncovered and urged her to continue.

"My fucking husband, that's what's wrong with me. He's playing around with some little slut." Katie's face now went blood red and you could tell she felt embarrassed.

Victoria reached for the photos and stood at the side of Katie as she pulled the first one from the envelope. As Katie glanced over the photo, her heart skipped a beat and she thought she was going to have a heart attack. Victoria grabbed her by the hair and pulled it down towards the counter.

"You dirty little slut. How dare you think you can sleep around with my fucking husband? I have been so good to you and this is how you repay me." She let go of her hair and as soon as she saw her full face, she slapped her with all her might several times.

"Nice ring you have Katie. Do you think I don't know where it came from?" Katie started to cry and the tears fell upon her cheek as she stood like a scolded child.

"Since when does my husband like kinky sex? You little whore! I bet this was all your idea wasn't it?" She held the photos up and showed Katie the remaining photos from the envelope. The shop assistant took a deep breath before she spoke and screamed at Victoria as she pulled away from her.

"No it wasn't my idea. Your husband is the kinky one and loves dressing up. He loves being spanked, and he loves that I do it all for him. If you wasn't so much of a prude and a frigid bitch your husband wouldn't have strayed. So you only have yourself to blame." Victoria stood gobsmacked for a moment and reached for the keys to the door.

"Get your stuff and get out of my shop. Never darken my door again you trollop. And as for Oscar you're welcome to him. He's nothing but a bald perverted bastard, so you should be happy together." Katie ran to door and grabbed her handbag as she left. As she passed Victoria, she spoke for the last time.

"It was your husband who came on to me. I told him no but he wouldn't leave me alone." Victoria screamed as she passed.

"Get out. Get out of my sight you dirty slut." As she closed the door, she fell to the ground behind it and sobbed her heart out. Within minutes, the sound of her husband's voice at the door made her sit up. The noise of him knocking sent chills through her as slowly she stood up to let him in.

Oscar walked into the shop as Victoria closed the door behind him. As he looked at her, he thought somebody had just robbed the shop and started to panic.

"What did they take? Did they hurt you?" Victoria stood in front of the photos and passed them to Oscar as she leant against the counter.

His face dropped and he looked directly at his wife.

"It's not me. Do you think I'm into all that dirty shit?" Victoria looked at him with hate in her eyes; she spoke to him in a disgusted manner.

"Listen, Katie's already told me about your perverted fantasies, so don't waste your breath. I want a divorce and I want it as quickly as possible." As Oscar tried to grab her arm, she spat directly into his face. "Take your dirty perverted hands off me. Don't ever touch me again. I will have your stuff ready in about an hour, so get round to the house and get it as quickly as possible, because I want every trace of you gone from my life as soon as possible."

Oscar tried to stop her leaving, but she kicked him in his legs and he soon realised he had to let her go.

Her legs felt like jelly as she opened the car door. She felt like she couldn't breathe and felt like she needed to be sick. As she sat in the car, she turned the engine over and drove off like a wild woman to get as far away from her husband as possible.

When she reached her home, she immediately phoned her friend Tina. She couldn't stand being alone at this time and needed someone with her to keep her sane.

Victoria ran up the stairs and pulled out all Oscar's clothes onto the bed. "Dirty, dirty bastard" she whispered as she threw each piece of clothing. She was in some kind of trance and ran round the bedroom collecting anything that belonged to her husband. It seemed as if his processions were poisonous and she touched them only to pack them into his suitcases.

An hour later and four suitcases containing her husband's clothing were packed. The phone had been ringing endlessly since she arrived home and she didn't answer it knowing it would be her husband trying to win her over. Tina used her key and entered the house.

The sound of her voice now filled the house and Victoria made her way to the top of the stairs to greet her. Tina's face was distraught when she saw her and she ran all the way up the stairs to hold her friend in her arms.

"Fucking knew it. Told you didn't I? The wanker. Who was he seeing, is it anyone you know?" Victoria led her to the bedroom and when Tina saw all the suitcases scattered round the room she knew her friend was for real and Oscar was well and truly out of her life forever.

Victoria had always been a strong woman and Tina knew she would never have Oscar back. As they sat down on the bed, she passed Tina the photos and watched her face as she gazed over them.

"Oh my god! I can't believe this is Oscar. What the fuck is he dressed like that for? He's a proper sick pervert Victoria." Victoria dipped her head towards the floor and felt so ashamed of what her husband had become. Once Tina discovered who the woman was in the pictures, she yelled out at the top of her voice. "The dirty little slapper! The way you've looked after her whilst she's worked for you. Tell you what love; you can't trust anyone these days." Tina looked at her friend and realised this wasn't the time or the place to go into anything. She threw the photos to the ground and hugged her. After a while, Victoria dried her eyes and smiled at Tina.

"Who would have thought Oscar was a kinky fucker. I can't believe he likes dressing up like a twat." Tina doubled over laughing and they both tried to see the funny side of everything. "Bet he has been wearing your knickers for years love. You better check if any are missing." Tina now stood up and started to lift her skirt up. "Bet he would love these. Might be a bit tight for him, but by the looks of his photos he likes them tight." Both women continued calling Oscar names and somehow it helped turn the situation around.

They both went downstairs and opened several bottles of wine and before the day was out they were both pissed as farts.

Oscar called to the house and Tina was the one who passed him his suitcases. He had asked to speak to Victoria, but Tina looked him straight in the eyes and told him she didn't want any more to do with him. She also told him Victoria was taking him for every penny he had and with the pictures, he didn't stand a chance in court.

They both watched Oscar leave through the small window in the dining room and they watched as he struggled to lift his suitcases into the car. Tina had made a comment that his thong was sticking in his arse crease as he walked and they laughed that much they missed him drive away.

★

Life for Victoria was strange for the first couple of weeks without Oscar. She felt alone and didn't know what to do with herself. As she sat at home, most evenings the walls just stared at her and she felt like she was going crazy. Everything in the rooms reminded her of time spent with

Oscar and as she poured another glass of wine for herself, she made a decision that would change her life.

Victoria looked at the holiday home brochure that Tina had left her and turned each page in amazement looking at all the beautiful properties. Tina had told her there was an agent in town that would help her make the right choice of property. She also told her they would go with her to view the property and stay with her until the entire sale was completed.

Victoria made up her mind there and then. Tomorrow she decided she would go into town and see someone about a property abroad. She needed to get away from the house and all its memories.

2

GERALDINE MILLS HAD always been a handful. Even as a child, she'd caused her parents so much pain. Her parents were quite strict and they tried so many times to change the way their daughter behaved.

Geraldine went to private school from the age of thirteen. This wasn't her parent's idea but her grandmother's. She told them she would pay all the school fees and hopefully it would give Geraldine a better chance at life, so they went along with it hoping she would be right. Even from an early age, they knew they'd have problems with her. She had boyish ways and loved climbing trees and playing football. Her parents often worried she was a trainee lesbian.

Barbara and John lived comfortably and Geraldine never wanted for anything, except love. Her mother had always run her own business and loved the income her estate agency brought her. Barbara specialised in properties abroad and she was always jet-setting around the world selling some property or another. Geraldine's father John was also involved in property.

Geraldine was one of two children, her older sister Marie was the perfect child and never crossed her parents. Geraldine's problems started when she was thirteen. She missed her parents so much and demanded attention whatever way she could get it.

The boarding school was set in a big estate in the middle of nowhere, somewhere in Yorkshire. Geraldine could remember her first day at the school. She felt terrified as they drove up the gravel path towards its entrance. The principal was a middle-aged man. He had a noticeable receding hairline. When they'd first walked into the school Geraldine was amazed at the high ceilings. Lots of artwork decorated the reception's walls.

The corridors that led to the reception looked wet. The polish on them made the floor look like a mirror. If you looked closely enough you could see your face in it. The smell of the white orchids in a vase near the double doors gave the place a lovely welcoming smell. Geraldine inhaled their scent as she sat waiting with her parents.

A few older girls from the school filtered through the reception. They stood impatiently outside the office waiting to see a member of staff. One girl leant against the wall and stood with a mischievous grin on her face. The girls looked Geraldine up and down and knew by her shy face that she was a newcomer.

The uniform was boring and nothing to write home about. It consisted of a maroon coloured skirt with a white blouse and a grey v-neck jumper. Some of the girls wore a black tie, but you could see by the way they yanked at it round their necks that it irritated them. Five minutes passed and Geraldine's mother kept telling her to stop fidgeting.

She leant towards her and tried to straighten her clothing. Geraldine, under protest, wore a floral print cotton dress and a pale blue cardigan. She hated the way the feminine clothes made her feel.

Geraldine acted like a boy in her mannerisms. She sat on the chair with her legs parted and her hands dropped between them. Her hair looked a fiery red colour and her eyes had an unusual shade of green about them. Several freckles thrived on her pale skin. Her sister always mocked her about the brown blotches and she hated them with a passion.

The principal finally came out of his office. John stood up and walked towards him with his hand stretched out in front of him. They all shook hands and followed him to his office.

The room was long and narrow. At the far end stood a worried looking student who looked like she'd been in some kind of trouble. Her eyes looked puffed through crying.

The office was old. The gold carpet, that had deep red circles on it, had clearly seen better days. There was a table in the middle of the room and the principal escorted them to it.

Geraldine's eyes focused on an old piano to the side of them. She would have loved to have a mess around on it. Her fingers fanned open and she tapped them on her knee as if she was playing the piano.

The sunshine glared in through the window and you could see it was affecting Mr and Mrs Mills' eyesight. The principal located a long pole at the side of them and hooked the red velvet curtains until the sun rays disappeared.

"Welcome to Bowker Crescent private school. I'm John Tate and I am the principal of the school. We are an all girls' school and we do our best with all our pupils here to make sure they can achieve to the best of their abilities." Geraldine's parents introduced themselves.

"My name is John Mills and this is my wife, Barbara." They all nodded at one another and all their eyes focused on Geraldine.

"And what's your name young lady?" he asked in a polite voice. Geraldine looked at him and you could see her face burning up as he prompted her. "Have you lost your tongue young lady? What's your name?" Geraldine swallowed hard and whispered her name as the other girl at the bottom end of the room focused on her.

"Well, welcome to Bowker Crescent young lady. You are going to be such a happy student here. You're going to make your parents so proud of you."

Geraldine smiled and gazed down to where the girl stood. She pretended to listen as the principal went through a few procedures with her parents. The meeting lasted another hour and at the end of it, Mr Tate offered to show her parents around the school and answer any questions they had regarding their daughters stay there. As they left the office, the girl at the bottom of the room waved slowly at Geraldine and looked as sad as ever now they were leaving.

Each classroom looked more or less the same. The desks were quite old fashioned. They had a small ink well at the top right of them, and the lid lifted up so you could see inside it. Every classroom had a tall blackboard at the front. At the left of it were several large windows that gave a view of the outside grounds. Geraldine walked over to the window and gazed outside. Everything looked so peaceful and all the flowers as far as she could see were in full bloom. Everywhere she looked was covered in greenery and there wasn't a building in sight. Once the tour of the school was completed, they all made their way to the dormitories on the top corridor.

The staircase was long and all the steps were shining as if someone had spent hours polishing them. The walls on the staircase were old wooden panels, and you could tell they'd been recently varnished as the smell still lingered in the air.

As they reached the top of the staircase, a set of dark wood doors stared at them with several glass panels inside. Geraldine felt nervous as they walked through the doors. She knew her life for the next couple of years would be sleeping here.

The dormitory had ten beds in it, five on each side of the room. The floors were dark oak and as you walked on them they squeaked. Each bed looked neatly made. All the bedding was matching. The beds displayed a crisp white duvet set on them and the pillows looked puffed as they sat on the top sheet. At the side of each bed stood an old bedside cabinet joined to a compact wardrobe. As she looked at each bedside cabinet round the room she could see there was no mess or clutter on any of them. The room had an odd smell to it, a bit like a wet dog.

The time finally came for Geraldine to say goodbye to her parents. She kissed them goodbye. Her grip round her father's waist looked desperate and she struggled to let go of him. Biting down on her bottom lip, she took a deep breath and put on a brave face. Mr Tate looked at Geraldine in a peculiar way and she could feel his eyes on her as she waved her parents goodbye. As soon as her parents had gone out of sight Mr Tate returned to the dormitory and looked at Geraldine who sat on her bed.

As he watched her pull clothes from her suitcase he came and sat with her on the bed.

"You will be fine my dear. It's always hard to be away from home at first, but in a few days you will be fine." His hands reached for her hair, they slid like a snake across it and he spoke in a strange way. "If you ever need anyone to speak to, you can always come and see me in my office. Don't worry, nobody will know about the reason you've come to see me, because I will always keep your time with me a secret." His hand caressed her leg. He looked deeply into her eyes and she could feel herself getting scared as his gaze lasted a little longer than it should have.

The doors flew open and in came several of the girls laughing and joking. As Mr Tate stood from the bed and made himself known, the silence returned and he introduced Geraldine telling everyone they needed to show her the procedures of the school.

As he left, the noise returned and several of the girls came round to introduce themselves.

"Hi I'm Jessica. I see you have met the principal." A few of the girls started to giggle behind her and one of them shouted, "Don't you mean Mr Tickle." The noise of the girls laughing made Geraldine smile and within minutes they were all sat on the beds getting to know each other.

The rest of the day went well and Geraldine thought things weren't as bad as they had first seemed. The girls went through a few of the classes with her and told her the ones that were boring. Jessica was in the bed opposite her and the two of them became great friends from day one. Jessica was a pretty girl and her long blonde hair had a slight kink in it. Her skin looked slightly tanned and she told her it was from a previous holiday to Italy with her parents.

That same night the clock clicked loudly on the wall and it seemed to hypnotise everyone to sleep. The clocks pendulum swung across at the bottom of the clock and Geraldine could just about see it.

That night she fidgeted and found it hard to sleep. She kept waking up and when she eventually started to drop off, she focused on a shadow next to Jessica's bed. She remained as still as a rabbit and placed her head nearly under the quilt feeling scared. Geraldine concentrated on her breathing and tried her best to keep it low. As she peered from her bed, she could see Jessica leaving. Jessica wasn't speaking to whoever she was with and she must have felt comfortable with them as she wasn't struggling.

The main doors shut behind them as they left. Geraldine sat up in her bed. She rubbed her eyes and doubled checked Jessica was missing. As she crept from her bed the floorboards squeaked and she stopped hoping she had not woken anyone.

When she reached Jessica's bed, she pulled the duvet back just to make sure she wasn't dreaming. The bed was empty. She was puzzled and returned to bed wondering what had happened to her.

The following morning, as light started to break through the dormitory window, she could hear the sounds of the birds tweeting wildly outside her window. As she listened carefully, the birds sounded like they were trying to tell her something. Their squawks were loud and deafening.

Geraldine rolled on her side and she heard the main doors open. She didn't look straight away. She closed her eyes tightly hoping nobody would know she was awake.

The noise beside her got louder and she could hear Jessica getting back into bed. She slowly turned to face where she lay and looked at the mound in the bed. The covers covered her whole body.

Soft sobbing emanated from the bed sheets. Geraldine's face looked concerned and thought she must have been extremely poorly to be crying like that.

Lying in the bed, she debated whether to go and comfort her. As she stood up her body froze. She felt like she was invading her privacy and made her way back into bed feeling helpless.

The alarm bell went inside the dorm, and everybody jumped from the beds as if they were on fire.

Geraldine watched the girls and jumped up with them. She followed them into the bathroom as they started to wash their faces.

Jessica was one of the last to come in to the bathroom and looked a mess. As she came to join Geraldine at the sink, she looked like she hadn't slept for weeks.

"You don't look well Jess. Don't you think you should go and get back in bed?" Jessica just stared at her and shook her head.

"I feel crap. I wish I could go home. I hate it here." Geraldine waited for the other girls to leave the bathroom and spoke to her.

"Where did you go last night? I saw you leave with someone and you didn't come back until early this morning." Jessica looked horrified and pulled Geraldine to the corner of the bathroom away from prying eyes.

"I had a headache and had to go and get a tablet to help me sleep." Geraldine could tell by her face she was lying and hoped in time she would trust her enough to confide in her where she was really going in the late hour.

The girls left the bathroom together and went back into the dorm. Geraldine changed into her new uniform and followed Jessica down for breakfast.

As they entered the large hall, around a hundred girls sat eating. The benches were long and girls sat facing each other. Geraldine grabbed a bowl of cornflakes and sat with Jessica at the bottom end of the table.

Breakfast went extremely quickly that morning. Before she knew it, she'd made her way to morning assembly. All the steel chairs faced the front stage. Mr Tate stood at the front reading from his notes. He told the girls about different events that were happening throughout the week and about some of the rules that some of the girls had been breaking.

Jessica sat next to Geraldine as he spoke and she could hear her muttering under her breath. She couldn't make out what she was saying but her face looked like she could have killed Mr Tate there and then. The assembly finished and they headed to their first lesson of the day. Jessica was now in charge of showing Geraldine the ropes. Their timetable meant they were together each day.

The first lesson started and both girls sat at the back of the class. The lesson was English and the teacher Mrs Sale was trying to make the lesson as fun as possible.

Jessica sat next to the window. Geraldine glanced towards her; she seemed distant and so unhappy. She nudged Jessica in the ribs as Mrs Sale asked her a question. Jessica seemed startled as if someone had scared the life out of her, and looked at everyone in despair.

"Jessica, are you listening to a word I am saying?" She could feel the eyes of everyone fixed on her face. Her face started to burn with embarrassment. Her heart was beating in her ears as Mrs Sale asked the question again.

Geraldine dipped her head into her arms and started to whisper the answer under her breath. Jessica spoke clearly and gave Mrs Sale the correct answer much to everyone's relief. Mrs Sale was a strict teacher and if anyone crossed her, she would make all the class pay and keep them all for detention after the lesson.

Jessica smiled at Geraldine as the teacher continued with the lesson. She knew she'd have to get her act together before she fell apart and tried to take part in the lesson.

Inside Jessica was crying. Her self-belief was extinct. Her once happy-go-lucky character seemed to be falling apart around her. Geraldine knew once they were alone she would ask the question that had been rolling around her mind all day – only this time she hoped she would get a truthful answer.

The lesson finished and the pair headed into the school grounds. The day was bright and the sun was out in full force. Jessica led Geraldine onto a lawn at the side of the building and away from prying eyes. As both girls sat on the grass, the smell from the flowers nearby lingered in the air. Geraldine inhaled, smelling the sweet scent from them. She loved flowers. The other girls flung themselves onto the grass. A few metres away another group of girls gathered like witches round a caldron.

Jessica reached into her pocket and pulled out a packet of cigs. As she lit one she asked Geraldine if she wanted one. Geraldine had never smoked before but didn't want to seem like a goody two shoes and accepted one cautiously. Jessica stretched her body flat onto the grass and inhaled, letting the nicotine seep through her body. Geraldine lay at the side of her and choked as she first took her first drag.

"Fucking hell, are you alright?" Jessica asked in a concerned voice. Geraldine had turned a pale white colour and it was obvious to her that she'd never smoked before.

"You need to take little drags at first, that's what I did."

Geraldine looked sheepish, she felt slightly embarrassed, and continued to smoke, taking tiny drags one at a time.

Once they'd finished their cigarettes Jessica lay staring into space. Geraldine thought it was the ideal time to ask the question. She lay on her front and kicked her feet behind her.

"Jessica is everything alright with you? You seem a bit stressed out?" Jessica felt numb. She wanted to tell her new friend the truth but couldn't.

"I'm fine. I just get a bit homesick every now and then. You'll know what I mean when you've been here a bit longer." Geraldine knew she should have left it at that but she couldn't keep her mouth sut and asked more questions.

"Oh I thought it was because you've have been ill. It must be tiring being up until the early hours feeling unwell." Jessica sat up and her eyes focused on her. She was fuming and Geraldine knew she'd hit a nerve.

"What do you mean feeling unwell? I haven't been ill or anything." Just as Jessica finished her sentence, she realised what she was talking about. She tried to back pedal knowing Geraldine had witnessed her being out of her bed until the early hours. "Sometimes I do feel ill, but it's only now and then. Anyway after a few tablets I'm right as rain." Geraldine knew she was lying and planned to watch her like a hawk in the future.

That night, the girls lay in their beds talking about their home lives and their parents. Jessica's had split up a few years before and they'd both came to the conclusion that boarding school was the only answer for her as they both had demanding jobs. When Jessica spoke, you could tell the whole set up had left her sad. She only spoke for a few minutes about her parents and lay flat on her bed remembering the good times when her family had been together. As the clock struck ten, the lights were turned out by one of the girls. The clock chimed its last and Jessica pulled the quilt over her body hoping to have a good night's sleep. The sound inside the dormitory was eerie, and you could have heard a pin drop. The routine in the school was quite strict and the girls knew if there was any misbehaviour there would be hell to pay from the head teacher.

The sound of a crying cat outside the window sounded like a baby and Geraldine sat up to listen to it more carefully. Jessica turned round and faced her as she too heard the noise.

"Spooky isn't it?" Jessica whispered and Geraldine nodded. "You will get used to all the strange noises once you've been here a bit longer. When I first came here, I use to lie awake most nights too scared to go asleep. You have to tell yourself it's your mind playing tricks on you and nothing is really out there." Geraldine lay back down on her bed facing Jessica. Her body was shaking inside and she really felt scared for the first time in her life.

All the other girls in the dorm were fast asleep. Both girls whispered to one another. Jessica told Geraldine she could get in her bed if she wanted and they both lay together trying to find sleep.

The girls only seemed to have slept a few minutes and the sound of the dormitory's door opening made them look into each other's eyes. Jessica knew exactly what the noise was and her body shook as the footsteps got nearer. The arms they both felt round their body pulled them both from their beds. Geraldine wiped her eyes. She could see the shadow of a large body in front of her guiding her through the doors. Geraldine could smell alcohol. The smell reminded her of her grandfather and the whisky he drank.

The girls clung to one another as they walked down the dimly lit corridor. Their feet were freezing as they crept along the marble corridors. They looked as if they were stepping on hot coals. Jessica knew exactly where they were going as she'd made this seedy journey several times before. Geraldine was shaking from head to toe as the breath from behind her warmed her body. Jessica wanted to tell her exactly what was about to happen, but before she knew it they were stood in Mr Tate's office.

The room was softly lit and the smell of cigars lingered in the air. The girls stood there as Mr Tate turned to face then both.

"Hello ladies take a seat while I pour myself a drink." Jessica sat on the chair facing his desk as Mr Tate pulled over the other chair for Geraldine to sit on.

"Why are we here Jessica? What have we done? Are we in trouble?" Jessica dipped her head and felt so ashamed that her friend was now a victim of Mr Tate. Her lips trembled and she couldn't reply knowing what was about to happen.

Mr Tate loosened the tie around his neck and slowly undid his top collar. He sat facing them both and slowly licked his lips as he spoke.

"You're probably wondering why you are here aren't you Geraldine?" She nodded and looked at Jessica for support, but her head hung low and she remained silent. Suddenly, it came to Geraldine why she might be there and the thought of Mr Tate seeing them smoking earlier in the day put the fear of God into her. The principal slurped at his drink. His eyes danced with excitement as he looked at the two young girls in front of him as he sat rocking in his chair. He began to speak to them both.

"You are very special young ladies. I want to show you how to get on in this school." Jessica took a deep breath and looked at Geraldine with sympathetic eyes. Mr Tate now told Jessica to take her position and Geraldine watched in horror as she pulled down her knickers and climbed onto his desk. Jessica bent over on all fours with nothing on but her t-shirt. Her eyes stared down at the desk as she waited for Geraldine to join her. Geraldine's heart pounded inside her chest and she felt like she was having a nightmare. Mr Tate made his way towards her and softly took her arm.

"Do the same as your friend young lady and all will be well." Geraldine wanted to scream and run away, but as she looked at her friend, she knew she couldn't leave her by herself. Slowly she pulled down her knickers and struggled to get up on the desk. Mr Tate was behind her and she could feel his warm hands on her backside helping her up. Jessica turned to her and told her it would all be over soon. She reached for her hand and squeezed it in her hot palm as their nightmare began. The room seemed silent until they could hear Mr Tate taking his pants down. They could feel the end of his penis rubbing on their supple buttocks. As Geraldine peeped behind her, she could see him with his knees on the table and his penis was erect with excitement. After a lot of moaning from behind, they could feel a warm wet liquid dribble onto their arse cheeks. Jessica looked at her and whispered it was nearly over. Mr Tate collapsed onto his chair. They could hear his excitement as he fell back.

As quick as could be Jessica pulled up her knickers and nodded to Geraldine to do the same. The tears in both their eyes were ready to erupt. God knows how they held them in as he spoke.

"Thank you girls, you can go back to bed now. Don't forget this is our secret and if anyone ever finds out there will be hell to pay for both of you." He sat in his chair as he waved them off. They left the room as if their feet were on fire.

Once they were out of his office, Geraldine turned and watched him with disgust as he sat in his chair with his dick hanging out. He looked proud of his accomplishments and had a perverted look on his face. Jessica pulled at her arm causing her to yell in pain. They hurried back to the dormitory. As the cold of the night hit their skinny frames, they both shivered. They ran like rats from a sinking ship hoping nobody would see them.

The dorm was lifeless and Geraldine was a little shell shocked as she flung herself on her bed. She wanted to scream at the top of her voice about what had just happened, but it was as if Mr Tate had cast a spell over her and stopped her from telling his sordid secret. Jessica cuddled in behind her. She placed her arms round her waist and tried to comfort the shaking wreck in front of her. Jessica felt responsible for what had just happened, yet somehow felt relieved that she wasn't on her own anymore.

There was no conversation between the girls that night. They both lay there feeling defenceless against Mr Tate's reign of terror. Geraldine was the one to wake first the following morning. The noise from the other girls caused her to open her eyes. She felt like a zombie inside and every movement felt like she was pulling a half a ton of iron about. Her eyes met Jessica's and still no words passed her lips. Jessica pulled herself from the bed and told Geraldine that she would have to hurry up and get ready before the monitor came in and saw her still in bed.

Geraldine finally found the strength to haul herself out

of bed. She slowly made her way to the bathroom as all the other girls ran round trying to get ready. As she entered, Jessica stood at the sink brushing her teeth. The bathroom was old fashioned and the sinks were square shaped and deep. The walls had white tiles from top to bottom and the ceiling was unusually high. Ten sinks were next to each other. The red quarry tiles on the floor were always a hazard from all the water spilt on them.

Geraldine wiped the mirror to see her face. As she looked at her reflection, she cringed. She'd changed so much. An angry face now faced her as if it was ready for war. She squeezed the toothpaste onto the brush and slowly started brushing her teeth. Once she'd cleaned her teeth she felt something on her bum. As she looked at it closer the signs of Mr Tate's ejaculation looked straight back at her.

She reached for her face cloth and rubbed at her arse as if her life depended on it. Her tears broke free and she fell to the floor like a bullet had shot into her chest. Jessica came to her side and felt the pain she was feeling too. She tried to help her up from the floor, but she was too heavy to lift.

"Please Geraldine, please. If somebody sees you like that, they will start asking questions. Please pull yourself together or we will both be in serious trouble." She looked straight into her friend's eyes and spoke from the heart. "Geraldine, he's a fucking pervert and we will make him stop. I don't know how and I don't know when, but believe me we will do it." Geraldine turned to her and kept asking why he'd done that awful thing to them, but Jessica was more concerned in getting her ready and started to speak.

"We will discuss it later, and sort something out, but for now let's get to class."

Both girls started to get ready and each piece of clothing that touched Geraldine's body felt like it was suffocating her. Today was Friday and the weekend was just round the corner. Jessica had promised Geraldine they would have fun. Apparently there was a boy's school a couple of miles down the road from them. Each weekend the girls would sneak out and have fun with the boys from the other school.

The day dragged. Each lesson seemed to take forever for both of them and Jessica could see that last night's events had hit Geraldine hard. She felt like she had to protect her friend and somehow the secret they shared brought them closer together. The lessons for the day were over and the girls jumped with excitement. The last lesson of the day was science, and Mr Tate had stepped in for a teacher who had suddenly fallen ill. When he first spotted Geraldine, he quickly turned from her and went slightly red with embarrassment. He started the lesson and slowly walked round the classroom as he spoke.

All the girls in the class knew there would be no fooling around in this class. They gave him their full attention. When he walked past where Jessica and Geraldine sat, he slowly bent between them with his arms on the back of their necks. His stale breath made their skin crawl. The memory of the night before was still fresh on both girls' minds. Geraldine wanted to pull his hand from her body and tell everyone in the class he was a kiddie fiddler, but as always, her lips were sealed. Mr Tate could feel the tension and quickly moved away to the two girls who sat in front of them.

Jessica kicked Geraldine's leg under the table. She knew she was finding it hard not to launch her books right at his head by the way she held her face to the side.

"He's a fucking pervert, and the sooner everyone knows it, the better" Geraldine whispered under her breath.

Jessica nodded and knew together they had to put an end to his reign of terror. Geraldine mumbled with her hand across her mouth to Jessica.

"How many other girls do you think he's abused, the dirty bastard?" She had a gut feeling that he'd done it before and wanted to stab her pen deep into his neck.

Geraldine had already planned the end for Mr Tate's reign of terror. She knew once she'd run her plans past Jessica the bastard would be locked up for many years, unable to hurt any more girls in his care.

The lesson ended and they left classroom. Once outside the classroom they smiled at one another and headed back to the dorm to get ready for the night ahead. When they entered the dorm they were alone and Jessica was the first to speak.

"He's a dirty pervert isn't he? I hope his fucking knob falls off. He's been doing that to me for around five months." Her head dipped and she looked in pain. "I wanted to report him, but how can you tell somebody that the principal is wanking all over your arse?"

Geraldine agreed and placed her arms round her neck. They both remained like that for a few moments. The secret they shared tore them both apart inside. Jessica lay on the bed and started to pretend to have a wank, just as Mr Tate had done night before. The faces she was pulling made Geraldine fall onto the bed with laughter and together they played the role of Mr Tate and his seedy secret.

All the girls who were sneaking out that night were ready. The only thing that kept them from a night of fun was the climb down the drainpipe next to their window. All the girls looked dressed to kill. Their faces had taken hours to makeup. Around ten girls were set to go out that night. Each of them stood near the window whilst the other girls kept watch. Jessica climbed out first, closely followed by Geraldine.

The night was warm and the sweat dripped from the girls' foreheads. The drainpipe was an old iron one secured to the wall by steel brackets. Over the years, the drainpipe had been the escape route for many girls who'd wanted a good time. If it could have talked, it would have got so many girls in deep trouble. As you looked, you could see three girls on the pipe at any one time. As soon as one girl got a quarter of the way down the next girl would set off.

After the descent, they scattered and hid in the grounds. They became like ninjas as they sneaked past the windows leading to the main entrance. Girls hid in bushes and you could hear them laughing as the branches scratched their legs. The main gates were only a stride away. Once they'd manoeuvred through them, they all cheered.

Several of the girls pulled stiletto shoes from their bags and put their flat ones back inside.

The word on the street was that one of the lads from the boy's school had organised some kind of a party. They linked arms and headed to a local shop to get their beer. The girls stood outside the shop and as usual, they argued who was going in to get the booze. They looked twice as old as they really were and Jessica ended up being the one who had to go in.

Pulling her top down she revealed two perky breasts. She collected the cash from them and took their orders. The girls hid round the corner and watched her head for the shop. Jessica was wearing white pedal pushers and a red sequined top. Her red shoes were her pride and joy and she knew the heel on them made her legs look as sexy as ever.

Reaching the counter she spoke confidently and asked the Asian shopkeeper for two bottles of vodka and a bottle of brandy. Once she saw no hesitation from him she added that she also wanted a tray of twenty-four lagers. As he reached for them, he chuckled and started to speak.

"You off to a party or something love?" Jessica smiled and a cocky look crossed her face. She started to speak with a giggle in her tone.

"Yes. It's my friend's engagement party and we're all going to her house for a good drink."

"Oh to be young again" he laughed. He placed the bottles in the bag and asked how she would carry it all. Jessica thought quickly and told him her sister was outside in the car. Jessica struggled at first to carry all the beer. Her grip was tight but she was struggling with the tray of beers. Just as she thought she was going to drop it a customer came in the shop and held the door so she could go outside. The girls suddenly reappeared and grabbed the alcohol.

The usual thing to do after buying their beer was to get pissed as quickly as they could and tonight was no different. They headed to a bus shelter a short way down the road and began drinking. Geraldine had never been pissed before and struggled to drink the brandy gripped in her hands. As she placed the neck of the bottle in her mouth, the girls began to chant. "Neck it, neck it."

The bottle remained in her mouth for several seconds and she could feel the brandy warming the back of her throat. Pulling the bottle from her mouth, the girls cheered. She felt like she had pleased them, and sat with a smile fixed firmly on her face. Geraldine took a cig from one of the girls, and lit it with a cocky face. Jessica watched as she started to smoke and hoped she wouldn't start to choke again. The smoke came from her mouth slow and sexy, and she even tried to make smoke rings.

All the girls were pissed as farts when they left the bus shelter. Geraldine and Jessica linked each other as they walked up the road. As Geraldine spoke, her words slurred and it was difficult to make out what she was saying.

"I think me and you are going to be friends for life. We're so much alike and get on so well don't we?" Jessica smiled and agreed. She knew the secret they shared would be with them both for a long time, no matter where life took them.

The party was rocking as the girls walked in looking like they owned the place. Geraldine and Jessica immediately started dancing as the boys looked on in disbelief. They both danced to the beat like they were hypnotised by the sound of the music and Jessica swung her hips like a Latin dancer. The other girls mingled and it wasn't long before they had hooked themselves up with a group of lads.

One of the lads saw the girls strutting their stuff and definitely wanted to get to know them both a lot better. He nudged his mate in the ribs as they walked past and cheekily grabbed Jessica's arse as she danced past them holding her arms in the air. Jessica turned and faced the lads and immediately knew culprit. His eyes danced with excitement as he watched her cocky face and he knew he had to prepare himself for a mouthful of shit from her.

"Who's the one with wandering hands then?" The other lads laughed and pointed to Malcolm who stood in front of them with a grin spread across his face. He stood tall and started to speak.

"I couldn't resist your sexy arse. It's like two eggs in a handkerchief." Jessica smiled at him and told him to fuck off. As she left, Malcolm followed trying to get her attention.

"So are you going to tell me your name then, or what?"

Jessica laughed and told him if he got her and her mate a drink she may consider telling him. He did as she asked shouting behind him, "do you want a can of lager, or something stronger? I can make you a special cocktail if you want." Jessica shouted to bring whatever he wanted and turned to Geraldine in excitement.

"He's alright isn't he? Should I ask him to bring his mates over to see if you like any of them?" Geraldine had already spotted one of his mates that she fancied and couldn't keep her eyes off him. She secretly pointed to the chosen lad and they both giggled as they started to dance.

Malcolm was back within minutes and handed them a large glass each. The drink looked brown and it smelt like coconuts. He placed two straws in each drink and watched as the girls tasted it

"Fucking hell! What the fuck is that?" Jessica screamed. She started to choke as Geraldine patted her back. Malcolm smiled as he watched her face and shouted his friends over to come and join them. Within minutes Geraldine had started talking to the lad she fancied. He introduced himself as Darren. He had fair hair and the most enchanting eyes she'd ever seen in her life. He told her he was fifteen, although he looked older. The party started to get louder. A lot more people arrived and the four of them went outside to get some fresh air.

Once outside, they all felt the summer breeze filtering throughout their bodies. Malcolm led them to a bench. Jessica was pissed. She struggled to sit up straight and Geraldine had to hold onto her arm to stop her falling onto the floor.

"Get a spliff made then" Malcolm said to Darren. He searched in his black jacket and pulled out a small plastic bag of what looked like tobacco. He started to place it into some cigarette papers he stuck together. Geraldine watched him eagerly as Jessica stood up and started to be sick in a nearby bush. Jessica was knelt on the floor and Geraldine knelt beside her as she held her hair from her face. The drunken mess was spewing up like a hosepipe on a summer's day. Geraldine covered her nose with her hand and couldn't help heave with her as she smelt the sick flowing from her mouth. She collapsed as she finally made the last heave from her body. The lads sat on the bench and cringed as they watched. They pulled their coats up and hung their noses deep into it to avoid the smell of her puke. Geraldine smelt something strange and sucked in the air deeply.

"What's that smell?" she asked in a high voice. "It smells like camel shit whatever it is." The two of them started laughing and nudged each other as she came to join them.

"I don't know how I'm going to get her home, you know. I hope she sorts herself out because I can't carry her, she's like a dead weight." She looked worried as she stood with one arm on her waist.

"Get a drag of this and stop moaning. She'll be fine now she's spewed up." Geraldine took the funny looking cig into her hands and took a drag as the lads watched with menacing eyes.

"Get another drag. Hold your fucking breath this time. You'll get a better rush that way." Geraldine did as they asked and within minutes, she could feel her body melting into the bench. Her vision became blurred as her body boiled with heat. Slowly she loosened her blouse. Her fingers struggled to find the small buttons and she found it hard to hold her eyes open. The lads laughed and made a clicking noise as they flapped their fingers about. They watched Jessica trying to stand up from the bushes and couldn't help but fall about laughing.

Geraldine was like a zombie. She looked like she was a step away from being fast asleep. Her body looked completely at rest and her face shook about slowly as she tried to stay focused. Darren leant over to her and slowly kissed her lips. She knew what was happening but it was as if her mind was awake and her body had fallen asleep without her.

Malcolm went to rescue Jessica and helped her back up towards the bench. As they slowly walked back, they could see Darren's hand down the front of Geraldine's pants. They looked like they were a step away from sex. Malcolm saw what was happening and quickly turned Jessica in the other direction. This was the code of conduct between them and if Darren was getting some pussy, he didn't want to spoil it for him. Jessica started to speak and it was clear she didn't want to leave her friend.

"Where you taking me? Take me back. I want to stay with my friend." Malcolm laughed and pulled her towards him and sunk his lips onto hers. As he kissed her, he could taste sick on her breath. He pulled a sour face but carried on regardless hoping he might get a bit of loving. Jessica accepted his kiss, but quickly reminded him she still wanted to go back to her friend. He admitted defeat and slowly headed back, hoping Darren had already shagged her brains out

As they arrived back, they could see Darren sat up straight and Geraldine trying to pull her pants up in a fumbled manner. Jessica flung her drunken body between them both and leant on Geraldine's shoulder saying "I feel so sick. I want to go home."

Her friend stroked her head with the side of her hand and agreed. The two lads whispered to each other and you could see Darren put his fingers under Malcolm's nose.

"Smell the fanny mate," he whispered as Malcolm pushed his hands from his face.

"You lucky bastard. That one of mine is waste a space, she's fucking frigid." Darren chuckled and placed his fingers to his own nose. The two girls struggled to stand up. They held each other up and walked away. Geraldine didn't really know exactly what Darren had done to her, but it never caused her any pain, and she liked what she could remember about it. The two lads followed them as they left and tried to get them to stay a little longer with no luck.

The street lamps were bright and they led them back towards the school. The next quest was to get back into the dorm without causing any noise. The job was going to be hard as they were legless. The climb up the drainpipe was set to be a nightmare. The school grounds were now in sight. They both sniggered in a drunken manner as Jessica told her what she'd seen.

"Fucking hell Geraldine, what are you like you dark horse. Darren was in your knickers for ages. What did it feel like?" she said poking her in the ribs. Geraldine stood still and her face looked serious before she spoke.

"I don't really know. All I know is that my fanny is a bit sore when I walk, but apart from that I can't remember." Jessica laughed and held her head in her hands.

"I don't know what was in that drink they gave us, but it was mind blowing. It knocked me out I can tell you." They slowly crept back into the school grounds and hid in the shadow of the bushes as they neared the building.

"Give me a leg up then," Jessica whispered as she tried to climb the drainpipe. Geraldine laughed and knew her friend would need her help to make it back into the bedroom.

Both girls giggled and after about three attempts, Jessica started to make her way up towards the slightly opened window. Geraldine followed quickly behind her and her body swayed as she reached the top waiting for Jessica to pull her body through the window. The darkness of the dorm made it difficult to see as Jessica fell to the floor with an almighty bang and caused a few of the girls to stir in their beds.

She held her hand over her mouth and tried to cover the laughter that was trying to escaping through her fingers. As she watched Geraldine's head hanging through the window she rolled about on the floor laughing.

"Fucking help me then, instead of sitting there laughing." Jessica peeled herself up from the floor and dragged her through the window by her clothes. They both sat wrapped up in each bodies laughing. One of the students had finally had enough of the noise and made it quite plain she wasn't happy.

"Will you two keep the noise down? People are trying to sleep." Geraldine focused on where she lay and tried to stand up. Her legs had a mind of their own and she remained seated. Jessica now hid her face into Geraldine's arms as her rant began.

"Listen Mrs stuck up your own fucking arse. We're having a good time, and if you want to be a goody two shoes, that's your business, so piss off and leave us alone."

The distressed pupil huffed and threw her bedclothes about the bed as she tried to get back asleep. She knew there was no point in trying to talk to them. She threatened to tell the principal the following day about their antics, but after that she remained silent. A few minutes later, the girls were in bed. The bedroom was spinning as Geraldine closed her eyes and she held on to it hoping the room would slow down.

Jessica was dead to the world within minutes and she missed the sight of her friend spewing her guts up at the side of her. The sick contained everything she'd eaten that day and at one point Geraldine thought she was going to choke to death. She contemplated cleaning it up but she needed sleep and flung an old sheet over it until morning.

★

The dorm was noisy. The sound of everyone getting ready for breakfast made Jessica open her eyes. She felt like someone had dragged her round the room by her hair all night long. Pulling the bedclothes over her eyes, she could hear the penetrating voice of one of the girls at the side of her.

"Oh my god someone's been sick all over the floor. The smell's knocking me sick." They gathered round the bed and looked at the sick as if it was a small puppy running round the floor. One of the girls whispered and Jessica held her ear to the blanket to hear more carefully.

"It must have been her" she said pointing her finger, "I heard her climbing in through the window last night. She was wrecked, falling all over the place. In fact, the two of them were a disgrace. They disturbed my sleep, the pair of slags." The girls looked at her and knew she was dicing with death gossiping about Jessica, especially when she was so close.

"Well let me tell you I'm not standing for it anymore. I'm going to tell the head. I need my sleep and I've got exams coming up in a few weeks anyway, I don't need the stress."

Jessica lunged out of her bed and grabbed the girl by her neck. Her face was on fire and the other girls could tell she was serious as they watched her grit her teeth.

"You won't be telling anyone you fucking grass, because if you do, you'll have me to deal with. Do you understand?" The girl pulled Jessica's hands from round her neck and quickly headed to the bathroom crying her eyes out closely followed by her friends.

Jessica looked at the floor. She knew that the room was due to be monitored any time now and started to nudge her hung-over mate. Geraldine's eyes looked like piss holes in the snow and she mumbled as she pulled the blanket from her body.

"What's going on, leave me alone" she mumbled. "I'm not feeling too well, fuck off." Jessica lay beside her and started to speak.

"You've spewed up all over the floor. We need to get it cleaned before the battle-axe comes round on her inspections. Geraldine hung her head from the bed and realised what she'd done. She stretched with her hands clenched above her head. Sitting up from the bed, she scratched her head and leant over to see the mess she'd created.

"Did I do that?" she asked in a timid voice.

"Yeah, so you need to pull your finger from your arse and get it cleaned up as soon as possible." Geraldine tried to pull herself together. As she started to wake up she felt soreness between her legs and the night before came flooding back to her. She didn't mention it straight away but as she started to walk her she told Jessica, "my fanny is killing; it feels like it's on fire. I don't know what he did to me last night but it feels like I've been horse riding or something." Jessica remembered exactly what had happened and smiled at her with a cheeky grin before she spoke.

"You got fingered, don't you remember?" Geraldine felt quite embarrassed and tried to make a joke of the whole matter.

"I was pissed wasn't I? Whatever he gave me, knocked me right out. What did I have?" Jessica shook her head and started to smile.

"Whatever you had was a leg opener. You were like a dog on heat when I saw you." Geraldine looked at her friend in horror as she remembered her first taste of sex.

"I'm never drinking again Jessica. He took advantage of my drunken state you know?" Jessica started laughing and they both set about cleaning the mess off the floor. Jessica grabbed two cloths and some tissue from the bathroom and they scooped up the dried lumps of food from the floor.

Once the mess disappeared, they both lay on the bed exhausted from the night before. They decided they would pretend to be sick, and both jumped into the bed waiting for the room inspection.

The bell sounded throughout the dorm. The sound of bantering girls hurrying down to breakfast made them hide their heads under their blankets. Within minutes, the room was quiet. Footsteps filled the corridor coming closer to their room. They looked at each other and knew room inspection was about to start, but as they lifted their heads it wasn't the usually figure stood in front of them. Mr Tate looked furious as he stood looking directly at them. They could see by his eyes he wasn't a happy chap.

"Why aren't you girls up and ready? You know the rules don't you?" his voice shook and he headed over to where they lay. They covered parts of their heads under the bed sheets as he approached. "Well I suggest you get your little bodies out of that bed and go and get washed. How dare you think you can lie in bed and disobey school rules?" He gripped the covers off the bed and yanked it from them. They kept their heads low and stood from the bed.

As they walked to the bathroom, they pulled their t-shirts over their bum cheeks. They could feel Mr Tate's eyes all over them like a rash.

Inside the bathroom, they ran the taps and started to throw the ice-cold water over their faces. Without any warning, Mr Tate appeared at the side of them and his eyes squinted as he watched them wash. Slowly he closed the bathroom door. He looked at them with the look they'd seen so many times before.

"If you decide to break the rules, you know you have to be punished don't you?" His voice was low and mischievous. They both struggled as he dragged both their arms and threw them against the wall.

"Get those knickers off and get bent over." Geraldine looked at Jessica and they obeyed his rules with tears in their eyes. As they took the position, they could see him pulling his pants down and stroking his erect member. Geraldine bent over first followed by Jessica and as they heard the grunts of pleasure from behind them they knew the ordeal was about to start.

The minutes seemed like hours as he yanked his cock over their arses. Geraldine bit onto her knuckle with a desperate face. She couldn't take it anymore and knew it had to stop. The words in her throat seemed like iron as she tried to get them out. Mr Tate's groans of pleasure were now louder than ever and they could feel his semen landing on their arses as he exploded with relief. Geraldine finally blew her temper and quickly pulled up her knickers, as Jessica watched in disbelief.

"You dirty fucking low life bastard. This is the last time you'll wank on our arses. As from today you tosser!" her breath struggled as she continued. Her face was white and her eyes were like saucers.

"If you ever, ever come anywhere fucking near us I'll make sure it's the last move you ever make. Do you hear me? You perverted cunt?" Geraldine moved her head to his and screamed into his face as Jessica joined in.

"Fucking pervert. Dirty, dirty pervert." Jessica spat right into his face. He fell to the floor as he keeled over as if someone had dropped a ton of bricks on to his body.

This once tall Mr Tate now looked like a small child, and shook like a scared animal. His reign of terror was over and the realisation of what he'd done hit him.

"Girls, listen to me. Don't go telling anybody about this, because I could end up in deep trouble. I promise you I will never touch any of you again. Please believe me; I'm so sorry I don't know what's wrong with me. I will stop I promise."

Geraldine saw his weakness and launched her feet into his body as he dropped to the floor. As she kicked him, she felt power like never before and she knew she was now the one who held all the cards. She crouched down to his face.

"It's not very nice is it? Do you feel scared Mr Tate?" She watched his face hid behind his shaking hands. "That's how you made us feel you dirty twat. Things are going to change round here aren't they? We're in control now, not fucking you. Well let's see how you feel when we abuse you. You'll do everything we say alright? Otherwise everyone will know exactly what a dirty little kiddy fiddler you are? Do you hear me?"

Mr Tate looked pathetic as he sobbed in the corner and he nodded his head letting the girls know he knew exactly what they meant. His eyes began to stream with tears and he looked as if he had seen a ghost. He slavered as his lips shook. Geraldine gave him one final kick to his body and left the bathroom. Jessica spat into his face but still felt scared of her abuser as he hid his face from them. The sound of the tap dripping was all he had for company.

Once they left him, Geraldine was shaking from head to toe. Her teeth chattered together and she hurried to her bed to throw her bedclothes round her for comfort. Jessica sat at the side of her and they both watched as Mr Tate crept from the room like a sewer rat. Just before he left, Geraldine shouted to him that they both would be spending the day in bed but he made no reply and hurried from the room. You could have heard a pin drop in the dorm at that moment. All the pair could hear were their chests breathing rapidly.

Jessica placed her arms around Geraldine and began to sob like she'd never cried before. The words they wanted to say dripped from their mouths. They looked paralysed. Gripping on to each other for dear life, they cradled each other. That day the girls came together as one and their bond would be forever. Once the silence broke Geraldine turned to Jessica and kissed her head as she lay in her arms. Her words were from her heart and her bottom lip quivered as she spoke.

"Never ever again will anyone make me feel that way. Promise me you'll always fight back if anything like this ever happens again. Mr Tate abused us both and perhaps we'll remember this for the rest of our lives. This is our secret and we need to keep it that way don't we?"

Jessica looked at Geraldine and her words were few. The terrible things Mr Tate had done to them both lay heavily on her mind. It was as if he'd sealed their lips with a key of truth and left them unable to speak. Both girls lay on the beds and felt completely exhausted. The day hadn't even started and yet they knew they wanted to sleep.

Over the next few weeks things seemed to change dramatically. Mr Tate left the school and nobody really knew the reasons why except Geraldine and Jessica. They heard on the grapevine he'd packed up and gone to live in Spain. A new head teacher took over the school called Mrs Boyle and she seemed to be very nice.

The new principal changed many rules in the school. She was always willing to listen to the pupils and their problems. Geraldine had only been to her office a few times and every time she went in to see her, the face of Mr Tate seemed to be lingering in the walls. She found it hard to cope trying to rid his memory from her mind.

The years passed and Geraldine was now sixteen years of age. Geraldine and Jessica had been ruthless over the years that had passed. Sex with boys just seemed the normal thing for them both to do every weekend. Some of the sex scenes they'd been involved in would have made their parents so ashamed. The girls had been involved in threesomes. It wasn't unusual for them both to put a show on for the boys they'd met. They loved to show off their curvaceous bodies.

Jessica secretly loved Geraldine and she'd been fighting her feelings for her for a long time. She felt protected by her and always knew whilst she was with her nothing would go wrong in her life.

The threesomes they shared were great for Jessica as it meant she got to hold and caress Geraldine. Sometimes the boy involved didn't even get a sniff during sex. Once Jessica got her grip on Geraldine, she didn't want to share her with anyone.

They were always rat arsed when they'd perform for the men. The following day Geraldine would continue her day as if nothing had happened between them the night before. Jessica felt so mixed up inside and a few days before they were due to go home she planned to tell Geraldine exactly what was going on in her mind.

All the classmates were ready for their last night together. The main hall looked completely different on the night of the party. Lots of balloons and banners stretched across the walls. The tables were set around the side of the room. The pink and gold balloons sat on the back of every chair. Everyone was seated and Mrs Boyle began her speech to say her farewells to the young women. Her voice was high pitched and she held her hands tightly clasped as she spoke.

"It seems only yesterday that all you girls were still children but as I look round the room today I see what lovely pretty young ladies you have all turned into. I hope in the future, you use your time at school to guide you to make the right decisions and make the most of your lives."

Everyone's eyes faced the front of the hall where the principal stood. For a lot of the girls this would be the last time they would ever see each other again. Life was ready for them and for some of them they would have a great journey in front of them.

Mrs Boyle was a middle-aged woman. She had a slender

figure. She always dressed in pencil skirts and neat blouses. Her brown-rimmed glasses took over most of her face and everyone commented on them. She looked like Deidre Barlow, a character from Coronation Street. Her hair was a mixture of blonde and brown. Tonight you could tell she'd taken the time and effort. She looked truly amazing. Once the speech finished the music started and all the girls hit the dance floor ready to strut their stuff.

The DJ was a local and he'd been used by the school several times in the past to cover any function they had. Some of his songs were cheesy, but he always played a mixture of past and present hits from the charts. The night was swinging and Geraldine and Jessica kept disappearing along with a few other girls to sneak a gulp of the vodka they'd hid in a locker nearby. All the other girls returned to the hall after the drinking session. Geraldine and Jessica stayed and finished the last few drops from the bottle. Jessica looked at Geraldine and knew it was now or never. Geraldine looked so pretty and the baby pink dress she wore made her look more stunning than ever. Jessica inhaled deeply and finally found the courage to start to speak. She placed her arms round Geraldine's neck.

"I can't believe our school days are over. What am I going to do without you to look after me?"

Geraldine smiled as she raised the bottle to her mouth and turned to face her as she drained the last bit of vodka from the bottle. "I know, it will be so strange without you, but we'll keep in touch won't we? You can come down to my house at weekend if you have time?"

Jessica cautiously moved towards her and moved her silken hair from her face. The love she felt inside was like a volcano and at that moment, she was ready to erupt.

"Geraldine I love you so much. You don't understand

that parting from you will be the hardest thing I've ever done. We've been through so much together and I can't imagine my life without you." Jessica felt that the moment was right and slowly moved her lips towards her. As their lips touched, she felt aroused and wanted to make love there and then with Geraldine. At first, Geraldine accepted the kiss and felt the passion between them both. She too felt turned on and continued to kiss her. They moved to a storeroom at the side of the corridor away from prying eyes.

Slowly Jessica lifted up Geraldine's dress and caressed her long thin legs. Once they were out of sight, they fumbled around each other's bodies. The light in the room was poor with several boxes piled high around it. Their breathing was loud. Geraldine's hands found Jessica breasts. As she touched them with her tongue, Jessica groaned with pleasure and was moments away from exploding into orgasm. The passion between these two young girls was amazing. They were confident with each other's bodies and looked like something from a porno film.

Jessica dipped her fingers into Geraldine's entrance. She commented on how warm and wet it was. Geraldine took Jessica's hands and placed them above her head. She peeled her dress from her hot sweaty body. Once her dress was off Geraldine noticed her erect nipples and caressed them as she slowly moved down her body with her silken tongue. Geraldine knelt between her legs and slowly pulled Jessica's knickers down her legs. She didn't know if it was the effects from the vodka that was making her feel like this or her friend's body stood. Whatever it was she liked it and continued as if she was on fire.

Even though in the past they'd previously had threesomes Geraldine had never given oral sex to Jessica.

This was all new to her. Jessica pulling her head towards her crutch with two hands. Geraldine's tongue began to do soft strokes. At first, she looked like she had placed her tongue on a P9 battery. Slowly she began to glide her velvet tongue in every nook and cranny. She could hear from above her head the groans of delight.

The taste of Jessica's fanny on her tongue was sweet and she could feel her wetness all over her face. Geraldine licked her fanny faster and she loved that she was doing a good job. Her fingers came into play. Within minutes, she felt a warm liquid running down her lips and by the sounds from above she knew Jessica had reached orgasm.

Jessica pulled Geraldine up from below her and greeted her with her lips. It was now time for her to repay the favour and immediately knelt before Geraldine. Jessica had only ever dreamt about this moment and now it was really happening she was going to make the most out of it. She loved Geraldine from the bottom of her heart. Before she left her, to move down her body she kissed her and told her how much she loved her. Geraldine was in a world of her own at that moment and all she could think of was reaching the orgasm her body was craving. Jessica licked Geraldine's pussy in a frantic way and added a finger just before she came. The fireworks finally exploded and Geraldine was panting on top of her like she'd been running a marathon.

Silence fell once both girls had finished and they looked at each other and smiled. Geraldine had never thought of herself as a lesbian but at that moment, she didn't care what she was because she felt like nothing on earth mattered and felt completely satisfied like never before. Once they'd straightened their clothing they slowly headed out of the store room checking each way first. That night had woken something inside Geraldine and she now questioned her sexuality. All night long, she gazed at Jessica and wondered why she was feeling this way, but the answer never came. She knew by this time tomorrow she would be at home with her family and Jessica would probably be a million miles away from her thoughts.

The morning light shone through the dorm window for the last time. Girls screamed and hugged each other. Tears fell and they said their final goodbyes before they left. Everyone headed to the car park. Many eager parents stood waiting for their children. Balloons swayed in the air and for some girls this was a sign that womanhood was just around the corner.

Geraldine and Jessica were alone for the last time. Geraldine felt strange as she looked at her and she fidgeted about, not knowing how to say goodbye. Tears formed in Jessica's eyes. Her emotions were ready to explode and as if someone had pushed a button, her tears fell.

"Don't cry Jessica, we'll keep in touch." Her sobs took over and she was broken in two. Geraldine continued to speak. "If you ever need me you know I'll always be there for you." Her words were like lashes of a whip across Jessica's body. She held on to her and buried her head into her chest.

That moment was memorable for them both. They walked to the car park together and Jessica knew her heart was well and truly broken. The morning was full of sunshine and the birds sang. Geraldine spotted her parents and ran to them leaving Jessica alone. Once Geraldine was by her parent's side, she swung around her father's neck and squeezed him. She kissed her mother and linked her arm tightly.

Jessica could only watch as her heart sank. Sitting on a small brick wall facing them she swung her legs rapidly.

Her parents were late to collect her and this just added to her torment.

Before Geraldine got into the car, she ran back to Jessica and hugged her one last final time. Bending her head slightly she whispered in her ear. She told her she would always love her and kissed her cheek. Jessica watched the back of her as she quickly ran to join her parents. The car pulled from the car park and Geraldine stuck her face up to the window. She could see Jessica in the arms of a man who looked like her dad. As the car passed them, Geraldine wound the window down and stuck her head out from it.

"Don't forget to keep in touch. I'll phone you when I get home." Jessica smiled but had to keep her head held down so she wouldn't break down and cry. She lifted her arm lethargically and slowly waved as she watched her disappear.

Over the next few months, Geraldine kept to her word and phoned Jessica most nights. As the months went by the calls got fewer and fewer until, finally they stopped. Geraldine's life changed so much. Her sex life was always on the go. She was addicted to kinky sex. She'd had strings of boyfriends but none of them had really ticked all the boxes. Geraldine loved fantasy sex and loved dressing up for her partners. She would always ask them what they liked during sex and she would always step up to the mark no matter what fantasy they had.

Over the years, Geraldine got herself mixed up in some dark holes. She'd been involved with drugs and was ready for a breakdown. Her parents caught her just in time and placed her in rehab. Geraldine spent many months at the drugs rehabilitation centre and tried to find out what was causing her to act this way. The centre itself was filled with lots of people and each of them looked as normal as the next to her.

As her time was nearing an end in detox, her mother told her she could come and work with her in the family business hoping that it would sort her out. The business was doing quite well and when Geraldine was set to work with her, she would be the one who accompanied clients to other countries looking for properties to buy. Geraldine had been scared of what lay ahead but knew she had to change. She was twenty-five now. She secretly wanted to settle down and have a family, but for now, she was concentrating on her career and trying to sort herself out.

Geraldine's first couple of weeks were hard and her body's craving for cocaine was never far from her thoughts. She hadn't had sex in months and knew her other addictions needed satisfying as soon as possible before she fell apart. Her first few days in work were hard but once she got her head round it, she seemed to cope. Her mother had arranged a meeting with a client that afternoon.

The woman who she was due to meet was in search of property abroad and had lots of money to spend. Apparently she'd just split up from her husband and had plenty to spend. That afternoon Geraldine met Victoria Greybank for the first time and really enjoyed talking to her.

Victoria told her openly of her husband's extra marital affairs. She never held back on any of the spicy details and Geraldine had to stop herself from laughing aloud on a few occasions. They spoke for hours like old friends. After a few hours passed, they decided they would fly out to Spain the following week to look at properties for sale. Geraldine had loads of men she'd call upon for sex, and once she'd left Victoria she made the call to a man called Mike. Mike was someone who she knew would drop everything at the drop of a hat to tend to her sexual needs. Once she'd spoken to him she went home to prepare herself for a night of hot steamy sex.

3

THE AIRPORT WAS JAM-PACKED with holidaymakers setting off on holiday. As Victoria and Geraldine checked in their suitcases they could hear children shouting and screaming. You could see they were doing their parents' heads in. Three children accompanied the couple who stood next to them in the queue. It was obvious the mother was at the end of her tether with her brood. The father was a tall man. As he bent over to fasten his child's shoelace the nick of his arse was visible much to the amusement of Geraldine.

The woman looked like a typical council estate housewife. She had bleached blonde shoulder length hair. Her arms rattled as she moved around with cheap tacky jewellery. Her skin was like that of a rhino and she looked like she smoked a hundred cigs a day. As she shouted at one of her children, Victoria hung her head in shame and felt so embarrassed.

"You little fucker. You'd better start behaving otherwise I'll smack ya arse till it's red raw." The young lad spun about on the floor and didn't listen to a word she'd said until she bent down over him and screwed up his face in her hands.

"Ya little bastard. Get your arse up off the floor otherwise ya going back home on ya own. You can stay at nana's house." She quickly dragged him by his ears and pulled him up to her level. You could tell the kid didn't give a flying fuck what she said because his eyes were everywhere and didn't look at her once.

Victoria and Geraldine checked their luggage and couldn't wait to get away from the family from hell. As they left them in the queue, they could still hear them arguing between themselves.

"I hope they're not sitting next to us on the plane" Geraldine sighed, "they shouldn't be allowed to travel if they can't keep their children under control." Victoria smiled as they walked towards the bar area. Geraldine wasn't feeling her normal self. After they'd ordered some drinks they sat at a nearby table. The silence was unbearable and Geraldine was the one to speak first after gazing round for what seemed like a lifetime.

"Are you alright love? You seem a bit quiet." Victoria shook her head and looked like she was going to cry but somehow she held back the tears and continued to speak.

"This is something I've wanted to do for a long time. I always thought when I'd go looking for a property abroad it would have been with my husband," her head looked down at the floor and she soon remembered his betrayal. "I'm moving forward now anyway aren't I and don't want to think about the wanker." Geraldine smiled and sipped at her orange juice.

There were many people in the bar and the atmosphere was really picking up. There was a group of girls who were near the bar and they were all wearing pink t shirts saying 'Girls on Tour'. Their skirts were up their arses and it was obvious they were in search of men. Geraldine smiled at the group and one of the girls came over to join them.

"Sorry if we are a bit loud, but it's my mates divorce party and we've promised her a week to remember." Victoria smiled and immediately started speaking.

"A divorce party? That's a really good thing to celebrate. I've just got divorced and never thought for a million years I could have celebrated it," her face tilted to the side and she grinned as she continued. "I thought people who'd just been divorced were supposed to sit there and mourn for the rest of their lives." The girl smiled and shouted the rest of the girls to join them. She introduced herself as Jackie and told them she was the one who had arranged this holiday for her best mate. Jackie spoke quickly before her friends came to join them her head bent down towards them as she spoke towards the floor in a low voice. "To tell you the truth girls I was fucking sick to death of listening to her constant moans about him. Her face was miserable twenty-four seven."

The group sat round them and the laughter filled the room. They were all drinking vodka and well on their way. Jackie now raised her glass to the ceiling and asked the others to as well. "Right ladies, this holiday is for my best friend in the whole world – Yvonne. We all know she's had it rough over the last couple of months but now it's all over and she has rid herself of that fat twat of a husband." The girls cheered and grabbed at Jackie as she continued.

"I think it's time to celebrate. Raise your glasses and let's toast to not giving a fuck about anything anymore and really enjoying this holiday." Their rants shook the roof and other people in the bar stood looking at them. They all stood from the bucket style seats and raised the glasses. Jackie started to sing a song by M people called 'Moving On Up' and everyone joined in.

Geraldine's mood lifted and she felt like joining the girls for the rest of the holiday, as she knew it would be one big scream. Jackie asked where they were staying in Spain and it happened they weren't really far from each other. They all sat chatting and arranged to meet up during the week for a good night out. Victoria loved the company and they both stayed with the girls until they boarded the plane.

They all boarded the plane and the girls from Manchester were seated at the other end. You could hear the laughter from them even from where they sat. No sooner were they comfortable and awaiting take off and the nightmare family from earlier came and sat behind them. The woman's gob was louder than ever and they looked at each other and laughed in desperation.

"Just our bloody luck. Of all the seats on the plane I just knew them lot would end up near us." Geraldine chuckled and could see Victoria was loosening up and the week ahead didn't seem so blue after all.

All through the journey the family behind were up and down out of their seats. The smaller child was kicking the back of Geraldine chair and she had to refrain herself several times from turning round and pummelling him. Victoria was new to all the commotion on a plane. Her journeys had always been first class in the past and this kind of situation was a first for her. She nudged Geraldine in the side of her waist and smiled.

"I know I haven't been much fun up to now but I promise you once we've landed in Spain I'll be a new woman." Geraldine felt relieved and immediately let her know so. She held her hand gently as she spoke.

"I'm so glad love, because for a moment I thought we were going to be like two nuns on tour. You know I love a good time and lately I've felt like I have lost myself. I'm going to show you how to have a good time and let your hair down."

During the rest of the flight, the two women became

one and Geraldine told her parts of her life and how she had ended up working for her parents. The bond was made between them and considering they'd only known each other for a short time, they looked like they'd known each other for years. The flight was nearly over and the captain came over the speaker. He told everybody to fasten their seatbelts. The heat in the plane was sickly and all the passengers were eager to land. The family behind them were now louder than ever. The children jumped about with excitement. The mother gave them their final orders and Geraldine and Victoria giggled as they listened.

"Right you lot, before we land I want some rules in place. Don't think for one minute me and ya dad are spending this holiday running round after you lot. We've saved all our cash for months for this holiday, so I don't want it ruining. Do you lot hear me?" The smallest child spoke in a disappointed voice.

"But mam you said we could go to the aqua park and that. Don't say we can't go now?" The other kids joined in the debate and the mother was fighting to keep in control.

"For fucks sake! I didn't say ya couldn't go to the water park did I? So stop moaning, believe me anymore fucking about and the water park will be cancelled." All the kids listened to her every word and you could tell it was something they wanted to do as they all sat back in their places and remained quiet until the plane landed.

Once they'd landed the doors opened and the heat from outside gripped everyone by the neck. Geraldine took off her cardigan and Victoria loosened her blouse. As they walked toward the exit, the kids from behind them were trying to push past. Geraldine's face filled with anger.

"Excuse me," she said in a high tone as the child tried

to push past, "you will have to wait your turn. We're all excited about getting outside, so just be patient." The lad was about twelve years of age and just stared at her.

"Missus, I'm sweating like a kebab man's arse. I just need some fresh air." His mother's arm reached towards him and grabbed the back of his t-shirt pulling him towards her. She gritted her teeth and looked him directly in the face whilst she held his cheeks.

"What have I told ya about speaking to people like that? Get back fucking here so I can keep my eyes on you." The woman looked at Geraldine and said sorry. They giggled as they her watched her drag him to her side clipping him round his head.

The view when they stepped off the plane was amazing. The blue skies were something you could only imagine on a painting. Once they stepped off the plane, the next task was to get their luggage from another part of the airport. The airport was busy and everyone was watching the small hole in the wall waiting for their suitcases to come through. Some people even jumped on the conveyor belt and walked round it until they found their luggage.

It was funny to watch everyone searching for their luggage because once they located it, it was as if they'd found a golden ticket. They quickly pull it off the conveyor belt and looked at people with a chuffed face, as if to say "I've got my suitcase, where's yours?"

Before long Geraldine located her suitcase and pulled it from the wide black belt with a chuffed face. You could see Victoria now looking flustered as she made her way to the front of the queue desperately searching for her baggage. Many of the passengers left the area and just a few suitcases remained on the conveyor belt. Victoria scanned each suitcase that came past even though she knew it definitely wasn't hers. After about ten minutes of waiting, she decided to go to the help desk to try to locate her luggage.

As they reached the large brown desk, about four people were in front of them. One of the passengers had obviously been in the same boat as Victoria and could be heard shouting at the person behind the counter. The airport's air conditioning helped keep them cool. The smell of cleanliness circled their nostrils. All the walls looked immaculate and not a spot of dirt was visible.

Geraldine gripped her luggage tightly as they made their way up towards the counter. The man looked stressed and he was constantly wiping his forehead. He looked around fifty and his white shirt clung to his body with sweat patches.

"Hello ladies can I help?" he said in a husky voice and he was trying his best to understand every word they spoke.

"My luggage is lost I think. I've been waiting at the pickup point for at least half an hour." Victoria was struggling to be understood and her words were coming out at speed. "I need my case. My clothes are in it. I haven't got a stitch to wear. Please tell me it's not lost." The man just kept his eyes to the notepad in front of him and passed Victoria a white piece of paper and a pen.

"Will you please fill out all your details and the address of where you are staying in case we find it" Victoria went bright red and she let him have a piece of her mind.

"What do you mean in case you find it? I need my clothes now. What do you expect me to wear whilst I'm here for the week?" Her lips were going ten to the dozen and she didn't stop for breath as she continued. "All my toiletries are in my case so I need my stuff now." Geraldine now came to her side and tried to console her, but Victoria was in a rage and couldn't be quietened. "How hard is it, to put a suitcase on the plane and give it to me when I reach the other end? Can you tell me that?"

The man looked at her and tried to tell her that it wasn't his fault but she looked like she would kill him. Eventually she gave up and trudged to the small table at the side of the window and started filling out the forms. Geraldine could see how upset she was and spoke to her in a sympathetic voice.

"I've got loads of clothes, you can share mine. We're about the same size so don't worry all is not lost." Nothing could make Victoria feel any better and once she'd filled out the form she flung it to the man behind the help desk.

"If you find my suitcase, that's where I will be staying." He looked at the form and nodded. You could tell he was glad to see the back of her and made no reply as she walked away followed closely by Geraldine. "What a start to a holiday. No bloody clothes, no toiletries, no underwear. It's the worst thing that could have happened. What am I going to do?" Victoria let out her frustration and tears fell onto her cheeks. Geraldine placed her arm round her neck and tried to make things better.

"Listen, it's not all bad. You can buy a few bits. Hopefully, they will return your case by tomorrow. You know what airports are like. It will probably turn up soon." Victoria tried her best to listen and was just glad all her money was in her handbag, then she realised something that put a smile on her face.

"You're right, I can go and buy all new outfits. I keep forgetting I'm a wealthy woman and why shouldn't I have all new clothes, half the stuff in there was old anyway. It's about time I treated myself."

"See, that's more like it. Told you every cloud has a

silver lining. When we get to the hotel, we'll check in and go straight out and get you what you need." They headed for the coach outside that was still patiently waiting for them. Victoria's face had changed and she beamed as she got on board.

The journey to the hotel took about an hour. Once they'd arrived they couldn't wait to get off the coach to stretch their legs. The hotel was painted white outside, palm trees shaded most of the walls. Victoria was the one who'd taken care of the hotel bookings. Geraldine knew there was no expense spared when she walked through the doors.

Once inside the air conditioning filtered cold air around their bodies. The marble floor looked like it was still wet. Victoria headed straight for the reception and told the woman who they were. After they completed a few forms, she handed them a key. The slender receptionist now spoke in Spanish to a porter and told him to carry their bags to their room. Once Geraldine handed him her case he looked at Victoria for her belongings. Her hands came out in front of her as she explained further.

"Oh I don't have any luggage, I did have, but it was lost at the airport. I'm going to have to buy all new clothing whilst I'm here, thanks to the airport." The man looked bewildered and didn't understand her completely.

When they reached the door, the man opened it and carried Geraldine's case inside. He quickly opened the curtains and opened the patio windows. The room was amazing and Geraldine could tell it was expensive. The porter stood at the door and smiled at them both. Victoria searched her handbag and quickly passed him ten euros. The room was spacious. A leather sofa sat in the middle of the room with a glass table slightly in front of it. The glass looked highly polished and not one bit of dust was present. Victoria inspected the rest of the room and she gave it her approval as she sat down to join Geraldine.

"It's a nice room isn't it? I've stayed in better but I can't complain."

Geraldine looked at her and smiled with a sarcastic face. "Well beggars can't be choosers. I think it's wonderful, just look at the view." They both walked out of the patio doors and looked at the holidaymakers who lay by the pool. Geraldine's eyes lit up as she spotted a gorgeous man lying near the pool. Without thinking, she spoke her mind.

"That's what I call a man. I will tell you something for nothing love, before the week is out he'll be in my bed making mad passionate love to me." Victoria giggled like a young girl and joined in the fun much to Geraldine's surprise.

"Well if you're having a leg over so am I. I'm sick of being on my own and if it's good enough for my twat of an ex-husband. It's good enough for me." She now pointed out a man who stood at the edge of the pool and commented on how tight his Speedos were. He looked like he was smuggling budgies down the front of them.

"Just look at him the poser. How tight are those trunks? He just wants everyone to see the shape of his knob." Her hands covered her face as she nudged her new friend in the waist. "Look, look. You can see the shape of it." Geraldine nearly choked as she laughed. She never thought in a million years she would speak like that. She loved that Victoria had a wild side too.

"Right let's go and buy some clothes, otherwise I'll be going out tonight in these and you don't want that do you?"

Geraldine opened her case and grabbed some shorts

and a vest top. She passed Victoria some shorts as the weather outside was boiling and they would have died from heat if they had kept the same clothes on. The girls made their way round the pool towards the exit. Geraldine made sure she caught the eye of the man she'd spotted earlier. When she was in his view, she gave him a sexy smile and knew he would keep until she was ready to take him.

The shops were busy and crowds of holidaymakers were buying gifts to take home. The shops were lively and one shop played a song Victoria loved as they entered. The song was 'Dance the Night Away', by the Mavericks, and once she heard it, she started shuffling her body from side to side giggling.

"I love this song. It always makes me want to dance, doesn't it you?" Geraldine had heard the song before and loved it too. Before long, they were linking each other dancing round the shop.

Money was no object to Victoria, and she knew exactly what she was looking for. Before long, she had many outfits under her arm. Victoria now hit the underwear section, and held a set up for Geraldine to look at.

"These are nice aren't they? I mean if I pull I need nice sexy underwear don't I?"

Geraldine helped her with her choices and gathered bras and knickers together for her to look at. Around an hour later, Victoria had replaced her clothing.

She even bought shoes, handbags, and new makeup. It was funny because this holiday was supposed to be about buying property abroad, not partying. Geraldine put looking for property to the back of her mind and concentrated on making Victoria have a good time. Back at the hotel they changed into their bikinis and headed for the pool grabbing the last few hours of sun.

Around the pool it was boiling hot. Before long, they were heading for a golden tan. Their skin was a lovely golden colour and as Victoria asked Geraldine to rub some sun cream on her back an older man came to join them. He hovered for a moment before he spoke.

"Hello ladies. If you need any cream rubbing on your backs, I'm your man." Geraldine turned to see who was speaking and was surprised at what she saw in front of her.

The man was in his early thirties and quite tall. His eyes were gorgeous. Once Victoria got a look at him, she started to talk with a cheeky smile on her face.

"So, do you do this service for all the ladies then?" The man smirked with a cocky face and looked at her.

"Well only the good looking ones. The mingers will have to get someone else to do it. My services are only for the finest looking ladies." The man introduced himself as Dave and told them he came from Alderley Edge.

Victoria got excited as she didn't live far from there and quizzed him about which area he lived. Geraldine knew at that minute that Victoria had put her mark on him and stood up and offered to go to the bar. "Anyone fancy a drink?" Victoria nodded and asked for Vodka and coke. She winked at Geraldine letting her knows she was over the moon with her newfound friend.

Dave asked for a pint of lager and told her that he would go if she wanted. Geraldine made an excuse that she needed the toilet anyway and didn't mind going. He positioned himself in front of Victoria to get her full attention. The attraction was almost instant between them and within minutes he had her doubled over laughing at his comments.

Geraldine stood at the side of the bar waiting to be

served. The bar was busy and several holidaymakers stood in front of her. Standing with her hand on her hip, she started to examine her new suntan. Through the corner of her eye she felt someone looking at her and lifted her head up to look at them.

The man she saw was the one from earlier and she smiled at him letting him know she'd seen him. Her eyes fluttered and she knew he wanted her attention. Once she'd been served she turned round and scanned the room for her eye candy, but he was nowhere in sight. Feeling a little bit disheartened she started to walk back to Victoria and struggled to carry all the drinks.

As she lifted her head, she saw him again. There he was like a gladiator waiting for the battle to begin. Her heart pounded inside her chest and her breath quickened as she prepared herself. As she took a few steps more her moment came and she quickly found the words to break the ice.

"Could you help me with these drinks, I think I'm going to drop one." He grinned and quickly came to her side. "Oh thanks, you're a saviour. I could feel them slipping from my grip. I'm just sat over here." The man didn't speak a word as they walked and she knew time was running out before they got back to the others.

"What's your name if you don't mind me asking?" He looked at her and she smiled revealing her pearly white teeth.

"My name's Ashley, what's yours?" That was all Geraldine needed and she introduced herself straight away. When they arrived back with the drinks Dave was rubbing cream into Victoria's back and she was roaring with laughter. As she saw her she tried to speak, but her laughter stopped her as Dave tickled her side.

"Geraldine please tell him. I only said he could rub

some cream in my back and he's tickling me to death."
Geraldine tickled her other side and Victoria rolled round
the bed struggling to breathe through laughing.

"She loves it really don't you?" Geraldine laughed and
turned to face Ashley.

"Grab a chair Ash, or do you have to go?" Ashley pulled
up a chair and started to talk to all of them. When he found
out Victoria and Dave had just met, he couldn't believe
it. He thought they were man and wife. Dave started to
ask questions of Ashley and Geraldine listened to his every
word.

"So where are you from mate?" Ash told him he lived
in Oldham and they all laughed because it was so weird
that they all came from near enough the same place.

"Fate it is," said Dave in his cheeky northern accent.
"These ladies have been sent to us Ash from the Gods
above. It's only fair we treat them to a good night out on
the town out to repay their hospitality. What do you think
mate?" Ashley loved Dave's cheek and carried on with the
banter between them all.

As the sun began to set the next task was to get ready
for a night on the town. They agreed to go out together
and arranged to meet in a bar not far from the hotel. Once
the girls had something to eat, they started to get ready.
They were both buzzing with the new men they'd met.
They couldn't wait to be reunited with them.

Victoria was the first in the shower. Her laughter from
within caused Geraldine to freeze on the spot. Geraldine
knocked on the door and asked her what was so funny. As
Victoria opened the door, she stood with a towel wrapped
round her body and was smiling like a Cheshire cat.
Geraldine looked at her and asked what was so funny. She
nearly dropped on the spot as Victoria dropped her towel

to reveal her fanny. All she had was a line of pubic hair just in the middle of her mound. It looked like Adolf Hitler's moustache. Victoria started to speak and tears of laughter fell from her eyes.

"It looks like a landing strip doesn't it? I only meant to tidy it up but before I knew it I got carried away and was left with this." Geraldine burst into laughter too and they both joked about her new pubic hair.

"Ay all you need is cat's eyes in it and it's definitely a landing strip," Geraldine giggled. Victoria picked up her towel from the floor and replaced it. She headed into the dining area. Geraldine followed her and she could see a change in her facial expressions.

"What's up love?" Victoria turned round and stared at her before she spoke.

"You know what? I feel like a young girl again. I haven't had this much fun for years and it just reminds me that I've wasted so many years with that husband of mine. Promise me you'll make me have a good time. I'm sick of being me and want to have fun." Her eyes looked glossy and she was close to breaking down in tears as she continued. "I've heard stories from my friends about all their sex antics and this time I want it to be me who is telling them the stories. Will you promise me that love?" Geraldine ran to her side.

"You want fun. I'll show you fun. I'm going to blow your mind tonight. You won't ever be that boring person again, I promise you." Victoria danced round the room with Geraldine and started to sing the song they'd heard earlier.

Once they were ready, they examined each other and knew they looked hot. Their golden bodies made their clothes look sexier than ever. They both set off to meet their dates for the night.

The bar was lively and the music was pumping as they got there. Everyone looked tanned and some of the people looked like lobsters. You could see bikini marks on some of the women's shoulders and some people had sunglass marks round their tanned faces. Victoria heard Dave's voice behind her and turned to face him.

"Come on sexy we've got seats round here." His words melted her heart. She couldn't remember the last time someone had called her sexy and she looked at herself up and down. She felt sexy.

The journey to the seats was horrendous. As they reached their seats, they spotted the nightmare family from the plane. Geraldine and Victoria looked at each other and hung their heads so as not be spotted, but it was too late.

"Hiya love," she shouted over to them. "Look at the colour of you two. You're really brown! What, have you been using chip fat oil?" The woman was laughing her head off and tried to carry on speaking but Dave pulled them both away as they waved goodbye to her.

Ashley sat in the corner looking uncomfortable. You could tell he felt better now that he saw them walking towards him. Geraldine sat next to him and he immediately commented on how good she looked. Geraldine was craving sex. She knew tonight would be the night that the old Geraldine would return. She wanted hot steamy sex and nothing was going to stop her getting her fix. The drinks kept coming and hours later, the four of them were legless. They'd been drinking shots of something Dave had got them from the bar and Geraldine could feel her head starting to spin.

"I need to get some fresh air Ash, are you coming outside for a minute?" Ashley agreed and they left Dave and Victoria in deep conversation.

The night was hot and muggy. Geraldine walked to the side of the pub and spewed up. As she looked up there were a line of people at the side of her doing exactly the same thing and somehow she didn't feel as bad. Ash came to her rescue and lifted her hair whilst she continued being sick. As she retched she farted and Ashley couldn't help but fall about laughing.

"Oh my god, have you just farted?" he asked. Geraldine tried not to laugh as she lifted her head up and denied it. He grabbed her and pulled her nearer as she wiped her mouth. His head touched hers.

"That farting business has really turned me on. I love a woman who can fart." Geraldine giggled and thought about what he said with a smile on her face. She headed towards a bench nearby and sat on it trying to sober up. As Ash sat by her side, she thought this was the ideal time to ask him the next question.

"So, come on then what turns you on, and don't say farting." Ashley threw his head back and laughed but then with a serious face answered her question.

"I love bald fannies. My fantasy would be to have you and Victoria in bed with me so you could both fight over my cock." Geraldine laughed because his fantasy was quite normal and she didn't seem surprised by it.

She looked at him with her head tilted to the side. "How would you like a foursome with Victoria and Dave?" His eyes lit up and she knew the thought of it all had already turned him on. Geraldine stood up and grabbed his hands. "Come on then, let's go and see if we can get this going. A foursome you want, a foursome you'll get."

Once back inside the pub, Geraldine got a second wind and felt a lot better. As she approached Dave and

Victoria she knew they were both as pissed as farts as they were swaying all over. She knew this was the time to put her question on the table in front of them. Once they sat down Geraldine just came right out with it as Ashley died with shame that his fantasy was now out in the open.

"Right you two. Ash and I have just been talking and he's told me that his fantasy is to have me and you fighting over his cock in bed." Silence filled the table for a moment, and then Victoria burst out laughing.

"What? You want a threesome with me and Geraldine?" She looked directly at him. Geraldine corrected her and told her he wanted a foursome. Dave looked interested at the word foursome and he leant over to listen further. Geraldine looked at Victoria for an answer and waited until she spoke.

"Are you joking with me love?" She threw her head back now and laughed out loud. "You must have told him about my landing strip fanny haven't you?" Dave looked at Ash and they both laughed wanting to know exactly what she was on about, but Victoria and Geraldine couldn't talk through laughing.

"Adolf Hitler fanny don't you mean," Geraldine giggled as Victoria rested her head on Dave's shoulder.

"Don't listen to her Dave she's just jealous of my new look." Dave cuddled up to her and whispered into her ear.

"Can I have a peep at it later, if I'm lucky?" Victoria smiled and felt alive inside. She felt like she was living in a dream world. Geraldine smiled at her and winked.

"So Victoria, shall we show these boys how to party?" Both men looked at her like gagging dogs and hoped they were in for a night of steamy sex.

Victoria felt on top of the world, but a foursome, was she ready for that? She'd heard about them before from friends but never in her wildest dreams did she think she would be part of one. Her thoughts went back to her husband and the photographs she'd seen, and her mind was made up. "Yeah why not? I'm sick of being prim and proper it's about time I let my hair down." Geraldine's focused on her and she reached her face over to kiss her cheek.

"Well that's sorted then. Let's get a couple bottles of wine and head back to our hotel. Both men seemed dazed and Ashley now looked anxious. Although he'd told her his fantasy, he'd never imagined it would take place. Dave grasped Victoria's hand under the table. He too was a bit scared of what lay ahead. Geraldine was so in control. She ordered the wine from behind the bar and nodded her head to them to let them know she was ready to leave. The walk to the hotel wasn't far and before long they were opening the door to their room. Conversation was lost because they all knew once the door closed, a completely new experience would begin.

"Who wants a drink?" Geraldine shouted as they sat themselves on the settee looking like they were waiting for the referee to blow the whistle to start the fun and games.

"Just bring the bottle, over" Ashley shouted. Victoria removed her shoes and placed her legs over Dave who started to stroke Victoria's long silken legs. He slowly caressed the calf first with long gliding movements. After a few stokes his hand was fully up her skirt. Geraldine came to join them and passed the bottles of wine round. They all gulped a large mouthful. Geraldine could see Dave's hand up Victoria's skirt and she could tell she was aroused.

Ashley didn't have a clue where to start and it was Geraldine who made the first move. Her hand caressed his knee. She teased him slowly by rubbing her hands across his firm cock. He felt like he was in a porn movie and couldn't believe what was happening. Dave was kissing Victoria and she could see his hands all over her legs. As she looked closer, she could see his finger teasing her fanny as he slipped his fingers in and out of her knickers. Victoria's groans were turning Geraldine on. She wanted the fun to start straight away. Slowly she rolled down her skirt and carefully took off her top. She stood in her black laced underwear and high heel shoes.

She looked at Ashley and told him to come and join her. Dave and Victoria were well under way. Geraldine knelt to where they lay, stroking Victoria's body near her waist. As Victoria looked at her, Ashley knew the fun was about to start. Geraldine leant her head to meet Victoria's and slowly moved in to kiss her.

At first, Victoria looked a bit apprehensive but as she continued, it felt so natural. Geraldine teased Victoria's lips with her tongue, as the two men watched with glee.

Ashley felt like a spare part at this time and knew he would have to get involved. After all, it was his fantasy. He leant in to them and caressed whichever body he could reach as Dave did the same. Within minutes, Geraldine and Victoria were both knelt up and exploring each other's bodies. Geraldine slid her mouth round Victoria's nipples as she groaned with pleasure. Dave was ready to explode at the noises they were making and quickly knelt behind Victoria.

Once he was there, he slid his throbbing cock inside her and started to stroke her hair. Ashley didn't waste time either and quickly inserted himself inside Geraldine as he watched the two women in action.

Dave moved his hand over to Geraldine and stroked what he could see of her minge. The four of them were now enjoying some mind-blowing sex. If anyone heard the noises from outside the room, they would have thought someone was in extreme pain.

The night continued until four hot and sweaty bodies fell to the ground. The sex between the four of them had been amazing. Victoria couldn't believe her body could bend in that many positions. She also felt like she'd been involved in something quite special. She didn't think of it as perverted. She thought of it as love making, but with a few extra guests. The four of them lay exhausted on the floor. Dave and Ash felt like porn stars. They lay with their erect penises still on full show.

Geraldine's eyes stared over to Victoria and her own body still wanted to lick her from head to toe. Victoria felt like a new woman. She felt sexy and desired for once in her life. She loved the way Geraldine made her feel.

"Am I a lesbian?" she thought as she lay with her fingers still stroking across her shoulder. Tiredness filled their bodies and the two men left with smiles fixed firmly across their faces. Geraldine and Victoria crawled into their own beds after they left.

The sound of children playing outside caused Geraldine to open her eyes. Her head was throbbing as she tried to lift it from the pillow. Her body felt like a lead weight as she looked towards Victoria's bed. Victoria was still asleep and she looked beautiful as she admired her. Stretching her body, she let out a loud yawn that caused her to open her eyes. Seeing Geraldine's face brought back the events of the night before. She slowly pulled the cotton sheet over her head and hoped she could go back to sleep. The noise of Geraldine going to the toilet let her know that the sheet she held over her wouldn't take away the night before.

Peeling the sheet away from her face, she sat up and waited for her to return from the toilet.

"Good morning honey. Did you have a good sleep?" Victoria nodded and fidgeted in the bed trying to straighten her pillow.

"You were great last night, you little minx. Thought you said you were shy?" Victoria's face went bright red as she spoke and you could tell she wanted the floor to open up and drag her inside.

"I am shy. I think I just had too much to drink. Did I embarrass myself?" Geraldine made her way to her side and moved her over in the bed, as she looked straight into her eyes.

"Babes you were amazing. Those two must have had the time of their lives. We could make a big business from what we provided those two with last night." Victoria smiled as Geraldine moved her over in the bed and joined her. At first, she felt uncomfortable with her at the side of her, but as she began to speak, her nerves returned back to normal.

"What did you think of last night? I didn't know you had such a gorgeous body. You're really sexy, do you know that?" Victoria smiled and tried to hide her face with the white cotton sheet as she giggled. Geraldine pulled the sheet away from her. As their eyes met, Geraldine felt a rush of excitement through her body and looked directly into her eyes.

The moment lasted a few minutes and Victoria felt strange inside. Geraldine placed her hand under the sheets and stroked at her legs. She glided her fanned fingers up and down them and watched her face as she continued. Victoria felt completely aroused and something inside her became alive. She could feel a throbbing between her legs and her heart beat like a ticking clock.

Geraldine moved her hands to her breasts and tickled her nipples. Her touch was soft and she looked at her for approval as she continued. This was the moment that two women decided they wanted to satisfy each other's needs. Geraldine's mouth moved towards her. She licked her bottom lip before she kissed her slowly. With her hands, she caressed all down her body. She could feel Victoria's legs slowly opening, wanting more. Within minutes, Geraldine had slid down the bed and was pleasing her with her tongue. The noise of a woman finding heaven soon filled the room and Victoria was on fire with passion as Geraldine's tongue pleased her. Victoria screamed with pleasure as her body shook with spasms of enjoyment. After a few minutes, she sat up to repay her.

She suckled on her breasts and licked up and down her body. Geraldine was mad with lust and wanted this woman to eat her. Her hands raised above her head as she knelt up and she rocked with pleasure as Victoria lay under her licking and caressing her vagina. Victoria felt wild. Never in a million years did she think sex with a woman could be this good. If this is how a lesbian felt when they made love, she definitely wanted to be one.

The warm liquid from Geraldine slid into her mouth and she felt crazy with excitement as she listened to her reach orgasm. When she'd finished they both collapsed beside each other on the bed and tried to calm down. Their lovemaking was electric. They held hands and gazed at each other. Geraldine folded the pillow under her head.

"Wow! That was hot. I can't believe how sexy you are. You turn me on so much." Victoria pulled Geraldine towards her and touching her lips with her long fingers.

"I feel so sexy when I'm with you. Do you think

I'm a lesbian? I've never felt like that during sex before."
Geraldine smiled and sat up to face her.

"Honey, whatever you're happy with. Man or woman it doesn't matter. Don't analyse it, just enjoy it." She jumped off the bed and paced over to the patio window, with no clothes on.

As she looked out of the window, she could see people gathering round the poolside. Today they were going to look at properties and she shouted over to Victoria who was still lying on the bed wearing nothing but a smile across her face.

"Shall we get ready babes? Let's go and see what Spain has to offer." Victoria smiled and kicked off the sheets and headed to the bathroom.

As she met her face in the silver mirror that sat on the wall under the sink, she smiled at her reflection and congratulated herself on the person she had become. The woman she once was seemed to be just a distant memory and a new sexy minx stood in front of her. The knock at the front door startled her as she wrapped a towel around her and quickly hurried to see a porter standing there with her suitcase at the side of him. Her face lit up as she signed his piece of paper. As she headed back, her smile filled her face. Within a short time, she was ready to go, wearing a white linen pant-suit with a silk lemon vest top underneath. She applied her makeup and headed back to Geraldine who was ready and waiting for her. Geraldine was wearing a navy pair of shorts and a cropped sleeved top. Her breasts looked as if they sat under her chin.

As they waited in the hotel, they both grabbed a few pieces of toast and a cup of coffee. They were waiting to meet Pedro who worked for a company in Spain selling houses and villas.

They were sat chatting when Dave shouted them. As they looked up, he approached them with a cocky face. "Morning ladies. How you feeling this fine morning?" Before they could answer, he continued. "I'm feeling fucking great." Geraldine and Victoria both smiled but their own secret after party when the lads had gone meant more than anything that had happened the night before, and they spoke to him with a coolly.

"Morning," Geraldine spoke in a sarcastic manner. Dave pulled up a chair and moved it closer to her before he spoke.

"Great night last night wasn't it. Best sex I've ever had. Are you up for it again tonight?" None of them spoke for a few seconds and Victoria was the one who answered.

"I think we all had too much to drink last night didn't we? I'm afraid I won't be doing it again. Don't get me wrong it was fun, but it's not for me."

Dave looked shocked and not a little gutted but before he could continue, a man stood at the side of them and introduced himself.

"You two beautiful ladies must be Geraldine and Victoria. I'm Pedro from Bella Properties." He reached towards them and shook both of their hands. Dave looked puzzled and struggled to speak as they both stood to leave.

"We'll meet up later and talk then. Is that okay?" They ignored him and headed off towards the front of the hotel with Pedro.

Pedro was good looking and about six foot tall. His dark hair complimented his hazel eyes. The stubble on his face made him look attractive. He wore cream canvass shorts and a white cotton shirt, with several buttons unfastened revealing his hairy chest. The girls waited at the front of the hotel while Pedro brought the car to the entrance. The heat was scorching and within minutes, Victoria had taken off her jacket. Pedro drove up a silver jeep and opened the door for them both to get in. He spoke very good English and told them that they would be at their destination within twenty minutes.

As they travelled towards the mountains everywhere seemed so small in the distance. Geraldine watched as Victoria sipped her water and smiled as she caught her eye. The connection between them was amazing and they both felt that they wanted to rip each other's clothes off then and there. Geraldine moved towards her as she offered her a drink of water and slowly touched her hand as she drank it.

Pedro told them they were nearly there and they both looked eagerly for the villa in the distance. The place looked dilapidated and the once white walls looked grey. The road was bumpy as they drove up towards it and none of them looked impressed as the car stopped. Pedro opened the door for them and started to speak.

"I know it needs a bit of work but that's what you always get with these kinds of properties." Geraldine took the paper from his hands that had the villa's information on it. It had eight bedrooms and two living rooms. The swimming pool only looked small on the picture. The price was great for the property but as they started to look around, they realised why it was still on the market. The villa was quite secluded and set on a hill. If you looked from the front entrance, all you could see were other villas set in the hillside.

Pedro kicked the dirt from the entrance and placed the key into the door. He pressed against the door with his hip to open it and invited them both inside before him. As they looked around, they got the shock of their lives. It looked like a film set inside. Each room had a theme and looked different.

The first room they went into was a bedroom; pink feathers were scattered all over the walls and a large brass bed stood in the middle of the room. They smiled as they continued the tour. The next room was painted white and had a hospital bed underneath the window. A sign hung from the top of the bed saying "Nil by mouth." Pale green curtains hung around the bed on a silver track. Geraldine's mind was working overtime as she looked into each room. What a strange place!

The tour lasted about twenty minutes. Victoria wasn't impressed. She wanted a holiday home to come and relax in and couldn't see beyond all the work that needed doing. The pool outside was average in size and full of debris. Pedro could tell by their faces they weren't interested. At last they headed back to the car and Victoria started to speak as Pedro looked at her through his rear view mirror.

"I expected something more inviting. I couldn't bring my friends over here to stay. It looks like a film studio." Geraldine agreed but her mind was elsewhere.

The journey back to the hotel was more or less the same. The heat was beating down on them and they felt sick because of it. Pedro asked if they would like to go and see more properties but Victoria was still hung over from the night before and wanted to fall asleep beside the pool.

Geraldine felt excited inside and couldn't wait until they left Pedro at the hotel. Once he'd gone they headed up to their room to get changed. Victoria wore a black bikini with white spots on it. Geraldine chose her old favourite, a red polka dot one. They quickly grabbed a beach towel each and headed for the pool.

Once they'd found a sun bed, Victoria went to the

bar to get two diet cokes. The complex was crowded and several kids were splashing about in the pool. The music from the bar was loud but not that loud that it deafened you. As they both took the sunbathing position, Victoria propped herself up and looked at all the different people round her.

A few families sat near them, huddled together under an umbrella. You could tell they were struggling with the heat. Gangs of girls strutted their stuff walking around the pool hoping to attract male attention. As the sun beat down on them, the girls applied a thick layer of sun cream. Geraldine was fidgeting as Victoria lay like a corpse and eventually she could hold her tongue no longer.

"We could make that villa into a great business you know." Victoria heard Geraldine's words and removed her canvass hat from her face.

"What do you mean a business?" Geraldine sat up fully and swung her legs off her bed.

"I think it was all that film set talk which gave me the idea. I think it would be a great opportunity for us." Victoria sat up and faced Geraldine.

"Well, tell me then. What's your idea? She moved in closer to avoid prying ears and looked straight into her face.

"Let's make it into a fantasy place." Victoria's face froze and you could tell she didn't understand what Geraldine meant, until she continued. "There are loads of people out there who love kinky sex. The film setting in each of the rooms are perfect to act out any fantasy. The hospital room for instance could be a sexy nurse scene. How many men out there have dreamt of a nurse touching them up, and bathing them," she looked from side to side as she continued, "we could create any fantasy we want and earn some money as well."

Victoria looked surprised, and laughed as she lay back on her sun lounger. Geraldine lay on her side and continued whispering her ideas.

"Look at what we did last night. Men would pay good money for that. I'm not saying us two do all the work. We can employ people for that. Victoria just think about it. It's a money making idea honey."

The conversation didn't stop there as Geraldine continued chatting about her wild ideas.

"We can have lap dancers, lesbians, super heroes, brides, and anything else they want. I know it would work, what do you think?" Victoria remained silent, and placed her hat over her face and shut her ears to drown out Geraldine's voice. All she wanted to do now was sleep and recover from the night before.

The plan was hatching in Geraldine's mind and as she looked round the pool, she looked at all the different kinds of people. Some were up their own arses and some were just glad to be on holiday. You could tell the working class people as they stood out a mile. Victoria stretched as she felt the heat melting her body. The hair at the back of her neck was wringing wet and she needed a cold drink as soon as possible.

Slowly she sat up and tried to focus. Finding her sandals she slipped them on and asked Geraldine whether she wanted a drink. Geraldine nodded and asked her to get her whatever she was having. As she stood to go to the bar, she watched her every movement as she pulled the bikini bottoms from the crack of her arse. Victoria was sexy and Geraldine had to fight the urge to make love to her.

Victoria stood at the bar and waited patiently. The bar staff were all Spanish and their dark hair looked sexy next to their skin. One of the men noticed her and made his way towards her.

He spoke in broken English. As he spoke, she smiled as she told him what she wanted. He never took his eyes from her as he poured her drinks. Her smile took over her face as she looked into his eyes. He winked at her and mumbled something in Spanish to the others. Victoria walked away but was fully aware all eyes were on her as she wiggled her arse back towards her sun lounger.

The smell of sun tan lotions filled the air as she squeezed past all the beds. As she neared Geraldine, she could see her sitting up awaiting her drink. Victoria passed her the drink and watched as she drank downed it in one big gulp.

"Bloody hell, was you thirsty honey?" she joked. Geraldine just grinned and watched as she sat on the side of her bed. Victoria thought about her idea and sighed as she started to talk to her.

"What makes you think it will work? This 'Fantasy Villa' as you call it?" Geraldine looked shocked and started to repeat her previous conversation.

"With the right people involved I know we could earn some big money. It's all about marketing and keeping it to those people we want to attract. We don't want the seedy perverts do we? We want businessmen and wealthy women. Let's go back to the villa and have a look at it again from a different point of view."

Victoria chuckled to herself and liked the idea more and more. After all, she was right; there was a market for it.

"Okay then, let's go back. I'm not promising anything but I do see the prospects of a new business venture. I can't believe I'm even thinking about it." Geraldine was excited and reeled off a few ideas as Victoria lay back down.

"We can get some dishy guys to do things like stripping and lap dancing, or even the dirty plumber scenes. We need girls as well. I don't think we'll have a problem with them. There are lots of places we can start to look for girls. I want this to be an up-market villa where we don't just let any riff-raff in. We can have it by invite only." Victoria lay on her side and asked what she meant by invite only.

"We can make it mysterious. I can make a website." Her ideas were flying now, "we can ask what fantasy they want acting out and tell them if they're picked they will receive an invite through the post. Of course, it won't say Fantasy Villa on it. It will be discreet. We can say it's a business meeting or ask the punter what they want us to write on the invite. There'll be lot of work involved into getting the place ready, but I'm sure we can do it"

"Wow you've really thought about this haven't you?" giggled Victoria.

"Nothing ventured, nothing gained I always say. We can go into the clubs tonight and start looking for staff. We need sexy girls and some dishy looking blokes" she sat scratching her head and looked deep in thought. "Phone Pedro and tell him we want a second look at the villa. The sooner we get this sorted the sooner we can start earning big money. I have some savings and I'll put it into the business, just to show you how much I believe in us."

The sun started to move round the tall hotel grounds and everyone started to leave the poolside. The two of them agreed that tonight they would delve into Spanish nightlife to see if they could find what they were looking for.

4

LONG LEGS WAS A well known lap-dancing club in the resort and lots of stag parties always headed there when they visited. Kimberley Kyte had been working there for the last two years. Her twenty-four year old body was toned and flexible. She had everything a man could ever dream of; her long blonde hair touched the small of her back and her blue eyes gave off an enchanted look.

Kimberley's thirty-four double D breasts looked firm as she confidently walked about the club. She'd originally lived in Manchester but her life there was nothing but torment due to family life. Anytime she met people from her home town, her own torment came flooding back to her and it reminded her of the reason she'd moved as far away possible in the first place...

Kimberley was one of seven children. Her mother Sarah had never had a steady relationship. All her brothers and sisters were from different fathers. Her mother had told her that her brother Simon shared the same father but that was always debatable as he looked nothing like her. Sarah loved each of her partners with all her heart but none of them ever stayed with her for more than a few years. She always said it was so hard for men to bring up someone else's kids and that's the real reason they never stayed.

She would always let the kids know this reason every time she hit the vodka and that was nearly every day. Her once pretty face looked haggard and the wrinkles on her face told the story of her life. Many a night she would sit alone downstairs with her only friend, the vodka, and cry at all the mistakes she'd made in her life. Her children knew to leave the room once she started drinking because it was only a matter of time before she turned on them.

Friday nights in the Kyte household were always the same. All the kids were out on the street causing chaos and Sarah was in the front room getting pissed out of her head without a care in the world. The lads from the family had their fingers in more than one pie. They earned cash from drug dealing, car theft and anything else they could to keep their heads above water. The girls from the family shoplifted and lived their lives trying to find a decent boyfriend who could help them escape the nightmare. Kimberley had two sisters, Jenny and Trisha. They were older than she was and tried to show her the ropes from an early age.

Jenny had auburn hair and green eyes. Her complexion was quite freckly. Her mum had always said she was the outcome of a one-night stand with an Irish navvy who was working outside the family home some years before. Jenny was a loud mouth and could fight with the best of them. She was short-tempered and Kimberley had seen the violent side of her many times before. Trisha was a lot quieter than the rest of her family and often wished they were all dead. She had hazel eyes and her plump figure didn't help her confidence. Kimberley and Trisha were Jenny's workers and whatever she wanted them to do, they did without a fight.

They all lived together in a four bed-roomed house in Harpurhey, on a notorious council estate. Many large families lived there and it was a dog eat dog environment. Very few households had a father figure and each of the mothers looked like they'd given up on life. The kids on the estate all seemed to get on well. There was an unwritten rule which meant if you fight one you fought them all. If anyone who gave them any shit they would all stick together and deal with them. This usually meant smashing their windows or slashing their car tyres.

The majority of the kids looked like life had given up on them. If you walked through the estate at any time, you could see them just sat about. School was just somewhere they got a warm meal and very few of them ever went. They sat on benches in the local park with tins of gas shoved up their sleeves getting high with the buzz it gave them.

Kimberley's brother sold drugs. He'd started selling for an older boy at first but as the months passed, he started to supply his own. Weed was a good seller but the profits were much bigger when selling smack. When smack first hit the streets no one wanted it until a few of the lads tried it. They told everyone about the buzz and it wasn't long before they were all on it.

Simon was wise and didn't try it himself. The friends he once knew who took the drug had turned into people he no longer recognised. Their faces turned white and dark circles appeared under their eyes. They would do anything for their next fix and some of them even sold their bodies. Nothing deterred him from selling smack. He loved the knocked off stuff the bag heads brought to him in exchange for drugs; gold chains, rings and televisions were common trades.

Simon never took any of his gains to the family home. He'd met a girl from a decent family and moved in with her straight away. His new home had all the luxuries he'd only ever dreamt of. Selling drugs helped him change his life. Simon was always smartly dressed and didn't look like he came from the same household as Kimberley. Every now and then, he would bung his sisters a fiver for food but those days were rare and his only concern was his own well being, not his family's.

The three sisters always played on the estate near Conran Street market. All the kids knocked around there. Mr Billings was a strange character who always sat out watching the children play, a cig always hung from the corner of his mouth. He was around fifty years of age and wore a white vest with navy braces hanging down from his shoulder. The white vest had several stains on it. Mr Billing was a well-known pervert on the estate. The story amongst the kids in the area was that his wife had found him in bed with a young girl and left him to fend for himself many years before. He'd always smile at the three sisters as they played near his front door. Jenny was always at his door cadging cigs from him. He liked their company and urged them to sit at his front door hoping to find out all the things they'd been up to.

Kimberley had often wondered why Jenny was always going in his house to use the toilet and why he would always follow her. It wasn't until one summer's day that she found out exactly why Jenny got the money she did from Mr Billings. Kimberley watched as Jenny entered the house and slowly crept in a few minutes later. The house had a damp smell to it and the smell of old newspapers filled the hallway. Kimberley was going to shout her sister but before she did, she listened to the noise coming from a small room to the left of her.

Feeling scared she progressed to the small gap in the door. She froze as she saw Mr Billing's pants round his ankles. She couldn't see anything else until she moved to the other side of the door.

"Go on love, fucking wank it!" Kimberley could now see her sister pulling on Mr Billings cock with a cig sticking out of her mouth. His face looked funny and she wondered what Jenny was doing to him. She remained silent until she heard a loud moan from him telling her he was shooting his load. Kimberley wanted to laugh out loud as she watched some kind of white stuff drop onto his fat belly but she was afraid they would hear her. Finally she saw a hand appear in front of Mr Billings' fat face.

"Where's my fucking fiver?" Mr Billings reached down to his and tried to recover his breath as he spoke.

"Hold on a minute you dirty mare, and I'll get it for you." Kimberley didn't wait around. She headed straight back to the front of the house to join her friends.

Minutes later Jenny came out of the house with Mr Billings following closely behind her. Jenny looked straight at Kimberley and told her they were going to get some cigs from the shop. When they were walking away Kimberley asked her where she'd got the fiver from. Jenny waved the money around in her hand and told her to fuck off and not to be so nosey.

It didn't take Kimberley long to work out exactly what was going on and as the months passed she also started wanking Mr Billings off for money. Jenny was none the wiser and Kimberley told him to keep it that way.

Kimberley loved earning the money from Mr Billings, and when she was sixteen, she entered her first brothel to begin work. It was her sister's idea and they both worked there to make ends meet. Their mother didn't give a flying fuck where they were, by this time she didn't even know what day it was.

A woman called Dawn ran the brothel. She looked after the girls and always helped them out, however she could. She knew Kimberley was only young, but with the help of makeup, she made her look at least eighteen. Dawn also got Kimberley into lap dancing. She took her one night with a couple of other girls and told them that's where the real money was. Girls could earn a fortune from lap dancing and that's what Kimberley wanted to do from the moment she walked in the club. She watched as the men caressed the bodies of the young girls and saw how turned on they were by it all. This lifestyle appealed to her and two weeks later, she started.

Kimberley's first night was terrifying but the other girls showed her the ropes and she practised the moves. Within the hour, Kimberley was bending over in front of a middle-aged man strutting her stuff. As she turned to face him she grabbed hold of his navy blue tie and slowly rubbed her breasts up his body. The man loved it and she felt like she had some control for the first time in her life.

Months passed and Kimberley was a favourite dancer for many of the men. She was taking home around five hundred pounds per week. Her clothes and her image changed too. She had long false nails and she now had a golden tan. Her hair extensions complimented her hair colour and she rocked most men's worlds when she danced for them.

Kimberley was twenty-four when her life changed. She packed her bags and set off to Spain with another lap dancer called Nicky who lived in Miles Platting on another council estate. Her family didn't bat an eye-lid when she told them she was leaving. By this time Jenny had turned to drugs and the rest of her family were too hooked on stealing and drinking to be bothered about her.

Kimberley packed her clothes on the day she was leaving. Looking out of her bedroom window, she shook her head at the estate that faced her. Dogs were fighting and kids stood drinking, the discoloured net curtains hanging from the window told her how bad things really were. Touching the window frame with her finger, she saw black slime round the edges. The sound of Nicky outside in the taxi shouting her made her hurry and close her suitcase. After a few minutes she dragged it down the stairway.

"Mam," she shouted in a high-pitched voice. "I'm going now, Nicky's here for me." Her mother lifted her head from the table and slurred her words.

"Go on you selfish twat. Leave me alone like every fucker else does." Kimberley froze and held herself against the wall. Her eyes closed as she screwed her face up listening to her mother's words. "No one gives a fuck about me. I'm left here as usual without a pot to piss in. Go on fuck off, and see if I care." Kimberley thought about going in the front room to see her but experience told her it was a no win situation.

Lifting her suitcase, she slowly dragged it outside and headed to the taxi. As she made herself comfortable, she could see her mother coming out of the front door. As she watched her drunken mother, she could see her struggling to stand. She watched her grip the doorframe to steady herself. Kimberley opened the window to hear her shouting abuse.

"Fuck the fucking lot of youse. You're all a load of toss pots anyway" Kimberley ordered the taxi to drive off and didn't look at her mother again. This was the life she left behind. As the taxi drove out of the avenue, she turned and looked for one last time. A tear fell from her eye. Nicky held her hand as she saw she was getting upset and no words needed to be spoken as they both set off in search of a better life.

The airport was empty for the time of the year. September was always quiet because all the kids were back at school after the summer holidays. Long Legs was the place to work for any lap dancer wanting to earn some decent money. They both hoped to get work there once they reached Spain. Nicky had come from a similar kind of home life as Kimberley and they both knew this job could change their lives for the better.

When they landed, they couldn't wait to get to the hotel. The journey lasted about forty minutes. They had only booked in the resort for bed and breakfast and the plan was to get somewhere proper to stay as soon as they started earning some money.

The atmosphere in Long Legs was amazing when they walked in on their first night. The heat was sickly as they moved towards the bar. Men were all over the place and you could see at least ten girls walking round with nothing but a bra and skimpy knickers on. The noise of everyone talking was deafening and the music played as some girls danced around.

"Two vodka and cokes please," Nicky shouted to the girl behind the bar. The girl had massive tits and a tiny belly top t-shirt, which left nothing to the imagination. Her thin waist held her shorts up. She looked gorgeous and you could tell all the men just sat at the bar so they could leer at her. Nicky gave her the money and wasted no time in finding out who ran the place. The barmaid was helpful and pointed to a tall thin man stood at the other side of the room.

As they looked over at the man he looked around thirty-five. He was stood with a few women and a couple of men. He was handsome and his designer stubble gave him that sexy 'just got out of bed' look. He was a darling.

"Fuck me he's gorgeous isn't he love?" Kimberley agreed as they searched for an area near him to stand.

Both girls looked dressed to kill. If they had learnt anything in the time they'd been lap dancing it was to dress sexy. Kimberley wore a white mini skirt with a bright pink vest that had sequins on it. Her high heels complimented her legs and she looked stunning. Her hair was in two pigtails tied back with two pieces of pink ribbon. Nicky wore black Lycra hot pants. She finished her outfit off with a black bra with silver diamonds sewn all round the edges of it. They were already drawing some attention as they stood chatting and it wasn't long before men were by their side trying to chat them up.

Drinks came free and easy all night. This was something both girls expected from the men they met. The night was soon in full swing and they loved the atmosphere in the place. From the corner of her eye, Kimberley could see the club owner checking her out. She kept her cool and never made eye contact as she watched him coming towards her. The music was deafening and the heat was causing her to wipe her brow as tiny trickles of sweat ran down her forehead. Kimberley turned just as he stood by her side and their eyes met for the first time. Words didn't come to either of them at first and they both just gazed into each other's eyes.

"Hello gorgeous," he smiled and grabbed her waist. "I've not seen you in here before, are you on holiday or do you live over here?" Kimberley's heart pounded inside her chest. Her words seemed stuck in her throat. Nicky heard the conversation and jumped to her side taking over the conversation.

"We're on holiday, but hoping to find work over here." James looked at them both and smiled.

"Well this could be your lucky night girls. I'm after some dancers if you're interested. You're just what I'm looking for." Kimberley nudged Nicky in the waist and she spoke for the first time.

"We might be interested but we're not desperate. We would have to discuss terms and conditions." Kimberley sounded intelligent and she surprised herself with the professional sounding negotiations she had just started. Nicky raised her eyebrows at her letting her know she was doing well.

"We can sit down and have a chat if you have a few minutes," James continued. Nicky knew they had to move quickly and pushed the chat forward.

"We're checking out all the other bars tonight as well, so if you want us to work here, grab us quick," Nicky chuckled, hoping she didn't sound too demanding.

James looked round the club and pointed to a corner that was deserted. He told them he would go and get some drinks and asked them both what they wanted. As he left, Nicky grabbed Kimberley's arm.

"For fucks sake he's gorgeous isn't he? Where the fuck did you learn to speak like that?" Kimberley's eyes were still on James and she slowly turned her head to listen to her. "All those big words you used. Terms and fucking conditions. You sounded professional. I loved it." Kimberley dragged her closer and spoke quickly.

"Right, we don't want to sound too eager. We want good money and somewhere to live. If we play our cards right we could be on a good little number here, so follow my lead and don't fuck it up." Nicky started to laugh.

"Fucking follow my lead!" she shrieked.

"Where the fuck is all this talk coming from," Nicky asked, "don't get me wrong I love it but I never knew you could speak the lingo with these posh fuckers."

James approached balancing the drinks in his hands. He positioned himself next to Kimberley. Nicky winked at her letting her know the ball was in her court as James made himself comfortable. As he spoke, his accent was familiar and Kimberley was sure he was from Manchester. As he continued, she asked him the question.

"Your accent is familiar. Where you from?" James laughed and stood proud as he told them about his home city.

"I'm from Manchester, England. I came over here about ten years ago when I was twenty. I miss Manchester sometimes it's a top place to live. Where are you two from?"

Kimberley spoke like an express train and now he'd told them he was from Manchester she felt like they were already part of a team.

"We're from Manchester too. Whereabouts did you live?" James smiled and took a large swig from his drink.

"I'm from Ancoats. The place of thieves, shoplifters, gangsters and dreams," he looked honoured as he continued. "I loved it in Ancoats. We were all like one big gangland family. If one had a fight, we all did. I go back every year and check out some of my old mates. It's changed a lot since I lived there. A different generation has taken over." The girls hung onto his every word as he continued. "Sad really, because I spent some top years round there. I remember the Seven Wonders, where we all used to go swimming. It was at the back of Ancoats hospital." He sat scratching his head as he tried to remember some more places. "The Brown Cow pub," he shouted, "fucking hell, The Brown cow. I had some great nights in there with my mates I can tell you."

Nicky moved closer and shouted out that she lived in Miles Platting that was just across the road from Ancoats. She went on to relay a load of names of different people in the area. She too knew a lot of dodgy characters.

Kimberley sat and listened and when he asked her where she lived, she told him Harpurhey. As he spoke, he started to smile.

"Fucking Harpurhey! I remember being there in the Foresters pub on Rochdale road. What a fucking rough place that was. I shit myself all night thinking I was gonna get done in."

Kimberley felt proud of the place she lived and began to speak with confidence in her voice.

"Harpurhey isn't that bad. I think because I was brought up there and know the people. Don't get me wrong, I've seen some terrible things that have gone on but ay, that's life where I live."

The ice was broken and they all shared stories about life at home. Kimberley couldn't stop looking at James and felt something strange stir inside her. The attraction was instant and as he spoke, she watched his mouth move. Nicky saw the change in her and changed the conversation towards work.

"So James, what can you offer us Manchester girls. Remember where we're from as well and who we know." James smiled and knew what she meant. She'd previously mentioned some big time names in their conversation and he knew they had a few contacts back home.

"I'll look after you don't worry. I'm after lap-dancers anyway. We can negotiate wages and that when I have seen you dance." They both looked at each other and laughed. As far as they were concerned, the job was theirs. They knew once he'd seen them dance he would know they were worth their weight in gold. The only thing left was somewhere to live so Kimberley asked the question while they were on a roll.

"So, what about accommodation? Is that with the job

as well? Only, we'll need somewhere to live won't we?" James looked directly into her eyes and spoke to her.

"You cheeky cow. Tell you what, you can come and live with me, until you find somewhere proper. I have an eight bed-roomed villa that I'm willing to share with you two if you want. You will have to pay rent though." Kimberley wanted to jump on him and kiss him from head to toe, but she held back and spoke casually.

"Thanks, we'll think about it." Nicky nearly collapsed and wanted to strangle her there and then, but watched as she continued.

"Well come on then. Let's show you what we can do, there's no time like the present." James stood up and directed them to a room to the left. He told them that one would dance for him and the other would dance for his mate Peter. He showed them to the rooms and left them to it.

Kimberley had done this dance a thousand times before, but she felt nervous inside. She sat on a red leather chair and looked round the room. The room looked dark as the deep red embossed wallpaper stood from the wall. A large mirror faced where she sat. The smell inside was stale and reminded her of Mr Billings' house back in Harpurhey. James could be heard from outside the room. She held her breath as the door slowly opened. She'd hoped she would have got the other man but as he entered she knew she would have to give it her best shot.

Silence filled the room as he seated himself in front of her. Kimberley peeled her clothes off slowly. She stood wearing a pink lacy bra and a pink and black thong that left nothing to the imagination.

She would dance to a song she loved by the Eurthymics called 'Thorn in my side.' Kimberley straightened her legs and perked her breasts in readiness. The song sent her into a trance and she was lost in the music as soon as it started.

Her hair swung round her face. James sat up and watched her every move as he touched his manhood. Her body was sexy and all her curves bent the way she wanted them to as she danced. She straddled him and let her long blonde hair brush across his chest. Leaning over him, she gave him a full view of her fanny. Her head touched the floor as she brought her legs up to his shoulders and flipped them over her head. James was gobsmacked as he watched her dance. He'd seen lots of dancers but this girl could move. She was like a snake charmer and he was transfixed. His cock stood to attention. All he wanted to do was fuck her brains out as he watched her. James knew the rules about touching the girls and gripped the side of the chair as the song continued. At that moment he knew this girl was special and he wanted her all for himself.

At last Kimberley finished the dance and stood in front of him. "Well do I get the job or what." James held his throbbing member in his trouser pocket. It felt like it was going to explode. He stood facing her and softly touched the side of her hair.

"You're not bad young lady. I've seen better but you'll do." He smiled as he watched her reach for her clothes and gently smacked her arse cheeks as he walked past her and opened the door.

The club was still swinging as Kimberley joined him. They both stood chatting until Nicky appeared with her newfound friend. Nicky was sweating as she walked from the other room and the man had obviously enjoyed her dancing as his eyes smiled at James. He held his shoulder and gave his verdict.

"Fucking little cracker she is mate. Definitely deserves

a job." Nicky watched James's face for some response.

"Right ladies, you can start tomorrow night. If you come in early I can go through how things are run here." Both of them hugged one another because they knew the dream had begun and they could start earning some decent cash.

James stayed with Kimberley for the rest of the night. It was obvious he wanted her and she felt the same way. She laughed at everything he said and her facial expression changed when she spoke to him. Although she had had lots of sex in the past, Kimberley had never been in love. Sex had always been a job to her. The feelings she had inside felt like nothing she'd ever felt before.

James kept the drinks coming all night long. By the end, they were all steaming. Nicky could sense a new romance blossoming as she watched Kimberley from the distance. As she watched them she could see them kissing. She mumbled under her breath. "Fucking gonna fall in love her I know it."

James and Kimberley were more or less an item from that day forward. He let both girls stay at his villa and Kimberley was the new lady of the house. James treated her like a princess and she fell in love for the first time in her life.

Months passed and James no longer wanted Kimberley to dance in the club. She was his property now and she shuld do everything to keep a smile on his face. She said it was love but everyone around her could see jealousy was setting in.

Night after night they would party until the early hours. Cocaine was a part of their lives now. At first, she had it for fun but lately she couldn't live without it. Kimberley was changing slowly and the drug was holding her hostage every single day. Each morning she would get up and reach for her hangover cure. The white lines on the table were her breakfast and she needed it to get by every day. Without the drug, she felt depressed and thought about all the bad things that had happened in her life.

Nicky was also hooked and James wanted her out of the villa. She was shagging anything that had a pulse these days and her looks were falling apart. The dream they both shared was slowing turning into a nightmare. None of them could see it as the drug blocked everything out of their minds.

The violence didn't start until Kimberley was dancing one night at an after party at the villa. James watched the way men were looking at her. His temper boiled over and he couldn't take it anymore. His body was like iron as he stood next to her as she danced. She never gave him a second thought until he pulled her towards the bedroom. The guests didn't know what was going on and just thought they were fooling around as he pulled her out of view.

James stood behind the bedroom door as he threw her onto the bed.

Kimberely thought he was just having a laugh. "Baby come and sit here with me," she slurred, "I want to fuck your brains out."

Her drunken words sent shivers down James' spine. His breath quickened as he watched her change her position. Kim struggled to focus and the room spun round as he slowly walked towards her. Her balance was lost and she rolled from the bed.

James sat at her side and looked at the photo of them together on the small pine bedside cabinet. His head shook as she spoke.

"Baby, what's wrong? Don't you want to fuck me silly?"

Her words were like bullets in his chest as he pounced on her.

"You dirty fucking trollop! All night I've watched you dancing trying to get fucking attention from everyone. You're a fucking dirty slut. What's up with you? Aren't you happy with just one cock?" His fist pummelled her face as he dragged her long blonde hair round the bed. Nobody heard her screams as she shouted for help. James ripped her clothes from her struggling body and threw her back on the bed.

"You want a good shag do ya? Well fucking let's see what I can do, or do you want somebody else's knob stuck inside you."

Kimberley struggled as he rammed his semi-hard manhood inside her. His body was firm and as he fucked her, he bit her body like a starving man. Her hair remained in his grip as he pulled her body to suck his cock. Her mouth was bleeding but it didn't deter him. Tears filled her eyes as she put his dick in her mouth. Her body felt like it was watching the abuse from another place in the bedroom. She was defenceless and carried on to avoid any further rage.

James reached orgasm after a long struggle. He rolled from her body to lie beside her. His breathing was rapid and the sweat poured from his body. As she tried to sit up his arm stretched out across her and he told her lie back down. Her head was spinning and she felt sick but knew if she moved he would hurt her.

James leant over to get his jeans and pulled out his cigs and lighter. He lit the cigarette and sat up as he looked at Kimberley lay next to him. He was like a different man and she no longer recognised the man she'd fallen for. His eyes filled with madness as he flicked the ash on her bare body.

She brushed it from her straight away and that seemed to amuse him. As he came to the end of the cig, he turned to her and stumped it out on her cheek. Pain filled her face as she screamed at him. He laughed menacingly. Her first thought was to run out of the bedroom, but as he watched her his voice was chilling.

"Don't fucking bother going out there, because I'll be straight out after you and sort you out big time." Kimberley froze as he held her face. She returned to his side. As she sat on the side of the bed, she gazed round the room that had brought her so much happiness in the past. The marble floor felt cold and her body shook as she turned towards him.

"Why have you done this to me? Why, why?" James sat up and reached for the bag of cocaine from his pocket. She watched him as he casually made cut two lines of sniff on the side table.

He snorted hard before offering the other line to Kimberley. Anyone would have thought she would have told him to fuck off but she took the fifty euro note from him and found comfort in the drug.

Once both lines had disappeared, he jumped up to leave and told her to get ready. It was as if nothing had happened. The door opened and she could see people stood outside the door. She walked to the mirror and touched the cig burn on her face. Her cheek felt boiling hot and she left the bedroom and ran straight for the bathroom.

Nicky had been looking for Kimberley for a while. When she saw her heading for the bathroom she followed her. The bathroom door was slightly open as Nicky approached. As she pushed the door, she could see Kimberley stood at the mirror touching her face.

"Fucking hell I've been looking for you. Where the

fuck have you been?" Kimberley made no reply and carried on nursing her face. Nicky came toward her and immediately noticed the big red mark on her face.

"What the fuck have you done? Your face looks a mess." Kimberley turned to face her and she noticed the rest of her body full of red marks. Her lip looked swollen and dried blood hung from her mouth.

"Who the fuck, has done that to you? Tell me now!" Nicky's voice was loud and she grabbed hold of her arm to look closer. "Fucking hell you're a mess, what's happened? Please tell me."

Kimberley washed her face in the small white sink and searched round for a towel. She stayed silent until she told Nicky to close the door. Once they were alone Kimberley told her what had gone on. Kimberley didn't seem that bothered about the attack anymore. The cocaine she'd taken numbed any pain she felt.

"I'm alright Nick. We just had a bit of a fight that's all. We're sorted now don't worry." Nicky looked at her wounds and started to shout at her.

"Are you right in the fucking head? Your man has just knocked ten bags of shit out of you and you think it's alright. You need to get a fucking grip girl!" Silence filled the bathroom and Kimberley moved towards her.

"Listen, I'm sorted now. I was winding him up dancing around near men, I deserved it love." Nicky felt sick inside and comforted her. Her own guilt for sleeping with her best friend's boyfriend now took over and she dipped her head in shame.

Over the next few weeks the beatings got worse. It wasn't long after that James threw her out. One night James was in a mood and placed all her stuff into a bin liner and threw them outside the villa's front door. He grabbed her hair and launched her out into the night. Not long after that he threw her clothes outside too. He told her never to come back and it was definitely over. It was lucky that Nicky had moved out a few weeks earlier and had a little apartment not far from where she lived otherwise she would have been homeless.

Kimberley was a mess when she left. Her makeup was smeared all over her face and her hair was shoved up in a ponytail. The light from the villa enabled her to pick up her clothes and as she looked back at the villa she was hoping James would come back out and tell her he was sorry but it never happened.

She slowly made her way down the footpath hoping to get a taxi to Nicky's house. Her heart was broken in two but the drugs held her together as if they were steel girders round her heart. Nicky welcomed her with open arms when she saw her stood at the door. She gripped her tightly and cried as she spoke.

"He's a no good bastard and the sooner you realise that the better. Why do you think I moved out? I couldn't stand that knobhead a moment longer." Nicky paced the room with a cig hanging from her mouth as she continued. "He speaks to you like a piece of shit and treats you like he owns you. You're worth ten of him love and the sooner you recognise that the fucking better." Nicky poured two larges glasses of vodka and sat by her side. Spain was still buzzing with holiday makers and you could hear the sound of drunken laughter in the distance.

They both decided that the job at Long Legs was over. James would definitely sack Nicky now knowing she had Kimberley living with her. He was like that, he liked to have control over people and she knew it was only a matter of time before she felt the force of his anger too.

It was decided between them that they both had to make changes in their lives. Drugs were the first things that needed to go, because they both looked like shit. The once beautiful Manchester girls now looked like a pair of smack heads. The days ahead were going to be hard but they were survivors and knew they would get back on their feet.

Kimberley hoped James would leave her alone now, because her body couldn't take any more pain. She also knew work would be hard to find because he had so many contacts in the bars and no one would employ her knowing she belonged to him.

Nicky and Kimberley finished their drinks and slept alongside each other. That's all they had now – each other. Tomorrow was another day and they just hoped they could find work and get their lives back on track.

The following night they called round to all the local bars hoping to find work but as predicted no one would touch them. James had won yet again and the two girls were getting desperate. Money was tight for them both and if something didn't come up fast, the only thing left was to go home to Manchester.

5

"VICTORIA PASS ME MY BLACK DRESS from the bed will you?" shouted Geraldine. They were hitting the town that night to check out a few lap dancing bars. Geraldine had a short black mini dress on and the biggest pair of heels anyone had ever seen. Her legs looked slender as she paraded around the apartment. Her hair was swept back from her face and held up with a diamond clip. She looked sexy and ready for a good time.

Victoria wore a red skirt and a white sequined vest top. Her skirt was short too and like nothing she'd ever worn before. Her breasts looked firm and the red straps from her bra hung off her shoulder. Her final touch was to put on some silver bangles and earrings and once that was completed she was ready to party. Geraldine stared at her and told her how nice she looked and walked over to her and gently kissed her neck. Geraldine towered over her and she liked the way she felt protected by her.

"Let's go and have some fun then. I'm looking forward to the night, are you?" Victoria was a bit scared of what lay ahead but something inside her felt like she was living again. If Oscar could have seen the new her, he would have died on the spot. She was a completely different woman from the one who left Manchester.

The pair of them headed out into the night. As soon as they walked outside the heat hit their faces and their hair frizzed almost immediately and the clothes they wore felt sweaty. The music pumped into the Spanish night and everyone seemed so cheerful. Some of the bodies they saw looked sore through sunburn. As they passed an old couple walking up the street she could hear the man telling his wife he had chub-rub. Victoria looked at him and smiled, and it was obvious that he knew she'd heard him. As he spoke to them he parted his legs at the top and pulled his shorts up with a smile on his face.

"Look at them sweetheart, I'm not lying." Victoria stood still as he revealed his red thighs, his wife moaning at the side of him.

"Stop being a mard arse. You're like a baby. I told you to put cream on them didn't I?" Victoria recognised the northern accent straight away. The couple argued amongst themselves as Victoria and Geraldine sympathised with him. The man's wife held her head up and repeated that she'd told him to put cream on but he never listened. The man nearly choked as he replied.

"Listen to her! She knows fuck all. Every time she gives me advice I end up like this. I said stay in England but oh no, Mrs Fucking Know-It-All said she wanted to come abroad. I'd never get burnt like this in England, I've got rhino skin." Victoria smiled and started to walk away. As she left she could still him moaning to his wife.

As they approached the first club, the Embassy, they looked at one another before they entered; it felt a bit perverted going into a lap dancing bar but the bouncers on the door smiled as they walked past.

"Good evening ladies, hope you have a good night. Any problems give me a shout and I'll be there in a second for you darling." The bouncer was around six foot tall and round in shape. His head was shaven and the few tattoos he had on his arm could be seen through his white fitted shirt. Victoria thanked him. As she walked into the club, she could hear him laughing with the rest of the bouncers saying he would shag their brains out given the chance.

The club was quiet as they walked through the double doors. A few girls were dancing on a silver pole on the stage. Several men watched their every move from the steel table in front of them. Geraldine went straight to the bar as Victoria watched the pole dancer with amazement. The girl who was dancing in front of her had long brown hair and her skin looked like silk. Every part of her body moved. Her arms looked strong as she held onto the pole and twisted her body up and down. As she slid up the pole the men in front of her leant forward with their tongues hanging out watching her every move.

The men looked like they were hypnotised, they had

that vacant look about them.

One of the men who sat watching took a drink from his glass and placed his hand on his penis, stoking it slowly. Victoria watched him with disgust. Dirty old bastard she thought. Her mind went back to her own husband and his sexual needs. Perhaps Geraldine was right about her idea, because the way the men looked at the girls, sex definitely did sell. Geraldine stood beside her and passed her a drink. She spoke quietly.

"Not that busy is it babes? Mind you, it's only early yet." Victoria was in a world of her own and her hatred for her ex-husband seemed to show in her face as she spoke.

"That dancer is amazing isn't she? I've been watching her dance I can't believe she can bend her body that much." Geraldine faced the stage and watched the girl slide up and down the pole wearing only a white bikini, with gold piping round the edges. "We need girls like her. We don't want any mingers. She knows how to tease the men and get them interested. Just watch how she keeps eye contact with that man as she slides up the pole."

Geraldine was right the girl's eyes focused on the man's face. She squatted down and opened her legs wide, knowing he loved what he could see. The dancer then walked up to the edge of the stage and smiled at the man who was holding a ten euro note in his hand.

They both watched with interest as the girl bent over and the man shoved the money in her bikini bottoms. His hand shook as he tried to feel every inch of skin he was touching. He looked like he was a piece of butter and she was the fire. His body melted into his chair as soon as he'd placed the cash on her body. All the men around the stage were like that. The money they paid gave them the seconds of pleasure they craved.

Men weren't allowed to touch or grab the dancers on stage and a large black and white notice displayed these rules in front of them. There were two girls on stage dancing and they seemed to fight for the men's attention. The other girl was blonde and had shoulder length hair but she wasn't a patch on her competitor. Once the music finished both girls walked from the stage and down to the bar.

Geraldine and Victoria sat down at a table as they watched everything that was going on around them. Some girls were seen walking to a small room with men following closely behind them. Geraldine looked and presumed that's where the private dancing would take place. Slowly but surely the night got busier. Lots of different girls came on the stage to perform.

Each girl had a unique style. Some used their breasts and some used the pussy shot to the men who sat near them. The money they earned throughout the night was huge. Each dancer left the stage with at least 200 euros hanging from their outfits. The girls dressed as nurses, sexy secretaries, super heroes and anything else they could think of that would turn a man into a sex crazed fan.

Victoria was on a high and started to talk to Geraldine as they watched the girls as the plans they'd discussed rolled around in their minds.

"We need to get some of these girls on board. They know exactly what makes the men tick. The more we get on board the better. I'll go and speak to a few of them and see how the land lies."

As Victoria stood up, her body swayed at first but with the help of the chair at the side of her she regained her balance. She slowly made her way to two dancers who sat near the stage. Her quest was to get them onboard. Geraldine was more interested in the other girls who'd she seen sat at the bar. They were both good looking girls. She wondered why they weren't working and headed towards them.

Geraldine stood next to them and smiled. They both looked depressed and one of them had her head in her hands stroking her hair. As she ordered the drinks she caught the eye of the blonde girl and smiled, that all she needed to begin conversation with them.

"It's boiling in here isn't it?" The dark haired girl smiled at her and answered her with sarcasm in her voice.

"It's all the heat from these horny men. I swear some of them are getting ready to explode." Geraldine smiled and took her drinks from the man behind the bar "Do you come in here all the time then?" Geraldine watched as she spoke to her friend to bring her into the conversation.

"We usually work up on the stage dancing in a different club but her ex boyfriend has seen to it that we can't find work anywhere, hasn't he Kimberley?" Kimberley joined the conversation and poured her heart out to Geraldine as if she'd known her all her life.

"I had it all you know. One minute I had a great job and life was good. He fucked it all up. As soon as he got a grip on me he slowly chipped away at any self confidence I had." Kimberley's eyes welled up and she wiped a tear from her eyes as she continued.

"We worked in his club. I didn't work for long, because the tosser got jealous, but Nicky did, didn't you?" Nicky told her part of the story and you could tell by her face she hated her friends ex-boyfriend.

"You should have the seen the state of her when she turned up at my apartment. The bastard had bit all her body and battered her black and blue." Nicky held her friend's hand as she continued. "She's better off without him but he knows she won't find work and will end up begging him for help."

Geraldine felt excited and asked them both to join her at the table across the room. The girls looked happy and didn't hesitate, after all Kimberley and Nicky were still nursing the same drink they'd had for the last hour. Their money was nearly gone and the only option left seemed to be to admit defeat and go home. Geraldine shouted Victoria over and watched her as she came towards them.

Everyone introduced themselves and they all sat chatting about things they'd done in life. Geraldine kept the drinks coming and by the end of the night she was ready to put her ideas into action.

"Me and Victoria might be able to help you two out with work. I'm going to run a few things past you and see what you think." The four of them moved in closer as Geraldine continued. "We're a bit new to all the sex scenes in Spain. We know a lot of girls lap dance and do extras, but we want to do something different. We are planning on buying a villa over here and turning it into a business." Both Kimberley and Nicky's eyes lit up in the hope that she was about to offer them a job. As they listened more they both looked shocked and remained silent.

"This is going to be a villa with a difference. We want it to be a 'Fantasy Villa'."

Kimberley laughed out loud and said in a cocky voice, "Fucking 'Fantasy Villa'. What the fuck is that?" Geraldine quietened her and told her to listen to what she had to say. Nicky was interested already and grabbed her arm telling her to shut up.

"We're getting ready to purchase a villa over here in Spain. It used to be a film set. A lot of the scenery is still there in each room and we think we can turn it into a sexual fantasy place. It's not going to be seedy. It's going to be up market. I'm going to design a website when I get home to Manchester. It's not going to say 'Fantasy Villa' on the website because we need to keep it discreet and above board, so I'm going to have to think about that part."

Nicky was now on the edge of her seat as she listened to every word.

"Our guests will hold a secret card that will be posted out to them as soon as they are accepted; only then will they know the location of the villa."

Victoria joined in, "the way I see it, men are dirty bastards aren't they?" Both girls nodded as she went on. "They will pay for anything so I want these perverts to pay thousands for what they want. We need to deliver a service like no one has ever done before. I'm not asking you two to have sex with them all. I'm asking you to come on board and help get girls who we trust and who can do the job."

Nicky was sold straight away and it didn't even bother her that she might have to sell her body. Kimberley, however, was more laidback and wanted to know more.

"I like the idea, but let's talk wages. What will our jobs be exactly and what money will we earn?" Geraldine moved closer to her and held her hand as she tried to sell her the job. "If this takes off honey, you'll be a rich woman and won't have to go running back to that cunt of a boyfriend." The words hit Kimberley hard and she knew what she said made sense. They all agreed they would go back to Victoria's room to talk further.

Nicky was acting like she'd won the lottery as she left the club and as she reached the exit, she placed two fingers in the air and shouted out into the night air. "Fuck you James, who's laughing now? Manchester girls always come back fighting. So watch your back, you fucking daft twat!"

Kimberley smiled and linked her arm as they followed Victoria and Geraldine to the hotel.

Geraldine was like a woman possessed and all her ideas were spinning round in her head. She grabbed Victoria by the waist and pulled her closer.

"It's all going to be great. I can see it now. We're going to be so rich," at that she stopped walking and kissed her on the neck. She wanted to have mad passionate sex with her there and then.

Nicky and Kimberley walked behind them and watched as they saw Geraldine kiss Victoria's neck. They looked at one another and thought the same thing but Nicky was the one to speak out loud about it. "Ay do you think they're lettuce lickers? The way she just kissed her neck wasn't normal was it? Say they're taking us back to the hotel and have two big strap-ons waiting for us?" Kimberley dug her in the side and giggled.

"I'm not licking any pussy love. I've seen my own in the mirror and it's not for me." Nicky teased her now and they both laughed loudly as the approached the hotel entrance.

The hotel looked like something out of a film as they entered. Small lights lit the pool and lots of people sat round it still full of life. The food on the table next to them told them this place cost money and as they passed Nicky said "Fucking lobsters. This place is definitely five star isn't it." She smiled as she continued and continued, "mind you love; you're used to five stars floating round your head when that prick hits you aren't you." Kimberley laughed and told her to fuck off winding her up, but she loved her sense of humour and loved how quickly she could make any subject a joke.

The holiday makers round the pool smiled as they

all walked past and one of them asked for them to join them. Nicky was ready to party with them but Geraldine thanked them kindly and told them they were all tired and ready for bed.

In the lift to their room Victoria and Geraldine giggled into each other's ears and Kimberley thought back to what Nicky had said. Her face looked white and she feared what would happen once they got to the hotel room. The lift door opened and they all walked from it. Three doors stood facing them. The smell of flowers hit the back of their throats and it was only when they walked a little further that they could see an arrangement of flowers and a small table. The door opened to the room and Nicky's eyes lit up. It was like something she'd only seen on TV. "Fucking hell, you two must have some cash to have a room like this," she shouted, "our place is a right shit tip compared to this."

She walked straight to the view from the patio windows and inhaled deeply as she took it all in. Kimberley was more apprehensive and sat down with her hands on her knees. She half expected them to come over to her and bind and gag her ready for a night of sex. Victoria came to her side as Geraldine poured the drinks. She made four large vodkas and cokes and placed them on the table before she sat down.

Nicky flung herself next to Kimberley and reached for her drink. She gulped nearly all of it down in one swallow and made a burping noise at the end of it.

"Oh I am sorry. It's the coke in it that gives me gas, I shouldn't drink it that fast should I?"

She now kicked her shoes off and placed her legs on the sofa over Kimberley. Nicky felt excited and began to speak.

"Right, let's talk more about this villa. I'm interested

in what it's all about."

Geraldine couldn't wait to go into detail and she too made herself comfortable before she began. "Men love sex, do we all agree?" Everyone nodded and she continued. "For instance let's see what we can use as an example." Her eyes looked up towards the ceiling as she searched for the answer. "Right, men always fantasize about nurses don't they? Well, I'll see to it that in the villa we have a room like a hospital and a sexy nurse, the rest as they say, is history. We can have a nurse and the client can be the patient. We need girls who aren't shy and can act out these fantasies as well." Nicky held her stomach and spoke.

"Oh my old mother always said I was meant for the stage. Don't think she meant this though but I see where you're coming from."

Geraldine continued and they all went through different fantasies they could act out and what men and women would want. They all seemed to relax and Kimberley sighed as she knew now she wasn't going to be any part of some big lesbian sex act. The four of them sat for hours talking about the plans for the villa and it was decided that Kimberley and Nicky would be in charge of finding the girls to work there. They gave themselves the name of managers and loved the thought that they would be making some money.

The villa would be a secret and it was decided that once it was set up on the website, only people who were invited would be able to come. If they were picked with their fantasy they would pay the fees and get an invitation through the post. The invitation would just say they were on a seminar and the dates they were required to attend. They all knew it was going to be hard work and the villa would need major repairs before it was ready for business.

The next day they all agreed to go up to the villa for one last look and set the ball rolling to get it ready for business. The four of them stayed in the apartment that night and sleep came easy to them all. The next day was going to be busy and lots of things had to be sorted before Geraldine and Victoria flew home.

The next morning they all ran round like blue arsed flies. Pedro was coming to meet them in less than an hour and they hadn't even had breakfast yet. They took turns in the shower and the two girls shoved on the clothes they wore the night before. They both borrowed flat shoes though because the heels they wore the night before weren't suitable for house hunting.

Nicky could see something between Victoria and Geraldine and knew they were more than friends. As she walked past the bedroom where they were, the door was opened slightly and she could see their two bodies lay together on the bed. As she watched further she watched Geraldine's hand sink into Victoria's lace white knickers and she froze as she watched. They looked so in love and as Geraldine caressed her nipples with her tongue Nicky felt excited. Half of her wanted to walk away but the other half wanted to go in and join them. Her body was tingling from head to toe and she opened the door slowly. No one heard her come in and she made her way to the side of the bed. Victoria's eyes were closed and Geraldine was too busy masturbating her to notice Nicky. Slowly as if she was hypnotised she started to stroke Geraldine's back and run her fingers through her hair. Geraldine slowly turned her head and looked shocked. Victoria opened her eyes and felt uncomfortable, but Geraldine guided her onto the bed and placed her over Victoria's other nipple.

The bed was rocking with the three of them and

Victoria had reached pleasure several times. Never had she dreamt that her body could be so fulfilled. Fingers reached places she didn't know existed and now Nicky was involved she tasted her first pussy.

At first Nicky sat next to her and stroked her body. Victoria also sat up as Geraldine still caressed her. Her head sunk in between Nicky's legs and within minutes she could taste the love juice she produced. She delved her fingers inside her and slowly penetrated deeper. It felt strange at first but as if she was teaching her Geraldine slid her finger inside her from behind and she copied her movements from Nicky.

Kimberley was sat alone in the front room and wondered what the noises were. At first she just listened but curiosity got the better of her and she went to investigate. The door was wide open and as soon as she saw them all she felt shocked. Their bodies were all entwined with one another and you couldn't see where one started and the other finished. Nicky saw her first and smiled.

"Come and join us love." Kimberley couldn't move or speak at first and felt embarrassed at the scene in front of her. It was only when Nicky spoke again that she peeled her clothes off and joined them on the bed.

"Fucking hell if this is a fantasy for one of you, I want paying." They all kissed and touched parts of each other's bodies and the sheet beneath them had several wet patches on it. The four bodies that lay together were something only a man could have dreamt of and as they made love they all looked so happy and relaxed.

The scene lasted around thirty minutes and breakfast was missed. When they had all finished they put on their clothes and headed back to the front room. Kimberley felt on top of the word and loved the freedom she felt during sex. She lit a cig and smiled as she spoke.

"Now that's what I call a fantasy. Imagine how much men would pay to watch something like that?" They all agreed and headed to meet Pedro who was now waiting in reception. Nicky felt incredible. None of them had done anything like this before but if this was what the job required they felt they both passed the interview with flying colours.

When they got to the villa Victoria and Geraldine walked round with a notepad and pen. They made a list of all the things they needed to get. Nicky and Kimberley were both giddy and walked into each room and laughed.

"Oh fucking hell, how cool is this all going to be. Our money troubles are over and one day we can go back to Manchester as very rich women. We need to work hard to make this work, because they're trusting us to get things done when they go back home. We need girls and men, and anything else we can get to make this place work." Nicky was on a roll and never shut up thinking of more ideas.

They all spent around three hours at the villa. Victoria gave the list to Pedro who had agreed to get all the repairs done while they were away. The place needed painting inside and out and lots of other repairs needed doing. Nicky's and Kimberley's list was just as big. They had to get beds, curtains, props and everything else they needed.

As they left Pedro he told them he would be in touch. He told them he would make sure all the work would be carried out before they returned. Lots of paperwork was signed and he assured them he would be managing the project himself.

Geraldine took control now and told him to make sure he got decent workers as they didn't want cowboys working at the villa. He laughed at the word cowboys and made her explain it. Once he knew he didn't stop saying it and it was obvious it would be in his vocabulary from now on.

Geraldine and Victoria had two days left before they headed home to Manchester. They had so much to do and lots of things needed to get sorted. Nicky and Kimberley were going to move into the villa in a few weeks, once the utilities were sorted out. All the furniture would be ordered and hopefully delivered before they moved in. Nicky and Kimberley now had the job of recruiting the staff they needed and as they spoke about it Nicky was already blurting girl's names out who she thought would be interested.

Victoria and Geraldine waved goodbye to them both at the airport and told them they would be back soon. They left them money for whatever they needed and gave them instructions about what they wanted completed before they returned. The plane left Alicante airport and headed to Manchester. As they sat together they held hands and sniggered like schoolgirls as they discussed the villa. Geraldine was the brains behind it all and the website she had planned to design, seemed to be just what they needed.

Their lives seemed so different to when they had landed in Spain. If Victoria was true to herself she had now completely changed. She was a lesbian now and she smiled inside as she said the words over and over in her mind. Geraldine had changed her and even the way she thought. She was once an unhappy divorceé who left a perverted husband. Her life now was a life of selling sex and helping people act out their fantasies. If Oscar only knew what she'd become he would have had kittens. His wife was now a mistress of sex, and boy did she love it and the way it made her feel.

6

GERALDINE STARED AT the computer screen. She had struggled for hours with the words she should use on the website as she tried to make it as professional as possible. She wanted men and women to trust the site and to fill out the application form that would give them the chance to be invited to the villa. The application form asked them their job description and other simple questions. It also had a section on how much they would pay for their fantasy to be fulfilled. The idea was that everyone would bid on the fantasy they wanted and the winners would come to the villa.

There were lots more questions and the final part of it asked them to describe in as much detail as possible what their fantasy would entail. It told the people that were reading it, that they weren't picked for the villa as of yet and they'd have to wait to be invited and of course pay the fee when and if they were successful. The fantasy they required could happen anytime during their stay at the villa and the element of surprise made the whole situation more fun.

Geraldine pressed the last button and the website was made. It was called "Dream a Dream," and no saucy pictures were present on the site. It was all above board and didn't look trashy. The home page was black and gold and soft music played as you entered the site. Victoria sat at her side and looked at the finished article.

"I hope people are interested honey. We've put so much

money into this already and I need it to be successful." Geraldine stretched back and pulled at her body. She had moved into Victoria's house with her and loved the thought that they were now a couple.

"Just give it time love. People need to go on the site first and I have to promote the site first to get people interested." Victoria rubbed Geraldine's neck as she stretched.

Oscar had been in touch with Victoria and wanted to meet her. He had heard she had just got back from Spain and had been waiting patiently for her to return. Geraldine had been a bit scared of her meeting him and wondered if she would return to her old life with him. He could give her everything she needed after all. After she'd spoken to Geraldine about him, she felt confident she would just go and see what he wanted without running back to him.

On the morning of the meeting with him Victoria was dressed to impress. She wore a black fitted skirt with a white blouse and her fitted black jacket. Usually she would wear a white bra underneath her blouse but today she wore a sexy black number and left the buttons open so you could see the top of it.

When Geraldine saw her for the first time her heart missed a beat. She looked so sexy. Geraldine hadn't realised that until that minute, she'd fallen head over heels in love with her. As she walked into the front room she stood from her chair that was facing the computer and held her in her arms.

"You look amazing honey. You look so sexy." She touched the top of her blouse and slowly slid her fingers into her bra. Victoria smiled and they kissed passionately for a few minutes. Geraldine slid her hand up her skirt and moved her knickers to one side with her fingers. As she dipped her fingers inside her she pushed Victoria onto the computers table. The lust between them was fantastic and it wasn't long before they were at it. Geraldine loved the taste of her and couldn't get enough of her. She licked every part of her and pulled her skirt up to her waist so she could get in deeper with her tongue.

Victoria loved it and opened her legs as wide as she could as she watched her tongue flick up and down. Victoria's breasts were hanging from her black bra as her head fell back and she began to orgasm. No man had ever made her feel like this and she guided Geraldine's head towards her vagina as she came.

Geraldine's fingers still continued penetrating her deeper and she never stopped till every inch of pleasure had left her body. When she had finished she lifted her head up toward her and stood facing her. Her face was covered in all her juices and she kissed her passionately letting her taste the enjoyment round her mouth. Geraldine didn't want anything in return and helped straighten her clothes. This was her reminder of how good sex was with her before she met Oscar. Victoria stood in front of her now as Geraldine sat down. She stood staring at her for a few seconds before she spoke.

"I think I'm falling in love you Geraldine. I feel different inside and the way you make me feel is crazy. Is this supposed to have happened, love?" This was music to Geraldine's ears and she reached for her and held her close.

"I feel the same. It's so weird isn't it? I love having sex with men but the way we make love never comes close to anything I've ever done. Oh baby it makes me feel so happy inside to hear you say that."

They held each other and squeezed each other. As from today they were a couple and no one would come between them. Victoria kissed her before she left and told her she wouldn't be long. Oscar was waiting in a nearby pub and she was already fifteen minutes late. Grabbing the car keys from the table she said one last goodbye and headed towards the car.

As the engine started she looked at herself in the mirror. She looked happy as she applied more lipstick. She licked her lips thinking of the sex she'd just had with Geraldine. Her hair was still held up with a grip and she quickly rearranged it to make it look neater. Driving from the house she tried to imagine what Oscar wanted and laughed at the thought of him knowing she was a lesbian.

The Whitegate pub was where they were meeting and as she pulled into the car park, she remembered how her life had been with Oscar. Now she felt free and for the first time in her life she felt like she wasn't pretending to be someone who she wasn't.

She walked into the pub as if she owned it. She headed straight for the bar and ordered herself a diet coke. Within seconds she felt his presence at the side of her. His Armani aftershave tickled her nostrils as she breathed and she turned to face him for the first time.

Oscar's face looked older now and she kissed him on the cheek to show she held no anger. He looked shocked and he asked her to sit down on the seats behind them. Victoria was flowing with confidence now. Oscar felt ashamed as he looked at her and felt sorrow in his heart as he watched his ex-wife sit facing him smiling like she didn't have a care in the world.

"You look great Victoria. In fact you look amazing." Her body was still tanned from her holiday and her eyes looked as sexy as ever. "I didn't think you would come and see me you know. I'm so glad you did. I've had this on

my mind for months and need to clear it from my head."
Victoria looked at him and reached for her drink as her
mouth felt dry. She watched him wriggle about in his seat
as he tried to talk and laughed to herself thinking his leather
thong must be irritating him. For some strange reason,
their past together didn't mean anything anymore and she
understood his need to feed his sexual desires. When he
finally stopped fidgeting she listened as he began.

"Victoria I miss you so much. Life hasn't been the
same without you. I still love you and want you back. I
know what I did was unforgivable, but I've changed and
promise you I will never be unfaithful again." He held his
head in his hands and looked desperate as he continued.
"You're my world and I need you to forgive me."

Victoria listened to his words and stared into his eyes
but felt no love towards him. All she felt was sympathy. She
took another drink from her glass and stared at him for
a few seconds without speaking. He looked nervous and
reached for her hand across the table. The few people in the
pub were oblivious to his request and nobody cared that he
was nearly in tears.

Victoria stared round the pub and watched the two
lads playing pool at the left of them. The pub was decorated
in cream embossed wall paper and she thought how good
it would look in the villa. Oscar spoke again and this time
he was more desperate than ever.

"We were good together. I can give you everything
you need. I will buy you a new car; diamonds anything,
just come back to me. Please." Victoria sat back in her chair
and finally replied.

"Oscar, our time has passed and I don't hold any anger
towards you. You had needs and I never gave them to you.
In the time we have been apart I've learnt so much about

myself and I kind of understand why you like kinky sex. It's over Oscar, I can only offer you friendship. I've changed too. I'm not the person you once knew." Oscar moved his chair closer and spoke with speed.

"Baby, I will never hurt you again, please believe me. I've changed - nothing means more to me than you, and I will do anything to get you back. I will never give up."

Victoria thought about the words she was going to use and slowly she told him she'd fallen in love with somebody else. His face changed and tears filled his eyes. He rested his head on her shoulder and people in the pub started to look at him as he sobbed.

"How can you have fallen in love? I love you. Nobody will love you the way I do. Please don't say that love, please. I'm nothing without you."

Victoria felt the eyes of the pub on her and felt embarrassed at the scene he was causing. Slowly she pulled him from her shoulder and spoke in a firm voice.

"Oscar, it's over. I can offer you friendship and nothing else. You have to move on with your life. What's happened to your lover?" Oscar started to cry as his words stuttered like a small child.

"Oh she went ages ago. All she wanted was money from me. I didn't want her anyway." Victoria listened to his story of the break up and felt he was getting what he deserved. She felt no attraction to him anymore and even as he spoke all she wanted to do was get home to Geraldine. She sat with him for an hour and listened to his story of how much he had changed but at the end of it she still felt the same. As she stood to leave she watched his face sink into sadness.

"Please Victoria; just say you will think about it, please." Victoria moved towards him and kissed his head. She took his hand and spoke softly. "Oscar, it's over love. You need to find happiness just like I have and move on. I'm sure in time you will. But as for us, it's gone." Victoria left and could hear his sobs as the people in the pub watched her leave. He was a broken man. She felt strong inside and held her head high as she swung the double doors open into the afternoon air. Victoria was free from him. Her head was clear with what she wanted from life and Oscar wasn't part of it. She reached her car and half expected Oscar to be jumping on the bonnet of it begging her to stay, but he remained in the pub heartbroken.

On the way home the radio played 'Laid' by James and Victoria sung along with the words loving every word. She loved who she was at the moment and felt like she could conquer the world. Oscar stayed in the pub on his own for a few hours more to drown his sorrows. He looked a shell of his former self and in his mind he was already planning to win Victoria back.

The weeks passed and everything was going to plan with the villa. All the things they needed over in Spain were sent over in a big container. The website was up and running and they were amazed at the interest they'd received. Some of the fantasies were sick and as they read through some of them they cringed at people's requests.

One man, aged sixty-five, wanted a woman to sit on a glass table while he lay underneath. He wanted to watch her shit from where he lay. The price he bid was £2,000 and the both of them were rolling about on the floor as they read it. Other requests were more straight forward. One man wanted to be part of two lesbians making love. He said he was willing to pay £600 for the privilege. He stipulated what they should wear, right down to the colour of their nail varnish.

All in all there were sixty two requests and now was the time to start the ball rolling. They wanted the villa up and running within a few weeks and they needed to move quickly to avoid losing any money.

The first customer they accepted had a fantasy that he was to be sat at a posh dinner wearing a tuxedo. He wanted the guests to be sat at the table and for a woman to be under the table sucking him off. The other guests would be none the wiser and he wanted to come while he sat there trying to hide his pleasure. He stated he wanted it all to happen slowly and he was to be teased all the way to ejaculation. His bid for this was £6,000. Victoria and Geraldine put him down as the first client and sent him the invitation. When he arrived in Spain he would be picked up by a chauffeur and driven to the villa. The price included all his food and drink for the week and any other services he required.

The invitation was embossed in black and gold on a card. The letter inside told him once the fees were paid his tickets would be forwarded, and everything else he needed to know about the visit. Victoria had kept in touch with Nicky and Kimberley since she'd left and they had now recruited six girls and two men to work in the villa. Nicky was shouting down the phone when she was telling her just how much the villa had changed. It looks so posh, yet a little sexy she told her.

The website was attracting more and more visitors as word spread. The money people were willing to pay was unreal. The following week seven more invitations were sent out and everything was set for the guests to arrive in two week's time. Victoria and Geraldine shopped online for every kind of sex toy on the market and every outfit that they thought could be used. As they were packing their bags they stood laughing at the thought of being searched at the airport. Victoria fell about as she spoke.

"Bloody hell, hope they don't search our suitcases. I'm going to be so embarrassed if they do. We will just have to say it's for personal use." They roared with laughter and sat on the cases to make sure they fastened. Their flight back over to Spain was in a few hours and they had so much to do before they left.

7

NICKY AND KIMBERLEY sat round the pool drinking cold lager. Sweat poured from their brows and the work they had completed had been enormous. All the rooms were ready for guests and each room had a theme. The outside of the villa was painted white and now all the pathways were clean and tidy, the place looked like heaven. Kimberley could imagine people walking up the pathway to enter the villa. Two Spanish men stood at the bottom of the path and were placing the last electronic gate on its hinge. Victoria wanted privacy and she wanted to see who was coming and going at all times. Spain was full of gangsters and she knew it would only be a matter of time before they wanted a piece of their action.

The girls had also employed a cleaner, she was an ex dancer and her days of turning men on were well and truly over. Melissa was a large lady and her tits were massive. Her arse should have carried a sign saying 'wide load'. Nicky told her she could start as a cleaner, but she could also earn extra money from doing tricks for punters.

All the employees knew exactly what the place was going to be and all agreed on keeping it a secret. Even the gardener was a dancer from one of the night clubs and loved that he was involved. The men who the pair had recruited came to join them round the pool and they all looked hot. Kimberley would have fucked all of them there and then without a second thought. They had a mixture of looks. Blonde hair blue eyes, brown hair hazel eyes, black hair green eyes, but the one thing they all had in common were the six packs stomach and tanned bodies.

When they'd spoken to each of the men about what they wanted from them, they all agreed to join them without a second thought. The men knew each other anyway from the club scene and they all got on well. Ray was the spokesman for them all and wanted to know the ins and outs of a cat's arse hole. He wanted to know why, when, who, and how.

Ray had dark hair and hazel eyes, he was definitely eye candy for the ladies. Ray was a Manchester lad and had been dancing in Spain for a few years. He told them he was bisexual and anything went in the bedroom with him. When he told them he liked men and women, Kimberley had whispered to Nicky he was greedy, and they both sniggered as he told them more about himself.

Ray came from Ancoats in Manchester which was well known for gangland activities. He was one of three children and had always wanted more than what Ancoats could offer. He started his life in Spain as a waiter in a club but after time he found himself dancing on stage and stripping. As they looked at his body they knew why the women would love him. In the interview Kimberley was the one who asked the question about his sex life.

"Why are you bisexual, if you don't mind me asking?"

Ray smiled and told them without any embarrassment at all.

"Ladies, I've had that much fanny in my life that I wanted something different, women throw themselves at me every day, and to tell you the truth if I had to lick another fanny I would do myself in." Kimberley smiled and played with her hair as she asked more questions.

"So you've had sex with a man? Have you got a boyfriend?" Ray thought for a minute and explained in more detail.

"Listen love I'm not saying I don't like pussy. I'm saying I like a bit of both, greedy perhaps. I don't like one on one with a man but if they are involved with a few women in the bedroom I would take part." Nicky looked at him and licked her lips. She hoped in the future she could be part of one the scenes and told him herself with a giggle in her voice.

The requests for sexual fantasies were emailed from Victoria to the villa. As they came in they set out to plan how they would happen. In a way it was like acting for them all. They wrote scripts and even planned how they would enter the 'scene'.

One of the requests had come from a forty year old woman. Her fantasy was to have sex with her chauffeur. She was a well-off lady and she had a chauffeur in her everyday life but never had the guts to have sex with them. She had put so much detail into her fantasy that she wanted everything to go to plan when she eventually got there.

The rooms looked the part. There was a room equipped with a hospital bed and lots of other medical equipment. The previous owners had left a lot of props and it helped make it the ideal place for a fantasy.

The fluff room was pink and black. A large metal four

poster bed sat in the middle, the black silk curtains were held back with two pink feather boas. The bedding was something Victoria had sent over from England and the bright pink lace bedding set looked ravishing. This was going to be the bondage and pain room. So many people who had requested fantasies were asking for pain. Some wanted ladies to stand on them in high heel shoes, others wanted to have their arses smacked with leather belts. Kimberley had pissed herself laughing when she read an email from Geraldine.

One fifty year old man wanted to wear a nappy. He wanted a woman dressed as a granny to take the wet nappy from him and for her to smack his arse for wetting himself. At first she couldn't see the pleasure he would get out of it, but as she read on she realised he wanted then to suckle on her breasts and be masturbated whilst he lay in her arms.

The sun was at its hottest and everything was set up and ready to go. The emails she received from Victoria told her they would have eight guests in the first week. They were all excited and the thought of performing the fantasies turned them on.

8

SUSIE WAS AN EVERYDAY WOMAN with three children living in Manchester. Her council house in Blackley had seen better days and some days she didn't know why she bothered cleaning it at all as it always looked a mess. Her three sons Martin, Lee, and Connor were every parent's nightmare. All three were into crime, drugs and anything else they could do to earn a few quid.

Susie was forty one but still looked stunning. Her

shoulder length auburn hair complimented her green eyes. Her figure was fantastic but the years were taking their toll and gravity was having its effect on her body. The kid's fathers were nowhere to be seen and if you were to ask Susie, she didn't really know who the true dads were, she just guessed to keep the lads happy.

Susie worked part time in the local chippy. Every night she would come home with her hair and clothing stinking of grease. She hated the way she smelt but bills needed to be paid and the kids needed to be fed. The lads were all old enough to look after themselves these days and many a night she would sit alone in the house staring at four walls. Boyfriends had come and gone and they all seemed to shag her brains out and move on. She'd promised herself that whoever came along next, her knickers were definitely staying on longer than the first date.

Paul owned the chippy where Susie worked and every now and then he would slip her one in the toilets. He was a kinky fucker and Susie just laughed when she heard some of the things he wanted to do with her. She smiled as she sat in the living room of her house remembering the time he'd rubbed mushy peas all over her fanny, and eaten the lot. He loved using food during sex and the things he'd done with the meat pies in the chippy would split your sides laughing. He liked to take a bite from the pie and release the juice all over her body. Then he would break the pie up and squash it all round her tits and lick every inch of it from them. Susie enjoyed sex with him but only really did it out of boredom.

Paul was a married man but his wife had no interest in him. His balding head and bright red cheeks framed a round face. He didn't paint a pretty picture. He also had teeth missing at the front of his mouth and he wore dentures to replace them. The 'Stud Muffin' as he liked to be called, looked misshapen and Susie often told him he didn't look normal. Paul loved kinky sex and had been known to see several prostitutes in the area. Susie was a bit wary of him when he came on to her for the first time but the £50 he gave her after sex helped ease her fears. Paul had also been to swinger's parties and loved the freedom everyone had when they were there. He'd offered Susie money to come along with him but she told him straight to fuck right off. He always spoke of the parties and how you could just fuck anyone's brains out. As he told her a story he held his belly at the bottom and nearly pissed himself laughing.

The party he told her about was one he had to pay £40 to enter. He told her how he lied to his wife to get out that night. She'd thought he was at a darts match. "If she'd have known the bullseyes I was aiming at she'd have carted me straight away" laughed Paul.

As he stood tall, he showed Susie all the actions of his love making. He even placed one leg on a chair at the side of him and showed her his penetrating moves. The swingers parties were the dog's bollocks in Manchester at the moment and a lot of them were advertised on the web. The one he last went to was in Bury and this is the one he started to tell Susie about.

"Fucking hell Susie, I thought I was a fat twat but the one who came on to me was like a fucking beached whale. I saw her watching me for a few minutes and knew she wanted my body. I tried to hide but as she came over she took my hand and led me to a nearby room." Paul sighed as he continued and his face looked serious.

"I was gonna tell her to fuck off but my cock was rock hard and ready – I'd taken a fucking Viagra pill an hour before and it was stood up like a fucking missile waiting to take off." Susie looked at him when he spoke and laughed calling him a bull shitter. Paul was always chatting shit and was well known for telling a few lies. As she laughed with him he continued with a cocky face. He quickly stepped to the door and looked both ways to make sure they were alone. Placing his hands on the doorframe he began to speak.

"As she got me on the bed I thought alright then, I'll just get a suck off her, but fucking hell the fat fucker climbed on my face and fucked it with speed. I couldn't breathe Susie; on my life she was suffocating me. Thinking fast I wiggled about under her and she got the message and moved her fanny from my face. I thought it was over but was it fuck; she sat on me, shoved my cock in and started riding me like a bucking bronco. It was alright I thought, and then the fucking dirty fucker pissed all over me." Susie looked shocked and asked him again to repeat it.

"What, she pissed on you?" Paul's face was red and his cheeks looked like big red tomatoes as he carried on.

"Fucking golden showers she called it. I didn't really mind that until she started squatting over me. I watched her as her face screwed up. I just looked at her and thought what the fuck? It was only when I felt something land on my legs I knew the dirty fucker had shit on me!" Susie doubled over laughing and he placed his finger to his mouth telling her to quiet. Once she'd pulled herself together he continued.

"Susie I'm open minded love but that was just fucking twisted. I fucking threw her off me and stood up straight away dropping the big turd on the floor. I didn't hang around much longer and fucked off leaving her to deal with it." Susie told him that's what he gets for being a big fat pervert but he laughed with her and told her he just had a bad experience and he had learnt his lesson now. The friendship between Paul and Susie was great. He helped her out with cash and she let him fuck her every now and then. It suited her well and she never moaned about it.

Paul was always taking her out for meals and dates, and she liked it that way because it meant she wasn't alone in the house all night. Susie's lads just thought they were friends and never doubted what she told them. The lads all called him pervy Paul and laughed with their mother about some of the stories they'd heard about him.

Paul's wife was never bothered by the way he flirted with the ladies and loved that he didn't harass her for sex. When she first met him she loved the sex between them, but as the years had gone by his sexual habits knocked her sick. In the past she had been to swingers parties with him but now she wanted a quieter life. Paul could do what the fuck he wanted as long as it didn't involve her. Night after night Paul would sit in front of his computer and check out all the new sites. His cock was always throbbing and when he entered a porn site he would usually wank himself off about some young girl.

Paul set himself up near the computer as his wife laid asleep upstairs. They had no children and the house sounded peaceful as he set up for his night of porn. Turning the lights down low with the dimmer switch he collected his normal things to have nearby him, like cigs, chocolate and baby oil.

Paul looked at the clock as the computer was setting up and stretched himself on the blue office chair. The room was cold as the night set in. The dining room was his favourite place in the house and the dining room table sat in the middle of the room. As he looked round the room he remembered times when he'd rammed his cock in his wife as she lay on the pine table. The room was decorated in a light yellow wall paper with embossed patterns on it.

Paul logged on and lit a cig. Once he'd found the site he was looking for he started to look at all the new groups that had been set up. As his eyes glanced through the list his eyes focused on one group in particular. As he read the words his face screwed up and he reached for his black rimmed glasses to see it more clearly. Reading the words he entered the site and wanted to know more. His fingers clicked away at the keyboard as he filled in the registration request. Once he had joined he checked his email to retrieve his confirmation notice. His heart was beating at speed as he wrote down the number he needed to confirm his registration. Once completed he read the words with a smile on his face. The word fantasies slid about on his tongue and even before he read any further he knew exactly what he wanted.

Paul read through the site and started to complete the request. When it asked him to put the amount he would pay for the fantasy he scratched at his head. Touching his manhood the thought of his dream coming true took over and he keyed in six thousand pounds. His fingers hit the keyboard.

He had thought about his fantasy time and time again and as he clicked the keyboard he made sure every detail was present. He giggled as he continued and thought about his arsehole being licked by a blonde sexy lady. All the parties he'd been to, he'd never had his dreams fulfilled. As he carried on writing he told them of how he wanted one girl sucking him off as one licked his ring piece. He finally finished and the fantasy was still fresh in his mind. He looked at the button that said submit and pressed it. His mind was working overtime and he prayed he would get an invitation to the villa in Spain.

Paul continued surfing the web and before long he was pulling his cock with delight. The baby oil was rubbed all over his knob and his pants were pulled down over his fat arse. His masturbating never took longer than a few minutes and before long he was stood in front of the computer screen squirting his load all over the girl's faces. As he reached orgasm he grunted like a pig and gritted his teeth together loving the way he felt.

At that moment he would have took part in any sexual act – even with men. Paul wasn't gay but he loved watching men fuck women in front of him. As he felt his blubber around his waist he knew he would have to go on a serious diet as his weight had rocketed in the last few months. He secretly blamed his wife for over feeding him and he was always telling her he wanted to eat healthily but when she placed mounds of food in front of him he usually ate it all. Paul felt fulfilled for the night and once he'd finished his wanking he turned the computer off and headed to the kitchen for a piece of the double chocolate cake he'd seen in the fridge earlier. Opening the fridge the light shone on all the treats in there. He knew he should have grabbed an apple or something but the cake looked nice as he pulled it from the shelf.

Paul stood in the kitchen cutting a massive piece of cake. As he put the rest back he grabbed a bar of chocolate as well. Chocolate was his downfall and he loved it so much. Many a night he'd taken a jar of Nutella upstairs to his wife and asked her to rub it on her fanny so he could lick it off but the response was always the same and his hunger was never fed.

When Paul opened up the chippy the next morning he couldn't wait to tell Susie what he'd done. He'd put her name down on the website too and wanted her to come along to watch him perform. Paul watched her every move and waited eagerly for the right moment. His wife told him she was nipping next door to get some change and he nodded watching her leave with a sly eye. As soon as she'd left he made his way to Susie who was stood making gravy at the old stove in the back of the shop. His apron was covered in dirt and grease and as he wiped his grubby hands he grabbed her waist from behind.

"Susie, I hope you have a passport, because you might need it in a few weeks if this plan pays off." Susie turned to face him and pulled the few strands of hair from her face. Her jeans were fitted and the red top she wore made her breasts look bigger than ever. Susie only looked little against him and her flat shoes didn't give her the height she wanted.

"What plan is that then?" Paul's words fired from his mouth and he could feel his cock getting harder as he spoke. As he grabbed it in his pocket he began to speak.

"I was on the web last night and found a site that invites you to come and live out your fantasy. It's costing me a fucking arm and a leg, but if I get accepted it's going be a dream come true." Susie looked at him and placed her hand on her hip.

"Well, why do I need a passport if it's a fantasy for you?" Paul grabbed her waist and pulled her closer.

"Because you're in it. I want you to come and watch me have sex and play with yourself as you watch me perform my magic." Susie nearly pissed her knickers and laughed out loud but as he continued she knew if she wanted a free holiday she would have to look more interested. "Listen, it's a free holiday for you, and you only have to watch. If you don't want to come, just say and I'm sure I can find someone else to fill your shoes."

Susie grabbed his thick waist and tickled his side. She hadn't had a holiday for as long as she could remember and the thought of escaping the Manchester weather appealed to her. Within seconds she told him she would go with him and asked how she would get the time off work without his wife becoming suspicious. Paul stood for a moment and scratched the top of his head. Nothing was stopping his new plan and his wife was the last thing on his mind.

"Leave it with me sugar bum. You know I wear the pants in our house and I'll just say you have family problems and have to go and see them." Susie looked at him with a serious face.

"What family problems! You can't say that and I come back with a fucking tan. It needs to be believable." Paul laughed and shook his head.

"Oh stop fucking worrying I'll sort it. So get on standby because as soon as I'm accepted we're off to the sunshine."

As Susie stirred the lumpy brown gravy she started singing along to 'Walking On Sunshine' by Katrina and the Waves as it blasted out of a nearby radio and shook her arse as Paul went about his business with a smile on his face.

Paul watched his emails like a hawk for the next few days. It was Friday night and his wife had gone to bed hours before complaining of a headache. He knew she had no headache and that was just his warning that she wasn't in any mood for his kinky sex tonight. Filling his face with cheese and onion crisps he shoved the last few in and sat licking his fingers like a cat cleaning its paws.

As he sat looking around the room he thought about having a wank but his cock was struggling tonight so he grabbed a bar of chocolate instead. Even the usual porn sites didn't interest him and his heart wasn't in it.

"Fuck it, may as well go to bed," he mumbled as he started to log off the computer. As he closed the final tabs he sat looking at his emails. Rubbing his eyes he saw he had one new message in his inbox. His fat fingers pressed the message and he moved his chair further to the screen to read every word.

Paul read the words carefully. "We are pleased to tell you" his heart jumped as he read on and he nearly came in his pants with all the excitement. As he read on he studied all the details in full. It told him all the information would be sent to him in the next few days to the address he'd stated.

As he checked the calendar he knew he would have to move his arse as his date was only two weeks away. The word 'fantasy' sat in front of his eyes and his penis got a second wind and stood to attention. His heart was beating ten to a dozen and he thought he was going to have a heart attack as he held his chest.

His mind was working overtime and he was already planning what he was going to tell the ball and chain that lay upstairs in bed. After a quick jerk of his manhood he found pleasure and wiped his come with an old tea towel that was on the side next to him. Tomorrow he would put all his plans into action so he could escape to his dream. He knew he would have to think of a good story to tell his wife. Turning off the computer he turned and set about locking all the doors. Once he was finished he struggled to get upstairs and made his way to bed.

As he pulled the covers back he looked at his wife fast asleep and slowly sneaked in behind her trying not to wake her. Once he was under the cover he planned in his head exactly what he was going to tell his wife the following morning. He was going to tell her his mates had asked him to go on a stag party in Spain for a week and he was thinking about going. Surely she would believe that, he thought. Within seconds he was snoring like a ten ton pig.

The next morning, Paul looked at Cathy in her long pink house coat and screwed up his face. She was a mess and her fat ankles hung over her fluffy slippers. As she stirred two cups of tea on the side he coughed before he spoke.

"Ay love I was speaking to Kevin last night. Him, and a few other lads are going to Spain on Peter's stag do. He's asked me to go but I don't know if I can be arsed." He watched her slyly from behind his newspaper and waited for her response.

"Peter, is that Pauline's fella from down the road?" she asked. Paul yawned and nodded as he continued.

"Yes, he's decided to marry the dirty fucker. Bet he wouldn't marry her if he knew what she was really like." Cathy loved gossip and started to talk of all the stories she'd heard about her too. Paul grinned from behind his newspaper and knew he would have no problems getting away to Spain. His mate Peter was really getting married and the stag party was in Spain at the same time. So once he'd told the lads to cover for him, there would be no problems.

Paul was buzzing round the kitchen that morning and a smile was plastered all over his face. All he had to do now was to pay the fees and get his holiday stuff ready. Once he'd told Susie all the details they planned together her quest to get a week off work and as the plan unfolded it was one hundred percent believable. Susie sat in the back of the chippy and wiped water on her face to make the mascara run down her cheeks. She positioned herself so she could see Cathy and as soon as she walked into the back room, she began to pretend to cry. Cathy came straight to her side and placed her arms round her neck. She'd always had lots of time for Susie and felt sorry for her.

"Oh love. What's the matter? Don't cry." Cathy looked round for some tissues and pulled four pieces from the box nearby. As she reached Susie, she passed them to her and asked again what was up. Susie lifted her head from her hands and began the performance of a lifetime.

"It's them little fucker's at home. I can't take much more, they are driving me crazy Cathy. All I need is a holiday to get away from them and they begrudge me that." Cathy pulled up a chair and asked her in more details what she meant. "I've met a fella Cathy and he said he will take me away for a week on holiday, but the kids are having none of it. They've told me they will chop him up if I go with him. They haven't even met him but won't have a man anywhere near me." Cathy huffed in a high voice and started to go mad at her.

"Fuck them, it's your life you deserve a rest. I mean they have their own lives don't they? What do they expect you to do, sit staring at four fucking walls every night?" Susie wiped her eyes and went in for the killer question.

"It's not just that love. I would need time off work and I know how you're fixed for staff at the moment." Cathy pulled Susie to her side and told her not to worry and that everything would work out. Once Susie told her the dates she needed off work, Cathy agreed and told her she would ask her sister Christine to cover for her as she knew she was skint at the moment and wouldn't mind the extra cash.

Susie smiled and thanked Cathy from the bottom of her heart. She felt a little bad for shagging her husband but not that much that it stopped her from taking her knickers off for him. Anyway she needed this holiday and nothing would stand in her way of hitting the sunshine. Paul now walked into the room and Cathy filled him in on the storyline.

"We need to ask Christine to cover for Susie as she needs to book a week off work. She's got a chance of a holiday with her new fella and her kids are causing a fuss. I've told her to go anyway. What do you think?" Paul's head nearly spun and fell off. His face became blood red and he grunted his words as he spoke.

"Do whatever but make sure we have cover. Are you alright Susie?" Susie snivelled into her tissue and winked at him as Cathy was looking the other way.

"I'm fine now. It's just them kids of mine they do my head in." Paul didn't stay long and left them to it but as he went back into the shop he smiled like the cat that had got the cream.

Over the next few days Susie went to Manchester town centre and hit Primark. The shop was well known for cheap clothing and accessories and she made the most of it purchasing all her clothes from there. When she told her kids she was going to Spain they went ballistic calling her an old tart but she just smiled and told them it was her life and to keep their noses out of it. Everyone thought she was going on holiday with her old friend from school Maria but it was only her who knew the truth about her seedy little secret.

As she stood in the mirror she looked at her new bikini and turned in different angles admiring her arse. She looked distressed as she spread her legs looking at her pubic hair hanging down from her swim suit. As she pulled at it she knew she needed some pampering before she hit the sunshine and laughed as she looked at the overgrown hedge. "Monkey fluff," she whispered under her breath as she started to take off her bikini and placed it back into her tattered suitcase.

Paul was excited and sometimes he wanted to shout out just how happy he was. When he was sat with his wife he wouldn't seem that interested in the holiday and made out he wasn't really arsed about it but inside his heart was jumping round and couldn't wait to play out his fantasy.

9

VICTORIA AND GERALDINE ordered the taxi to the airport and both sat waiting for the adventure to start. They had already earned a lot of money from the requests and they had a couple of days when they got there to make sure everything ran smoothly before the guests arrived.

The airport was busy and once all their luggage was checked in they headed for something to eat. They both ordered a full English and when it arrived they ate it like starving animals. The bacon was crispy, just how they liked it and the egg was just cooked enough so the yolk didn't go everywhere. As they sat looking around Geraldine started to speak in a calm quiet voice.

"I can't believe it's all happening. We're going to be so rich. Do you know that?" Victoria smiled and nodded, as she changed the topic to the fantasies they had to perform. As she spoke she held her head in her hands and chuckled.

"There are some weird people in this world aren't there. I never knew all this existed till I met you. You have led me astray." Geraldine laughed and told her that she could return to her boring husband if she wanted, but Victoria grabbed her arm from across the table and told her she was only joking.

The months that had passed had changed Victoria that much that she didn't even recognise herself anymore. Her life was so different and the sex life she had was amazing, like nothing she had ever experienced before. She loved Geraldine but in her heart she knew she preferred the man-woman relationship but for now she just carried on loving the experience.

Once they were seated on the plane the journey began. The plane was packed with passengers and the leg room they had was tiny. As the plane took off Geraldine nearly shit her knickers. She hated flying and she only settled when they had been in the air for at least twenty minutes. Once they had landed a car was sent to meet them at the airport. Nicky and Kimberley had everything waiting for them and they couldn't wait to meet the staff and see what the girls had done with the place.

As they came through customs they saw a man holding a card up with their names on. Geraldine nudged Victoria as she looked at the handsome man in front of them.

"Fucking hell, Victoria where have the girls got him from? He's gorgeous!" Victoria blushed as they made their way to his side. Geraldine was like a dog on heat.

"Hello babes, you must be for us. We are Victoria and Geraldine." The man looked at the card to double check the names and nodded as he spoke.

"Yes, I'm here for you ladies. I've been ordered to bring you to the villa by Nicky and Kimberley." As he spoke he smiled and chuckled at the orders he was responding to. "I've been told to treat you two like queens by your girls." Geraldine walked by his side as Victoria trailed behind them pulling her suitcase. The man was around six foot tall and wearing a white short sleeved shirt with black pants that made his bollocks look massive. As Victoria walked behind him she admired his arse but was pissed off because Geraldine was all over him like a rash. His dark hair looked healthy and the shine from it looked amazing. His eyes were an enchanting dark blue colour and his tanned skin made them stand out. As they reached the black limousine they both smiled as he opened the door for them. He told them to get seated as he placed the luggage in the boot.

The limousine had white leather seating and a small drinks compartment in front of them. Geraldine grabbed a miniature bottle of brandy and drank it straight from the bottle. She asked Victoria if she wanted one but she declined. Geraldine didn't even know she'd hurt Victoria's feelings and carried on necking lots of different bottles. Victoria loosened her pink blouse as the heat filtered into the car and she felt sweaty. Geraldine had now moved towards the small window in front of them and sat talking to the driver. The driver was called Lance and Geraldine joked with calling him Lancelot.

As they neared the villa they both looked through the open window and couldn't believe the changes that had been made. The villa looked amazing. The white walls stuck out like a sore thumb in the distance and the place itself looked like something out of the movies. Lance stopped at the iron gates and spoke into the intercom as they both hung their heads from the window taking in everything around them. Once the gates were open they could see another hunky man gardening in the distance. Geraldine looked at Victoria who still had a face on her and spoke.

"This place looks amazing. The girls have really done us proud, come and have a look." Victoria moved her head towards the window and briefly glanced through it. She was right, the place looked superb and it had totally changed.

As the car stopped Lance came to the door and opened it.

"Here we go my ladies, hope your journey was comfortable." Geraldine went over the top and laughed out loud as Victoria thanked him. As they stepped out of the car they could see Nicky and Kimberley stood at the entrance of the villa waiting eagerly to greet them. Lance took care of the suitcases as they both walked a short distance to the front door. The doors looked fabulous and as they approached Kimberley pushed them both open and joked with them both.

"Welcome to your kingdom." Geraldine was the first to enter, as Victoria followed her slowly touching the wooden doors. The smell of paint could be smelt throughout the villa and everything looked so clean and new. They all hugged as they went into the first room. The reception room was painted in a light almond colour and complimented the brown leather sofa that sat in the middle of the room. A few pictures hung from the walls and it seemed to be just enough decor for the room. The white marble floor shone like ice as they walked across it and Victoria felt like she was sliding as she walked.

The four of them sat down in the front room and Kimberley told the maid to bring four glasses of red wine. Victoria looked at Kimberley and smiled telling her how organised she was. They all chatted for a while and then it was time for them to meet the staff they had recruited to work in the villa.

Nicky ran round like a headless chicken and wanted it to be a big moment. She stood proud and asked the girls to come in one by one. Victoria kicked her shoes off and told the maid to open the patio doors that led to the pool as her body was on fire with the heat.

Nicky shouted for the first girl to come in and as she

walked in she watched Geraldine like a hawk. The girl introduced herself as Connie and her legs looked long and sexy. Her long dark hair came to her waist and as they looked at her as she seated near them and smiled. Geraldine was asking her lots of questions and asked what experience she had in the business. They all listened as she spoke and her Yorkshire accent made them laugh. She told them she had been in Spain for a few years with her mate Jessica and they had both worked the bars and done lap dancing. They spoke to her for a few minutes more then the next girl was shouted in to join them. As the next girl came in Geraldine nearly collapsed and couldn't speak as she recognised the face of her old friend Jessica from school. Jessica didn't notice Geraldine at first but as soon as she did she ran to her and threw her arms round her.

The rest of the girls just sat staring at them both, and waited for an explanation. Geraldine was caught up with so much emotion and wiped the tears from her eyes. Jessica couldn't speak and sat by her side holding onto her arms with a grip. Within minutes Jessica spoke with a breathless voice.

"Geraldine it's been so long. I can't believe you're here. I've tried finding you for years but didn't even come close to." Geraldine hugged her again and both of them sat chatting as if no one else was there.

Victoria felt her heart break and she knew by the look on Geraldine's face that there was history between the two of them. Jessica remained at Geraldine's side as the rest of the staff were introduced. The girls were stunners and each of them shone in their own right. The men were hunks and one of them was hung like a donkey. As he walked into the room they all cast their eyes on his package in his tight white shorts. Nicky had already sampled his manhood a few weeks before and rated him a ten. Mark was their prize guy and they knew he would satisfy whoever he attended too.

Now everyone had met the tour of the villa began. Geraldine was joined at the hip with Jessica and brought her round the tour as if they had never been parted. Each room looked exactly as they had planned it too. Victoria walked in the bondage room and touched all the leather belts hung on the walls. At this moment she wanted to take one from the wall and strike it right across Geraldine's face, because her blood was boiling and she couldn't hold onto her temper any more. Every second they were laughing together and she couldn't take it anymore.

As they left the room she grabbed hold of Geraldine's hand and told her she needed a minute with her. Jessica was about to follow them both but the look on Victoria's face told her not to move an inch further. Jessica kissed Geraldine cheek as she passed her and told her they would catch up later and she agreed as she followed Victoria into the front room.

As they entered Victoria closed the doors so no one could hear and all hell broke loose.

"What's your fucking game? Do you think I'm some kind of idiot who will just sit there and watch you strut your stuff to anyone who'll have you? First it was Lance and now it's fucking Jessica. Don't you give a fuck about me and how I feel?" Geraldine sat down and remained calm. She couldn't see what she'd done wrong.

"What do you mean strut my stuff? Just because I like to talk it doesn't mean I'm flirting. Anyhow I've known Jessica for years we were good friends back in the day. Don't tell me you're jealous, because I will tell you now, I'll never be owned by anyone. I'm my own person and nothing will ever stop me from being me. If you have insecurities, that's your problem not mine." Victoria came and sat by her side and tried to explain how she was feeling but Geraldine stood up and walked around the room sighing.

"I can't believe what you have just said. We have something special between us and you're ruining it. I won't be a prisoner to be scared of speaking to people because you're paranoid. I'm me honey and you know what I'm about don't you?" Victoria felt bad but she hated Geraldine's flirty nature. She stood and walked to her side and placed her hands around her waist. Geraldine looked around the room but wouldn't look at her face. Geraldine listened to her and at the end of the conversation they were on good terms again. Inside Victoria felt her heart had been ripped out but she held her cards close to her chest and carried on looking around the villa.

Everything in the house was spot on and it felt like a hotel the way the staff walked and buzzed about. The kitchen assistants were cooking tea and the menu was displayed on a pink and black card in the dining area. The dining area had about ten chairs seated round the table. The table cloth was black and all the candles were a light pink colour. Victoria and Geraldine sat at the table and looked at the menu. It looked appetising and Geraldine ordered a cheese and bacon omelette and potato wedges with a side salad. Victoria scanned the menu and ordered the same. Her appetite was lost but she didn't want to seem too upset and ordered anyway.

All the staff came to the dining area and sat at the tables. They all had one more night free before the games began and they planned to make the most of it. They had organised a party for the same night. Jessica sat on a table where she could see Geraldine and it was like she was hypnotised by her. The sound of everyone eating and laughing filled the room and the atmosphere was lively. Once they had eaten Geraldine stood up and tapped at her empty glass with her knife. Once everyone was quiet she began her speech.

"Where do I start? I'm speechless that everything we've planned has become a reality. This place is going to be a success and with everyone who's here, I know we can all make some big money. From the bottom of our hearts we are grateful and tonight is going to be one hell of a party. This place will put us all on the map and you have all helped to make it happen." Everyone clapped and cheered as she finished her speech and they all agreed the villa would be something different and special.

The night was set to be a long one and everyone was in the party spirit. The bar in the back room was fully stocked and Nicky had secretly got hold of a big bag of cocaine to help the night along. Everyone was told to dress in a sexy outfit and Geraldine made sure she looked extra hot as she smoothed her legs with moisturizer. She wore a short red skirt with a black vest top with sequins on it. Her wonder bra made her breasts full and perky. As she looked at her shoe collection she decided on her long black boots to finish the outfit off. Her hair was back combed and sprayed in a messy style.

Victoria's heart wasn't in it tonight and she struggled to find the right outfit. As she emptied her suitcase on the bed she looked at her figure hugging silver dress. Pulling it from the case she held it near her skin and loved the feel of. She shouted Geraldine and asked her what she thought and she agreed that the dress always looked nice and sexy on her.

Victoria applied her makeup and styled her hair. As

she placed her silver diamante shoes on her slender feet she looked in the mirror and she started to feel sexy. Geraldine came to her side and felt she had slightly overreacted earlier and kissed her cheek telling her she was sorry. She forgave her instantly and touched her face hoping to kiss her but Geraldine pulled away and told her they needed to be ready because, after all, they were the hostesses.

Kimberley had bought some cheap disco lights and placed them in the long front room. The red, green and yellow lights flashed around like bolts of lightning. All the food was spread across the table on the back wall and looked like a feast fit for a king. The kitchen staff had made a great effort to display the food. Chicken legs, bowls of pasta, rice salad, all stood out from the buffet.

Nicky sorted out the music in the corner of the room. Dance music was her favourite but she knew she couldn't have it on all night and placed some other more relaxing tunes on the system.

Victoria and Geraldine walked into the room and all eyes focused on them both. Everything was perfect and everyone looked sexy as they'd requested. Geraldine was like a child in a sweet shop and secretly looked at all the hot bodies surrounding her. Jessica stood on the other side of the room and played with her hair. Her low cut pink vest top revealed her perky breasts and her light denim shorts stuck right up her crotch. Jessica stood against the wall and pulled her shorts out of her fanny. She stood tall in her white stiletto heels scanning the area for some signs of fun. Her plan was to get Geraldine on her own and catch up on old times but she could see by Victoria's face the job wasn't going to be easy. She could see Victoria watching her every move from the corner of her eye and felt uneasy. Jessica played with her long white beads round her neck and twisted them with her fingers as the party began.

Lance looked so fuckable, his oiled body hypnotised all the ladies. He wore a tight pair of jeans that strangled his bollocks and a fitted black t-shirt that showed off every inch of muscle he had. His black sandals looked sexy somehow, if anyone else had worn them other than him they would have looked a right geek.

Music played and talking filled the room. Nicky was loud and her gob drowned out the music. She had decided that her black Lycra dress was her sexy outfit. Kimberley danced up against Jessica and showed her some of the moves she did as a pole dancer. Her body was flexible and her long blonde hair flicked all around her as she twisted her body up and down.

Geraldine saw her dancing and escaped Victoria's side leaving her talking to another girl. The smell of fresh meat lingered in the air and Geraldine was keen to make a kill. Jessica smiled as she came over. She stood watching with a glass of brandy in her hand. Her lips were on fire as Kimberley came face to face with Jessica and she felt like she needed to get Jessica's attention.

"I would love to learn how to pole dance; can you show me some of your moves Jessica?" Jessica smiled and moved Kimberley out of her way as if she was barging past a customer at the Christmas sales. She walked to the middle of the room and told Geraldine to copy her. The disco lights flickered and Geraldine was now stood in front of her as she placed her hands round her shoulders in a seductive fashion.

Jessica smelt her hair from behind her and fresh lemon fragrance filtered up her nose. She wanted to lick her soft silky flesh and smell every inch of her body. Pulling her body towards hers she encouraged Geraldine to rotate her hips and follow her lead. Within minutes Geraldine was grinding her slender body up and down as Victoria watched with an evil eye in the distance.

Victoria had never been into drugs but she needed something to numb the pain she felt inside. Geraldine was the life and soul of the party and she felt her slowly slipping away from her. She felt like she was holding a bar of soap in her hands and the more she was trying to hold on the more it slipped away. Feeling like shit she sneaked off to the toilet and found Nicky preparing the lines of cocaine on the side of the sink. She looked like a Chinese chef as she sliced and cut into it with speed. When she had finished two neat lines stared at her.

Nicky felt uneasy as she stared at Victoria but within seconds she thought fuck it and rolled a note up and snorted one of the lines. Victoria watched as the white powder disappeared from the surface like a Hoover had picked it up. She watched her stand up fully as the sniff took effect. Nicky now passed the note to her.

Victoria felt her heart pounding and couldn't decide whether or not she wanted to snort the white powder. She froze for a moment and slowly took it from her hand. It felt like she was back in school and all the kids were round her egging her to do something naughty. In the past Victoria had always been a let down on things that had been wrong but tonight her mind was in a different place and she wanted to be ruthless for once in her life and not give a fuck about anything.

As she bent down to the line Nicky coached her through what she needed to do. All she could hear was Nicky's voice saying "snort it." The sniff penetrated deep into her nostrils and her body froze as it hit her brain. At first she thought she was going to die there and then but after a few minutes she felt like Ms. Confident and could tackle anyone or anything that stood in her way. She stood tall and looked in the mirror in front of her.

The mirror had small lights dotted around it and it reminded her of a film star's dressing room. Pulling her eyes towards the mirror she opened them as wide as she could and scooped the clump of mascara that had gathered in the corner. Once that was done she was ready to face everyone again. Nicky told her if she wanted any more sniff just to give her a shout, as there was plenty to go around.

Victoria walked back into the room like she was queen of her domain again. Her head was held high and she felt on top of the world. Looking towards Geraldine she saw her still flirting with Jessica and thought she would give her a taste of her own medicine. She felt strong inside and nothing would pull her back into a depression, not even her horny lesbian lover Geraldine.

Making her way to Lance she caressed his face with her long silver nails. She felt different inside now and had no inhibitions. He welcomed her touch and rested his elbow on her shoulder as he spoke. He was looking deep into her eyes and she felt she wanted his cock deep inside her there and then. The lesbian life she had chosen now seemed old and the thought of a real man stuck inside her turned her on.

She playfully touched his body parts and slid her fingers across his lips as she told him to be quiet. Lance was ready there and then to fuck her brains out, but he needed to be sure that's what she wanted. He'd taken a Viagra tablet minutes before and his manhood now stood like a launching missile inside his trousers.

Nicky shouted Victoria as she walked past a few hours later and she knew it was time for her top up of drugs.

Her hair looked like she had been outside in a hurricane, and her mascara looked like it had melted. The heat was sickening and the night air was clammy and still. As they prepared for more drugs Victoria sat on the toilet with the door opened. Her head hung between her legs and she wobbled as the sound of her pissing filled the air. Searching for toilet roll she heard Geraldine's voice as she entered the room.

The toilets had four cubicles and she hoped she wouldn't notice her. As she stared at the side of the cubicle she felt she was back at school and wanted to use a magic marker to scrawl her name on the surface. Smiling to herself she wiped between her legs and yanked her knickers up. As she walked out of the toilet she saw Geraldine and ignored her. She walked straight up to the line of cocaine. Geraldine leant onto the sink and watched her in disbelief. As she began to roll the money in her hands Geraldine came to her side like a shot.

"Hold on, hold on, what do you think you're doing?" Victoria focused her eyes and looked at her directly in the face.

"What does it look like? I'm having some fun, not that you care." Geraldine grabbed her arm and tugged her away. Victoria struggled and freed herself from her grip as Nicky left the toilets feeling that World War Three was about to kick off.

"Are you right in the fucking head? That's Cocaine you're taking!" Victoria nodded and shrugged her shoulders.

"So what? I'm a grown woman aren't I? And if that's what I want to do, leave me alone and get back to your fancy piece." Geraldine had been into drugs a long time ago and they'd taken over her life at one point. She too felt the urge to vacuum the lines she saw in front of her. She could tell Victoria was hurt and stood in front of the sink.

"Honey what's the matter? I've only been talking to everyone. I can't be at your side every minute of the day." Victoria screwed her face up and let her have it.

"You're just like everyone else aren't you? You think you can pick me up and put me down whenever you feel like it. I'm not a fucking toy. I have feelings you know." Geraldine cradled her in her arms and said she was sorry, but she hated the way she felt trapped by her. Their relationship had been great when it was just them two but now she was seeing a side of Victoria she didn't like. The business had just started and she knew she would have to console her to stand any chance of it working, so for now she ate humble pie and apologised.

"Babes I'm sorry. I didn't think it was a problem, but now I know I will stay by your side." Victoria felt in control and wrapped her arms round her but still wanted the rush of the cocaine. She smiled at Geraldine and asked in a low voice.

"Do you want some? We can both share it and feel the same way together?" Geraldine had wanted to say no, but something inside her mind told her how good it felt and within minutes they were both high on the drug.

The night was rocking and the Spanish air made everyone feel upbeat. The music played and as the night went on a few of the girls were in the fantasy rooms having hot steamy sex with the men. Kimberley had wanted Lance from the moment she'd seen him, but Nicky had pounced on him first and fucked his brains out, but that didn't deter her. She knew his love pole was massive and wanted to feel the girth of it inside her. Nicky had told her in great detail how good he was in the bedroom and as she saw him walking into the kitchen she followed him in hope of some sex.

Lance chewed a piece of quiche as he walked into the kitchen and swigged a mouthful from his bottle of lager. The fan on the ceiling was turning like a cyclone and he stood underneath it lifting his t-shirt up from his body. Kimberley could see his six pack as she entered. As she walked past she touched his stomach commenting on his toned body. Lance thanked her and tucked his hand down the front of his jeans.

"Tell you what love, my knob is on fire. I took a Viagra before and it feels like a baby's arm. Here have a feel." Kimberley didn't need to be asked twice. She squeezed her fingers together and slid them down the front of his jeans as he breathed in. Her pussy had a beat and the throbbing inside her wanted soothing.

As she felt his warm cock he smiled as she commented how big it was. He told her it was his main selling point and in the past he'd made women scream with pleasure. She didn't want to sound desperate and nodded her head and told him she'd experienced bigger in the past. His face dropped and he looked crestfallen. Lance pulled her closer and pressed his firm throbbing cock into her waist.

"The proof's in the pudding honey. You can sample it for yourself if you want." She didn't need asking twice and she followed his lead into a room at the left of them. The room was dimly lit and as the light shone in from the pool she realised she was in the bondage room. Lance dragged her towards him and twisted his tongue around in her mouth. She hated his technique and told him to slow down.

Lance had something to prove to her and didn't waste any time freeing the beast from his trousers. His trouser snake landed on his legs like a piece of meat slamming on a butcher's block. Her eyes had never seen anything so big and she laughed as she asked him did he have a licence to carry it round, as it definitely should be classed as a dangerous weapon.

Lance kicked off his jeans and stood in front of her wearing only his figure hugging t-shirt. She felt like all her Christmases and birthdays had come at once and stood looking at the black leather whip on the wall. She had always wanted to be in control during sex. Her last boyfriend had tortured her physically and mentally so now was her chance to pay men back.

As she put on some red plastic boots and grabbed the whip, Lance smiled. He loved a dominant woman and to get his arsed whipped would be the turn on he needed. Kimberley kicked off her skirt and pulled her polyester black nylon top over her head. She now stood with her boots and her sexy black lacy underwear on. The knickers were skimpy and the black lace at the front of them showed her lips from her lady garden. Her bra strap hung from her shoulder and she lifted it back into her shoulder with a sexy movement.

The room was painted in a dark red paint and the black silk bedding shone under the moonlight. The small side light was switched on by Lance and he now lay on the bed waiting for action. Kimberley rolled the black whip round in her hands, she wanted to make sure she knew how to use it and practiced her movement a few times on the floor.

The noise of the whip cracking onto the floor turned her on and she tried it three or four times before she walked towards him. Kimberley was now in the character of the porn queen she'd always wanted to be. She'd watched lots of porn movies in the past and knew lots of movements in the bedroom. Even the way she spoke changed. She adopted a German accent and placed one of her long legs on the side of the bed. Lance watched her with excitement. She now cracked the whip on the floor and told him to sit up straight from the bed.

"Sit up you lazy man, quickly! Come on, I haven't got all day!" Lance obeyed and sat on the edge of the bed. She stood tall in front of him and told him her orders in a strict tone.

"Lick my pussy, you dirty, no good bastard." She whipped his legs and he screwed his face up in pain. "Do it now you scum bag or feel my whip across your arse." The pain of the whip surged his body and his legs felt like they were on fire as the pain travelled down them.

With shaking hands he pulled her knickers down and caressed her legs as she lifted her legs up to take them off. Her fanny had been shaved that day and she looked proud as he saw it for the first time. His tongue looked like a thirsty dog after as he tasted her for the first time. As he opened her flaps she struck his arse with the whip.

"Stop fucking around and lick my pussy, you lazy twat." Lance knew she meant business and thought she was taking the role a bit far but carried on anyway. As she felt his warm wet tongue inside her groove, she knew it wouldn't be long before she came all over his face.

The whip now dropped from her hands and she held her hands up behind her neck pulling at her long locks of hair. Her groans were loud and Lance knew he could now take control. Taking her thighs he pulled her towards him and threw her onto the bed. Her orgasm was hanging by a thread and she knew he would only have to touch her one more time and she would explode with pleasure.

Lance teased her and laid her flat on her back. He lifted one of her legs onto his shoulder and teased the end of his penis near her entrance. Her nails plunged into his waist and she pulled him nearer to her. As the beast entered her she struggled for breath, she felt as if she was being ripped apart. His girth was incredible and as the rest of him entered her she shouted with pleasure. She felt as if she had put a load of sweets into her mouth and couldn't chew them all to get the full taste of them. Her pussy was full, and it was a kind of painful, yet pleasurable experience.

His rhythm was long and hard and the Viagra he'd taken was at full effect. His love shaft looked swollen and ready to burst. As she shouted out with pleasure he forced himself as deep as he could inside her. The sweat on her brow rolled down her forehead and as she screwed her eyes together it rolled down onto her eyes. Heaven was felt for Kimberley and now she had been satisfied she pushed him from her and knelt in front of him.

The job in front of her looked impossible, but she stretched her mouth as wide as she could and placed him inside her warm, wet mouth. There wasn't much room in her mouth for any tongue teasing, and as he slid in and out of her mouth she heaved a few times as his member touched her tonsils.

Lance grabbed her head and held it with two secure hands as she sucked him off. She felt dizzy and sick but still continued wanting to please him. Within seconds Lance's body stiffened as if someone had stuck a pin in his arse and he shot his load right across her face. Kimberley hated the taste of spunk and dodged the spurts as they came flying onto her face. He groaned and his face looked angry as he reached orgasm. They both collapsed onto the bed and Kimberley grabbed a nearby towel to wipe the spunk from her face.

★

Victoria and Geraldine danced the night away together as Jessica watched from a distance. Jessica felt cheated and planned to get Geraldine on her own. Taking a triple vodka and coke she came to Victoria's side and passed it to her.

"Come on get that down your neck." Victoria thanked her and gulped the drink quenching her thirst. As the night went on the vodkas kept coming and before long she keeled over on the sofa. Her head lay on the side of the sofa as her legs dangled at the side of her. Geraldine laughed as she looked at her and pulled her up trying to get her to bed.

Victoria was like a corpse as a few of the lads helped to get her in bed. As they opened the bedroom door they headed towards the large bed placed under the window. They held her on the side of the bed as Geraldine pulled her dress over her head. Once it was off they laid her on her side and slid her shoes off. The room was lit only by the outside lights and the white silken sheets shone under the moonlit sky.

For a moment they just all stared at her and laughed. Slowly they headed back to the party. The night was nearly at an end anyway, and lots of them had already gone to different parts of the villa. Nicky was talking to one of the guys and her hands were all over him as they spoke. The music was turned low now and the disco lights were turned off.

Geraldine plonked herself onto the sofa and lit a cigarette. She felt like she'd been in charge of a children's party and now they had all gone she could relax. Jessica saw her opportunity and sat with her. As she sat next to her she nudged her up with her bum cheeks as the sofa wasn't that big. To start with the conversation was basic and just about the night, but Jessica wanted to know more about Geraldine and how her life had turned out.

Reaching for a cigarette her body hovered over Geraldine. As she got the ashtray she could smell Geraldine's scent. This woman had always been her heroine and for years she never stopped pining for her. Resting her slender hands onto her lap, she tapped her fingers and looked into her eyes.

"I still can't believe I'm here with you. I've had some shit in the years gone by and always wanted you to be near so you could make things better." Geraldine felt slightly embarrassed but smiled.

"Honey, my life hasn't been plain sailing either. It's been a mixture of one disaster to the next let me tell you." Jessica reached for her hands and slowly held her sweaty palm in hers. Geraldine wiggled her fingers about as she held her and tried to straighten her ring. Jessica whispered as she spoke.

"I've never forgotten what happened to us and how you saved me from him you know. That fucking, perverted headmaster ruined my life. I drink to forget his ugly face and take drugs to try and nurse away his sick perverted acts. Every night I close my eyes and he's still there in my head as if it was yesterday. I've slept with loads of men to try and get over it but he's scarred me inside and I can't seem to get past it." Geraldine moved the hair from her face and felt her pain. She had dealt with their ordeal in a similar way and told her that.

"I know where you're coming from babes. I've done the same thing. I've been a sperm bank for years and most men I've met have left a deposit." Jessica smiled and rolled into her lap. The years had passed but there was something about their friendship that made them that little bit closer than her other friends.

Geraldine still felt like her protector and as she played with her hair lifting it up and rolling it around in her fingers she knew she had to put her straight about a few things.

"Jessica, that was such a long time ago and I've moved on; or at least I'm trying to. Me and Victoria are an item, you know that don't you?" Jessica rolled her lips with her teeth and looked into her eyes with an endearing smile.

"Yeah I know honey, but I can't help the way I feel about you." Geraldine felt slightly uneasy and slowly lifted her head from her lap.

"We all have a big day tomorrow so let's get some sleep. We need to be bright eyed in the morning." She looked at her gold bracelet watch which told them it was nearly half past three. The guests were due tomorrow afternoon and she rounded the last few people up like a cowboy leading them to the bedrooms. Jessica thought when they had all left she might come back to her to talk some more but as she stared at the empty room she knew she would be alone for the rest of the night.

Geraldine peeled her clothes off and slowly slid into bed next to Victoria. She placed her right arm across her body and pulled her closer to her. She could smell her Chanel perfume all over her and snuggled into the small of her back hoping to find sleep.

Lance and Kimberley ended up spending the night together and if you listened carefully inside the villa you could still hear her sexual moans like a wounded animal in the night air.

Jessica lay in her bed and a few of the other girls were already asleep to the left of her. Their room was like a dormitory and five single beds were spaced out evenly along the white walls. Her mind was playing with her thoughts yet again and the past she hated was there in full force. She pulled the white cotton sheet over her face and tried to hide from it. Usually she would have a man or woman at the side of her to help ease the loneliness she felt inside but tonight she was alone and at war with her memories.

Searching for her bag, she fumbled around in it until she found the bottle of tablets. As she pressed and screwed off the lid at the same time she emptied two small white Diazepam tablets into her hand. The doctor had told her a few years before they would help relax her but he failed also to tell her they would start to rule her life if she took them for long enough. Panic stricken she searched for a drink around the room and her eyes focused on a half empty glass near one of the girls beds. She crept over and reached for the drink trying not to wake anyone. The drink was warm and tasted like Malibu and lemonade as she threw the tablets into her mouth. Jessica knew that it wouldn't be long before the tablets worked and prepared herself for her body melting into the bed.

She undid her shorts and slid them down her slender legs. Her bra had been digging in her all night and she couldn't wait to take it off and rub underneath her breasts. All but her pink lacy knickers remained on her bronzed body as she fell back onto the bed and tried to find comfort in the Spanish heat.

10

The morning light came faster than they all had wished as

the sound of the cleaners moving glasses and plates about woke Geraldine from her sleep. Her eyelids felt like lead weights and she practised opening them a few times first before she finally awoke. Victoria was dead to the world and her night of drugs and alcohol had knocked her out. Geraldine stared at her back and slowly slid her long fingers up and down her spine. Victoria moaned at first and kicked her legs as if she knew someone was invading her dreams.

"Come on lazy bones, the day has finally come to make our dreams reality." Victoria moaned but didn't budge from her horizontal position. Geraldine gave it a few more minutes and pulled the sheet from her.

"Oh, stop it please I'm not a well woman." Victoria sat up but still had her eyes were closed. She tried to pull the sheet back over her body and steal a few more minutes. Geraldine laughed as she played with her and let her think she had won the sheet of comfort back. Within seconds Victoria was laid back down again and holding the sheet round her with a tight grip. Her knuckles had turned white she was holding it that tight. With one almighty tug Geraldine stood and pulled the sheet completely off her. Victoria looked like a shaking drug addict as she lay in the bed with his knees pulled tightly to her chest.

"Come on babes, we have a busy day in front of us and have to make sure everything runs smoothly. There are guests to be picked up from the airport and fantasies to be fulfilled. Come on honey, we need to meet the staff and go through the needs of our guests."

Victoria stretched her body and tried desperately to open her eyes. She patted the side of the bed and asked Geraldine to come and sit with her for a minute. As Geraldine sat by her side she sat up and like a small child who'd been caught doing something mischievous she started to apologise.

"You must think I'm a right one don't you? I acted like a smacked arse last night and I hope you can forgive me." Geraldine smiled and spoke to her with a high pitched voice.

"You were over the top alright. I thought you were going to a have a nervous breakdown or something," she teased her now and smiled as she dropped her head onto her body. "Everyone gets insecure at one time or another and I know you're not really the jealous type. I think it's all that cocaine you had that made you paranoid love." Victoria hung her head in shame and wanted the floor to open to swallow her up. She decided there and then that drugs weren't for her. They cuddled for a few minutes and Geraldine was the one to break the moment.

"Right, I'm going to make sure everyone's up. Do you want any breakfast babes?" Victoria couldn't face any food at that moment and told her she would grab something later. Geraldine left the bedroom in her knee length black shorts and a plain white vest top she had dragged from the wardrobe. The villa smelt like a nightclub on a Sunday morning and the smell of stale cigarettes and alcohol spread throughout the walls. The cleaner had already started in the kitchen and the smell of lemon gel had already eliminated most traces of the musty smells.

A few of the girls were already up and sat round the pool drinking coffee with the men. They looked quite fresh considering the night they'd had. Some sat reading scripts and some of them were laughing as they acted out some of the fantasies they had to perform. Kimberley was sat next to Lance and she smiled from head to toe following her latest love conquered mission. Her white housecoat hung from her shoulders and her bare skin could be seen as she sipped her coffee.

Geraldine noticed Jessica wasn't there and searched each bedroom until she found her. Once she saw her lay in bed she made noises as she walked round the bedroom trying to wake her. Jessica opened her eyes and squinted as the morning rays shone through the large window. They made eye contact for the first time and Geraldine spoke to her with a firm voice.

"Come on Jessica, everyone's up but you. It's a big day and the guests will be arriving soon." Jessica pulled herself from the bed and stood in front of her with nothing on but her pink knickers. Geraldine looked shocked as she watched her stretch. Her breasts looked firm and tanned and her nipples were large and flat. As she looked closer she could see her tan marks where her knickers had moved over. Jessica knew what she was doing and teased her all the more knowing she had her full attention.

As if by magic Geraldine woke up from the trance she had put her under and walked to the door. "Hurry up love; we're all by the poolside." Jessica gave a cocky smile and told her she would be there soon. No more words were spoken and Geraldine left the room with her heart beating ten to the dozen. Jessica was like a drug and now her body was craving her no matter how much she tried to deny it. She cleared her mind and joined everyone round the poolside. The sun was beaming down and it seemed a blessing was being cast upon them all as Victoria joined them and told them what she expected.

"This afternoon, we have six guests arriving. From the minute they step foot into this villa they need to be treated like kings and queens. They have paid for a service and that's what we're going to provide." She quickly read through her paper work and read some of the fantasies of the guests.

Lance was handed his job sheet and he was to pick a lady up from the airport. She was the lady wanting sex with her chauffeur and he'd already planned how he was going to treat her for the week ahead. The element of surprise was a big part of his job and he promised he'd give her a full service once she arrived.

Nicky had her piece of paper in front of her and she planned how she would suck her client off while he was eating his dinner. She told the others how she would position herself under the table and how the seating plan should be arranged. Kimberley's job was to have sex with a man while his partner watched. As she read the rest of the fantasy she held her stomach and heaved at the thought of someone farting in her face.

The villa looked like any other hotel; the cook was already preparing the menu for the day ahead and the cleaner was just getting rid of the final touches and the traces of the night before. The grounds were being cleaned and the plants on the driveway were being pruned. Everyone set off to get ready and plan for the day ahead. A black people carrier had been organised to pick up the guests and the car looked amazing with its tinted windows, which gave the discretion the punters desired.

The rooms were all ready to go and some Spanish music was being played around the poolside. Table and chairs were set out around the pool and sun canopies were opened up in the middle of them. All drinks were placed in ice buckets and the bedrooms were given a final inspection.

Victoria chose to wear a long white dress made from cotton. She combed her hair to the side of her face and placed an artificial flower clip by her ear. She wore gold beaded sandals and her freshly painted toe nails shone a shiny pink colour. Geraldine felt her nerves kick in and she doubted whether or not it had all been a bad mistake. Herself and Victoria had put a hell of a lot of money into this project and if it all came crashing down in front of their eyes, she would feel responsible for Victoria losing her money. They had both spent over thirty thousand pounds to kit the villa up. The Jacuzzi they installed took a lot of that money, as did the sauna. However, the extension had made the villa more spacious, allowing for a higher capacity of people to stay and the chance of making more money.

Geraldine wore a long blue patterned dress and gripped her hair up with a gold slide she'd found in the bedroom. Her white open toed shoes were dragged from the wardrobe and she struggled to walk in them as she placed them on her feet. As she finished getting ready she stood at the window like a sergeant watching his troops getting ready for war and smiled.

Both Lance and Peter left to drive to the airport. Lance left in the limousine and Peter took the people carrier. Lance was dressed in a crisp white shirt with a black Jacket and neatly pressed trousers, he didn't wear his hat yet and placed it on the passenger seat. After making sure he had the name card of the person he was picking up he set off down the drive way as the others cheered with excitement.

Peter followed a few minutes later and the rest of them sat around the pool. Geraldine said once they got the call from Lance telling them they were on their way back, they would all have to set about their business. Geraldine didn't want the guest to come and have everyone staring at them and told them all, she wanted them all to look as busy as they could be when the cars pulled up. Walking around the grounds she flicked her D&G sunglasses over her eyes. It was hot alright and she could even feel the heat through the floor. Standing alone she looked at the villa in full view from the main gates, she placed her hand on her hip and nodded in approval. The place looked the business and fit for a king. Even though they were all in Spain it still felt like a Manchester project as most of the staff had previously lived there. The Manchester people seemed to have a lively feel to them and their humour was something that kept them amused for hours. They were one big, happy family and Geraldine felt like the mother of the house.

In the distance Victoria could be seen walking towards her and she set off back to meet her. When she reached her Victoria was on her mobile phone and she could be heard given instructions to someone. When she'd finished the call she shouted to everyone that Lance and Peter were setting off back to the villa now. Everyone started to run round like headless chickens as Geraldine hugged Victoria.

Lance held the laminated piece of paper up at the arrivals in the airport. The holiday makers were eager to get out into the sunshine and started to stampede past him. He didn't know what the lady looked like he was meeting and tried to make eye contact with a few different ladies as they passed him but they just walked past thinking he was flirting.

Five minutes had passed and he was pissed off. His arm ached now as he'd been holding the card up for ages. He scanned the area another few times and was going to sit near the exit, when a middle aged woman tapped him on the shoulder.

"I think you're here for me aren't you?" Lance turned

his head to the left and there she was, stood before him. He introduced himself and looked quite shocked at the woman he saw in front of his eyes. She looked around forty and was dressed very classily in a cream suit with a black vest top underneath it. She looked fantastic as he scanned her body and although her skirt wasn't that short, it was enough to show off her lightly tanned legs. Lance took her silver case from her and wheeled it towards the exit. Mrs Jones then introduced herself.

"I'm Gaynor, my friends call me Gay, but for some reason I prefer Gaynor as it gives people the wrong impression otherwise." Her smile filled her face as she spoke and she casually took off her jacket as they walked. Gaynor had honey blonde hair and underneath it stripes of dark brown. Her eyes were green and her makeup was a bit over the top. Lance had noticed her makeup straight away when he met her. It looked as if it had been applied with a trowel it was that thick. Her skin looked quite greasy and as he looked closer and he could see the pot holes on her face. Her perfume was strong and Lance imagined being in a garden centre near the roses as he walked with her. As they left the airport he escorted her to the car.

His own heart was beating fast because he knew he had to plan his next move very carefully. He placed the case in the boot and opened the door for Gaynor. Once she was seated he came and sat with her and asked what she would like to drink. Champagne had been her first choice and as he poured her some into a glass she watched him with caution. Once she held the drink in her hands he moved to the door to leave and placed his hand on her leg. Gaynor smiled and kicked off her shoes as she placed her sweaty, tired feet onto the chair. The door was closed and Lance made his way to the driver's seat. He had planned to take her on a detour and hoped she would be okay.

The engine started and he checked over his shoulder as he pulled out of Alicante airport. His hat was placed on the passenger seat as he turned the music up that played in the back of the car. His choice of music was light and slow and Paloma Faith seemed to set the mood for the trip.

The roads were bumpy and he checked his map to make sure he was going the right way. The script he'd made was close to him and he kept glancing at it going through his words again and again. He pressed the button that released the window so he could see in the back of the car and looked through his mirror as he spoke to Gaynor.

"Is everything alright in there for you my lady? Do you want the air conditioning turning up?" Gaynor told him she was fine and crossed her legs slowly as he watched through the mirror.

"Shouldn't be that long now sweetheart. If you need anything just give me a shout." The button was pressed to close the compartment and Lance continued to his destination. Trickles of perspiration could be seen on his forehead and he wiped it with the back of his hand as he continued. He breathed his warm breath into his cupped hands and smelt it. Not sure of the smell he reached into his pockets and grabbed a chewing gum.

Gaynor was never in a million years expecting her fantasy to begin today and sat in the back listening to the music sipping her chilled champagne. She felt a little uneasy about the whole set up and earlier that day at the airport she nearly turned back.

Lance drove up the bumpy hillside and he was minutes away from beginning the fantasy. Rubbing his crutch he squeezed his manhood and gave it a wakeup call. Gaynor sat on the back seat and she shouted where the hell they were going as she bounced from side to side in the back of the car. Lance brought the car to a halt. Gaynor looked out of the window and wondered what on earth could be wrong. Lance left the car and made his way to the back wheel and started to kick at it softly hoping she would get out of the car. His white shirt was now opened and his hairy chest could just be seen. He could hear her shouting and popped his head in the left hand side of the car.

"Looks like we've got a puncture Gaynor." She sighed and pulled at her clothes.

"How long do you think it will take to change the wheel? I'm sweating and need to get out of these clothes I'm boiling hot." He smiled at her with a cheeky grin and suggested she took them off anyway. Gaynor's eyes lit up yet she felt uneasy.

She sat for a moment and decided to step out of the car. As she did, her high heeled shoes made a crunching noise on the uneven gravel which caused Lance to turn around as he pretended to look in the boot of the car. His cock was rock hard now and he knew exactly what to do next.

"You don't mind if I take my shirt off do you, only I don't want to get it dirty. You know what it's like when you change a tyre." As he unbuttoned his shirt he watched her face and knew she liked what she saw. Her legs buckled when she saw the toned body of the love god in front of her and she rested her body on the car with her legs stretched out in front of her. As he bent near her she wanted to rip his bollock-grabbing trousers off him but she held back and tapped her long pink nails on her teeth instead.

Lance was on count down for the act to begin and he scanned the area before he began.

"Mrs Jones can I tell you how sexy you look today, I

hope you don't mind me saying that?" She seemed a little shocked at what he'd said, but smiled and thanked him. He bent near her with the wheel brace and placed it on the floor near her feet. As he looked he knew it was now or never and slowly he rubbed her calf. Her leg felt warm and smooth and he looked up at her as he slid the rest of his hand up her thigh.

"You feel really firm Mrs Jones. Do you go to the gym?" Her words were jittery and she didn't realise this was her fantasy beginning.

"I work out; you need to when you're my age." Before she knew it he'd placed his hand up her skirt and touched her white cotton knickers. Her eyes danced like an Irish dancer and she felt a rush of excitement run through her body. He slowly pulled them down her legs and she panicked knowing she'd worn the knickers all day and hoped they would be clean. Lance pulled them to her ankles and lifted her leg to take them off. Her vagina was pumping with lust and her legs parted as she felt his finger investigating her.

Lifting her skirt over her bum cheeks he looked up at her and raised his eyebrows. His tongue slowly came out of his mouth like a tortoise from its shell and he tasted her for the first time. Her head fell back onto the car and she felt his warm wet tongue for the first time. At first he was like a kitten with a saucer of milk, but as time went on he was like a lion with a piece of meat. His hands stretched up her top and pulled her breasts from her bra. Within minutes he had pulled her onto the bonnet of the car and his pants were completely off as he penetrated her. At first she screamed with pain as the heat from the bonnet burnt her arse and back, but as he moved her further down she slid on to his cock. His voice was husky and sexy as he continued.

"Mrs Jones, forgive me for fucking you. You're just so fucking sexy, you're a little minx." Gaynor's dreams were coming true and no man had called her sexy for years. The sex she'd had in the past was like dipping a biscuit in a cup of tea – wet and soggy – and often left her wanting more. Her legs were hitched up now and she could see his face as he pleasured her. The words she'd wanted to say for years were there on her tongue and she began to shout with years of frustration leaving her body.

"Fuck me you dirty bastard. I love cock and I want you to ram that pole deep inside me." Lance seemed a bit shocked but he encouraged her to shout some more as she dug her nails deep into his shoulder blades. The noise of a few birds could be heard tweeting in the distance and the only other sounds you could hear were that of Gaynor yelping like a dog. Sweat ran down both their bodies and her top was now open and her breasts were hanging from it. He pulled her down from the bonnet and turned her round as he took her from behind. He grabbed her hair back and spoke in a strict voice.

"Tell me you want more, come on tell me." Gaynor shouted out like she had won a line at bingo and as his movements quickened he heard her shout she was coming. Within minutes they both fell to the yellow gravel and tried to recover from the mind blowing sex they'd just had. Their bodies were lay next to each other and Lance turned to face her.

"Mrs Jones, I'm so sorry. Can you ever forgive me for what I've just done?" She knew now her holiday had begun and played her part well.

"As long as it doesn't happen again Lance, I won't speak a word of it, but don't ever try and fuck me again." Her tone was light as she finished her sentence and he knew she wanted as much of his cock as he would give as the dirty little minx was gagging for it. After a few minutes he stood and offered his hand to her to pull her from the ground. As she stood up she tried to locate her knickers and the rest of her clothing but as she turned Lance held them in his hand. He slowly passed them to her and pulled her closer as he did. His kiss was sexy and left her wanting more, but he knew she would have to wait as seven days were a long time and he didn't want her getting bored already.

They both got back into the car and headed to the villa. Lance didn't speak to her much because he wanted to keep it professional and they only spoke when they neared the villa.

"Well Mrs Jones we are nearly here. I hope this holiday is one you're going to enjoy." Gaynor smiled at him through his rear view mirror and nodded telling him she had a funny feeling this was going to be the best holiday she was ever going to have.

As the journey finished Lance stepped from the car and walked to open her door. Her smiling face greeted him and he held her hand as she carefully got out of the car. She looked like royalty as her slender legs touched the white gravel and she stood proud as she watched him get her luggage from the boot of the car.

Her eyes scanned the area – it looked like a famous footballer's home. She inhaled the fresh aromas of the flowers in the garden. People sat around the pool as she neared and she placed her sunglasses on to try to cover the sin she'd just committed. Lance followed behind her as they entered the villa and headed to the reception area.

Everything smelt fresh and clean as she stood fidgeting. Geraldine came straight away to tend to her and she removed her sunglasses to talk to her. Lance winked at Geraldine slyly and introduced Gaynor.

"This is Mrs Jones, Geraldine and she has reserved a room for one week via the net." Geraldine asked her for her invitation and she pulled it from her purse like a piece of gold. Her eyes looked at the invite and she passed it to her feeling a little apprehensive. Lance thanked Gaynor and told her he would be driving her for the rest of the week. Gaynor felt her face blush and didn't speak; she just nodded and acted as if she didn't take any notice of him. Geraldine watched him leave and told her to sit at the small pine table in front of her. As she pulled a chair out Geraldine was at the side of her with a clipboard and a fountain pen.

"Can I just ask you to fill out a few details; it's only for our records." Gaynor took the silver pen from her hand slowly as her eyes cast over the writing on the white paper. Once the form was completed, Geraldine spoke to her about the villa. She passed her a timetable of all meal times and told her of a few rules and regulations. Gaynor was dying of embarrassment and hoped she didn't talk about the fantasy she'd requested. Five minutes later the discussion was over and Geraldine showed her to her room, without any mention of the reason she was there.

The room was painted white and looked fresh. The patio doors were opened and the long patterned curtains were pulled aside. Outside her room she noticed a white plastic table with two chairs placed round it. An ash tray sat in the middle of it and she could hear another couple laughing. Once Geraldine had shown her round she left her the key and told her she hoped she would enjoy her time there. Gaynor thanked her and followed her to the door locking it behind her.

Falling into the bed Gaynor kicked her legs up and

down with excitement. She felt sexy like never before. The sex she'd just had was still fixed firmly in her mind and she closed her eyes to recapture some of the moments. As she kicked her shoes off, she located her suitcase and pulled it to her double bed. As she hung from the bed she searched for something comfortable to wear. Her eyes lifted as she saw a man outside her patio. Quickly she bent down and tried to avoid eye contact.

"Hello love, have you just got here? We got here today didn't we Susie?" As he spoke a woman came to his side and introduced herself.

"Bloody hell I'm sweating like a camel's arse." As she noticed Gaynor near the window she quickly changed her tone and continued.

"Oh I'm sorry love. I didn't see you there. Listen to me being so common." She smiled at her and continued.

"I'm Susie from Manchester, where you from babes?" Gaynor stood from the bed and came out onto the patio and pulled her sunglasses over her eyes.

"I'm Gaynor. I'm from Prestwich in Manchester. It seems everyone I've spoken to is from Manchester so far, how weird is that?" Susie smiled and rambled in her Manchester accent.

"Mancs are the salt of the earth love, straight talking and no bullshit. That's us isn't it Paul?" Paul was already weighing Gaynor up and down and quickly tried to answer the question.

"We sure are sweetie. Tough cookies we are and stand alone amongst other places on the maps." The conversation was over quickly as Susie pulled Paul's arm toward the pool.

"Come on let's have a look at your sexy Speedos then." She tugged at his bright blue beach towel round his waist as he laughed and tried to keep a straight face. He turned to Gaynor as he left and laughed as he shouted.

"Nice to meet you, see you later. She's a crazy fucker this one isn't she?" Paul's body was wobbling as he left and he smiled, departing Gaynor's side leaving her to head back inside trying to locate her black bikini.

Once she was ready Gaynor slipped a chiffon dress over her bikini and headed for the poolside with her book held firmly under her arm. Pulling up a sun lounger she rolled her yellow fluffy towel out on the bed and made herself comfortable once she'd removed her dress. As she lay she checked her legs for any signs of cellulite and positioned them so they looked toned. Glasses pulled down and oil applied she opened a book and started to read as she listened to Susie and Paul larking about in the pool. She could hear his loud mouth and as she looked over her book she could see him bombing Susie in the pool.

A few more people were starting to arrive but Gaynor just kept her eyes on her book. She wondered about the other people present and surmised they were all here for a fantasy request as well.

Geraldine and Victoria stood watching them have fun like proud parents. This was a busy time for them both and they met with the staff to start the procedures for the night ahead.

Mr Ferris's fantasy was that he wanted to be sucked off while he was eating his meal. He wanted everybody to be dressed in tuxedoes and the ladies to be wearing cocktail dresses. In his email he had even described what they would be eating at the time of his fantasy.

Geraldine had given Belinda the job of acting out his fantasy and she was sat there at the side of them reading through his desires.

The dining table was being set already and several large silver candlestick holders were placed in the centre of the table with six red waxed candles inside them. The table cloth was gold cotton, and as they placed it on the table it looked so regal.

The food was almost prepared now and the cook stood to look at it with a smile on her face. The feast looked fit for kings and queens.

Victoria poured two diet cokes and handed Geraldine one. They had every day planned out and if everything went to plan the customers would be all leaving with smiles on their faces.

Nicky and Kimberley had gone shopping and left about an hour ago. Geraldine was moaning about them leaving and told Victoria she shouldn't have let them go especially on the first day of everyone arriving.

11

NICKY AND KIMBERLEY needed a break from the villa if the truth be known. They had worked their arses off every day for the last couple of months and now they wanted to chill for a bit before their big night began. Their drive into Benidorm took around thirty minutes. The heat was blazing and Kimberley was finding it hard to breathe.

Nicky had wanted to go into town because she needed some cocaine for the party nights ahead and she knew exactly where to go for it. Dennis was a friend of James and he could get you whatever you wanted at the drop of a hat. Nicky had text him earlier that day to tell him what she wanted and she now told Kimberley her plans as they pulled up outside the shops.

"Dennis is going to sort the sniff out for us. I've already told him what we need. He's going to meet us at Tommy's bar in about an hour." Kimberley checked her watch and pulled Nicky towards some clothes shop she'd spotted.

The streets were packed with people in summer dress. The men walked around like they were Greek Gods in their shorts and bare chest. Some of the men were overweight and their bellies looked massive but they didn't seem to care. People sat outside the bars and the atmosphere was a happy one. Music played from almost every shop with The Mavericks, 'Just Want to Dance the Night Away,' making Nicky sway her hips.

The shops seemed to sell everything from groceries, to cigarettes, novelties and even rock. Kimberley thought about her family and looked at some of the ornaments. As she held an ashtray in her hand, she read the words on it, 'With Love from Benidorm' and smiled. She looked at all the bright colours on it and loved the style of it. Her mother smoked loads of cigs a day and she placed the ash tray back thinking it would never be big enough to hold all her cig ends.

Nicky held her belly and told Kimberley she was starving. They both agreed they would grab something to eat after they'd picked up the few things they needed. They strolled up the streets and sipped the freezing water they'd just purchased. Kimberley was dressed in a pale blue cotton dress and a pair of flip- flops. Nicky wore her bright yellow bikini and an oversized white pair of canvass shorts that hung from her waist. They spoke as they walked and Kimberley seemed a bit concerned when she spoke about Jessica.

"Jessica seems nice doesn't she? But there is just something about her that I can't put my finger on. She's got some serious issues if you ask me. Have you seen the way she looks at Geraldine?" Nicky agreed straight away and didn't hold back on her opinion.

"She's a fucking bunny boiler if you ask me. I haven't spoken to her much but you can tell a mile off she's got the hots for Geraldine. I can tell Victoria knows as well because since she arrived she's been a little off with everyone, don't you think?" Kimberley screwed her face up and tried to make up her mind on Jessica.

"Well she's one to watch isn't she? We'll have to keep a close eye on her because if she steps out of line we'll land on her like a ton of bricks. That's all we need – a psycho loose in the villa isn't it?" They both giggled and entered a café near the sea front.

Once seated they looked at the menu and decided they both wanted the full English breakfast with two pieces of toast. They both agreed that it reminded them of home and talked about when they last ate one. The waitress came over and took their orders and left them talking at the table while she went to get them two coffees.

It was Kimberley who missed home the most and these last couple of days she felt the urge to walk the streets of Manchester once again. She spoke to Nicky about it and hoped she felt the same but as she told her Nicky exploded with disagreement.

"What the fuck. Why are you missing home? We have it all going on here love and what's back in Manchester? I'll tell you, fuck all!" She reeled off all the good things in Spain and hoped Kimberley was just having a moment with herself. Kimberley listened and knew deep inside she was right, but the need for home was still strong inside her.

The waitress brought their food over and they sat

eating it as if they had never been fed. Nicky had ordered extra mushrooms, while Kimberley ordered extra black pudding. They threw bacon on to the toast and dipped it in the bean juice. Nicky laughed as she watched her eat.

"We're so common aren't we? We use our bread to soak up any juices from food so we don't miss out. I'm the same with anything that has gravy on it. I need bread to soak up anything that's left on the plate." Kimberley nearly choked with laughter and shouted out so everyone could hear.

"Us northern girls love gravy, don't we?" A few onlookers smiled and knew exactly what they were talking about as they folded their bread and dipped it in anything they could. Nicky checked her watch and told her they would need to hurry as Dennis would be waiting for them.

Five minutes later the hunger pangs had vanished and they left the café to go and meet Dennis. As he was a close friend of James's they knew he was dicing with death meeting them but Dennis had always had a big crush on Nicky and would do anything to get into her knickers. People said he had mental issues but Nicky thought he was an alright kind of guy.

Walking to meet him was like the walk of death. Everyone's eyes seemed to gaze on them as they located him. Once Dennis had seen them he nodded and told them to sit down for a minute while he was finishing talking to some guy at the exit. Dennis was a large man and had thick black hair. His hairy arms were toned and he resembled a gorilla. His tracksuit bottoms hung from his arse and you could see the top of his white Calvin Klein boxer shorts. Even the small of his back was covered in a mass of black hair and Nicky nudged Kimberley as she laughed.

"Fucking hell I bet he never gets cold with all that hair. He looks like cousin IT from the Addams family." Kimberley giggled and nudged her in the waist.

"Shhh he'll fucking hear you. You know what he's like. He's a fucking stress head and he won't see the funny side of it." Dennis stared over to them and they immediately stopped laughing. He wobbled toward them and told them to sit down in the corner of the pub. Tommy's was quiet at this time of the day and the music was soft and low as Kimberley looked round. Once they were all seated he sat with his hands down the front of his pants and played with his cock. His legs were stretched out and he didn't seem embarrassed that they were watching him. Dennis was from Newcastle and spoke with a Geordie accent.

"Right ladies, what can I do for you?" but before they could answer he spoke to Kimberley with a concerned voice. "Fucking hell, James would shit bricks if he saw me talking to you two. Word on the street is that when he finds you he's gonna do you in big time." Kimberley sunk her head while Nicky answered.

"What's up with him the daft twat? Kimberley's not been with him for months. He needs to get over it. He treated her like a slave anyway, what does he expect?" Dennis agreed but told her to watch her back as he had heard through the grapevine he was still looking for her and knew she was working at some villa.

"Right, let's get you sorted out. I've got be out of this place in a minute. People to see, places to go, you know how it is don't you?" Nicky moved towards him and kept her voice low and told him she wanted a gram of white and twenty Ecstasy tablets. Kimberley asked why that many tablets and she laughed and told her it was party time and everyone needed to relax.

Dennis walked away from them and went into the gents. He was only gone a few minutes and he returned and passed her the drugs. She handed him the cash and he shoved it straight into his pocket. Dennis now gripped Kimberley's shoulder and warned her about James. He also told her not to stay long in town because he knew someone somewhere would have spotted her and been on the blower to James filling him in on her actions. Dennis now looked at Nicky and winked. He told her how good she was looking and asked for her to come and meet him but as usual she fucked him off leaving him in a foul mood.

Kimberley shit herself and panic ran through her veins. She didn't know he was still looking for her and urged Nicky to get the fuck out of here. They both left Tommy's like rats leaving a sinking ship and Kimberley kept her head dipped as they made their way towards the car. Once inside Nicky started the engine and her temper blew.

"Why's that cock still thinking he owns you? He's a proper tosser if you ask me. He should be moving on instead of getting busy on you." Kimberley agreed but her heart sank thinking of him on her trail. They pulled away from the town centre and headed back towards the villa in silence.

From a distance James sat in his black Audio with the window opened slightly. He threw his cigarette end from the window as he set out to follow the girls. When he'd received a phone call telling him Kimberley was in Tommy's his heart skipped a beat. He immediately left what he was doing and jumped in his car, only wearing a white pair of shorts and his trainers. He'd seen Kimberley from a distance and had wanted to deal with her there and then but he gritted his teeth and thought he would wait until the time was right.

James drove quite far behind them and knew they didn't have a clue he was following them. He sipped his chilled bottle of Stella Artois and placed it between his legs as he drove. The music played in his car and it was his favourite song by The Smiths 'This Charming Man.' He sang along with the words and nodded his head slowly as he watched the girls in the distance.

James was getting bored of the driving and wondered where the fuck they were going, when he saw them take a side road and head up it. Scratching his head he followed them and saw them heading towards a large white villa at the top of the hill. James pulled up and watched their every move. He scratched his head and wondered who the fuck lived there. He knew when he got back home he would get his people on it and find out exactly what she was up too.

"Fucking little slag," he whispered. "Well let's see what happens to you and your little mate now. You dirty fucking slappers." He turned on the car engine and skidded from the side road, leaving a cloud of dust behind him. Every second he drove his temper was exploding and he wanted to know who was protecting her. He tormented himself with all the different scenarios and couldn't deal with the thought of another man loving her. James still cared for Kimberley but he'd wanted to rule her and have her at his beck and call. Even when he was with her he still slept around with other women but she was his comfort blanket that made him feel safe at night and he wanted her back where she belonged, under his thumb and under his spell once again.

James pulled up outside his home and screeched the car to halt. He searched for his mobile phone and started the investigation to find out exactly what his ex-girlfriend was up to. Once he found out what she was up to he planned to deal with her good style.

Kimberley was strangely quiet when they entered the villa and Nicky had to tell her not to let the bastard get to her. She hugged her and told her everything would be fine and not to worry, but Kimberley knew in the back of her mind James wasn't a person to mess with but for now she put it to the back of mind and plastered a smile on her face and pretended all was well.

12

THE GUESTS WERE GETTING READY for the evening meal and they were all dressed in evening wear. Nobody knew that tonight one of them was going to get the fantasy they had requested. The seating plan had been set out and Belinda was practising her moves under the table to make sure she would fit underneath without being detected.

Mr Ferris looked in the mirror in his room and straightened his dicky bow. He had no idea that tonight was the night his sexual desires would be fulfilled. He'd wondered about the other people at the villa and wondered if they were all there for the same reason as him. To the onlooker it just looked like a holiday villa and everyone was still doing what you would expect to see in any holiday resort. He sprayed his clothing with his Gucci aftershave and looked for the key to his room. As he walked out of his door Paul and Susie were on the small corridor. He smiled at them and he could tell Paul looked uncomfortable in his suit. Susie was standing in front of him straightening his bow tie and you could tell by his face he was angry. As he listened further he smiled at the Manchester accent. Paul looked at Mr Ferris and started to speak.

"Fucking can't stand anything tight round my neck, that's why I've left the Mrs at home," Paul laughed his head off and introduced himself. He reached his hand out for him to shake it. Mr Ferris thought about telling them his proper name but thought against it straight away.

"I'm Mark, nice to meet you." Paul nodded and Susie was all over him like a rash.

"I'm Susie, and I'm here with my good friend to make sure he doesn't get himself in any trouble." Susie liked what she saw in front of her and wanted to let him know she was a free agent. They all walked to dinner together and once they reached the dining area they checked their names on the little white cards that were at each place around the table.

Mark was sitting facing Susie and Paul and was quite relieved they weren't sitting next to him. The rest of the guests started to arrive and they all looked amazing. As they were all seated Geraldine and Victoria came to join them at the table.

Belinda waited under the table and dodged people's feet as they uncrossed their legs. All she could see was black pants and highly shined shoes. The ladies round the table were like a sea of colour. All the dresses were bright and pretty. Belinda laughed as she saw one lady pulling her dress up to scratch her fanny. She had to hold her mouth so her giggles couldn't be heard. She watched the women kick their shoes off and knew the night ahead would be filled with the unexpected.

The night was going well and Paul kept everyone amused with his tales and jokes. He was a true comedian and Geraldine loved his sense of humour, he reminded her of Bernard Manning, a famous comedian, and when he pulled some of his faces she pissed herself laughing.

Jessica sat at the table and her wine glass was never empty as she gazed at Geraldine from across the table. Her heart was breaking when she looked at her and she wanted to be at her side where she belonged instead of across the table where she couldn't be near her. She frowned as she looked at Victoria next to her and knew she would have to get rid of her, if she stood a chance to be with Geraldine.

Mark started his meal and loved the way it was all set out. His roast potatoes were crispy just the way he liked them and all the vegetables were crunchy and not over cooked. As he sliced his turkey he felt something cold on his leg. At first he just used his other leg to try and move it, but as it continued he felt his face go blood red.

Belinda was knelt under the table and she struggled at first to get herself in a comfy position. She tickled his legs first and stroked them up and down. Mark now knew that his dream was about to come true and felt his cock swell. Belinda slowly unzipped his pants and unshackled his beast. At first she struggled to pull his trouser snake out but once it was freed she set about teasing it with her tongue.

People spoke to Mark round the table and he found it hard to answer the questions they asked. Belinda knew when he was talking and played with his cock harder and faster to listen to him struggle. She found it funny and did it all the more. Mark's shoes were pulled off and she watched his feet curl as she took his throbbing cock to the back of her mouth.

Geraldine secretly watched Mark and knew he was in heaven as his eyes rolled and he kept covering his eyes every now and then when the pleasure was too much for him to hide. Belinda had been teasing him for around ten minutes and now she wanted to finish him off. She pulled at his pants and encouraged him to slide them down a little. The large table cloth covered everything that was going on and no one had a clue he was getting sucked off under the table.

Belinda licked his bollocks and caressed his love shaft as she started to bring him to orgasm. She guided her finger up towards his arse hole and she heard him cough loudly as she entered him. His arse felt tight and she slowly slid in and out of him. His ball bag was quite hairy and large. She nibbled at them causing him to move his arse about a bit. She was determined now and set out to make him shoot his load.

His manhood slid in and out of her mouth as her finger penetrated deep inside his arse. Her other hand was caressing his legs and she could feel any moment now he was going to explode. Her hands were that busy it reminded her of trying to pat your head and rub your stomach at the same time.

Mark hung his head and wiped trickles of sweat that had appeared on his forehead. At one point Paul had asked him if he was feeling okay and he had to lie and say he was feeling a bit under the weather, saying he had a terrible irritating cough that was causing him stress. He smiled as Belinda sucked him off and within minutes he was closing his eyes feeling the pleasure inside. He'd wanted to shout out and tell everyone what was happening but he managed to maintain his composure and shot his load all over Belinda's face as she finished him off under the table.

Geraldine noticed Mark's face changing and raised her eyes to Victoria telling her to check him out, and she too had seen his face change and smiled knowing it was another job performed well.

Mark felt his spunk fire out and squeezed the table cloth in his hands to help with the feeling. When he'd finished he slowly lifted the table cloth and saw a pair of big hazel eyes smiling at him. He winked at her and placed the table cloth down over her. He slowly pulled his pants back up and zipped his fly trying to recover from the experience.

Belinda was now stuck under the table and she felt trapped and needed to stretch it out. She felt horny now and felt like she had missed out. Looking round under the table she could see Jessica's long legs and thought she would have a little fun with her.

Making her way to her she crept up between her legs and pulled the tablecloth up so she could see her. Jessica smiled and pushed her head back but her laughter escaped and she had to pretend she had thought about a funny story. Belinda carried on along the table and did the same thing to the other members of staff round the table and it had the house up with laughter. The guest thought they were all crazy and looked at each other feeling a little left out.

Once the meal was finished they all went into the party room and the drinks and music started to flow. Paul was whispering to Susie and stood at the back wall with his back against it, moaning as usual.

"When do you think I will get what I've paid for? Hope it's not at the end of the week, I want it now." Susie stood at the side of him and kept her voice low.

"They said in the email it could be any time in the week and you might get it twice if you're lucky so stop fucking moaning and wait." Paul mashed his face up and grabbed Susie's arse.

"Well I suppose I can fuck you until then can't I?" Susie grabbed at his nuts and laughed as he squealed like a pig with the pain.

"Ay you cheeky fat fucker, I'm here for a holiday, not to get rammed by you every night. You said all I had to do was to watch you that's all, so think again if you think you're emptying your sack on me tonight." Paul laughed loudly as she let go of him. He told her that he loved the way she spoke to him and knew she loved him really. Susie just shrugged her shoulders and secretly watched Mark from the corner of her eye.

A few of the girls had dressed up and preformed pole dancing round the pool to entertain the guests. One of them had got up and tried their hands at it and had the place up with laughter as her stiff body collapsed to the floor. The pole was silver and cemented in the ground, it had been Jessica's idea and she loved the freedom it gave her when she danced around it.

The night was pleasant and a cold wind filtered through the villa. The floodlights from above lit up the grounds and the swimming pool looked magical as the lights shone on it. Jessica now danced for the guests and Geraldine walked over to look at her in action. Victoria was on her way accompanied by Nicky and Kimberley.

The song by the Eurhythmics played and Jessica mimed the words to 'Thorn in My Side' as she danced. Her black bra top looked full and her breasts looked fantastic. Her oiled body looked toned and her legs seemed to have a wet look about them. Geraldine lit a cigarette and sat on a table watching her from a distance. Jessica felt her presence and slid up the pole like a coiled snake. Her eyes looked sad as she danced and years of torment seemed to be trying to escape from them as she folded her body round the pole. Geraldine felt a chill as she watched her dance and she felt sadness for the years that had gone by. The secret they shared seemed to be pulling them towards each other and it was only Victoria's voice that broke the trance that Geraldine was in.

"It's all been a dream come true hasn't it love?" Geraldine shook her head and realised it was her she was talking to and answered her as she was seated at the side of her with Nicky and Kimberley.

"Yeah it's been amazing. If this week is anything to go by, we're all on a winner." She went on to tell them that the emails were still flying in and it looked like they were booked up for the next three months.

Kimberley was sat with her pink cardigan hung from her shoulders. Since they'd spoken to Dennis she couldn't stop shaking and even the thought of seeing James sent shivers down her spine. Nicky was high as a kite on coke and she'd had requests from some of the guests to supply them with drugs too.

Paul was sat at the next table alone and watched Susie strut her stuff with Mark. He didn't get jealous but he wanted something to happen for himself before he exploded with desire. He'd already taken a Viagra tablet just in case tonight was the night and he sat with his rock hard cock feeling rather embarrassed at the size of it in his pants.

Susie had clicked with Mark and they sat chatting inside the villa like they had known each other for years. Mark loved her northern humour and cringed at some of the things she said but he liked her even though she wasn't someone he would meet in the normal world.

Gaynor had requested to be driven into the countryside to sightsee and Lance knew she wanted more of what she'd received earlier. Geraldine had told him not to fuck her again tonight and he knew it was going to be hard to refuse as he could tell by Gaynor's face she was rampant for him.

The night came to an end and a lot of the guests were disappointed that their fantasy hadn't happened but they knew they couldn't predict when or where it happened and that made them even more excited knowing it could be sprung on them at any time during the week.

Paul went to bed alone and left Susie with Mark still drinking and laughing. He felt like a spare part as he sat with them and eventually left them to it.

The last fantasy of the night was for Mrs Bell. Her name was Clare and she'd requested in her email that every night when she went to bed she wanted seven men to come into her room, dressed in tiny black shorts and a dicky bow, so she could take her pick of which one she would have sex with. She had stressed in her email that all the men should be covered in baby oil and carrying a silver tray.

Clare was sixty years of age and looked like an egg on legs. Her fat legs looked like she needed to pull all the fat up to stop it drooping round her ankles. Her face was pretty but her treble chins hung onto her breasts like they had given up years ago trying to look perked. Clare had very thin grey hair and she had no style to her shoulder length mess. Geraldine rounded all the men up and told them exactly what was needed from them. They had to bring the gardener in, as Lance had left them a man down and they needed one to fill his place. Once the oil was applied by Nicky and Kimberley she made them stand together against a wall so they could take a look at them. Once this was completed Nicky marched them to Clare's room and knocked at the door. At first there was no answer and they had to knock again before they could hear a soft voice telling them to enter.

As they entered Clare was lay on the top of the bed with a pink transparent gown on. You could see the concern on the men's faces as they saw her for the first time. Her fat spread across the bed like a duvet sheet and as she lay on her side trying to look sexy her breasts came together and formed one big mound of tit.

Nicky was dressed in a black pencil skirt and a crisp white cotton shirt. She looked like a school teacher with her black rimmed glasses hanging from her nose. In her hands she held a clipboard and a silver pen. As the men lined up in front of her she spoke to Clare with a firm soft voice.

"Mrs Bell, these are the love slaves for tonight. Can I ask you to look over them and tell me which one you would like to use tonight." Clare licked her lips and twirled the grey strand of hair that had fallen onto her face. The men stood tall with their shoulders back like soldiers on parade and secretly hoped they didn't have to fuck the beached whale in front of them.

Clare's eye's looked over them and she cast her eyes to the second man in the line up. Looking down at his crotch she felt excitement and knew his package looked like it could satisfy her needs. Once her mind was made up she told Nicky her choice was made and the others left the room with a smile on their face. Nicky now spoke to her and cast her eyes over to the man of her choice.

"Mrs Bell, I hope Ben will satisfy your needs. If you have any problems with him please tell me and I will make sure he will be whipped for his actions." Clare nodded and told her Ben looked like the obeying type and she didn't think she would have any problems with him. Nicky told her she hoped her night would go well and left the room leaving Ben looking like a lamb being sent to the slaughter. As she left the room she was greeted by the other men who were falling around laughing.

"Fucking hell poor Ben. I'm so glad she picked him. She looks like a pig in a fit." Nicky told them to quieten down and moved them along the corridor at speed. As they neared the other rooms she laughed with the men.

"Ay I wouldn't laugh if I was you. Remember she wants a different man each night, so it's only a matter of time before she had her wicked way with you lot, so be warned." The smile dropped from their faces but they still found humour in that Ben was the first one to part Clare's tash.

A few of the men left the front room now and Nicky stayed with the ones who remained drinking and snorting cocaine. Kimberley had gone to bed early and Nicky knew it was the thought of James finding her that had changed her into a nervous wreck.

Jessica came to join Nicky and she too sniffed the white powder laid out in lines on the glass table. Jessica looked troubled and as soon as she had a minute Nicky asked her if she was alright.

"What's up chick, you seem a bit down are you alright?" Jessica fell back onto the leather sofa and felt the effect from the drug before she commented.

"I'm fine honey, just a bit of shit in my head that I have to deal with. Don't worry about me I'll be fine." Nicky turned the music up and started to dance round the front room trying to get the men dancing with her, but with no results. Jessica watched her and knew she too was lonely and needed attention. Pulling her body from the sofa, she stood and started to strip for the men. As she danced she looked fierce and every beat of the song came with a movement.

Paul heard the music from his room and thought he was missing something. Grabbing his clothes from the side he took his hard cock to investigate. As he entered he looked at Jessica stood there with just a black thong on. His eyes danced with excitement as she saw his face. Walking towards him she touched his neck with her finger, and teased him with her movements as she squatted down in front of him.

All the men's eyes were on her and Paul was chuffed that she had picked him to dance with. With silver high heeled shoes on, she stood with one leg on the chair and the other on the ground as she swung her hips. As she bent down you could see her fanny and Paul nearly came in his pants there and then.

Once the music had finished Paul made his way to where she fell. He was like a dog on heat and didn't care if she was pissed out of her head he still wanted to fuck her brains out. As he spoke Jessica tried to focus on his face but couldn't see straight. All she knew was that she didn't want to sleep alone and she grabbed his face and kissed him. Her tongue teased his and she could feel his weapon pressing against her side.

Paul asked her if she wanted to come back to his room and he pulled her hand up as soon as she said yes. He hurried her away from the room before anyone saw him leaving with her. That's all he needed, some caring friend looking out for her, he thought as he left.

Jessica walked the corridor in her thong and Paul's over sized t-shirt on her body. As they got to the room his hand shook as he couldn't get the key in the door fast enough. Once inside Jessica wasted no time and pushed him onto the bed. She loved being in control in the bedroom and made no secret that she was the boss. Paul pulled his clothes from his body as if they were on fire. As she tried to focus her eyes she found the fat man on the bed.

Jessica sat on top of him and pulled her black thong to the side as she guided him inside her. Her legs looked like she was sat on the toilet and she began to thrust to and fro on his cock. Her hair flew about her body and she swished it about his skin as she jerked harder on his fat cock. Paul loved it and tried to move his arse up and down until she slapped him and told him she would do the work. Paul thought all his Christmases and birthdays had come at once and lay still enjoying the pleasure she was giving. As she rode him she held her right nipple in her hand and twisted it with force. Her rhythm quickened and her body tensed as she found heaven. Paul's arse was now like a sewing machine needle and he quickly found his orgasm.

"For fucks sake," he shouted as he felt himself ejaculate deep inside her. Jessica didn't stay on top of him for much longer and she fell off him like she'd just realised who he was. As she lay at the side of him she cringed with despair and started to cry. Paul tried to comfort her and tried to make light of the matter.

"Fucking hell love I'm not that ugly am I?" Jessica ignored him and stood swaying from the bed. Her eyes could see where the door was and she made her way there as fast as she could. She never said goodbye to Paul and as she left she didn't look at him once.

Once she'd gone Paul smiled to himself. Things like that had never happened to him and he knew once he got home and told the story, no one would believe him as he'd been a bullshitter all his life.

Jessica found her way back to her bedroom. She felt

sick inside and wanted to end her life. Previously she'd attempted to take her own life six times but had always been rescued before it was too late. In her mind she wanted the one thing she couldn't have and felt completely at her wits end. Everyone was asleep in the bedroom as she fell onto her bed. The room was spinning and she held onto her bed to steady herself. A plan was starting to unfold in her mind and she knew Geraldine would be by her side at the end of it. She laughed to herself and closed her eyes leaving a menacing look all across her face.

13

GERALDINE AND VICTORIA were living the dream and all the guests left the villa with a smile on their faces. The next lot of guests were due to arrive that afternoon and everyone was running around getting everything ready.

Despite the success of the venture, Geraldine looked worried as she sat by the pool drinking her ice cold drink. There was something bothering her and she felt uneasy. For a few nights now she'd been woken in the early hours by a strange noise outside. Every time she walked outside she couldn't see anything. She knew something was there but nothing could be seen. Walking around the grounds she checked for evidence. She didn't know what she was looking for but she needed something to reassure her.

Victoria walked at her side and asked her if she was okay. She'd seen the change in her lately and worried she was doing too much work. Taking her hand in hers she kissed her finger tips and smiled.

"What you thinking about honey?" Geraldine turned her head and looked into Victoria's face.

"Something is keeping me awake each night. I know something is out here each night but I don't know what." Victoria pulled a chair up and sat with her legs crossed.

"Something like what? Why haven't you told me this before?" Geraldine lit a cigarette and inhaled deeply.

"I don't want to worry you love. It's been happening a few nights now and it's really winding me up." Victoria looked into the distance and told her all about the CCTV they had and she was just being foolish. She reached for her drink and started to sip at it slowly. She could hear the phone ringing in the distance and told Geraldine they needed to move their arses as that was the call to say the guests were on their way.

Geraldine stood slowly as Victoria waited. Grabbing her hand Victoria told her they would go and check the CCTV to put her mind at rest.

"Told you didn't I! Who the fuck is it?" As they stared at the small TV screen they could see a shadow running in the grounds. Victoria rubbed her arms and felt sick but Geraldine carried on watching.

"I fucking knew it. Who the fuck is he? Do you think he's a pervert or something? Because, he's not actually doing anything, he's just sat there smoking his cig looking at the villa."

The man looked tall and his black clothes made him look spooky. A baseball cap was hung over his eyes and his face couldn't be seen. They checked the video and realised this man had been there each night for the past week and his movements had always been the same.

"We need to call the police, don't we?" Victoria walked to the phone on the small office table and picked up the receiver.

"No! No!" Geraldine shouted, "you can't fucking

phone them. We're running a business here. We don't want them knowing all our stuff. Just let me think for a while."

The mini bus pulled up and the guests walked from it with smiles across their faces. As Victoria watched them from the small window in the office she nearly collapsed.

"It's Oscar!" screamed Victoria. Geraldine lifted her head from the TV and looked at her for a second.

"Who? What did you say?" Pulling the blinds back they peered through the small gap.

"What the fucking hell is he doing here?" Geraldine moaned. Victoria's face was white as she walked up and down the small room looking for answers.

"Geraldine, go outside and see what he's up to. He must have booked in a snide name. Get his details and I will check his stuff on the booking form." Geraldine walked to meet the guests and spoke in a warm voice.

"Hello everyone I'm Geraldine and I hope you're going to enjoy your time here. If you just follow me to the reception, I can sort out your rooms and give you all the details you need." A few of them cheered and started to follow her. She kept her eyes on Oscar and looked at him in more detail.

Oscar was third in the queue and he stood looking pissed off as she dealt with the others. When he came to the desk he was grumpy and he couldn't wait to grab the key from her hand. The form he'd filled out was in the name of Mr Samuel Jones. Once he'd taken the key she shouted to one of the men to come and take over. Quickly she took his details to show Victoria.

"Samuel Jones he's signed in as love. Get his details up and let see what he's up to." Victoria logged in the computer and typed at the keys as fast as she could. She sat watching the screen tapping her fingers on the desk as she waited.

"Here he is the twat." Scrolling down the page she started to read his fantasy. "The dirty cunt. Have a read of this." Geraldine leant over her shoulder and together they read word by word what he wanted to happen.

"I'll whip the dirty fucker. He's paid four grand as well to wear his gimp mask and get slapped about." Victoria was ranting and raving, clenching her fists as she read over it again and again. Geraldine held her shoulders from behind her and sniggered.

"Why don't you dress up and do it? He would never know, just keep him blindfolded." Victoria nearly choked as she tried to speak.

"Not a chance, he's a dirty bastard. He told me it was a stage he was going through and here he is still being a perverted twat."

Her blood boiled at the thought of him being so close to her. As she inhaled she smirked and stood from the chair.

"I can't let him see me. That's all I need that nosey fucker on my case." Geraldine held her waist and tried to calm her down.

"What you should do is be his mistress and give him the fantasy he's paying for. Wait until he's finished then reveal yourself. He will shit bricks."

Victoria chewed on her bottom lip and swung her body from side to side as she stared at her with mischievous eyes.

"You know what, I just might do that. Imagine his face when he sees it's me." She laughed out loud and asked Geraldine did she mind.

"No love you go for it, it would be so funny to see him get his payback. Make sure you whip the bastard as hard as you can though, make him squeal like a pig." Victoria grabbed her hands and bent her over smacking her arse as if she was her mistress.

"And that's for being a dirty perverted fucker, when you had a lovely wife at home." She slapped her arse cheeks softly and giggled as she started parading round the room.

"He's going to die isn't he? Revenge is sweet isn't it? The bald fat fucker will have kittens when I reveal myself." Geraldine just smiled and enjoyed seeing her laughing for once.

Victoria ducked and dived round the villa for the next few days. She wore her sunglasses twenty four hours a day. Every time she saw Oscar coming near her she quickly moved to another spot and kept her identity hidden. She watched him from behind her sunglasses. His Speedo trunks made her smile. He'd always worn them on holidays with her and she hated the way he thought his knob looked massive in them. The trunks were red and his fat belly hung over them as she watched him sit on the sun lounger facing her. He'd aged so much since they'd been together. She looked sad as she started to read the newspaper. She had never come to terms with the way her marriage ended and even though her life had changed so much since her days with him she still thought he had serious issues. She lay back and stared at the newspaper thinking about her ex-husband.

A couple from Liverpool had also arrived today and their accent kept the crowd amused as they gathered around the swimming pool. To look at them all, you would have never guessed in a million years they were sex addicts. The fantasies had all been quite basic this week and nothing really shocked Victoria like it had before. Sat alone she re-read Oscar's request. He'd described everything so well, even down to the words he wanted her to use. Victoria didn't know her ex-husband anymore as she leant on the windowsill reading his sordid little fantasy.

Geraldine was still sat in the grounds and wanted to go to the place she'd seen the intruder. She quickly jogged down to the position she'd seen him on the CCTV and kicked at the white gravel. Her eyes were drawn to a small gap in the fencing. Pulling her dress up she tiptoed up to the fence.

"So that's where he's been getting in," she mumbled. She placed her body in the gap and looked what lay on the other side. As her head squeezed through the gap she wriggled her body to the other side and stood on the outside of the grounds. Looking left then right she dusted her dress.

The view was breath taking as she took in the Spanish landscape. Everywhere looked peaceful and she could hear a few cars in the distance. Walking down the hill she headed for the front entrance of the villa.

"Right, I will catch the twat," she whispered. Pressing the buzzer on the gates she asked for them to be opened. The voice seemed shocked when she told them her name and she could hear them speaking to each other. She kept her plans to herself and walked up to the main entrance. As she approached Jessica was stood watching her and smiled as she came to her side. "Where have you been?"

Geraldine winked at her and told her she had been to see a man about a dog and sniggered. Jessica remembered her dad using that saying when she was a child and knew it was her way of saying don't be nosey. Jessica loved being by her side and she looked liked a devoted puppy as she walked with her. Geraldine chewed her chewing gum like a horse with an apple and thought she would do a bit of flirting with her.

"You look amazing Jess. I wish I could look like you." Jessica smiled and jumped at the opportunity.

"Let me give you a makeover. I've always been good with things like that, what do you say?" Victoria had been locked away all day hiding from Oscar and at the moment Geraldine was bored shitless so she agreed.

Back in her room, Jessica pulled out her box of makeup and placed a white head band round her hair. Her hands were shaking slightly and she tried to calm herself down. She plonked herself onto the bed and placed a folded pillow between her legs, she patted at the pillow telling her to come and lie there.

"Your eyes are gorgeous, do you know that?" Jessica smirked. Geraldine smiled and looked up towards her. She could see the insides of her nose and chuckled. She started to relax and closed her eyes and began to speak.

"We had some good times didn't we. Remember that pervert in school, hope he's dead now don't you?" Jessica didn't answer straight away and Geraldine opened her eyes to see what she was doing.

"Oh, don't get upset love. I'm sorry for talking about it, it's just that I thought you'd be over it." Jessica sobbed and tears fell from her eyes as if years of emotion had been unleashed.

"I'll never get over what that cunt did to us both. He ruined my life, you know? You saved me. If you wouldn't have come along that twat would have gone on forever. I wonder if he's still teaching?" Geraldine sat up and turned to face her with a look of fear on her face.

"If he's still teaching, he'll still be fiddling with the kids. Fucking hell I never thought about that. Do you think we should make a phone call and check him out?"

Jessica wiped her eyes and looked anxious.

"We don't even know where he works, so how can we find out?" Geraldine looked towards the ceiling and bit her lip.

"Surely there must be a phone number for the education department in England. If not we will write a letter to the police in Manchester with his name and what he did to us." Jessica pulled at her hair and dipped her head.

"Geraldine that's a life that's behind us now. I couldn't cope with anyone knowing what he did to us both."

"Well you're not coping by the looks of things and that dirty wanker could still be out there making girls lives a misery." Jessica sat with her legs still apart on the bed and sunk her head. Geraldine could see Jessica was upset and calmed her as she climbed up onto the bed and sat next to her.

"We can write a letter anonymously. We'll give them all the dates we were there at the school and tell them exactly what he did to us. He's probably wanking over somebody's arse as we speak." Jessica sobbed and tears fell from her eyes. Geraldine cradled her and looked like a big sister holding her sibling.

At last Jessica agreed, "Okay let's do it. You're right he deserves everything he gets, but please don't mention our names. I couldn't cope with the publicity it would bring."

Black tears fell from her eyes and she sniffled as she patted at the pillow again for her to lie down. In her heart she wanted to tell her just how she felt about her and as she looked down, she took her chance. Her breasts could be seen through her dress and the bare skin looked sexy. She wanted to touch her so much. Slowly she slid her fingertips onto her warm skin and stroked it slowly as she spoke. "I've never forgotten what we shared in school. In a way, I still haven't got over you. You were my hero and you saved me in more ways than one. In fact I think I'm still in love with you."

Geraldine held her breath as she felt her hands on her skin. Her words had hit her like a bullet to the heart and no matter how hard she'd tried to deny it to herself, she felt the same way. Jessica's long hair tickled the side of her face as she leant forward and slowly kissed her lips. Their eyes now met and the reality of what was happening hit Geraldine.

"I'm sorry," Jessica whispered but it was too late she was now sat up and was holding her head in her hands. Her face was still covered and Jessica sat at the side of her. She paused for a minute and slowly peeled her fingers one by one from her face.

"It was only a kiss. I'm sorry, but I love you so much. Do you know how hard it is every day, watching you and knowing you don't feel the same way?" She lifted her face up and took it into her hands. "I love you Geraldine. I know I shouldn't but my heart won't let go of what we shared so many years ago."

Geraldine stared into her eyes. This was the same girl who'd meant so much to her years before. Caught up in the moment she moved her head closer to hers and kissed her slowly.

"I feel we have shared something special too and I'm fighting with my heart every time I look at you." Geraldine now stood and walked to the door with her head dipped. Jessica felt her world falling apart and sighed. She watched her every movement and got ready to throw herself onto the bed and cry her eyes out.

Geraldine locked the door and stood with her back

pressed against it. She checked the door was locked one last time and walked to the patio windows. Pulling them together she turned and stood looking at her. Her emotions were now on fire. Jessica came to the side of the bed and smiled. They wrapped their arms round one another and fell back onto the bed.

"What about Victoria?" Jessica whispered, but no reply was given as they kissed each other passionately.

Clothes were pulled from their bodies and within minutes they were both rolling around naked. Jessica licked her nipples and caressed her body slowly. Her hand stroked along her legs to find her legs ready to accept her. Dipping her fingers gently inside her she could hear her breath quickening. Geraldine always liked to be the one in control and stopped her movements as she rolled free. Jessica moved her long blonde hair from her face and knelt up to meet her lips. Their hands caressed each other's bodies and they both satisfied each other's needs as they kissed. Their tongues danced with each other and the passion and lust could be seen between them.

Lying in one another's arms they felt safe and as if nothing else mattered. Their lovemaking lasted around twenty minutes and they both shared a cigarette after they had finished. The cotton sheet was spread across them and you could see the shape of Geraldine's hand moving slowly up and down her body. The two lovers were entwined – Jessica was safe once again and she opened her heart to Geraldine telling her how she would like things to turn out.

"Let's leave here. We can both be so happy." As if a hot drink had been split on her, Geraldine jumped up from the bed.

"Listen Jess, I'm not ready for anything like that just

yet. We've had a good time, but we don't really know each other do we? I mean it's been years since I've seen you."

Jessica sat up and looked hurt and she could tell by Geraldine's face she had said the wrong thing and quickly back pedalled.

"I didn't mean to sound demanding. I just think we could have a great life together. I don't think Victoria is what you need." Geraldine sat back on the bed, and felt a bit silly for over reacting.

"Victoria is a lovely lady and I would never hurt her. She has been through so much you know?" Jessica raised her eyes to the ceiling and shrugged her shoulders.

"We all have a story to tell honey, but it's all about being happy. If you can hold your hand on your heart and say she is everything you want in life, then I will gladly walk away, but I know by looking at you, that something is missing."

She reached for her and kissed her slowly as she kept her eyes wide open. Geraldine looked in heaven and she could feel the passion in her kiss.

"You're like a drug Jessica. And I think I'm addicted." She laughed and threw her body onto the bed. She dug her head into the pillow and kicked her legs like a spoilt brat.

"Why can't I stay faithful? She has never said a bad word to me or treated me badly, but here I am with you." Jessica loved it and spoke with a cocky tone.

"Admit to yourself, you need me like I need you." The bond they shared from years before was still there no matter how much Geraldine tried to fight it.

14

VICTORIA HAD PUT ON a black rubber dress. It had taken her ages to get it on and she felt a little stupid as she looked at herself in the mirror. The dress had holes in it for her breasts to hang out of and the metal studs round it made them look sexy. The black stockings had little pink bows on them and her black patent boots made her legs look sexy. Her black leather hat was twisted to the side of her head, and she held the pink mask in between her fingers, looking apprehensive.

"Do I look a twat?" she asked as she looked at herself in the mirror at every angle. Geraldine shook her head.

"You look like a sexy minx. Make sure you whip that fat fucker's arse until it bleeds." Victoria giggled and walked up and down the bedroom cracking her whip against the marble floor.

Oscar was sat in the bondage room wearing a black gimp mask and a dog collar. His red thong looked a little tight as he wriggled about on the bed trying to get comfy. Checking his watch he'd previously placed on the side he became quite anxious. The door opened and he could hear an Irish voice shouting at him telling him to keep his head facing down.

"Don't you dare look at me, keep your head down you dirty perverted cunt." Victoria stood tall as she entered the bedroom and came to his side. Her hat peak was nearly touching her nose now and the small mask she wore hid her true identity.

"Get on the floor. How dare you sit on my bed?" The man in front of her fell from the bed and curled into a small ball as she kicked at him softly were he lay. Victoria smiled as she pulled his thong from up his arse. "That's because you eat too much isn't it. I hate fat men." She cracked the black leather whip against his arse cheeks and she could hear him squealing like a pig. Looking at him she felt in control and quite turned on by his humiliation.

Lying on the bed she pulled one of her legs up towards her chest. Her crotchless knickers could be seen as she leant over the bed and poked at the fat pudding of a man still curled at the side of her.

"If you're hungry I've got some pussy for you to eat." He quickly moved from the floor and placed his head between her legs. Quickly she grabbed his head and slapped him. "Have you no manners, you dirty little low life. Ask me if you can taste my fanny first, don't just dive in. Do you hear me?" she could hear him mumbling underneath his mask and sunk her nails into his back. "I can't hear you, what did you say?" He sounded like he was in pain and she could just make out what he was saying.

"Please my lady, could I taste your vagina?" Her legs widened and he pulled her knickers to the side. Sitting up on the bed she could see his pink tongue sliding in and out of her. Quickly she pulled at his head and told him to slow down.

"Stop being greedy and save some for the others." His rhythm slowed down and she found herself loving the way she was feeling. Within minutes her orgasm was found and as she came she let out words she never knew existed.

"Eat my come you fat fucking animal. Eat it, fucking eat it." Her face was angry and she played her part well.

Oscar was sweating in his mask and loved the way his mistress was treating him. She climbed on his back and made him crawl round the room on all fours. His knees were hurting him but he continued wanting to please her. Victoria whipped the fuck out of him and her own tormented years with him seemed to be in every crack of the whip. His screams were at their highest now and she sat on the chair looking at the man she once loved.

"Get on your feet scumbag and play with your poor excuse of a penis - if you can find it!" Her head tilted to the side as she gritted her teeth. "I bet you've never satisfied anyone with that poor excuse of a manhood have you?" She touched her mask and thought about revealing her identity, but held her fingers still as she continued.

"Do you have a wife dirt bag?" She watched him as he shook his head and grasped her leg near his wobbling body. With a swift kick she shouted as she bent down to where he was. "I said stand up and fucking answer what I've asked you. How dare you remain silent when I'm asking you a question?" She held the whip in her hand and brought it behind her waist to get a better swing. With one almighty swish she whacked his body with the leather straps. "Have you got a wife, you perverted twat?" His voice was tragic as he spoke like a small child who had been caught in the act.

"I've been married but I'm divorced now mistress." Victoria wanted to know more and whipped him making him howl with his own pleasure. "Why did you get divorced? Wasn't she enough for you?" She was sure she heard him snivel as he continued and her heart missed a beat knowing he was talking about her.

"My wife was a lovely lady mistress. It was me who was unfaithful."

Her whip struck him several more times now and she had to stop and think before she hit him again as his skin was starting to bleed. The lines of lust on his back looked red and burnt and she sat down to steady her nerves before the conversation went on. Her voice was calm and low and sadness filled her as she heard the man she once loved tell her about his estranged wife.

"I liked kinky sex," he paused and sat down with his eyes still looking at the floor, "my wife wasn't into all that. She found out about me and my needs and got rid of me after that." Oscar crossed his legs in front of him. His head lifted and he seemed to be looking at her through his mask. She pulled her hat over her eyes and made sure he didn't recognise her.

"Did you ever ask her if she liked kinky sex?" he huffed and shook his head.

"No mistress, I felt so ashamed of what I liked in the bedroom. She was prudish and I know she would have been mortified by the whole thing." Touching her legs she stoked from her calf to her thigh with him looking at her every move. Tapping her teeth with the end of the whip she continued.

"I'm pretty sure your wife would have done anything for you given the chance. I think you underestimated her didn't you?" His reply was muffled as she kicked him in the ribs with the heel of her boot.

"Right take off your thong, and let me see what you have to offer a woman." Peeling it off, he stood with his small penis erect waiting for instructions. Victoria looked at him and felt strange.

"I think I still love him," she whispered to herself. Beckoning him to her side she kissed him. As she inhaled the smell of his aftershave it brought back the years they had spent together. He'd always worn expensive aftershaves and tonight was no different. The voice she'd used all the way through his fantasy was weak now and she struggled to keep up the Irish accent.

Sex began and his fat arse moved like never before on top of her. Geraldine was a million miles away from her thoughts and everything felt so right between her and her ex-husband. Even though the sex was rough and fast, he still remained gentle in his touch. She somehow forgot her role and as she neared her pleasure she shouted out his name.

"Faster Oscar, fuck me baby." Oscar carried on for a moment but stopped dead in his tracks. Lifting his head up slowly he tried to look at her face. Realising her mistake she scratched his back and made him continue by biting his skin.

Once it was over, she lifted her shaking body from the bed and collected her equipment. Oscar was still on the bed in a world of his own. She was just about to walk out of the room and as if it was a magnet pulling her back she turned and faced him. The words were playing on her tongue and she couldn't bring herself to tell him who she was.

Oscar could sense she was still there and asked would she help him unbuckle his mask. The straps were fastened behind his head and she knew it would be a real struggle for him to get it off by himself.

"Bloody hell, who fastened these straps?" she chuckled. Her voice sent a shiver down his spine and he recognised it. Not thinking he spoke her name.

"Victoria, is that you?" her head spun and she dipped her head trying to do her Irish accent again. He raised his body from the bed and lifted her hat. She tried to struggle but he just pulled it away. He nearly keeled over as he saw the colour of her hair. Everything looked so familiar and as he lifted up her face mask, her identity was revealed. At first he was gobsmacked and he rubbed his bald head pacing up and down the room. She felt dirty at this moment and pulled at the rubber dress to try and cover her legs.

"What the fuck's going on Victoria?" His temper was exploding now and his face was red as he wiped the trickles of sweat from his forehead. Covering his body with a nearby towel he sat by her side with his head shaking from side to side. "I don't believe what's happening I'm in Spain and my ex wife is working in a fucking brothel performing sex acts for every Tom, Dick and Harry." Her shame couldn't be hidden and he grabbed at her wrist as he shouted in her face.

"Come on then, what the fuck's going on. Am I dreaming or something?" As if her courage had been found she fronted him with a cocky voice and spoke like she was in control.

"Oscar I think you're forgetting why you came here aren't you? You're the perverted cunt who paid for all that stuff; I just did it to prove to you that I'm not as stuck up as you thought. The business is mine and Geraldine's and when I saw you get off the mini bus I knew what you'd come for. I thought you'd changed?" His eyes danced from her face to the wall and anywhere else he could look. Silence fell and they sat on different sides of the room. Oscar kept sighing and tried to get his head round what had happened.

"If it's any consolation to you, I thought you were amazing and worth every penny I paid." Choking, she placed her drink back on the side of the chest of drawers.

"Was I?" She waited for his comment and stretched her legs out in front of her. As he spoke she unzipped her boots and began to take them off.

"You were amazing. Where did you learn all them sexy moves from anyway?" Laughing she tilted her head and stuck her tongue out at him.

"I've always been a star in bed. You just never gave me the chance. Many a night I wanted to shag your brains out, but all you ever wanted was a quick wham, bam, thank you mam."

His round body waddled back over to the bed and jumped beside her. As their eyes met they both pissed themselves laughing as he said the word mistress over and over again. Their laughter filled the walls and they were like a young couple who had just met.

★

Sex, drugs and music filled the villa's rooms. Each room was fulfilling someone's fantasy and some of them had even found rekindled love. The night was nearly over and Nicky and Kimberley were ready for bed. They had both been involved in a foursome and now it was all over they sat by the pool having a nightcap.

"Fucking hell, I feel like a sperm bank love. Those two blokes were the ugliest fuckers I've ever had sex with in my life." Kimberley laughed as Nicky wiped her mouth.

"I can still taste his sprout come in my mouth." Kimberley broke into fits of laughter.

"What the hell is sprout come?" Nicky's face was serious as she swilled the brandy round her mouth.

"That scruffy bastard from before. His spunk tasted like sprouts." She giggled and she stood dancing round the pool taking the piss out of the men's sexual rhythm in the bedroom earlier. Her waist gyrated as she pretended someone was in front of her. Kimberley nearly pissed herself as she watched her performing.

From a distance, in the shadow of the night, James watched her as he lay flat in the corner of the villa's grounds.

He gritted his teeth together and dug his nails into the dirt as he watched her.

"Fucking dirty slut. You think you can leave me do you? We'll see you slapper, just wait and see what I've got planned for you." Resting his head on his folded arms he lay lifeless in the still of the night.

Finishing their drinks Nicky and Kimberley walked back inside. They had a quick chat in the kitchen then both made their way to bed. Kimberley thought about seeking some loving from Lance, but remembered he was pleasing another guest tonight.

"Oh well," she mumbled and trudged to her bedroom.

James moved to see when Kimberley was in her room. He knew once he saw her light go on, the time would be right to make the bitch pay for all the torment she'd caused him.

The villa was quiet and each room held the passion of the night. Victoria lay in Oscar's arms, and Geraldine cradled Jessica on the bed while she slept. Tormented by the sounds of the night Geraldine slowly moved Jessica from her. As she released her she clenched her fist together because it felt numb. Peering through the patio windows, she decided to go and check whether the intruder had decided he was giving them a visit tonight.

Picking her clothes up, she slowly slipped her dress over her head. Sitting for a moment she stared at Jessica's face. She looked so angelic while she was sleeping. Taking her index finger she kissed it and placed it on her head before she left.

The night was warm as she walked towards the main gates. Her eyes were all over the place trying to find any signs of the stalker. Lighting a cigarette she stood still and inhaled the Spanish air. James had spotted her almost immediately and scattered back through the hole in the fence.

"Fucking nosey cow," he grunted. "What the fuck does she want?"

His body squeezed through the gap in the fence and his heart was beating faster than usual. His breathing was deep and as he waited in the bushes on the other side of the fence, anger filled his mind. Geraldine searched every nook and cranny in the area and felt like she could relax when she found no sign of him. The soft lighting round the poolside made her feel calm as she headed back.

"What am I going to do? Why do I always get myself into this sort of shit? Fucking hell I have everything I need with Victoria." Her head rested on the table beside the pool and she ran her fingers through her hair lifting it up and down as she talked to herself.

She decided that she couldn't sleep in the same bed with Victoria tonight. The guilt she felt was tearing her apart. Lying on the sofa in the reception, her eyes flickered and sleep was soon only a moment away.

Like a cat in the night James sneaked back in through the hole in fence. He was carrying a petrol can in his hands. With his body dipped he dodged his way up towards the villa. His baseball cap hid his face and his black clothing helped him blend into the darkness. Pulling at the patio door of Kimberley's bedroom he slowly opened it. His eyes stared at the woman he'd once loved who lay on the bed fast asleep. Kimberley was wearing a small pair of green knicker shorts with white spots on them and a white vest top. One of her legs was hanging from the bed, and the cotton sheet was tucked between them. The room smelt of perfume. As he took in the scent his nostrils flared. James stood still against the wall and planned his next move.

Moving towards the bed his mind was made up. Placing his hands across her mouth he sat on the edge of the bed. He watched her face as she struggled for breath and kicked her legs frantically. She didn't recognise him at first, but as the moon moved into the room she panicked.

"Little slut," he whispered into her face as his head met hers. "Told you not to mess with me didn't I?" Resting his lower arm onto her chest he continued. "Selling your body for money are you?" he ripped at her top and bit down onto her breast. Using his other hand he gripped her hair and squeezed it tightly. His eyes looked menacing and she could smell the alcohol on his breath.

"One bit of noise from you and I'll cut you up. Do you hear me?" He released his hand from her mouth and she quickly sat up bringing her knees up to her chest. She was shaking from head to toe and her hands shook as he gripped her. "Scared are you? Well you should be. You've been a naughty little girl haven't you?" He looked at her and chuckled. He tugged at his crotch.

"I should fuck your brains out before I sort you out shouldn't I?" Kimberley made no reply and he could tell she was frightened of him. Pulling the roll of white tape from his pocket he looked at her and hated what she'd become. As he covered her mouth with the tape he pressed hard over it causing her to moan with pain.

"Shut up bitch. It's what you deserve. With your mouth shut, no cock can ever get in there can it?" She wriggled about on the bed as he taped her hand and legs together, he quietly spoke under his breath. "You haven't even said you're sorry have you. I've been waiting for months for you to come back but you've been too busy here haven't you with your slutty fucking, cock loving mate."

Kimberley's lay flat on the bed with no movement, only her eyes danced about looking petrified. Rummaging in his pocket he pulled out a small bag of white powder.

The cocaine was on the end of his key as he shoved it up his nose and snorted loudly. He looked fearless as the rush hit his body. Holding his head back he flicked the lighter and watched the small flame before his eyes. James opened the outside door slowly and brought in the petrol can. She couldn't see what he'd brought in as he she watched him bend down and place it on the floor. A noise outside the door caused him to freeze and he quickly came to the side of her and gripped her by the neck. As silence fell, he picked up the green can and placed it on her stomach. The smell of petrol was under her nose. As she smelt the fumes from it she kicked her legs and tried to free her body.

"Oh, doesn't the little baby like the smell?" He chuckled with an evil look in his eyes. "You're going to burn in hell you slut and all these other dirty cunts with you." He stood from the bed and picked the can up from her stomach. Holding one arm underneath it he started to sprinkle the petrol all round the bedroom. Her muffled voice could be heard as he came over to where she was.

The wet liquid was poured all over her body and she managed to roll off the bed and land at his feet. Looking down at her he swung his leg back and kicked her in the ribs. Her body doubled up in pain as she groaned near his feet. Pulling her hair up from the floor he looked directly into her traumatised face.

"Goodbye bitch, see you in hell." Pouring the last bit of the petrol on her he stood at the side and searched his pants for a lighter. Holding the flame in his hand he pulled the cotton sheet from the bed. Holding one corner he held the burning flame to it.

The sheet started to burn immediately. As the flames reached his fingers he threw it on the bed and watched the bed start to burn.

With one last look over his shoulder he spat at where she lay and fled into the night. His legs looked shaky as he ran and sweat poured from his body. Running like his life depended on it, he made his escape.

15

KIMBERLEY BANGED HER head against the door as the fumes started to hit her. She made it to the door and for the last few minutes her weak frame had been screaming for help. The flames crackled in the bedroom and the room was filled with black smoke. Her semi naked body now collapsed and there she remained still behind the door.

Nicky had fallen asleep with one of the lads who worked there. The thought of going to bed without any fun hadn't appealed to her. As she slept in the arms of a man she barely knew she was unaware her friend was burning to death.

Black smoke crawled from underneath the bedroom door and started to filter into each room in the villa. Oscar and Victoria were fast asleep and dead to the world.

As if someone had poked a knife into her waist Geraldine jumped from the sofa in reception. She sat up for a minute and rubbed at her eyes. They felt itchy. Reaching for her shoes she stood up and swung them over her shoulder. As she made her way to the corridor she stood still. She inhaled deeply and sensed something wasn't right. She traced the smell to the other corridor.

Her pace quickened and as she turned the corner smoke hit her. Pulling her dress up over her mouth, she began to panic. Her words were stapled to her tongue and she struggled to speak.

"Firreee" she yelled. The first door she opened she could see someone lay on the bed. She shouted again and watched the body move quickly towards her.

Smoke was filling the corridor at speed. The man who'd just joined her now started to run to all the doors shouting at full pelt. Each door was opened and within minutes people were running around screaming.

Geraldine pointed to the exit and grabbed a few people by the neck telling them to hurry up. The next door she opened she saw Oscar and Victoria lay together on the bed without any clothes on. At first she panicked and turned away, but quickly she turned back and shouted Victoria's name.

As she shouted their bodies remained lifeless on the bed. Smoke was now filling the room and she knew she had to get them out as quick as she could.

"Get up, wake up. You need to get out of here the place is on fire!" Her voice was desperate and when she saw Victoria open her eyes she quickly pulled at her.

Visibility was poor now as the three of them left the smoke filled room. The last door on the left was the only door she hadn't opened. Oscar tried to pull her along with them but she insisted she needed to check no one was in the room.

Pushing at the door she could only open it a little bit. She could feel something was behind it but couldn't see what. Pulling and pushing at it she managed to poke her head in the small gap, she couldn't see a thing. As she left to run and join the others she worried if someone had been left inside the room. All the guests were stood at the main entrance. Some of them were still wearing stocking and suspenders, and one man was dressed in a white doctor's jacket with a silver stethoscope hanging from his neck. They all stood shaking as they watched the villa go up in flames.

Geraldine was the last to come out and she shouted to everyone who was there.

"Has anyone phoned the fire brigade?" Pedro came to her side and placed a cream coloured cardigan over her shoulders and told her he'd already made the call. Casting her eyes round everyone she searched for all her staff members.

Suddenly Nicky screamed at them all and began to run back inside until Lance grabbed her by the arm.

"Nicky, what's the matter? You can't go back inside there you will be burnt alive."

"Kimberley's still in there I can't find her anywhere." Panic took over and Lance grabbed a jumper from one of them. Geraldine screamed at him as he set off running toward the flames with the jumper tied round his mouth and head.

"For fuck's sake Lance are you mad. Please come back, please." Her voice fell on deaf ears and all she could see was him bending down with his arms held up in front of his face as he entered the front doors.

Visibility was poor and he could feel the heat as soon as he entered. The sound of burning could be heard and he stood running from one place to another trying to remember which her bedroom was.

"Lord help me please" he cried. Tears ran down his face as he shouted her name.

"Kimberley where are you. You daft cunt where the

fuck are you?" His voice was low as he continued. The fire was in full blaze as he turned the corner. As if boiling water had been poured on him he froze. He could see very little, but he knew her bedroom was to the left of him just a little bit further down the corridor. Pulling the jumper tightly over his mouth he ran with speed towards the bedroom door.

He held the brass door knob, but quickly released it. He knew by the door handle that the room was ablaze. Blinded by the fumes he held his head down and used his shoulder to push at the door. The door opened slightly and with one last blast he ran at the door opening it a little further. Squeezing his body through the gap his legs was stopped by a large lump on the floor. As he pulled the jumper from his eyes he could see it was a Kimberley. Her body was covered in black ash. Panicking he pulled her lifeless body from the floor.

"Oh, Kimberley, please help me." His words were tormented and he knew by the ceiling collapsing on the other side of the room he didn't have long. Pulling her body up, he bent down and threw her over his shoulder like a rag doll.

The fumes were choking him now and as he struggled to get back out the door he could see large flames in front of him. His strength was weakening as he struggled to remember which way it was to get out. He knew time wasn't on his side and ran through the flames blinded by smoke.

"He's out and he's got someone over his shoulder!" shouted Nicky as he emerged from the blaze. They all ran to his side as they saw him keel over near the entrance. A few of the guests now ran to assist him and the man dressed in red suspenders and a black basque, helped them to pull her away from the blaze. Lance coughed loudly and struggled for breath as Nicky screamed over Kimberley's lifeless body. He quickly removed the tape from Kimberley's body.

"She not breathing, please someone help her." Nicky crawled on the ground to her side and placed her head on her chest, but by her face you could tell there was no heartbeat present.

The fire service had now arrived and the ambulance wasn't far behind them. They had to smash down the electronic gates with a large lump hammer to gain entry. Five or six Spanish firemen now rolled the hoses from the fire engine and ran looking about for the water point. Using a metal rod they opened the grid and connected the hose. They now ran towards the fire with three different hoses under their arms. They could be heard shouting at each other, as the guests stood like zombies watching them.

The medical team moved all the people from Kimberley's side. You could see them holding her wrist checking for a pulse. The medic was dressed in a green boiler suit and he looked as if he was melting as sweat poured from his body. A woman now joined his side and passed him different tubes from his black holdall.

Nicky was shaking with shock and one of the onlookers placed a long black shawl around her shoulders. Her words were heartbreaking as everyone watched her go to Kimberley.

"Please don't leave me Kimberley. We're a partnership, what will I do without you? We are girl power remember." Tears streamed down her face and Victoria came to her side to offer support as she fell to the ground in desperation.

One by one the guests received medical treatment. The police car now could be seen driving up to where they all stood. Geraldine looked at Victoria and they knew they would have to get their story straight before they spoke to them. Oscar gripped Victoria's arm as she left Nicky. But she looked at him and stared deeply into his eyes.

"I need to sort some things out with the police, I won't be long." Oscar tried to get into a big conversation with her but she ignored him.

Geraldine was now moving herself round the guests whispering to each of them.

"If the police ask what's been happening here tonight, just tell them we were having a fancy dress party." One of the holiday makers looked mortified and tried to follow her asking more questions, but Geraldine turned and threw her a look that would kill.

Looking at the man in suspenders she pulled him to one side away from Lance who was now on his feet still coughing. She told him the same and nervously laughed as he remembered what he was still wearing. All the staff were passed the same information and they all stuck to the same story.

The medics had finally found a slight heartbeat with Kimberley and rushed her to the hospital with sirens blaring. The fire was still fierce and everyone watched as they could see the villa falling apart in front of their eyes. Hours later the firemen won their long battle with the flames. As they pulled the hoses back towards the engine they looked exhausted. Their faces were black with soot as they pulled off their heavy clothing.

Tears were shed all night. The police had briefly spoken to Geraldine and Victoria, but as the fire service were finishing off, they asked them both to accompany them to the police station. Geraldine tried to sort out some transport for the traumatised guests and asked a few of the staff to take them to a local hotel in the town centre.

Looking over her shoulder before she got into the police car, her head fell back and she pulled at her hair. The car started moving and the broken English spoken between the police was enough to let them know what was happening. The black leather seats felt cold against her skin as she moved her legs over to be closer to Victoria.

"I'm shitting myself love. I don't know about you but my heart is pounding in my chest." Victoria looked in the rear view mirror before she spoke. She placed her hand up over her mouth and whispered.

"Just keep to the story we haven't done anything wrong just remember that. At the end of the day people have come to us for a good time and that's all we have done, given them what they have asked for." The police radio could be heard now and she watched the driver as he spoke in Spanish to the voice on the other end.

The journey seemed to go on forever and the lighting was poor as they drove along the bumpy roads. As they pulled into the car park, there was one cream two storey building facing them. The Spanish flag flew from the top of it and as they walked in they knew a challenge was facing them.

Once a translator was brought two policemen came to join them in the small office with six chairs around the table. A small white fan gave off little comfort, but it was better than nothing. Drinks were provided and the interview started.

Every now and then Geraldine kicked Victoria under the table when she was waffling on too much. Geraldine tried to do most of the talking but every now and then Victoria would add her input. As the interview came to an end, they both looked at each other and raised their eyebrows. They were told an investigation would now take place to find the cause of the fire and that they might need to speak to them again in the near future.

Days passed and most of the tenants from the villa went home. They'd told Geraldine that they had a wonderful holiday in the time they'd stayed there, but they were desperate to go home now due to the stress of it all.

The bill was paid at the hotel where they all stayed and it was lucky that Geraldine still had her handbag wrapped around her shoulder when she'd fallen asleep, otherwise they would have still been waiting for cash from their banks. Kimberley lay in the hospital bed and her barely conscious state left the doctors with little hope. As Nicky walked in she broke her heart crying as she fell at her bedside. Her once blonde hair was still covered in the black remains of smoke, and her face looked thin and drawn. Four tubes seeped into her body and a machine with her heartbeat stood at the side of her.

Police had been at her bedside since the fire and she was their only hope of finding out who'd set the villa ablaze. The evidence from the fire service proved that the fire was set intentionally. When everyone had heard the news that some arsonist had tried to kill them, fear set in. Each of them had wracked their brains working out who would do such a thing, but the answer was always left blank.

Kimberley licked her lips slowly as Nicky watched. She reached for a nearby jug of water and poured a small glass of water. Placing her finger in the glass she slowly placed it on her friend's lips to moisten them. Her lips looked cracked and sore. As she ran her finger over them she felt every line and began to speak to her.

"Don't you think you have chilled for long enough now, you lazy cow?" Her tears fell onto her face as the emotion she'd stored for days finally gave in. "Just open your eyes Kimberley. I'm all alone without you. Us Manchester girls need to stick together. Open your fucking eyes will you." Nicky sighed with desperation and felt her fist clench together. Taking a deep breath she sat back on the chair and started to sing a Wham song they'd sung together years before in Ancoats Youth club in Manchester.

"Wake me up before you go go. I'm not planning on going solo."

Tears fell as she softly sang the song. Her heart was low and she didn't hold much hope for her best friend. After sitting in the hot sweaty hospital for a few hours Nicky went outside for a cigarette. She listened to a lot of Spaniards shouting at each other and laughed at how fast they spoke.

Nicky inhaled deeply as she took the first drag from her cigarette. She saw an elderly woman nearby and watched her eagerly. The woman wore a long black dress with a matching shawl and her face had deep lines on her face. Her hair was grey and held back with a few a plastic grips. As she watched her pray she noticed some Rosary beads in her hand. The woman was mumbling something as Nicky watched her holding one tiny silver bead at a time. The woman's eyes were closed and you could see the determination in her face as she said some kind of prayer. Nicky wasn't a big church goer but the Catholic faith had always helped her in times of need.

Sitting on the wooden bench just outside the entrance Nicky sat next to her and placed the two palms of her hands together. Closing her eyes tightly she began to pray. Watching her face you could see her mouth moving but no words were coming out. After a few minutes had passed she opened her eyes and became aware of people watching her. Feeling embarrassed she made a quick sign of the cross on her forehead and went back inside. As she trudged down the long corridor everything in her world seemed to have fallen apart – without her best mate, what would she do?

Opening the door to Kimberley's room she felt depression strangle her. Pulling a booklet from the side she started to try and read the Spanish. As she sounded the words she chuckled to herself. Her singing also began and another song freed from her lips. The two of them had always loved Diana Ross, and the song 'I'm Still Waiting' was a favourite. With her head held down she swung her right leg and looked at the pictures in the leaflet.

Kimberley opened her eyes and the bright lights caused her to squint. Her body felt heavy and her legs didn't feel like her own. As she lay for a few minutes she heard singing and a smile appeared on her face. The words she wanted to say didn't come straight away but when they did they were low and husky.

"You could never sing that song as well as me," her eyes closed again as she struggled to open them. Nicky froze and looked over her shoulder trying to locate the voice. As she moved from her chair she looked outside the small window to see if someone was outside the room. Kimberley spoke again.

"Where the fuck am I? My head feels like a lump of lead." Closing her eyes she screwed her face up and tried to move. She had been awake a few times over the last few days but this was the first time she had been conscious.

She was weak as she tried to move, her frail frame looked lost in the bed. The doctors were in the room now and they were checking her pulse. Shining a little silver torch in her eyes they started writing on the notes that were positioned at the end of her bed held by a clipboard. Nicky was by her side holding her hand. She watched the doctors finish their checks and pulled the chair up next to the bed.

"I shit myself you know? I thought you were a gonner." Kimberley raised her eyebrows and a worried look appeared on her face. Her voice was low and she pulled Nicky closer to her.

"James did it."

Nicky stared into her eyes and waited for her breath to return.

"The bastard taped me up and threw petrol on me." Nicky held herself and her mouth opened but no words came out. "Please don't tell anyone it was him. He will make sure he kills me this time if I grass him up." Kimberley was fidgeted under the covers and Nicky could tell she was getting anxious.

"The dirty low life twat. Who does he think he is?" Nicky's face was white and drained of colour. Her knuckles turned white as she clenched her fists tightly. Kimberley was tired and the little time she had been awake had already made her exhausted. The doctors had told her she was lucky to be alive and told her to take things easy. As her eyes closed she drifted back to sleep and left a furious Nicky still gobsmacked by her bedside.

Thoughts of revenge were written all over her face. She kissed her friend's cheek and looked at her lying in the hospital bed.

"Revenge is sweet love and mark my words that tosser will pay," she whispered as she left. She looked like she had the worries of the world on her shoulder as a tear dripped from her eye.

16

TWO MONTHS HAD passed and even though the police knew it was an arson attack on the villa, they still had no suspects. Geraldine, Victoria and the rest of the staff were still staying in a local hotel but at the end of the week they'd all decided it was best to go their separate ways.

Oscar was like a fly around shit. He never left Victoria's side for a moment. It was obvious they were back together as his hands were always touching some part of her body. Geraldine was going to wait for the right moment and try to set things straight between them, as she too had drifted back to Jessica. Nicky and Kimberley were like a hinge and bracket – inseparable.

The next night a flight had been booked home to Manchester for them all. Manchester was the place they were all heading and they hoped to set up the same kind of sex scene there. Lance had jumped on the bandwagon with them and secretly hoped Kimberley and himself would become an item when Nicky eventually let her out of her sight. The insurance claim on the villa was all going through and the girls had given them their address in England to send any correspondence too.

Nicky sat smoking a cigarette. She stared into thin air and looked worried. Kimberley came and sat with her and told her they were all going to hit town that night as it was their last full night there. Nicky smiled and agreed they needed to chill and joined them all but she had a plan of her own to put into action.

Everyone looked great and considering what they'd been through, the smiles on their faces looked genuine. Heading into "Jumping Jacks" night club they were all pissed. Geraldine had seen Victoria heading to the toilets on her own and quickly followed her.

The toilets stunk of piss and wet toilet roll was scattered around the floor. A few women stood at the mirror straightening their hair. As Geraldine stood waiting she felt upset at the thought of speaking to Victoria. Placing two arms around her waist she waited for Victoria to come out of the cubicle.

"Come on pissy arse, some of us are bursting out here." Victoria smiled as she saw her and moved out of the way to let her past.

"Don't go yet honey," she shouted. "I want a quick word with you." Victoria looked up to the ceiling and turned to face the mirror on the wall. She'd dreaded this moment for weeks now and as she heard the toilet being flushed she turned to face the toilet door. Geraldine straightened her dress as she came out and stood next to her. Slowly she began.

"We've not had a moment by ourselves have we chick? I think we need to talk don't you?" Victoria agreed and Geraldine went first, confessing her sins.

"I never meant it to happen, it just did. I feel devastated that I've let you down. Me and Jessica go back years. I knew when I first saw her that I still had feelings for her, I just tried to block them out." Her eyes welled up and Victoria didn't act the way she would have thought, instead she put her arms around her and squeezed her tightly.

"I've been so worried about telling you too. Me and Oscar were the same. It just happened and all our old feelings just came flooding back." Geraldine put her head onto her shoulder and sobbed. The moment they shared was special and they knew they didn't have to go into any more detail as they both were happy with the choices they'd made.

They spoke for a while and decided when they got back to Manchester they would search for premises to continue their work. This time they had Oscar behind them and that meant money would never be a problem.

Jessica entered the toilets and she looked embarrassed as she walked towards them. Victoria placed one arm around her neck and started to speak.

"Jessica, this is one special lady in front of you," Geraldine smiled and took hold of Jess's waist as she continued. "I hope you two are very happy and I wish you all the luck in the world. I'm so glad you both found each other again after all these years." Jessica looked relieved. She was dreading the truth coming out but looking at the two of them she could see they would always remain friends.

Oscar didn't have a clue about Victoria's and Geraldine's love affair and that's the way Victoria wanted to keep it. He knew they'd been close but never dreamt in a million years they were lovers. Everyone was having a great night. Even Oscar hit the dance floor with Victoria and showed his dance moves. The two of them looked so happy and perhaps they both realised how much they still loved one another. Victoria told Oscar she'd changed since their time apart. Their sex life was wild and hot now and nothing like the sex they'd had when they were married. She accepted his kinky sex habits, only this time she was the one whipping his arse and not some slapper he was paying. He'd asked her how she knew so many new moves and she just laughed and told him she'd always been wild in the bedroom she just lacked confidence.

Jessica was in heaven. Geraldine was stood at her side by the bar as she whispered into her ear.

"I'm never going to lose you again. I love you so much." They placed their heads together and shared a passionate kiss as onlookers nudged each other.

"Have you seen Nicky?" Kimberley asked as she swayed in front of them.

Geraldine shrugged her shoulders and looked at Jess for her answer.

"She was over there before, but I've not seen her since then." All their eyes focused on the last place she was seen. Kimberley walked across the dance floor and checked every nook and cranny of the club. She was talking to herself as she swayed across the room.

"Bet you're in some little corner with a hunky guy aren't you, you little minx." Her eyes were finding it difficult to focus as she looked amongst a crowd of people in the corner. Standing for a minute she asked one of the lads near her if they'd seen her.

"I don't suppose you've seen my friend round here. She's this big," she lifted her hand out flat and raised it up above her shoulder. The young lad smiled and took his chance trying to flirt with her.

"No love but what's a nice girl like you, doing in this club on your own?" Kimberley was just about to answer him, when a hand gripped her waist from behind and spoke in a deep, cocky voice.

"She's not on her own mate, she's with me." The lad looked shocked and offered his hand to Lance.

"No problems mate, knew it was too good to be true," he shrugged his shoulders and turned away from them rejoining his mate's conversation.

Lance swung her round to face him and bent his knees to kiss her. Kimberley forgot all about looking for Nicky and enjoyed every minute she had with him.

At that moment, Nicky was waiting in the car park behind Long legs. Her body shivered as she sat behind a black car where she could get a good view. The lighting was poor and she struggled to see directly in front of her. In her long dress she held a knife which she planned to lunge into James's heart. Her fingers stoked along the blade as she held it in her hand. Thoughts were dancing in her head and at one point she'd changed her mind and headed back to the club but the urge for revenge pulled her back.

Drugs and alcohol made her unsteady. As she sat on the small wall she knew her mission wouldn't be far away. James usually left the club at about three o'clock in the morning and she hoped he didn't have a tart with him. Nicky knew his every move and he usually took the money from the tills home each night before he started partying with any women.

The car park was quiet. All she could hear were people walking past shouting at each other. Pulling a dark green scarf over her head she tried to keep out of sight. The old security man from the club could be seen near the far wall smoking a cigarette. He was a peculiar man and Nicky cringed when she thought of how he looked at all the young girls in the club. She watched him stand, flick his finished cigarette to the floor and head back inside.

James was a big man and she knew she would have to be quick. Chewing on her bottom lip she played with a few stones on the floor. Nicky had dressed like an old Spanish woman. A saggy long black dress covered any curves her body had and she looked quite fat and old. Nicky had already checked for any CCTV and knew no one would be able to see what she'd got planned. She hated James with a passion and hated the way he'd treated her friend. The secret she shared with him had kept her awake for many a night and now was the time to silence him.

Nicky had never told anyone she had seen James in

the last few weeks. She'd told him she was going to make sure the police knew exactly what he'd done. He was the arsonist and she wanted him to rot in jail. When she finished telling him her plans he'd laughed in her face and spat at her.

"Do whatever you have to do slut, but don't forget I'll make sure your best friend knows exactly what kind of a friend you really are." His words surprised her but she knew he was dangerous and couldn't take the chance of him revealing her secret.

Nicky had had a short affair with James when Kimberley was off her head on drugs. It had started suddenly and before she knew it, she was fucking him most nights while Kimberley slept. It didn't take Nicky long to realise he was an out and out bastard and she left his sorry arse behind telling him it was over. Yet she knew that if Kimberley found out their friendship would be over forever.

The sound of crunching gravel startled her. Raising her head Nicky looked underneath the cars to see if she could see James's feet – it was now or never if she was to make her move. Squeezing and rubbing her hands she tried to stop them shaking. As she raised her head she could see a large frame coming towards her.

"Come on you fucker," she whispered. Her heart pounded in her chest.

Tying the scarf firmly round her head she waited for the figure to pass her, like a lioness waiting to make her kill. As he turned to get into his car, Nicky saw James's familiar profile and dived onto his back, thrusting the silver blade deep into his back. She plunged it as fast and as hard as she could, gouging as deeply as she could. He mumbled something as he fell to the ground. Checking the area she knew she didn't have long.

Bending down she saw his eyes were rolling with his final, struggling breath. His trembling hand covered his chest where blood pumped from him. His white t-shirt was now covered in it.

"Payback. You tosser. Thought you could blackmail me did you?"

James started to shake and his legs were scuffling around the floor where he lay. Dipping her head she knew her job was done and she headed back into the night, checking over her shoulder to ensure no one had witnessed her brutal attack. Her head was spinning and at one point she felt like she was going to collapse. Before she headed back to the hotel she made her way towards the sea front.

The sea was calm as she stood looking out at it trying to compose herself. The small waves seemed to be laughing at her as they rolled onto the shore. She plunged her hands in her pockets and felt the blade. She knew she needed to dispose of it.

Looking in all directions she gripped the knife in her right hand and pulled it from her pocket before launching it into the Spanish sea. The sound of the sand crunching underneath her feet sent shivers down her spine. Only a few lovers saw her leave the beach but they were too involved in one another to notice the nervous wreck passing them. As she washed her hands in a large silver foot washer near the end of the beach, the blood ran off them swirling round and down the plughole. She checked her clothes for blood stains but it was difficult to see in the half light.

Music played along the sea front and holiday makers could be seen swaying from side to side. Nicky removed her scarf from her head and stuffed it into a pocket. Suddenly she was felt violently sick and started retching over the sea wall. Holding her hair back from her face she found it hard to breathe. Wiping her mouth she started to walk back towards the club. Her feet didn't seem to be moving and everything round her seemed to be in slow motion. Pulling her dress from round her neck she felt agitated. Tears fell from her eyes as she gritted her teeth and sighed.

"Got what he deserved, the no good cunt. He won't hurt anyone else ever again will he?" People passing her in the street stared at her but they assumed she was just another drunk. She hailed a taxi and headed back to the hotel. The driver watched her fall from one side to the other in his rear view mirror. He'd already told her if she was sick in the taxi she would have to pay to have it cleaned, but his words went over her head as she nodded at him.

★

Lance held Kimberley's arse as he rammed his cock deep inside her. Her moans of pleasure kept the other guests in the hotel amused for hours as they listened. Although their sex was rough and hard Lance held deep feelings for her. His hairy fingers caressed her curves and he watched her face as she turned to face him from behind.

"Fucking hell your cock's massive," she smiled arrogantly and as he changed his rhythm to circular movements and heard her groan with more pleasure.

Lance and Kimberley had conversations throughout sex. At one point he couldn't concentrate and told her to "shut the fuck up," but this only made her more determined to make him laugh.

"We Manchester girls can multi-task. We can talk, fuck and suck all at the same time." Her giggles made him weak at the knees and he fell off her telling her he needed a break for a while as they'd been shagging for the last hour and a half. They lay together with a smile on their faces as they rested. He twirled her long hair with his finger as he spoke.

"You know what? I could fall for someone like you," her eyes stayed looking outside at the moonlight and she felt unsure of the way she felt.

"It's amazing that the moon lights up all the sky in the world isn't it?" Lance chuckled.

"What the fuck does the moon have to do with anything I've just said?"

He rolled on top of her and pressed down with all his weight as he held her hands above her head.

"How do you feel about me then?"

He played with her hands twisting them about in his grip and nibbled at her neck. Her naked body wriggled about as he chewed at her skin.

"Oh, please stop it, you know how ticklish I am." The sound of a pig grunting come from his mouth as he continued and laughter exploded round the bedroom.

"Okay, okay, I hear you. Please stop now please." She slowly looked up into his eyes.

"I will be honest with you Lance. At the moment my head's up my arse and I don't know how I feel. I mean I love having sex with you. I mean who wouldn't; you're hung like a donkey." His faced looked disappointed and he knew he would get no sense out of her. Feeling deflated he rolled off her and lay with his hands looped underneath his head. Seeing she'd hurt his feelings she rested her head on his smooth chest and stroked her fingers across his stomach.

The hotel bedroom was basic. A small wooden unit separated the two single beds and one small drawer was at the top of it. Previously they'd pulled it from its position and joined the two beds together. A light green cotton sheet was pulled over their legs and they both had one leg freed from underneath it.

"Lance?" she whispered, "I know you think I'm being horrible to you, but I'm not. I just don't want to get hurt." Lying in silence he turned on his side removing her from his chest. He coughed and folded the pillow under his head. The light from the moon shone inside the bedroom and seemed to focus on his eyes. They looked glossy and full of love for her as he spoke.

"I'm not asking for much. I'm just saying if you gave us a go, who knows what could happen. We could be good together. We get on don't we?" She agreed and brought her hand up to touch his cheek. In her heart something was happening and she told him about how she truly felt.

"I think I could love you too Lance but I need you to promise me that you'll never hurt me." Now it was his turn to wind her up and he spoke in a sarcastic manner.

"Ay I never mentioned love. I just said I could fall for someone like you that's all. Fucking hell you bunny boiler." She kicked at him as she hid her head under the sheet. He could tell she felt embarrassed and popped his head under the sheet to be with her, feeling his presence under the blanket she started to laugh.

"Fuck off now. You've hurt my feelings. I'll never open up again." The giggles from under the sheets let you know she had forgiven him and the shape appearing underneath the sheets let you know he was now on top of her.

Nicky swayed into the hotel and entered the lift. The receptionist didn't notice her as she pressed the button for the floor she required. When number fifteen appeared in the display she trudged to her hotel room. The apartment was in darkness as she entered. Throwing the key to the door on the side she made her way to the bedroom. Just before she opened it she could hear the sound of moans and knew the rest of her night would be spent on the small sofa in the front room.

Sitting with her head held in her hands she started to pull at her clothes as if they were burning her skin. Turning the small pink lamp on, her eyes focused on the packed suitcases in front of her. The buckle on the case seemed stuck and as she pulled at it, she sobbed.

"Fucking daft bastard suitcase, fucking open!" Her hands were trembling in front of her. Pulling the grey leather strap from the buckle she unzipped the suitcase.

Searching through it she found a plain pink t-shirt and a pair of jogging pants. Heading into the bathroom she saw herself in the mirror. Pulling at her eyes she knew she had to pull herself together before anyone noticed she was upset. Turning the shower on, she ripped her clothes off her body like they were full of ants. Wrapping them into a small ball she placed them behind the door before standing underneath the warm jet. She pressed the soap hard against her skin but no matter how much she rubbed she could still feel her sins. Holding her head back she wet her hair and reached down for the green shampoo on the side. Foam fell onto her face as the water rinsed her hair clean and at last she felt fresh.

With a small white towel wrapped round her she made her way back onto the sofa. Despite the cool shower she still felt hot and sweaty but once she stood on the veranda for a few minutes she cooled down. She was exhausted. Lighting a cigarette she stared out into the night. She would soon be on her way home and hopefully she could put this nightmare behind her. The moon shone brightly in the Spanish sky, it seemed to smile at her as she exhaled the cigarette smoke. That big silver ball in the sky knew exactly what she'd done and she hung her head in shame as the reality set in.

The drugs she'd taken earlier had worn off now and she felt ready for sleep. Flicking her cigarette butt from the balcony she made for the sofa and rolled up on it in a small ball with her legs drawn to her chest. Staring round the room she located a bath towel and stretched over to get it, placing it over her she snuggled up and tried to fight with her conscience.

17

"COME ON LAZY BONES. We need to be out of the room by half past ten." Kimberley stood over Nicky wearing Lance's t-shirt that barely covered her arse cheeks.

Nicky had not long since been asleep and her heavy eyes showed her tiredness. Kimberley moved her over on the sofa and sat beside her. Her head was bent over her and she looked directly at Nicky's closed eyes.

"He told me he loves me. I can't fucking believe it. There we were just having a knee trembler and he blurted out how he really feels."

Nicky kept her eyes shut as Kimberley shook her body.

"Are you listening or what? For crying out loud, I have a trauma and need some advice. Wake up."

One by one her bloodshot eyes started to open. The tears she stored were ready to explode and she choked back her emotions as she continued to listen. Kimberley moved herself further onto the sofa. Bringing her knees to her chest she pulled the red t-shirt over her legs.

"I think I'm in love. It's all so wild I just don't know

any more. What do you think?" Nicky asked for a drink. Kimberley heeded the advice and hurried to the sink to get her a glass of water.

"Here, get this down your neck." Nicky sat up and reached for the drink, downing the lot in one go. With a smile on her face she placed the glass on the floor and lay back onto the sofa with a large yawn.

"Right, fucking love bug what's going on?" Kimberley blurted out all the ins and outs of the night and sat looking at Nicky for her advice. When she'd finished, Nicky held her head to the side and paused for a minute.

"I'm so made up for you both. You've been through so much lately and deserve some happiness. Go for it. What do you have to lose?" Kimberley rubbed her hands in excitement and dived on her friend.

"I love you so much Nicky. You're the best friend I've ever had." She kissed her on the cheek while she squeezed her half to death and jumped up quickly remembering they needed to get ready to leave. "I've packed all our stuff. It's just the last few bits that need going in the case." Kimberley left the room and headed to get washed.

Closing the door behind her she noticed more of Nicky's clothes left in a ball on the floor.

"For fucks sake, I thought I'd packed all the clothes" she snarled. Bending over to pick them up she noticed that patches of the clothes felt hard. Lifting the scarf up towards the light she could traces of something on them and thought Nicky had spilt food or drink on them the night before. Thinking no more of it she threw the clothes outside the bathroom and shouted to Nicky to make sure she remembered to put them in the suitcase.

★

Geraldine and Jessica were up and ready and had left the room early to go and get some breakfast. Oscar and Victoria joined them and the four of them sat facing each other as they started to eat. Oscar wasn't much of a breakfast person. He held his slightly burnt piece of toast in his hand and nibbled. The rest of them were eating a full English and they all looked starving as they tucked in. The atmosphere was quiet as they ate, as the waiters were cleaning vacant tables around them as more holiday makers arrived.

Nicky and Kimberley had packed all the stuff and sat in the hotel room for the last time. Lance had left minutes before to pack his own suitcase.

"Well it's home to Manchester now then isn't it? At least Geraldine and Victoria are going to set up again. What are we going to do until then?" Nicky waited for the answer and saw Kimberley shying away from the question. Resting her hands on her face she leant forward.

"I'm sick of doing the club scenes now. Lance has said we should both give all that kind of stuff up and try and just get a normal job." Her eyes focused on the ground as she waited for her response.

"Oh like that is it? Are you selling me out then? I thought we were a team?" Nicky stood up and paced the room. She kicked the sofa as she walked past it. "What about me? I've done a lot for you and now you're fucking jumping ship." Kimberley tried to backpedal as she could see how she'd hurt her feelings. Nicky grabbed her suitcase from the kitchen area and remained silent as she dragged it to the lift. Her eyes pumped tears and she looked in a world of her own. Kimberley sighed and left the hotel room shortly after her. Once they had put their luggage in the allocated area, they both headed for breakfast. As they entered they saw the rest of the group. Pulling a chair up at another table Nicky smiled at them.

"Late night?" Jessica giggled. Nicky's eyes looked black underneath and her usually bubbly nature had left her. Kimberley sat facing Nicky and passed her a coffee.

"Nicky, please don't go on one. I need to sort myself out. I can't keep doing what I'm doing for the rest of my life can I?" Nicky's bottom lip quivered and she held back her emotions. She too had wanted to change her life, but at the moment she couldn't afford to.

A middle aged holiday maker, sat not far from their table, started to speak in a loud voice.

"A man was murdered last night in the town centre. Stabbed to death they say. I think he was only young. An Englishman as well." The woman who brought the news was fat and flabby, she wobbled as she reached for her morning coffee. Her suntanned bingo wings nearly touched the table. She had everyone's attention at both tables nearby now and she sat back and crossed her arms telling them the whole story.

"One of the Scottish lads told me the news on the way down here. He said the police are all round the area near Long Legs nightclub. Tape is around the scene he said." Nicky's heart stopped and her eyes widened. Taking a deep breath she tried to change the subject but nobody listened to a word she said and carried on listening to the woman. Geraldine's face betrayed her thoughts. Jessica held her body and shivered as the thought of a murderer being on the loose took over, "I'm so glad we're going home and away from all this," she said.

Oscar looked at Victoria and nodded his head. He looked like he was talking to a small child as he continued. "Manchester's police would have made an arrest by now. These Spanish police just seem so laid back and don't seem to care. They think they have all the time in the world."

Nicky felt physically sick. Holding her stomach she quickly left the table and told Kimberley she was off to the toilet. Kimberley looked at her as she left. She stood to follow her but slowly sat back down as Geraldine started to talk to her.

"Are you all packed love?" Kimberley looked towards the door in anticipation and made herself comfortable in her chair again.

"Yeah. I didn't have a lot to pack did I? Most of my clothes were lost in the fire. My suitcase is empty near enough." Geraldine gave an endearing look and agreed.

"I'm the same love. Never mind when we get set up again the money will be rolling in and you can get a whole new wardrobe again can't you?" Kimberley nodded in agreement and reached down on the floor to grab her leather shoulder bag.

As she entered the toilets she could hear someone wretching in one of the cubicles. Standing still for a second she banged on the middle door.

"Nicky is that you in there? Are you alright? Open the door." Kicking at the bottom of it softly she heard the bolt being slid from the door inside.

"Fuck me. You look rough. What's the matter with you?" Nicky turned and sat on the toilet lid. Her hair was swept from her face with a gold clip and she sat pulling toilet roll from the holder to wipe her mouth. The white tissue paper skimmed across her mouth. Slowly she scrunched it together in her hand, and rolled it together in her fingertips. Kimberley stood in front of her and slowly placed her arm round her neck.

"You look like shit. Do you think you need to see a doctor?" Shaking her head she looked up towards her.

"I'm fine now. I'll feel better when we're on the plane and away from this shithole."

"Come on love, do you want me to get you a cold drink or something." She helped her up from the toilet and opened the door. Nicky went straight to the large mirror on the wall and wiped the smudged mascara from round her eyes with the tissue and prepared her face to re-join the others.

Geraldine and Victoria were walking towards the pool when they came to the top of the stairs and decided to go and join them. Sun loungers were placed all around and a sea of bright coloured beach towels were spread out on them. Spanish music played quietly in the background and a few children were swimming. The sun hid behind the clouds as they took their positions for some last minute sunbathing. Nicky lay on her side and placed her brown imitation D&G sunglasses over her eyes. The rest of the group came to join them and laughter filled the air.

Lance was by Kimberley's side and he nudged her in the side asking what was wrong with Nicky. Covering her mouth she mumbled to him that she was feeling under the weather. All eyes cast over to the pools entrance as three police officers came strolling in. They were talking to the bar staff and looking round the surrounding. Nicky was fast asleep as the others started to talk.

"I bet they are here over that murder aren't they," boasted Oscar. "It's about time they got off their arses and done a bit of investigating." Swigging his ice cold orange juice he sat up from his bed and discussed the murder again.

"It's scary isn't it, that one human being could kill another. They must have a slate loose or something. I mean you just don't wake up and think, 'Oh today I will kill someone' do you?"Victoria had to agree.

The poolside was busy now and the music was getting louder. Kids ran around chasing each other and water was splashing all over as children bombed into it. Nicky opened her eyes but kept her sunglasses on. Stretching her body she called to Lance.

"Have you got a drink there love? My mouth is so dry." Reaching down to the concrete floor he picked up a plastic cup full of Coke. The fizz from it had vanished and it looked as if it had been there for a while. Bringing the cup to her mouth she swigged it back in one gulp. Her head was tilted back as she finished the last mouthful. Wiping her mouth she looked round and grabbed Lance's wrist to look at his watch. The silver face told her she didn't have to wait long before they would be on their way to the airport. The sleep had done her good and her spirits had lifted. Standing slowly she walked to the pool and secretly bent down to fill the plastic cup with water. As her feet hopped about on the boiling floor, she held the cup behind her back.

Kimberley was lying flat on her back with one leg raised up. Nicky's face changed and a mischievous smile appeared on her face. Lance saw the cup in her hands and covered his face ready to shout out, but she placed her index finger to her mouth quickly and told him in a low voice to be quiet. Now Lance realised he wasn't the intended victim he relaxed and watched her stand directly over her friend. Her hand was held up high in the air and the plastic cup was tilted facing Kimberley. The rest of the group shifted positions to watch the prank and get out of the way. The water poured straight onto Kim's face and her body folded together. Turning her head from side to side she tried to work out what was going on. Everyone was doubled over laughing and Nicky leant down to comfort her.

"Oh I might have known it was you. You daft twat. Can't we tell you're feeling better ay?" Kimberley was sat up now and used the beach towel to wipe her face. Nicky sat at the side of her and rested her head on her shoulder.

"Oh babes, it was only a bit of fun. Come on forgive me." She made the movement of praying and jerked her body up and down in front of her to the amusement of the others. Kimberley smiled and stood.

"Right Lance, grab her!" He hesitated for a second and dived to where she was as Kimberley joined him ragging at her body.

"Oh, fuck off will you. These are the only clothes I've got," she screamed out as Lance picked her up and Kimberley tried to hold her legs together. She was now laid out flat except for her legs scuffling trying to break free.

"One... two... three...!" Nicky was in the air just over the pool. The splash was huge as she was entered the water. Holiday makers round the pool side sat up to watch the entertainment, within seconds her face appeared from under the water with black mascara dripping from her eyes. A smile filled Kimberley's face, as she clapped her hands together.

"Not so funny now is it?" Nicky swam to the nearby steps and pulled herself from the pool. Her clothes were dripping wet as her legs reached the top. She bent down to her long gypsy skirt and twisted the purple material together. A pool of water appeared at her feet as she pulled her vest top up revealing her stomach to wring out her top. Pulling her hair to the side she twisted it in her hands and mocked them all.

"I only poured a little cup of water over her and look

at me." Holding her arms out in front of her she looked towards Geraldine.

"I've got no other clothes so I will have to go home like this. I could die of pneumonia you know." Her face held a sarcastic smile.

Geraldine stood to hug her and told her she had some spare clothes she could borrow. She thanked her and turned to Kimberley who was sat on the sun lounger behind her.

"You know it's war now don't you, honey? Remember if you live by the sword, you die by it." Her face was alive with amusement as she moved to Kimberley to hug her.

They hugged one another and their forgiveness was obvious.

"Right Geraldine can I get them clothes from you now because I feel like a right scruff." Geraldine looked at her gold watch on her wrist and gathered her belongings from the side of her.

"Come on you lot. The coach will be here in half an hour." As if they'd shit their pants they all jumped up and headed to collect their belongings.

18

The coach pulled up outside the Flamingo Benidorm hotel and they all waited on the pavement for the driver to open the luggage compartment. The driver's dark black hair looked like you could fry an egg on it. The side of the coach held a storage point and as he took each case he threw it inside without a care in the world, then the journey to pick up other holiday makers began. Every pick up point added more passengers. As they boarded the coach some of them looked pleased to be going home and some looked upset as they waved to their new found friends from the windows.

Oscar now stood from his seat as they passed Long Legs. He could see yellow tape all round the murder scene. As he shouted out to the others they all came to the right hand side of the coach to take a closer look. Nicky remained seated and chewed on her bitten down nails. The skin round her fingers looked red raw. Her head remained low as they passed the scene and she sat looking out of the window on the other side. The noise on the coach was loud and some mouthy kid was sat two seats in front of them talking to a woman. As Nicky concentrated she listened to the lad who looked about fifteen years of age.

"Some sickos about isn't there mam? I wish I would have known, I could have gone and had a good look myself." His mother screwed her face up.

"John, just because you have watched a bit of CSI doesn't make you a detective." The teenager wobbled his head and reached his hands out in front of him shaking them in the air. .

"I know you muppet, but I could have helped them find some new evidence, couldn't I? I know exactly what to look for." His mother shook her head and turned to the window. She was used to her sons chatting shit so smiled as she tried to ignore him.

The journey to the airport lasted about forty minutes and as they headed onto the motorway Nicky looked through the back window of the coach. She stared at the rear view for a few minutes watching every car behind them. The airport was busy when they arrived and a lot of people lay on the grass verges with their suitcases next to them. The palm trees looked like something you would only see on a postcard and Geraldine commented on how nice they looked. The queue to check their luggage was long and people stood sighing in front of them.

Before Nicky joined the line she grabbed a small plastic bag from the trolley and told Kimberley she just needed the toilet.

"Hurry back. We shouldn't be long. The line is moving fast so be quick about it." Nicky held her hand up and acknowledged the comment.

The airport was busy and different nationalities were scattered at different check-in points. The duty free shops were hammered and people were running about grabbing last minute presents. Nicky hurried past the perfume shop and inhaled deeply. The smell of vanilla hit her as she held her breath taking in the aroma.

The toilets were just a few metres from the perfume shop. As she turned the corner to go in she could see an elderly lady with a cleaning trolley. She was dressed in a sky blue tunic and looked busy. Trying not to bring any attention to herself Nicky sneaked past her. Once inside she stood for a second as if she was gathering her thoughts. Stepping into the toilet she could hear voices. With her back against the door, she held a white plastic bag up tight to her chest and her knuckles turned white as her grip tightened.

Once the talking outside had stopped she pulled the white toilet lid down and sat on it. Sweat was visible on her forehead as she tugged at her cotton shirt as if it was strangling her. Slowly she untied the bag. Sticking her head inside she pulled out the clothes she'd worn the night before. As she felt the material her face screwed up with disgust and she shook her head.

"For fucks sake," she whispered. Nicky froze and her eyes stared at the door. Pulling at the clothes with her fingertips she placed them on her lap.

The sanitation bin at the side of her looked like a good way to dispose of them but as she bent over to lift the small silver lever up she hesitated. Having second thoughts she placed the clothing back into the bag and tied it tightly as if it held her secrets inside.

Unbolting the door she peered from inside and emerged looking both ways. Slowly she walked up to the large silver swing bin and pressed the bag deep inside it. Standing there she froze again. She quickly gripped the bag back out of the bin. Nicky decided she would take the clothes back home to Manchester. At least that way she would be able to burn them and be rid of them forever.

Nicky didn't wait a second longer and headed back to the busy airport with the clothes still with her. As she hurried back she could be seen smelling her hands and wiping them on her thighs. The walk back to the check-in seemed to last forever. Every time she passed a police officer or someone who looked suspicious she dipped her head and kept her eyes low. The queue had gone down by the time she returned and three people were stood in front of her. As she passed the others in the line to get to Kimberley a few people moaned. Nicky heard the moaning and just ignored them shouting "excuse me" as she passed them all. She found her suitcase and quickly placed the clothes deep inside it.

"Have you got your passport ready?" Lance asked. She searched in her brown leather handbag and placed it on the floor to get a better look as Kimberley moaned at the side of her.

"It's a good job your tits are in your bra love; otherwise you would lose them as well." Nicky looked at her and gave a sarcastic laugh.

"We can't all be perfect can we?" Nicky pulled her passport from her bag and held it up in her right hand.

"One passport ready for use your highness." Kimberley raised her eyebrows and softly kicked at her while she was still looking in her bag and chuckled.

The suitcases were now lifted onto a grey conveyer belt. The assistant weighed it first and placed some stickers round the handle. The words Manchester in bold black print made Kimberley's hair on her neck stand up. Rubbing her arms as if she was cold she turned to Nicky.

"I wonder what Manchester's like these days. I bet nothing has fucking changed." Nicky stood with a cocky look on her face and placed one hand on her hip.

"Nothing ever changes there love. It's just the same shit every day." Lance agreed and none of them were looking forward to the grey clouds of home.

Geraldine and Victoria were at each other's side for most of the journey. A lot of bridges had been built between them. It was decided that Jessica was to move in with Geraldine and Victoria would be going home to Oscar. Kimberley, Lance and Nicky were also going with Geraldine and they hoped they could soon get their new project up and running as soon as they got home. Oscar had told them of a few nice discreet places that were for sale and hoped he could get them cheap as he knew the estate agent very well.

They handed their boarding passes to the air hostess. Nicky commented how nice her uniform was and told them that when she was a young girl she had dreamt of flying all round the world. As they passed her she gripped Kimberley's hand and whispered in her ear.

"I fucking love that uniform. As soon as we get going in our new place that's going to be one of my outfits.

Do you think it would suit me?" Kimberley pushed her playfully and told her of a few more outfits she'd been thinking about getting. When they finally boarded they sat in their seats ready for takeoff they could hear the pilot telling them the emergency procedures. A flight attendant stood in the middle of the aisles and held her arms up to the side showing where each exit was.

The sound of the engine could be heard. Geraldine gripped the edge of her seat and sneakily looked out of the window. Jessica was at her side and saw her nerves were getting the better of her.

"I didn't know you didn't like flying?" but Geraldine struggled to speak.

"It's just the taking off and landing that does me in. I'm fine once we're up in the air." She moved her hand to take hers and stroked it softly as she watched her lean back in her chair. The leg room was small between each seat and Jessica found it hard to get comfy. Once the air hostess had finished her talk and they were up in the air the refreshment trolley came round. Nicky's nerves were terrible and as she reached her hand out to give the assistant money for her vodka and coke, Kimberley commented on it.

"Look at your nerves. That's too much beer, if you ask me." Nicky took the drink from the young woman and turned to face her with her usual arrogant face.

"I'm hungry, that's why my hand is shaking. I've not really eaten anything all day." Kimberley just huffed and didn't want to go into it, so she remained silent.

Looking out from the small window Nicky chewed on her lip. The secret she held was eating her up. Reaching out in front of her she placed her hand in some black netting at the back of the chair in front of her and grabbed a magazine. Flicking through the pages she tried to make conversation with Jessica at the back of her.

"Have you seen the prices of the perfumes?" The magazine she'd grabbed was the planes duty free book and she held the pages up over her head to let Jessica read it.

Jessica was blown away by how much some of the products were. She even made a comment that the watch they had priced at one hundred pounds would only be around forty quid on Manchester's streets. Geraldine went on to tell them that you wouldn't believe all the daft things people would try and reproduce. She told them about batteries and toothbrushes she'd bought in the past in Cheetham Hill. Nicky added her penny's worth and told them that there was even snide vodka about. The vodka she'd bought in the past had been on the news. She giggled as she continued.

"I was watching Granada Reports when I was last at home when I heard them talking about this fake vodka. Apparently it was sending people blind. As soon as I heard that I was up at the mirror checking my bloody eyes and doing eye checks on myself. That vodka gives another meaning to being blind drunk doesn't it?" Kimberley nudged her in the waist at the side of her and laughed.

"You're a fucking nutter you. No wonder I love you." The look they shared for the moment was endearing and they squeezed each other tightly as Lance commented that he felt left out. Nicky reached over from the window and dragged the side of his head down onto their laps. She told him they loved him too and to stop being jealous.

Oscar was drifting to sleep as Victoria stared over to where the laughter was coming from. She looked at Geraldine and smiled softly. The memories they shared were magical and she would keep them close to her until her dying breath. Victoria had learnt to live again thanks to

Geraldine, she'd taught her that whatever you like in life you should grab it with both hands. Sex is whatever you want it to be and if you want kinky sex, so what, go for it and enjoy it. Feeling a little sad that their time was over she looked at Oscar who now was fast asleep and resting on her shoulder.

"I'm a new woman now Oscar," she whispered, "I hope this time we can make it work and be happy together." Her words circled the inside of the plane and no one heard them but herself. Snuggling into Oscar she closed her eyes and slept for the rest of the journey.

19

The weeks passed and all their plans seemed to be paying off. They'd found a big eight bedroomed house in Cheshire to set up their business. The website was set up again and new staff were recruited. Geraldine and Jessica were as happy as ever and were never far apart from one another.

Lance and Kimberley fizzled out once they got back to Manchester much to Nicky's relief. He started escorting for some money to get them by at first, but as time went on he got more than familiar with a fifty year old woman. Kimberley knew something strange was going on but just put it to the back of her mind. The presents he'd received were only something she could have dreamed about; Rolex watches, a new car, the list went on and on. One night after he'd come home late he woke Kimberley up so he could talk to her. She had a feeling it was bad news as she watched him turn the small bedside light on. He held her hand with tears in his eyes and began to tell her the heartbreaking news.

Lance told her he still loved her but the life his mistress could give him was one he could only dream of. She was taking him to America the following week for an exclusive two week break. The news hit Kimberley hard, but she knew chances like that didn't come along every day and cried as she told him she'd always love him. For all the days she'd worked in brothels and clubs, she'd prayed for someone like that to come along to whisk her away from her troubles and she fully understood where he was coming from.

As she watched him leave, Nicky stood by her side. Once he drove away from the car park Nicky placed her arms round her and spoke.

"Looks like it's just me and you now isn't it? I will look after you love, don't worry." Kimberley sobbed all through the night and Nicky slept her side.

Weeks passed and Kimberley's heart was on the mend thanks to Nicky. They'd had plenty of nights out in Manchester and met up with lots of old friends. Kimberley's mother had made a change for the better now and she had rid herself of her old habits. The first time she went back to the family home she'd nearly fallen over with shock. As she walked into the house she couldn't believe how clean it looked. The smell of tater ash filled the kitchen and her mother was sat there repairing some clothes.

When her mother saw her for the first time she dropped the pair of jeans from her hand and ran toward her with her arms open wide. The moment they shared was heart warming and as she looked at her mother's face she saw tears in her eyes. Kimberley spent all day there with the family and caught up on all the local gossip. Her mother had found love again and for the last year she'd turned her life round. She didn't drink anymore and her forty cigs a day habit was down to ten. Her new man was Irish. She'd met him on one of the market stalls in Harpurhey. They started out as friends and within time they fell head over heels in love with each other. He'd told her from day one that she'd need to sort herself out and that's exactly what she had done.

Nicky never went back to see her family. She'd asked a few questions in the neighbourhood about them but realised they were worse than ever and decided to stay well away. She'd had enough of the heartbreak when she lived there and she couldn't stand the trauma that went on in her household.

Victoria and Oscar had decided to remarry and the following morning they would pledge their undying love together once again. The house Oscar had told them about came through and the website had already got clients booked in for the fantasy services. The business was incredibly popular and even Oscar commented on how well it was all looking. Each room in the house had a theme. Any fantasy you could have dreamt of was catered for. Nicky did as promised and went out to get her air hostess uniform and lots of other costumes as well. The night before the wedding they all met at the new house and partied well into the early hours.

20

OSCAR STOOD AT THE FRONT of the registry office. His face looked flushed as he watched his bride walk towards him. Victoria looked stunning in her long ivory dress. Everyone from the villa was present, even Lance turned up to celebrate their love. Her four bridesmaids looked amazing in their black silk dresses. Geraldine, Nicky, Jessica and Kimberley all stood to the left of her as she reached the front of the room. Comments on how sophisticated she looked could be heard from the guests as she faced the registrar. 'Breathe Again' by Toni Braxton faded out as the guests sat down.

Victoria's shoes were crippling her feet. She could be seen twisting her foot under her dress and whispering to Oscar that she couldn't wait to get them off. Oscar looked into her eyes as they exchanged wedding vows. His eyes leaked tears as he told her that he would love her forever. Sobbing could be heard from the guests as the service continued and everyone was shocked to find out it was Nicky who was so emotional. Kimberley placed her hand to her side and grabbed Nicky's hand trying to comfort her. Every woman dreamt of this special day and Nicky now realised that her dreams of becoming a bride were receding quickly.

The guests all headed back to the venue. The Orangery was Victoria's choice and everything was set once they stepped in through the doors. Around one hundred people were sat down for the meal. The tables were round and eight seats were at each and small gold name cards were placed all round them. Once the meal ended it was time for the speeches. Geraldine had written hers over the last few days and cried every time she had read it.

The long oblong table held the bride and groom and all the bridesmaids and best man. Bottles of wine were placed on each table. Nicky had already downed one bottle on her own and Kimberley was now watching her drink intake. The time came for Geraldine to make her speech. Everyone cheered as she stood up and silence fell. Clearing her throat she took a white creased piece of paper from handbag. She quickly glanced at the words she'd written and started to speak in a low voice.

"I would firstly like to thank Victoria and Oscar for such a lovely day." The other guests clapped and shouted out remarks to thank them. Once the noise died back down she continued.

"In my life I've met very few people who have inspired me the way Victoria has. In a way she has shown me how to love again." The words hit Victoria's heart and a single tear fell from her eye.

"I've known Victoria for some time now and she always sees the best in people. She doesn't judge people and takes them as she finds them. I hope Oscar knows how special she is and treats her as the princess she deserves to be." Her voice became emotional now and she raised her glass in the air and toasted the happy couple. The cheers went on for a few minutes and Victoria gave a small speech thanking everyone for coming. She also presented each of the bridesmaids with a gift. The presents all looked the same except for Geraldine's. She held the small box in her hand and when all the ceremonies were over she secretly took a look what was inside it under the table.

Lifting the small purple lid from the box she could see a shiny white gold ring inside. A diamond sat on top of the ring and a small white piece of paper was at the side of it. Checking no one was watching she slowly unfolded it. The writing inside it was Victoria's. The words read 'I've had your ring engraved. The words just seem to say it all.'

Lifting the ring out of the box she slipped it onto her middle finger. She held her hand out underneath the table and admired it. Quickly she took the ring off her finger and screwed her eyes up as she tried to read the message inside it.

At first the words were blurred but as she focused a smile appeared on her face. The words 'Northern Girls Love Gravy' were engraved inside the ring with two small kisses at the side of it. Her heart melted as she rolled the ring round on her finger. She looked to where Victoria was sat and smiled. Victoria winked at her and blew her a kiss, the message meant so much to Geraldine and she placed it on her finger promising herself she would never take it off.

The night went on and a good time was had by all. Victoria and Oscar were married again and the journey of man and wife began again. They had stayed at the new house for the wedding night and without saying you knew they would be having a night of naughty, kinky sex. Once they had waved the happy couple off Nicky and Kimberley went back inside for one last drink. They knew they would be starting work at the fantasy villa in the morning so with that in mind they thought it best to go to bed.

★

Morning light crept in through the thick checked curtains. Nicky and Kimberley lay in the double bed with their legs and arms sprawled over one another. The room was bright and Kimberley hid her head further under the sheets to escape the morning light. As her head ventured under the quilt she nearly choked. Her eyes opened straight away as she inhaled the smell of Nicky's fart.

"You dirty animal!" she shouted as she grabbed the corner of the quilt over her mouth. Nicky opened one eye and stretched slowly. Kimberley kicked at her legs under the covers and caused Nicky to wake up.

"You're like a fucking bloke. I don't know what you've been eating but that stinks." Nicky smiled and inhaled the fumes. As she giggled she pulled the covers from the bed and held it up with her legs letting the smell escape. They both struggled fighting for the quilt and laughed loudly.

Once the smell had disappeared they both lay there with big smiles on their faces. None of them had enjoyed any male attention for months and Nicky was the one to bring the matter up.

"I think my fanny's got cobwebs on it now, it's been that long." Kimberley agreed as she nodded her head.

"You're not on your own love. I feel like a virgin again. Well at least when we start work we will get a bit won't we?" Nicky jumped on her and held her hands above her head as she screamed out playfully.

"Oh no! I can't stand the thought of big fat horrible perverted men inside me again. The thought of letting one of them break me in again is unthinkable." As she tickled at her body their eyes met. They'd both slept together in the past and a dirty thought came into Nicky's mind.

"I suppose you could lick my fanny. It's better than nothing isn't it?" Kimberley wriggled from underneath her and freed her grip.

"I don't think so love. If anyone is licking pussy, it's you." Lying back on the bed they both stared into space. Nicky felt her hand had a mind of its own as she watched it crawl under the blanket towards Kimberley's thighs. Within minutes Nicky was caressing her legs and slowly teasing her over her knickers. The moment was explosive and the two sex starved girls attacked each other. Their kiss was passionate and they both needed each other at that moment. Nicky's mouth suckled round Kimberley's ripe breast, her tongue flicked her nipple slowly and she could feel by her thrusting pelvis she was getting excited. Slowly they both rolled on their sides and guided fingers into each other.

Orgasm wasn't far away when Nicky disappeared under the covers. Slowly she opened Kimberley's flaps and caressed her clitoris with her tongue. The long soft strokes made her feet curl up at the end of the bed. Kimberley's hands were hung over her head as she tugged at her hair. Her eyes flickered as her orgasm began. Once Kimberley had reached heaven she took the place between Nicky's legs. Spreading her arse cheeks open she licked carefully at her bum hole. Her long movements continued up towards her fanny. A sneaky finger slid into her arse hole and Nicky sighed with pleasure.

The whole episode lasted no longer than fifteen minutes. They both lay in the bed with nothing on but their small vest tops. Nicky looked over to Kimberley and commented on how bushy her lady garden was. Laughter filled the air and they both enjoyed the banter.

The morning was set to be busy. They'd both booked in a local salon to have their nails done. The image they had to portray was hard. Everything about them had to be perfect. Both girls had booked to be waxed as well. Nicky went for the completely bald look where Kimberley had what she called a Hitler moustache. The beautician had her work cut out with both the girls, but they knew at the end of it they would be stunning again.

Geraldine was in the office at the new house in Cheshire. As she sat facing the computer screen she concentrated hard and shook her head.

"Victoria, come in here a minute and have a read of this." Victoria entered the office and looked at her face.

"What's the matter love you look stressed out?" Victoria came to her side pulling a spare chair towards the computer.

"Have a read of this email and tell me what you think." Victoria leant forward and screwed her eyes together. Holding one hand to her mouth she stoked her thumb nail across her lips. When she'd finished reading the email she looked at Geraldine with a puzzled look on her face.

"How does anyone know Nicky is here?" Geraldine stood from her chair and reached for her cigarettes.

"That's what I thought. It seems a bit weird doesn't it?" Placing the cigarette in her mouth she flicked the lighter and inhaled quickly.

"Unless it's one of her old punters. She might have given them the website address."

"Yeah I never thought about that." Victoria said with a sour face. Geraldine carried on talking about the email's contents. The man had requested some really kinky stuff. After a few minutes they agreed they would tell Nicky as soon as she came into work. The opening night went to plan and the four guests arrived as expected. Another two guests were expected the following night. The people who came to the house could stay as long as they wanted. Some only booked for one night where some had booked for the full week.

Kimberley's first job was a large African man. When she had found out what he'd wanted to do to her she nearly dropped down dead. In his request he wanted to be joined by another man and for her to suck them both off at the same time. That wasn't that bad she thought, until she read that she would have to swallow both the men's come. Spunk made her heave and the thought of swallowing it made her stomach churn. Victoria had told her that she would have to stomach it, as the other girls were all busy with their clients. This left Kimberley in a low mood.

Nicky stared in the mirror as she concentrated putting

her mascara on. Her mouth was opened fully as she guided the small round brush from the black mascara. Victoria had told her about the email from the man requesting her company and she racked her brains trying to think who it was. The man was due to arrive tonight and she felt a little anxious. Nicky back combed her hair and stuck the occasional clip into it to break it up. Her silk red knickers were pulled up her legs as she looked in the mirror at them. The underwear was something the client had requested and she touched the front of them feeling the softness. Once her black suspenders were on she stepped into her black high heeled shoes. The red and black bra complimented her tits and she smiled as she pulled them together. The last thing to go on was a transparent netting housecoat that just covered her arse cheeks. After one last look in the mirror she squirted her Paris Hilton perfume on and headed down to the room where the man was waiting for her.

Victoria had told her that the man requested a video recorder in the room and a black sheet to split the room in half. He'd told them in detail that he wanted it pinned from the ceiling and to make sure the girl couldn't see him until he was ready to reveal himself. On the way down the narrow corridor Nicky could see Kimberley getting ready in a side room. Sliding one leg round the door, she paraded her look to Kimberley. Kimberley told her her outfit looked sexy and carried on pulling the large Velcro rollers from her hair. Seeing a bottle of white wine on the side, she grabbed a nearby glass and filled it to the top. Nicky knew by her face she was in a mood and tried to make light of the matter.

"Oh, you're still not moaning over swallowing a bit of jisbo are you?" Kimberley stood up and threw a roller at her.

"I fucking hate the stuff. I don't mind it on my body, but fucking two of them shooting their load in my mouth that's beyond a bastard joke." Nicky could see there was no point in arguing with her and downed her wine in one go.

"Right I'm off to my weirdo. See you in a bit, demon semen." She could hear her shouting abuse at her as she left the room and smiled as her housecoat opened as she plodded to her destination.

The white door looked clean as she knocked on it. She waited till she heard a reply telling her to enter and walked into the room. The room was painted dark red and a black sheet hung from the ceiling hiding the other half of the room. It didn't separate the room completely as you could see the television on the wall mount on the other side of the room.

The male voice she heard told her to sit down. Looking behind her, she located a red leather sofa. As she looked carefully she could see the silhouette of a fat man behind the black material. His voice was slow and deep as he spoke and he sounded pissed. Men were generally pissed when she'd performed her acts on them and he didn't seem any different. Sitting down she made herself comfy and crossed her legs. She pulled at her netted housecoat and started to speak.

"Hi I'm Nicky and I'm your lady for tonight." She shrugged her shoulders and positioned her ear towards the curtain waiting for a reply. There was an eerie silence and all she could hear was rummaging.

The voice told her to watch the television on the wall. His tone was dominant. She faced the screen and waited. She could hear coughing and waited patiently. Usually men would want her to watch porno films with them, but this seemed different as she watched the screen. Her eyes tried to focus as she heard the volume being turned up. The picture looked just like a black screen and all she could see were cars parked up on a car park.

As she watched closely she noticed a man wearing a white t-shirt appear on the screen. She watched the man walk to his car and then from nowhere she saw a woman jump onto his back attacking him with what looked like a knife. Her mouth became dry as she stood up from the seat. Her heart was racing as she recognised the woman as herself. Her body shook as she pulled the material from the ceiling revealing the man's identity.

"Hello Nicky. Long time no see ay?" Struggling for breath she turned to leave the room but he grabbed her hair.

"Not so quick, you little slut. Did you think you could get away from what you've done?" Her head was now pulled to her waist as he grabbed her hair. Spitting into her face he threw her onto the floor.

"James tried to kill us all. He set the villa on fire. He was a fucking nutter." Her words were wasted as he sat near where she lay. His face was tormented as he continued.

"I saved you from being arrested you know." Her eyes looked towards him and she looked puzzled. "That night I forgot to give him the money I owed him and followed him out, but you had already done him in hadn't you?" Her head dipped and she sat up in front of him like a scared animal. "I found him in a pool of blood. He was already dead when I got there. I had to think quickly and ran back inside the club to check the CCTV." Nicky remained still and remembered she had checked where the CCTV had been positioned but as he continued she realised she had dropped a bollock.

"When I watched the video I switched it to the new camera James had put in. I knew it was there as I was there with him when it got fitted." He remained silent for a second and leant down and touched the side of her face. "I studied the evidence and saw it was you. Me being a quick thinker I replaced the blank tape back inside and got out of there as soon as I could." He reached his hand out to her and helped her from the ground. Patting the sofa he told her to come and sit next to him. As she did he sat back and continued.

"You've been on my mind for a while now, so I did a bit of research and tracked you down to here. It was quite easy really, well that's if you're in the know like I am." Her fists gripped together and she squeezed them down at the side of her. Her mind couldn't focus and she needed to know what he wanted from her. Her words were shaky as she spoke.

"What do you want from me? It's quite obvious you haven't come all this way for nothing." Nicky remembered who he was now, a security man from James's club. Reaching into his pocket he pulled out a small red box, and handed it to her. He watched her as she looked at it. She didn't have a clue what was in it and continued.

"What's that for? I don't understand." His face now filled with joy. Lifting the hinged lid he revealed a ring. The ring looked new and had several diamonds in it.

"I want you to be my wife." Nicky stood up and gasped.

"Get a fucking grip mate. Do you think I'd marry a fat twat like you? You can fuck right off." His face changed and he gritted his teeth as her words stabbed his heart.

"Well you don't have much choice. You either marry me or spend the rest of your life locked up in prison." She ran at him with rage and pounded her clenched fists into his face.

"You dirty blackmailing bastard. I would rather rot in jail than be with your fucking sorry arse." He chuckled loudly as he grabbed his coat from the bed.

"Well it looks like I'm taking this tape to the police then doesn't it." He walked to the video recorder and knelt down to press the eject button. As he grabbed the tape he turned and faced Nicky who was stood in front of the door.

"Do you think you can stop me leaving?" He laughed out loud. His face looked menacing as he placed his hand on her shoulder ready to rag her from where she stood. She put her arms around his neck and knew if she had any chance of keeping his silence she would have to keep him on her side.

"Please stay a while. I need to talk to you. You can't just spring this on me and expect me to jump to your command." He saw the defeated look on her face and held his head back as if he was thinking. Slowly he dropped his head and looked her in the eyes.

"Hurry up then I haven't got all day. The way I see it, it's very easy. You either say yes or no." His heart melted as he looked at her. He'd fancied her for ages but knew she wasn't in his league. He was just the old security guard and nobody really took much notice of him until now. She was everything he'd ever wished for in a woman and now as he looked at her, he knew she was nearly his wife.

Nicky knew she didn't have a choice and held his hand in hers. His face changed and he placed his arms round her neck.

"I'm not that bad. I will look after you. I've got quite a bit of cash behind me now. We can live a great life in Spain together."

Nicky folded her housecoat around her. She wanted to hide any part of herself from him. She played with her hair and twisted it at the side of her head. His words were excited as he spoke and it was obvious he'd planned all this before he found her.

"We can fly back at the weekend. You don't have anything here to stay for. I'm not saying to get married, straight away. We can wait and plan it all. I can see it now, 'Mr and Mrs Tate.'" The words strangled her body. To become his wife would be a fate worse than death. She watched his movements as he scratched at his body. His white shirt was bursting open and the buttons were just about hanging on by a stitch.

Nicky had no other choice but to accept his offer. Her face couldn't hide her pain and she held her hands over her face as she sold her soul to him.

"Okay, I'll do it."

She saw him purse his lips together and watched as he moved his face in towards her. His kiss was wet and he used his tongue wildly. His breath made her heave and she could smell old fillings in his mouth. The kiss was short but enough for him to relax.

Nicky needed fresh air and told him she was just going to get a cigarette from her room. He looked at her with a smile on his face and told her not to be long. As she left the room she held her body against the wall outside. She struggled for breath as tears streamed down her face. Jessica heard the sobs from outside her room and came to investigate.

"What's the matter love?" Nicky placed her shaking finger up to her lips and urged her to remain silent. Jessica looked horrified as she dragged her to the other end of the corridor. Once inside the small bedroom she stood with her back against the door.

"What's fucking going on love. What's happened?" Nicky fell to the floor and curled up with her legs to her chest. Her housecoat was gripped tightly as she tried to cover her body. Jessica moved away from the door and knelt down pulling her hands away from her face. "Just tell me what's wrong and I can help." Nicky sobbed and lifted her head up. Her lips trembled as she tried to speak.

"I'm in big trouble love. No one can help me now." Jessica held her in her arms and tried to get some sense out of her. Nicky had got on well with Jessica in the past and decided to tell her the truth.

"It's the security guard from James's club. Do you remember him? The one who always stood at the end of the bar weighing us all up?" Jessica shook her head and didn't know who she meant. Nicky stood from the floor and walked towards the small window. As she wrapped her arms round herself she started to tell Jessica what had happened.

Jessica sat on the bed and her eyes widened as Nicky carried on telling her what had happened. The hairs on the back of her neck stood on end as the words murder came from Nicky's mouth. When the truth was out, Nicky turned from the window to see her white face looking straight at her. She walked to her side and knelt in front of her.

"He tried to kill us all, don't forget that, I did it for Kimberley. He would have never left her alone otherwise." Jessica sighed deeply. She knew this was way out of her league. She looked deep in thought and told Nicky she was going to get Geraldine. Nicky was shaking and knew she would have to go back to the bedroom before Mr Tate came looking for her. She kissed Jessica on the cheek and sobbed as she left.

"Please help me. I'm not a bad person." Jessica hugged her tightly and told her she would be back soon. As Nicky went back into the room she could see Jessica running down the stairs trying to find Geraldine. Once Jessica found her, she told her the story regarding Nicky. Geraldine was horrified but Nicky was part of them and she knew she needed to think quickly. Geraldine marched to the room and smoked her cigarette with speed. Jessica sat on the chair and waited for her to come up with a plan.

"We will offer him some money. How can he refuse that? Go upstairs and tell Nicky I want her. Don't mention anything to them and try to act as normal as possible. We don't want to scare him off do we?" Jessica headed back upstairs and softly knocked at the bedroom door. Once the door was opened she could just about see the feet of the man who was blackmailing Nicky. She kept her cool and in a calm voice she spoke.

"Hello sweetheart, Geraldine just wants a quick word with you. Can you come downstairs a minute?" Nicky looked over her shoulder and waited for the approval of her guest. As she watched him nod his head she grabbed her cigarettes from the side. Jessica was more than curious and made her way into the room.

"Can I get you a drink sir while you're waiting?" The man spoke for the first time and Jessica nearly had a heart attack as she looked at him closely.

"Yes love. Can you get me a large brandy?" Jessica's eyes squeezed together as she concentrated on his face in the semi-darkness. Once she was sure of who he was she left the room as quickly as possible and ran back to Geraldine with tears streaming down her face.

Nicky was stood in the room talking to Geraldine as Jessica entered. As soon as they saw her face they ran to her side. Geraldine was now shaking as she tried to get some sense out of her.

"Speak to me Jess. What's the matter?" Jessica sat on a chair and stared into space. Her words were broken as she spoke for the first time.

"It's him Geraldine. I thought he was dead. I didn't recognise him at first until I heard his voice." Geraldine was at her side and she looked angry.

"For fucks sake, who are you talking about?" The words "Mr Tate" left Jessica's lips and Geraldine shook her body to make sure she'd heard her right.

"Say it again. Did you say Mr Tate? The Mr Tate who we both know. Fucking headmaster Tate?" Jessica nodded her head. Nicky stood looking bewildered. She watched their faces and knew something was seriously wrong. She tried speaking but Geraldine turned to face her and told her to be quiet. Nicky had never seen her look like this before. As she watched them both she could see fear in their faces

"The dirty no good bastard. So he's still alive then?" Jessica stood and placed her arms tightly round her.

"Geraldine, I know it's him. As soon he spoke I recognised his voice." Geraldine patted her back and looked towards the ceiling. Nicky was now at the side of them and looked towards them for answers.

"Will someone please tell me what's fucking going on? I'm in deep shit here girls and need some help otherwise I'm going to prison for a long time." Geraldine knew they would have to tell her their secret and sat her back down in a chair. As the truth unfolded Nicky wanted to run back upstairs and stab him to death as well but as Geraldine spoke she knew her problem would be sorted.

"Right Nicky I want you to wait here. Jessica you're coming with me." Jessica felt scared and tried to stay with Nicky but as Geraldine raised her voice she knew she had no option.

The walk up the stairs seemed like the walk of death to them both. As the bedroom door opened Geraldine took a deep breath and stood tall before she entered, Jessica followed behind. The room still looked dark. As they closed the door behind them they saw Mr Tate for the first time. He looked different. His hair had gone now and he had a pot belly. Geraldine looked around the room and finally found a chair near him. Jessica stood against the wall and pulled at her clothing like a small child who was about to get in trouble. Taking a moment before she spoke Geraldine began with a confident voice.

"Hello Mr Tate. Nicky's told us all about her situation and we are here to help her." His face looked cocky as his head fell back and he chuckled to himself.

"I don't think you can help her love. The way I see it is, if she doesn't do what I say, she will be going to prison for a long time." Cringing at the voice, Geraldine composed herself and played with him now like a cat playing with a captured mouse.

"I'm sure you can walk away from her can't you. I mean we've all done things in our lives that we're not proud of haven't we?" Mr Tate screwed up his face and felt uneasy and tried to get back on top again.

"We all haven't murdered someone have we? Listen ladies, she knows what she needs to do, so leave her to deal with it and keep your noses out of her business."

Jessica knew what was coming and came to Geraldine's side. The man she had feared all her life was now sat in the same room as her and she felt a wave of courage pass through her body.

"You look familiar to me Mr Tate. Have we ever met before?" Mr Tate felt uneasy and wiggled about on the chair having little looks at the girls. As he remained still he looked at them in detail and didn't think he knew them.

"Mr Tate, from Bowker Crescent. The old perverted headmaster." He looked horrified and he stood from the chair feeling uneasy. Geraldine now stood up with him and Jessica stood in front of the door.

"Are you still kiddie fiddling Mr Tate? Remember us do you? Geraldine and Jessica." They watched his face collapse and he tried to pretend he didn't know what they were talking about.

"I don't know any of you and don't have a clue what you're talking about." Jessica flew into his face and years of torment came to the surface as she spoke.

"Oh you do remember us, you sick cunt. That's why you left the school. Do you remember? Fucking once a pervert always a pervert." Her words were like swords into his heart and his lip trembled as he remembered both the girls.

"Listen that was years ago. I've paid my price for what I've done to you two. I left my family, my job, everything to start a new life." Geraldine now played her ace card and told him to sit back down. Once he was seated she began as she watched him crumble right in front of her.

"We all hold secrets don't we? The way I see it is that if you want to send Nicky to jail for her crimes it's only fair we send you as well. The difference is that perverts in jail don't really stand a chance, especially ones who mess with little girls." His hands covered his ears and he shook his head about so as not to listen to anymore of her words, but it was too late they were both in his face shouting insults at him. Mr Tate exploded with emotion and stood up. He knew he was beat and tried to grab the video from the side. Geraldine grabbed his hand and looked him straight into his eyes.

"Put that down. You don't need it do you?"

His eyes looked menacing as he stared at her for a few minutes. His grip was released and his head sunk. As he walked to the door he turned and spoke to the girls for the last time.

"I'm not as bad as you think. I won't bother her no more." Jessica came to his side and looked straight into his eyes.

"I know you won't Mr Tate, because if you did I would be straight at the police station giving them a full statement about you and your dirty habits." He looked deflated now and he opened the door to a gobsmacked Nicky standing in front of him. She had heard every word and couldn't wait to give him a piece of her mind.

"You dirty old bastard. How dare you judge me when you're a fucking sex case?" Her fist pummelled the side of his face as Jessica came to pull her from him. She was like a wild woman frothing at the mouth as she shouted more abuse at him. Mr Tate left the house like his life depended on it. Nicky saw the video in Geraldine's hands and sobbed as she got hold of it. Her words were emotional as she spoke.

"Thank you so much girls. I'm not a bad person I just couldn't watch him destroy my friend any longer." They all hugged and agreed never to mention it again.

Suddenly the sound of Kimberley wretching from across the hallway broke the silence and they all ran to see if she was alright. The toilet door was open and Kimberley had her head hung over the toilet basin. Nicky remembered the fantasy she had to act out and burst into laughter. Within minutes the toilet door was locked behind them and they all pissed themselves laughing as they watched her wipe her mouth.

★

From that moment the business grew from strength to strength. The secrets they all shared never left their lips and life looked rosy for all of them. Lots more houses were opened in different areas and in time Nicky and Kimberley became madams in their own rights. They were getting richer by the day and loved how successful they'd become.

So if you are ever walking around Manchester in the late hours and hear a cat crying out, take a second to listen more carefully because it could be one of Nicky's and Kimberley's houses opened near you.

THE END

BLACK TEARS

A NOVEL BY KAREN WOODS

"MANCHESTER'S ANSWER TO MARTINA COLE"

WITH EVIL GORDON locked up in Strangeways for 5 years, the characters from Karen Woods' debut novel 'Broken Youth' come to terms with life without him.

Misty, now married to Dominic, gives birth to Gordon's child, Charlotte. Her former best friend Francesca also gives birth to one of Gordon's children, Rico, while staying with Gordon's heroin addicted brother Tom.

Meanwhile, as the clock ticks down on his sentence, Gordon broods on the injustice of his situation and plots sweet revenge on those on the outside.

Other novels from Empire

THE CARPET KING OF TEXAS

PAUL KENNEDY

"TRAINSPOTTING FOR THE VIAGRA GENERATION"
SUNDAY MIRROR
"DRUG-TAKING, SEXUAL DEPRAVITY... NOT FOR THE FAINT HEARTED."
NEWS OF THE WORLD

This shocking debut novel from award-winning journalist Paul Kennedy tells the twisted tales of three lives a million miles apart as they come crashing together with disastrous consequences.

Away on business, Dirk McVee is the self proclaimed "Carpet King of Texas" – but work is the last thing on his mind as he prowls Liverpool's underbelly to quench his thirst for sexual kicks.

Teenager Jade Thompson is far too trusting for her own good. In search of a guiding light and influential figure, she slips away from her loving family and into a life where no one emerges unscathed.

And John Jones Junior is the small boy with the grown-up face. With a drug addicted father, no motherly love, no hope, and no future, he has no chance at all.

The Carpet King of Texas is a gritty and gruesome, humorous and harrowing story of a world we all live in but rarely see.

ORDER THIS BOOK NOW FOR JUST £6
WWW.EMPIRE-UK.COM